## Praise for the *USA TODAY* be... Jennife...

"Fun, heartfelt and far too good to miss."
—*Bookish Jottings* on *Sweet Home Alaska*

"Prepare to have your heartstrings tugged! Pure Christmas delight."
—*New York Times* bestselling author Lori Wilde on *An Alaskan Christmas*

"Heartwarming, romantic, and utterly enjoyable."
—*New York Times* bestselling author Melissa Foster on *An Alaskan Christmas*

"Set in the wilds of Alaska, the beauty of winter and the cold shine through."
—*Fresh Fiction* on *An Alaskan Christmas*

"Jennifer Snow's Alaska setting and search-and-rescue element are interesting twists, and the romance is smart and sexy... An exciting contemporary series debut with a wildly unique Alaskan setting."
—*Kirkus Reviews* on *An Alaskan Christmas*

"This first title in the Wild River series is passionate, sensual, and very sexy. The freezing, winter-cold portrayal of the Alaskan ski slopes is not the only thing sending chills through one's body."
—*New York Journal of Books* on *An Alaskan Christmas*

"*Alaska Reunion* has a little bit of everything—drama, humor, friendship, and love. It's a well-written story that will draw readers in."
—*Harlequin Junkie*

**Also by Jennifer Snow**

**Wild Coast**

*Alaska for Christmas*
*Sweet Home Alaska*

**Wild Coast Novellas**

*Love in the Forecast*
*Love on the Coast*

**Wild River**

*Alaska Dreams*
*Alaska Reunion*
*Stars Over Alaska*
*A Sweet Alaskan Fall*
*Under an Alaskan Sky*
*An Alaskan Christmas*

**Wild River Novellas**

*An Alaskan Christmas Homecoming*
*Wild Alaskan Hearts*
*A Wild River Match*
*A Wild River Retreat*
*An Alaskan Wedding*

For additional books by Jennifer Snow,
visit her website, JenniferSnowAuthor.com.

# JENNIFER SNOW

# Second Chance Alaska

HQN

**HQN®**

ISBN-13: 978-1-335-44865-1

Second Chance Alaska
Copyright © 2023 by Jennifer Snow

Love in the Alaskan Wilds
Copyright © 2023 by Jennifer Snow

Recycling programs
for this product may
not exist in your area.

For questions and comments about the quality of this book,
please contact us at CustomerService@Harlequin.com.

HQN
22 Adelaide St. West, 41st Floor
Toronto, Ontario M5H 4E3, Canada
www.Harlequin.com

**Printed and bound in Barcelona, Spain by CPI Black Print**

# CONTENTS

"In order for the light to shine so brightly,
the darkness must also be present."
—Francis Bacon

# Second Chance Alaska

# PROLOGUE

Dear readers,

Never in my wildest imagination could I have envisioned that you would have embraced the love story about a sea serpent queen and a lonely fisherman the way you have. Writing this story was something I'd wanted to do for a long time, but lack of courage to follow my heart has always been my greatest fault. As a resident of Port Serenity, Alaska, I finally felt it was my duty to give this story within me life-space to breathe. I wanted to give Sealena a voice in a way she's never really had, exploring her wants, desires, struggles.

This trilogy is a love story that surpasses all time and space. It speaks to the agony of a love that shouldn't be, it offers hope and inspiration in our darkest moments, and it shows that love is all that truly matters.

Thank you for the fan mail. I've read each and every last letter, email and social media comment, and I cherish the support and encouragement. Your passion for these stories is my motivation and inspiration to continue writing Sealena's love adventure.

I've kept my identity a secret for a lot of reasons, and I'll just say that, for now, that path serves me and my life. I'm not hiding behind a pen name out of fear or guilt or embarrassment, but out of respect for the true star—Sealena, the Serpent Queen who courageously guards the waters and shoreline along this rugged, majestic Alaskan coast. She is the protagonist of her own story and I want to let her shine.

Know I appreciate every one of you, dear readers, and this community of Sealena fans continues to grow every day because of your praise and support of this series.

Keep believing that dreams do come true and lasting love is always just a serendipitous moment away.

XO
Y.C. Salwert

# CHAPTER ONE

SHE WOULDN'T BE standing there, practically naked, in front of half of Port Serenity if it hadn't been for that damn tail.

But Carly Walters's worst nightmare was indeed happening. Standing center stage in the Serpent Queen pub, under the bright, blinding spotlight, she stared out into the shocked, horrified, slightly amused expressions of people she'd known her entire life.

Wearing only her Little Miss Sunshine days of the week underwear and a shiny gold sports bra.

Her Sealena costume had been ripped from her body when the serpent-like tail had snagged on a raised wooden floorboard as she'd proudly walked across the stage when her contestant number was announced. Lucky number thirteen, her ass.

How she'd even allowed herself to be talked into participating in this silly yearly tradition, she'd never know. Tequila shots had definitely been involved. And a bet—at least she had fifty dollars coming to her. Small consolation for the mortification she was currently enduring.

The town's annual Sealena costume contest was held every year at the end of June in a closed event at the local pub named in the Serpent Queen's honor, open to locals only. A catered, open-bar kickoff party to the official start of tourist season—a way to pre-thank the community for the hard work they were about to endure for the next two months when the small Alaskan coastal town saw a huge influx of tourists. The town's generations-old claim on the mythical sea creature made it a hot-spot destination for those in search of the elusive, the unknown. Families flocked to town hoping to spot Sealena for themselves and the local businesses had thrived in providing that opportunity.

Thank goodness this event was closed to the broader public, otherwise Port Serenity would be newsworthy for a different type of sighting.

Onstage, her fellow competitors sent her sympathetic looks as Carly struggled to tug the trapped fabric toward her. "Come on," she muttered.

"Spotlight off, please," Dex Wakefield called out to the stage technician from his position behind the bar.

Immediately, the light went out, providing more privacy, and Carly sent her cousin's fiancé a grateful look as she continued to try to pull the tail free. From far back in the crowd, she could see her friend Rachel approach the stage. *If* she could actually call Rachel a friend. She was pretty sure Rachel had been the one to suggest Carly participate in the event. At thirty-four years old, she really had to stop giving in to peer pressure.

She motioned for Rachel to hurry up, but her friend was held up by the thick crowd gathered around the stage.

"Hey, hold still. I got you," a male voice said from the front row.

Carly turned toward the man as he climbed onto the stage, one hand shielding his eyes to give her privacy. She appreciated the gesture, but it also blocked her view of his face. She squinted in the dim neon lighting, taking in the designer jeans, expensive leather shoes and light gray Henley that hugged the man's muscular frame—a muscular frame she didn't recognize and one she surely would have noticed if she'd seen it around town before.

The event was locals only. New man in town?

If so, he would be the first one in forever. Things didn't change much in Port Serenity. People didn't change much. It was both a blessing and a curse at times. Especially times such as this, when anonymity might make this mishap less mortifying, but the familiarity of the crowd made it a safe zone.

Next to her, the stranger bent and quickly detached the ten-foot tail from the splintered plank of wood and offered the fabric to her without looking.

Grateful, she wrapped the costume around her exposed body. "Thank you…?"

"Is it safe to look?"

"Yes," she said, glancing down to make sure. Not that it mattered. It was too late now anyway.

He lowered his hand from his face and extended it toward her. "Sebastian Grant. I'm the new head of tourism development in town."

Carly's mouth gaped. Of course he was. She'd heard the rumor that Mr. O'Doyle was retiring from the position he'd held for over thirty-five years and she knew the mayor's office was hoping to hire a replacement by the start of tourist season, but she hadn't known they'd found someone.

Or that he'd be a young, handsome guy with a savior complex.

"Nice to meet you," she said, feeling her cheeks flush with heat even more than they had seconds ago. "I'm Carly Walters—I run the Sealena Bookstore and Museum on Main Street."

"Ah! Yes!" The man's eyes lit up. "Great to meet you.

Mayor Crinly said you'd be my greatest resource on all things Sealena."

As somewhat of a local expert on the Serpent Queen, Carly was heavily involved in the tourism department. She sat on the local planning committee and helped to arrange a lot of the town's events, such as the Sealena Festival happening the following month. Mayor Crinly had already given her a heads-up that she'd be spending a lot of time with whomever took over the position.

"I, uh, guess I didn't make a great first impression."

Sebastian shook his head as he helped her descend the stairs from the stage. "On the contrary," he said. "You've impressed the hell out of me—definitely shows commitment to participate in something like this. You wouldn't catch me up there." He shuddered at the thought. The other contestants had dispersed, and the judging had commenced. Music had resumed, and luckily, everyone had continued on with their evening as though the costume malfunction hadn't happened.

Carly laughed. "I was winning too, until that stupid plank of wood." Her costume had been the best by far. Once she'd agreed to participate, she'd gone all in on the design and, being a Sealena expert, made hers as authentic as possible with a likeness to the Serpent Queen that none of the other competitors could have hoped to duplicate, with a multiple snake headdress that had taken weeks to sew together. Her body-painted scales of various greens, tans and gold had taken three hours to apply with an airbrush and stencil. She'd even temporarily dyed her long dark hair an ocean shade of green for a more authentic look than the wigs worn by her fellow competitors. The gold tank top she wore matched the long serpent appendage she'd fabricated from a mermaid tail she'd bought the year before when she'd signed up for a mermaid swim class, where she'd quickly discovered that her abs were just not up to the challenge.

She'd had this win, hands down.

Now it appeared the trophy and bragging rights belonged to Amelia Fisher, the first-grade teacher, who was graciously accepting her award from the judging table.

"There's always next year," Sebastian said.

Carly laughed and shook her head as she turned toward the back room, where she had a change of clothing waiting. "Not for me. This was a once-in-a-lifetime event."

"Glad I was here to witness it, then," he called after her teasingly. His gaze drifted over her with obvious interest and she felt her cheeks warm again.

When was the last time a man had looked at her that way?

Longer than forever. A serial monogamist, she didn't do casual and didn't like to waste her time on relationships that weren't going to lead anywhere.

"I look forward to talking to you about the Sealena Festival," she said, pushing open the back staff-room door.

"Likewise," he said. Then he jogged toward her and lowered his voice to a conspirator's level. "And, uh, Carly?"

Her pulse picked up slightly. "Yeah?"

"It's Saturday."

She frowned. "Huh?"

"Your underwear said *Friday*," he said with a grin and a wave as he headed back to rejoin the group seated at the mayor's table.

Carly watched after him, an odd feeling washing over her. Had they been flirting just now? It had felt like flirting, but it had been so long since she'd flirted or been flirted with that she couldn't be sure. And did she want to flirt with a man who was going to be a colleague of sorts?

Rachel finally caught up to her in the hallway, dressed in a tight, lime-green body-con dress and matching six-inch heels. It was no mystery why her friend had taken so long to get through the crowd. Carly would never be able to walk in such tight fabric with stilettos. Rachel was from Seattle and she still dressed like a city girl despite having lived in the casual small town for almost a year. "Holy hotness. Who was your sexy rescuer?" she asked, her gaze on Sebastian.

"Sebastian Grant, the new head of tourism development," Carly said, pushing through the staff-room door of the pub.

Rachel followed her inside. "New head of tourism? So, essentially your new shadow for the summer?" she said with unconcealed pleasure at the turn of events. Her blue eyes sparkled and Carly could already see the matchmaking wheels turning in her friend's mind. Recently engaged, Rachel had love on the brain 24/7 and she was constantly trying to convince Carly to sign up for relationship apps, speed dating events... She'd even suggested a reality dating show, which, luckily, Carly had not succumbed to the pressure of.

Yet.

"Who just saw me in my underwear," she said as she carefully removed the snake headdress without yanking out pieces of her stiff, dyed hair. She was going to need a really great hair conditioning treatment after this.

"Everyone just saw you in your underwear," Rachel said, helping to unzip the tail from around Carly's waist.

She breathed in deep as the tight fabric was removed. "Thanks for the reminder."

Rachel laughed. "It wasn't that bad, and having a gorgeous man come to your rescue couldn't have been that horrible either," she said with a raised, suggestive eyebrow as she looked at her through the mirror. Obviously, her friend wasn't ready to drop that conversation.

Carly sighed. Sebastian *was* a gorgeous man and he *had* rescued her in her moment of need and they *would* be spending a lot of time together that summer. All of that was true.

Unfortunately, it was also a truth universally acknowledged that Carly's heart wasn't up for grabs. It was—and would probably always remain—in the clutches of the one man in town who hadn't been there to see her in her underwear that evening.

And probably never would.

"PORT SERENITY'S LIGHTHOUSE has stood tall on the cliffside overlooking the North Pacific for over a hundred years. Timeworn and fragile, the structure serves as more of a beacon of the past, shining light on maritime history, than—"

A loud emergency response alarm that echoed throughout the lighthouse tower the next day interrupted Rachel's spiel, giving Oliver Klein a welcome respite. "Hold that thought," he told her as he and his daughter Tess sprang into action inside the historic building.

Rachel sighed loudly behind him, but Oliver didn't have time to worry about putting off the local historian blogger who had been harassing him for an exclusive interview since the day she'd moved to town. This "emergency" couldn't have come at a better time.

"6.7 earthquake. Go, go, go!" he told Tess.

"I've got the tower," she said. Dressed in her lighthouse tour guide T-shirt and shorts, his ten-year-old daughter sprinted up the winding, concrete tower stairs, her little legs moving at the pace of lightning.

Oliver hurried inside the showroom where the historic

artifacts were on display to check the main floor wash-rooms. He knocked once on each door, then went in, check-ing all stalls.

All clear.

He opened the records-room door and scanned, but there was no one inside. The seating area with the library boast-ing books about Port Serenity's heritage was empty as well.

Everyone must be in the tower.

As Oliver reentered the main room, a group of people de-scended the tower stairs carefully but quickly as the alarm continued to wail, echoing for miles across the marina.

Oliver frowned as he surveyed the group. There should be eight people. A quick head count revealed only seven. His daughter appeared at the rear. "Injured male. Fifties. About two hundred pounds," Tess reported, pointing up the stairs.

Shit.

Oliver moved past her on the stairwell and his thighs burned as he made the fast climb toward the injured man at the top of the tower. Why the hell were there so many stairs? Maybe they should reconsider letting tourists into the tower. Did they really need to see the beacon up close? Or the view of the ocean from that vantage point?

Might be a hard sell for the tourism board if they re-moved that aspect, and unfortunately, with the coast guard having assumed official control over the lighthouse, Oliver was more tour guide than anything else, despite being an honorary member of the Coast Guard Aids to Navigation crew, which currently maintained the functioning of the lighthouse. Upgrades in technology meant there was little maintenance on the place these days.

Ten seconds later, he reached a man in his late forties, sitting on the floor, his back to the concrete wall, a pained expression on his face as he groaned, clutching his left leg. Oliver bent next to him and assessed the injuries. "Can you walk?" he asked the man, helping him to his feet.

The man's leg gave way and he shook his head. "I don't think so."

Fantastic.

Oliver sighed as he bent, braced himself for the weight and heaved the man over his shoulder. The guy was definitely heavier than two hundred pounds. Tess needed to work on her assessment skills. At thirty-five years old, Oliver liked to think he was still in good shape, but the aching of his muscles and the slight panting for breath after the sprint up the stairwell had him rethinking it.

Carrying the man, he headed back downstairs, careful not to trip over the chipped concrete edges of the stairs. He could see the others from the tour group were already outside, so he brought the man out and set him down on the grassy, safe muster area.

Tess was dismantling the camera tripod they used to capture the tour group photos. She quickly secured it in the underground bunker several feet away from the lighthouse.

With everyone safely outside, Oliver got to work closing the storm shutters on the outside of the windows, then headed back up to the tower to apply storm panes for the lantern rooms to protect the optics. With the exterior of the building secure, next, he and Tess got to work wrapping the threatened artifacts and displays in the museum room with plastic and tape. He gathered the artifacts and paper records and the two of them exited the lighthouse, closing and securing the door.

Oliver stopped his stopwatch. "Eight minutes and forty-eight seconds," he said to Tess. "We beat the record." Rehearsing their response to disaster warnings was something they did regularly throughout the year, but especially before the start of tourist season, when groups would be coming through the lighthouse.

It was important to have a plan and to ensure its proper execution. There was no room for improvisation in the wake of a disaster. Good planning sped recovery and minimized loss. Most importantly, being ready with a detailed, well-organized disaster response plan increased everyone's safety.

During the year, there was only the two of them to worry about. But when tourist season started the following day, the lighthouse would host tour groups three or four times a day during the week. They had to ensure they were prepared to evacuate in the case of a sudden emergency. Like the fake earthquake they'd just simulated with the help of volunteers.

The lighthouse where Oliver and his daughter lived was a tourist favorite in the small town, just as most lighthouses attracted visitors for their mystery and history. But a lot of people underestimated the dangers. Lighthouses were put in places to warn of risk. Their purpose was to mark landfalls and passages. They were positioned in locations fully exposed to storm waves. Visiting them was a great way to learn about a place's history, but people needed to be aware of the potential hazards.

Oliver could understand the appeal of the Port Serenity lighthouse. At one time, this lighthouse had charmed him as well...

Tess held up a hand to high-five him, but he folded his arms. "Could you have picked a heavier victim?" he whispered, as their volunteers applauded their speedy efforts.

Tess grinned, displaying three missing teeth in the sides of her mouth. "You need to start working out again, Dad. You're a little winded from those stairs."

He ruffled her hair and they dismissed the volunteers with the promised homemade cookies for their participation. As everyone dispersed, he checked his watch. "Okay, let's get to work on resetting everything."

The training exercise over, they needed to get the place ready for the actual visitors arriving the next day.

"That was really cool," Rachel said as she approached him.

Shit, he thought she'd left with everyone else. "Thanks... Sorry, I can't chat right now. We have a lot to do."

"Would you like some help?" she asked.

"Yes!" Tess said.

Oliver shot his daughter a look before turning to Rachel. "No, thanks. We've got it."

The Seattle native nodded, her red hair falling around her shoulders. "Well, since I'm here, maybe I could ask you a few questions?" she asked casually. "I can just follow you while you work. I promise not to get in the way."

He'd known she had an agenda when he saw her name on their volunteer sign-up list that day. Rachel had moved to town when she'd met and fallen in love with a coast guard officer on a trip to Port Serenity to dispel the myth of Sealena. She'd since become a firm believer in the mysteries of the sea and had been hounding him to do this story about the lighthouse and his family's connection to it. "Listen, Rachel, I know you're hoping to really explore the history of this place, and your article on the lighthouse sounds great so far—" not that he'd really been listening "—but I'm just not comfortable with the idea of my personal life on display to several hundred people."

He'd dealt with enough scrutiny years ago.

She nodded quickly, her gold, dangly earrings swishing from side to side. "It's 4,863 people actually, but I totally understand."

He doubted that.

"But we don't have to talk about…what happened," she said quietly and gently, as Tess was still within earshot, resetting the camera tripod. "Just the history of the lighthouse. How it was passed down in your family, that kind of thing… The future of it."

"It's mine next," Tess said confidently, appearing next to him.

Oliver's gut twisted slightly. That would normally be the plan—to pass the torch to the next generation. The job of watching the coastline had been passed along through his family for decades, and despite automation of the systems themselves and the US Coast Guard's control over the operation, Oliver was the fourth-generation lighthouse keeper in Port Serenity.

For how much longer, he didn't know.

And he certainly wasn't sure he liked the idea of his daughter following in his footsteps.

"I'm sorry, Rachel, but the answer is no," he said firmly.

Next to him, Tess pouted; he knew she'd love to be featured on Rachel's blog. His little girl loved the local community and the family heritage revolving around the lighthouse, but he struggled with an uneasiness that maybe too much of their lives were tied up in the antiquity of the town.

"It's just not the right time," he said by way of excuse. "I still have a lot to do before the season starts."

Rachel nodded. "Okay, sure…another time." She touched Tess's shoulder. "Great job."

Tess beamed. "Thank you."

"Before I forget, here is the invite to Darcy's birthday party next week," she said, handing a pretty light blue–themed party invitation to Tess.

His daughter's eyes lit up again. "This is going to be so fun. She's been talking about it for weeks."

Darcy was Rachel's stepdaughter of sorts, her boyfriend Callan's adopted niece and Tess's best friend. Despite the three-year age gap, the two girls were inseparable, as Tess had become like an older sister to the younger child. During the summer months, they tried to have playdates and sleepovers as much as possible. Oliver was grateful that Tess had such an amazing friend. Having lost her older sister three years before, he knew having Darcy helped to relieve some of that longing for a companion.

"I'll reach out again when things are less busy," Rachel said to Oliver with a wave.

He had no doubt that she would, and unfortunately, he'd left the door wide open for his scars to be exposed to all 4,863 of her followers.

## CHAPTER TWO

CARLY PEEKED THROUGH the blinds of her bedroom window the next morning and then let them quickly close again before the long line of people standing outside Sealena Bookstore and Museum could see her.

July first and the crowds were just in time.

Summer in Port Serenity, Alaska, saw a huge boost in tourists from all over the world, as children were on vacation from school and the weather was nice and warm. The North Pacific icebergs visible in the marina melted and moved farther away from the coastline, making access to the port town easier by boat and cruise ships that sailed from all over the USA. The town's famed mythology was the biggest draw, but once visitors realized the beauty of this part of Alaska, surrounded by large mountains and wilderness with pristine lakes and waterfalls—an outdoorsman's dream—they often returned for more than simply a chance, rare encounter or sighting of Sealena, the Serpent Queen.

However, just in case visitors didn't get to see the real thing out on the various boat tours in town that "promised" a sighting, Carly's Main Street store sold everything a Sealena fan could want—T-shirts, hats, books, figurines, replicas of historical documents...

From now until Labor Day, the lineup outside the store before 9:00 a.m. would be long. It was great for business, but within a week, Carly would be looking forward to her own well-deserved vacation at the end of the summer season.

With the official Sealena Festival four weeks away, there was so much to do. Her store built one of the floats featured in the parade that kicked off a week of Sealena-themed events and activities throughout town, and locals expected a different design each year. After thirty years, there were only so many unique concepts for the Serpent Queen's ride, but Carly was determined to make sure she didn't let the community down. So much of its economy depended on the next several months and the annual parade was a huge draw.

She showered and dressed quickly, braiding her long, thick dark hair, that still held remnants of the green dye on the ends. Then she applied mascara to her naturally long lashes and lip gloss to her lips. She didn't bother with much makeup. She never had. Growing up with her nose stuck in a book, she'd never been interested in spending hours in front of a mirror. And sensible shoes were the only option for fourteen hours on her feet as store hours were extended until 10:00 p.m. in July and August.

That year, she'd finally hired an assistant to help run the store—a university student home for the summer. Melissa was studying history and folklore at the University of Alaska, and while her résumé had lacked any retail experience, Carly had taken a chance on her, knowing the work experience would help the girl's future employment success. Having just arrived home the day before, Melissa was scheduled to start that afternoon and Carly hoped training her wouldn't just end up being even more work for herself. Ideally, she would have preferred training someone during the slower lead-up to the season.

In her kitchen, she placed an espresso pod into the new

coffee machine that she'd splurged on as a birthday gift for herself the month before, and the instantaneous scent of delicious caffeine filling her senses relieved her guilt over the extravagant purchase. This time of year, coffee was life. She deserved this.

Five minutes later, carrying her Sealena-themed coffee mug, she headed downstairs to the store. She unlocked the door that connected the storage room to the front salesroom and flicked on the interior lights.

She smiled as the place lit up. After four hours spent preparing the night before, everything was in place and ready. At least, until the mob outside descended.

New T-shirts with that year's date on them, featuring various designs and sayings, had replaced the old stock. Sizes from children's small to adult's triple XL hung on the clothing racks. Five hundred copies of the latest Sealena-themed picture book, graciously signed by the local author, made a magnificent tower display near the front window. They'd disappear within the first week. The long-running children's series featuring the adventures of the Serpent Queen were a hit, and Carly's store was the only independent that sold them.

Protected within glass cabinets throughout the store were Sealena figurines and collectibles. Designs portraying the Serpent Queen rescuing ships and battling fierce ocean waves were on display with price tags that ranged from fan to obsessed.

Portraits and paintings from local artists hung on the walls, and the historical documents that told the original story of how the mythical creature was adopted as the community's mascot were displayed in a special glass case near the counter. Included was the original signed letter from Earl Wakefield four generations ago. A duplicate was in the local Serpent Queen pub on the marina.

Carly loved the history all around her. Loved being a part of a deep-rooted community with its traditions and culture. There was nowhere else she'd rather be, nor anything she'd rather do. She held a teaching degree with a major in history and put the skills to good use by offering Sealena School twice a week at the store.

Her mother had run the Sealena Bookstore and Museum before her, officially retiring two years before, so Carly had grown up surrounded by the mythology that was Port Serenity. Being related to the Beaumonts on her mother's side had meant juggling her passion for all things Serpent Queen and loyalty to her family's civil servant legacy. But with her cousin Skylar breaking the Wakefield/Beaumont family feud by falling in love with Dex Wakefield, the lingering tension around town, that had spanned generations, seemed to evaporate.

Carly sipped her coffee, letting the hot liquid bolt of energy seep in as she scanned her float concept drawings on the counter, where she'd left them after midnight the night before. That year, she wanted to go bigger and better than ever. No friendly-looking Sealena lurking beneath smooth waters. She wanted huge, threatening waves and a fierce, strong female protector fighting the elements. She also wanted to honor the coast guard with the design, showing how the two were not opposing forces, but working together for the same goal—protecting those at sea. Therefore, the float needed to be much longer and slightly wider than previous years. The night before, under the cover of darkness, she'd measured the width of Main Street, taking into account the spectator zone, and she thought they could safely push the boundaries on the width restrictions by an inch or two.

Her phone chimed with a text message from where it lay on the counter. She reached for it and read:

It's not too late to run away together.

Oliver.

If only he meant it…

Her heart warmed at the sight of his photo appearing above the message. The picture of him and his daughter Tess had been taken that Christmas before at the tree lighting ceremony, and it was one of her favorites, as his expression was happy and relaxed—a true rarity, as he always seemed to be carrying an unspoken heaviness…

They always started their day with a text. Just a quick one, but it was the highlight of her mornings. That chime sounding made her heart race at the thought that he started his day thinking about her just as she did him. Even if it was just in a best-friend kind of way—at least, from his perspective.

His text sounded casual enough, but she knew he was stressed about facing the start of his own busy season, with lighthouse tours being offered three or four times a day Monday to Friday. Unlike her, he at least had the weekends off, but these tours were tough on him.

Having lost his wife, Alison—Carly's best friend—and his eldest daughter, Catherine, at sea three years before, Oliver was struggling to raise Tess on his own, still battling with the mystery of what happened that peaceful summer's day at sea when the family's new sailboat had disappeared.

Having strangers from all over the world invade his home was difficult enough, but especially so since Oliver's tragic story was almost as much of a draw to curious visitors as the lighthouse's history. The disappearance had made national news and Oliver's quiet life had been on full display. Most of the time, it was easiest to stay in the shadows of the town's popularity, but tourist season brought everything to light all over again.

Three tickets to Bali sounds nice...

She texted back and sighed. Three tickets to anywhere with Oliver and Tess would be a dream come true, but so far, that dream of becoming something more had eluded her, and besides some casual flirting when he seemed to forget all the reasons he shouldn't flirt with her, Oliver had given her no indication that their friendship status would be changing anytime soon.

Carly tucked her phone into her pocket as the clock on the wall chimed, indicating the hour. With a final scan of the store, she took a deep breath and flipped the Closed sign to Open and unlocked the front door.

"Hello! Welcome to Port Serenity's best souvenir shop," she greeted the first customer in line as they entered, hoping her smile lasted the fourteen hours until closing.

"Is IT TRUE that all lighthouse keepers eventually go mad?"
*And here we go.*
Luckily, Oliver didn't have to answer the question they inevitably received at least once every tour group.
Tess was an expert on the subject.
Oliver watched her now as she led the first official lighthouse tour group of the summer season through the main room of the lighthouse, stopping at the base of the spiraling staircase up to the tower.

Tess laughed as she shook her head. "Not anymore, thanks to modern science," she said, standing in front of the eight people with such confidence and pride, it brought mixed emotions to Oliver's chest.

Sometimes, he felt like he was drowning in them.

Living there, haunted by the tragedy of his past, was hard. As time passed with no answers, he thought maybe he *might* be slowly losing his mind. And yet he felt compelled to stay. Loyalty to his family's legacy—loyalty to the town—was rooted deep in his core.

"It's true that in the nineteenth century, lighthouse keepers had a high frequency of madness and suicide. But it had less to do with being solitary in the tower than people assume," Tess told the crowd, who were now captivated.

"One of the greatest lighthouse inventions back then was the Fresnel lens, which increased and intensified the range of the lighthouse beacon. The rotation speed of the light was important and the best way to ensure its accuracy was to float the light and lens on a circular track of liquid mercury." She led the group toward the artifact on display that showed the older instrument in action.

Without real mercury, of course.

"When the mercury got dirty, it was the lighthouse keeper's job to strain it through a fine cloth to clean it. It was the exposure to the mercury fumes that drove them to madness," Tess concluded with a wide grin, happy to be the smartest one in the room.

The crowd applauded, enlightened, and Oliver winked at Tess over their heads as she continued toward the stairs. The best part of the tour was getting to see the beacon at the top of the tower, and he knew Tess loved seeing the expressions on the visitors' faces when they saw the incredible view up there for the first time.

Knowing the group was in more than capable hands, Oliver headed to the records room, where he kept a log of the weather each day. He opened the door and entered, a familiar musky smell filling his nostrils. Same smell since he was a child. One that used to fill him with his own sense of pride when he'd help his father perform the same duty, but these days, it was just another reminder that he'd been in the same place, doing the same thing, for a long time.

Maybe too long.

Switching on the light, he scanned the old wooden bookshelves where hundreds of logbooks were preserved. Old, worn leather and yellowing pages of decades ago stood in line with the year etched on the spine. Newer books were evident on newer shelves. Less dust, less fading from time and from sunlight streaming in through the small round window directly across.

The weather log was also automated now on a spreadsheet, shared on the coast guard's internal database, but the town wanted to continue the paper records in the old leather notebooks to preserve the history and keep with tradition. Generations from now, the lighthouse would still be standing there, long after everyone in the town was gone, a new generation carrying the community forward, and these current weather reports would be historical documents.

Oliver reached for the recent logbook and checked the temperature gauges for outside; then he documented the temperature, wind and ocean patterns, including that day's force and wave height. He sighed as he wrote the date. Two days after the anniversary of his wife and eldest daughter's disappearance. Lost at sea on a day as clear and calm as this week's forecast.

An experienced sailor, his wife had known the waters better than most. She'd been a competitive sailor for ten years before they'd started their family. There had been no reason to suspect that taking the boat out that day would have resulted in them not returning home.

The lack of closure was the hardest part. Not knowing. Always looking. Always waiting.

He wasn't sure he'd ever find the answers he was searching for.

He closed the logbook and placed it back on the shelf. Then, turning off the light, he left the room and locked the door. Footsteps on the tower stairs indicated that the tour was wrapping up, so he headed outside and waited for Tess and the others.

The old-fashioned camera was set up on the tripod on the grassy area in front of the lighthouse and he took his position behind it to capture the photo of the tour. It was an add-on feature that, to Oliver, only amplified the touristy element of the whole thing, but the mayor's office insisted on it. They said people loved to receive the printed black-and-white photo in the mail weeks after arriving home from their vacation. A little reminder and incentive to return.

"Okay, everyone, line up over here," Tess instructed. She positioned the group with a great backdrop of the lighthouse tower and the ocean in the background, tallest in the back, shortest in the front. "And…smile!"

The group of tourists did and Oliver snapped the photo.

"Copies will be mailed out in two weeks. Thanks for coming. Be sure to sign the guest book as you leave," Tess said, happily accepting tips from several of the group.

Oliver grinned. He doubted he'd get tips if he ran the tour. Tess was special. She knew the town's history better than anyone and relished the old stories.

"Generous crowd today," she said, flashing him the bills as she approached.

"By end of summer, you'll be able to afford that new bike

you've been wanting," he said, wrapping an arm around her shoulders.

"I'm actually saving for a kayak," she said, and his gut clenched slightly. He'd never stop her from going out on the water. She loved to swim and fish and enjoy the local tour boat for whale watching, but each time she was near the water's pebbly edge, his chest tightened and it was difficult to breathe. He longed to move somewhere a little farther inland, but he knew being away from the ocean would crush his daughter's spirit.

"But first I'm going to get an ice cream," she said. "Want one?"

"Your treat?" he teased.

"Why not?" she said with a grin before skipping off toward the ice cream hut on the beach.

Oliver stared out at the calm water and sighed as his daughter waited for their frozen treats.

Yet another tourist season to survive.

# CHAPTER THREE

WHO WOULD HAVE known the Sealena-themed socks she'd ordered would be such a hit?

A week into the season and Carly had seen four tourists wearing the knee-high socks with their sandals around town; she couldn't keep the product on the racks. She'd need to place another order that week. The unexpected bestselling product of the season.

Last year's had been the snake hats that resembled the Serpent Queen's tiara. She glanced toward the pile of them now in the clearance bin. Not such a hot seller now. It was impossible to guess what the next trend would be. Tourists continued to surprise her.

What wasn't a huge surprise was the success of the new Sealena-themed fantasy romance series, which had been flying off the shelves. Author Y.C. Salwert's debut, the first book in the series, *A Forbidden Obsession*, had hit the *USA TODAY* bestseller list for six weeks in a row. Local support for the series was understandable, but Carly was a little surprised by how far across the country the series—and the town's mythology—had reached. Originally, her store had been the only place stocking the title, but when the online version hit number one on Amazon, the small Alaskan press publishing the title expanded distribution to all brick-and-mortar stores across the US and Canada.

The second book in the series, *Love at Sea*, had been

released the day before, two months ahead of its original release date, as the publisher wanted to ride the wave of success of the first book. Carly was already placing another order for more copies. The third book wasn't scheduled for release until winter, but the publisher had sent promo and preorder sign-up sheets for the store already.

Carly glanced at the display in the front window that had replaced the children's series, and seeing the pile getting low, she headed to the back of the store and grabbed another box. They were all signed already and she stared at the cover as she positioned them in the window. The images on both covers shared a similar aesthetic—an image of the sea serpent queen in the background and the picturesque image of a sleepy fishing village, featuring the story's hero in the forefront. The overall vibe was hauntingly seducing...or at least, that was how the promo pack put it.

Carly's phone chimed, and reaching into her pocket for it, she saw a message from Rachel.

Two more for book club.

Book club in the small town was a big deal—a favorite night out for many of the locals, even the ones who didn't do the required reading but liked to enjoy a glass of wine and listen to lively debates. All were welcome, with the only requirement being that they at least purchased a copy of the novel. But none of the book selections had garnered as huge a turnout as the new Sealena series, and it appeared that everyone was actually reading them.

We're running out of space. Stop inviting people.

The local fire marshal would shut them down if they surpassed the thirty-five people maximum in the store.

Have you finished book two yet? Dying to discuss.

Rachel was truly obsessed with the series, which was ironic, seeing as how the woman had originally come to Port Serenity to dispel the myth of Sealena. When Carly had pointed that out, Rachel had claimed that love was universal and that it was the romance between the pages of the novel that appealed to her most, not the fantasy element.

I'll be done soon. XX

Read faster! xx

As she tucked the cell phone away, a knock sounded on the front door. She checked the time and frowned. She didn't open for another hour, but some tourists could be really pushy. If they saw her inside, they expected her to open. The town's welcoming "we cater to tourists" vibe was to blame. She was tempted to ignore the knocking, but what if it was someone with an early-morning flight, who'd left their Sealena souvenir shopping to the last minute?

She'd hate to think there was a Sealena fan out there expecting a Serpent Queen souvenir who would be disappointed when their relative or friend returned from their trip empty-handed because they'd failed to plan ahead.

Carly sighed and set the box aside. She smiled, seeing not a tourist, but Oliver standing outside. She ran a hand quickly through her hair and straightened her skirt as she opened the door.

"Hey, you," she said, her heart warming at the sight of

him, as it always did. The dull longing she could do nothing about never subsided when it came to the one man in town she couldn't have in her life in any romantic way. Dressed in a pair of faded jeans, a gray hoodie and running shoes, he made casual look hot. His messy dark hair that rarely saw a comb and the two-day-old stubble along his jawline gave him an adorably unkempt appeal. At least, to her. He was attractive without trying. Attractive despite *lack* of trying.

He held up a paper bag with the local diner's logo on it. "Figured you hadn't eaten anything substantial in days."

How on earth was she supposed to not be in love with him?

He was gorgeous, kind, thoughtful and considerate. He was as much a landmark in Port Serenity as the Sealena statue in the center of town. He was a fantastic friend and an amazing dad—and he knew when she'd be too busy to eat.

"You figured right," she said, taking the bag and looking inside. The smell of her favorite bacon-and-egg muffin drifted from within and her stomach growled. "Extra bacon?"

"Would I dare bring you anything else?"

She laughed. "Do you want to come in?"

He shook his head. "Just wanted to drop it off before the crowd started to gather. We have four tour groups today," he said, his voice revealing how he felt about it.

She knew he'd fought with the tourism office for years about the tours. He didn't like doing them or having strangers in his home. Unfortunately for Oliver, the town had approved his living quarters off-limits, but insisted the lighthouse itself was the town's property and part of the coast guard, so the tower and the history rooms were open to the public from July 1 until after Labor Day weekend.

Carly looked out past him for Tess. "Speaking of, where is the famous tour guide?"

"She's at the diner, finishing her breakfast. She said to tell you that she'll be here this afternoon to help you with Sealena School."

Sealena School was the instructional course Carly offered two afternoons a week during high season to teach tourists about the history and mystery surrounding the Serpent Queen. Tess was the most Sealena-knowledgeable person in Port Serenity and Carly appreciated the little girl's familiarity and enthusiasm, but... "You sure you can spare her?" If Oliver had to lead the lighthouse tour himself, those tourists would be getting a very shortened version. "I can ask Melissa to help." Her seasonal help was turning out to be a fast learner, to Carly's relief. She'd only had two shifts so far, but she'd caught on to the register immediately and didn't mind cleaning between customers—when she wasn't sneaking off to read a copy of *Love at Sea*.

Oliver nodded. "I should pull my weight a little. Of course, my groups will be getting the condensed version of the tour," he added with a smirk, confirming Carly's suspicions and causing her heart to skip.

She loved that smirk. It was better than a smile because it was real and she knew few people got to see the real Oliver. He hadn't always been so guarded. Years ago, he was lighthearted and funny and felt comfortable around anyone, in any social setting. Since the accident, he'd become more withdrawn. Choosy about who he spent time with. Who he trusted. Carly was honored that she'd made that inner circle. After losing Alison and Catherine, she wouldn't have been able to cope with losing Oliver and Tess as well.

Which was why she kept her real feelings close to her

chest, for fear of scaring him away. Having Oliver in her life as a best friend was better than not at all.

At least, most days she could convince herself that was true.

"How's the new staff member doing?" he asked.

"She's good. I'm not sure why I hadn't thought to hire additional help sooner." That year she'd had no other choice, for reasons she hadn't yet disclosed to Oliver—or anyone.

"Because the store is the most important thing in your life," Oliver said with a touch of respect in his voice.

Carly forced a smile. Oh, if only he'd allow her to change that.

"Hey, sorry to interrupt," a voice said to their right, and they both turned toward it.

Dressed in a tan suit, light blue dress shirt open at the collar and dark brown leather shoes, Sebastian approached the store, looking a lot more professional than he had the night he'd rescued her from mortification at the pub.

Carly's face flushed at the memory. "Oh… Hi, Sebastian. Good to see you again," she said politely.

Just like the other night, she could appreciate his handsome looks, but there was not even the tiniest spark of interest that spurred within her at the sight of his dark blue eyes and dimpled chin. Especially when he was standing right next to Oliver. No one would measure up to her best friend.

How depressing.

"Nice to see you too. Although, I do miss the green hair," Sebastian said with a charming smile.

"Green hair?" Oliver asked, eyeing the other man with an expression Carly couldn't quite decipher. There was definitely a hint of judgment. And the way he'd folded his arms across his chest when Sebastian had appeared was telling. Oliver didn't trust him.

Suits in the small town were generally a bad sign.

Sebastian returned Oliver's appraising look, eyeing the casual clothes and seeming to deem Oliver as nonthreatening, then turned his gaze back to Carly. In the doorway, she shifted uncomfortably from one foot to the other, feeling caught in a tense triangle of some sort between her friend (secret love of her life) and the new man in town, whom she'd be working very closely with that summer.

"What's he talking about?" Oliver asked her, finally tearing his gaze from Sebastian.

"Long...embarrassing story," she said quickly and dismissively to Oliver. He wouldn't be impressed to hear about her participating in the Sealena costume contest. He wasn't exactly a huge Serpent Queen fan. And if she'd been spared him having to witness her embarrassing moment, she'd prefer to keep it that way. "Oliver, this is Sebastian Grant— he's the new tourism manager in town."

Oliver seemed as surprised as she'd been that the town had hired someone so young and city-ish. But he seemed to relax slightly, his expression indicating he expected the guy to last a week at most. Carly wasn't so sure.

"Carly here has graciously offered to help get me up to speed on the whole town's mythology thing—as soon as possible with the festival in four weeks," Sebastian said, sending her a look that definitely held more than just gratitude.

Carly felt her cheeks warm under the obvious attraction.

"You took the job not knowing anything about the town?" Oliver asked, a slight irritation in his tone. His guarded stance was back.

Unoffended, Sebastian had the decency to look slightly embarrassed. "I was the mayor's second choice of candidate. Apparently, the first one had to turn down the position, so I only found out that they were reconsidering my application two weeks ago. There was only so much research I could do online before arriving here."

Oliver nodded but still looked unimpressed. Carly didn't necessarily disagree with her friend's opinion. She'd have hoped that the town would have hired someone who knew the history and culture of Port Serenity. But she suspected Sebastian's appeal was his young age and more professional appearance. Their latest poll suggested that their marketing campaigns appealed to an older demographic, and with an aging population, Carly knew the town was hoping to bring in a younger crowd. Tourists needed to be a renewable resource, otherwise the industry would suffer. Repeat visitors would only spend their limited vacation dollars on this Alaskan trip for so long before wanting something different.

And nothing was ever different in Port Serenity—at least, not until Sebastian showed up.

"Well, you've come to the right place," Carly said in the awkward, tension-filled silence. "And actually, this is Oliver Klein, the local lighthouse keeper. He is quite knowledgeable as well," she said, ignoring the look Oliver shot her way. The two men seemed to be getting off to an inexplicably prickly start, and they'd need to work closely together as well. The lighthouse was a big part of the community. A peacemaker and people pleaser at heart, Carly didn't do well with conflict, and the awkward tension simmering between the two men was making her uncomfortable.

Sebastian turned to Oliver with a look of interest now. "Oliver Klein. Great to meet you. I was actually planning to come see you." Gone was his slight air of arrogance, replaced by a tone of comradery.

Odd.

"Oh?" Oliver asked, seemingly more distrusting now.

"Yeah, there's a few things I'd like to discuss and I'm dying for a tour of the oldest lighthouse in Alaska."

Well, he'd done his research on something, at least.

"Tours run four times a day," Oliver said. Then he caught Carly's pointed stare and cleared his throat. "Of course, you're welcome to stop by anytime." The offer was said begrudgingly.

But Sebastian smiled. "You'll be seeing me."

"Wonderful." Oliver glanced at his watch. "I should get going," he said to her, then paused. "But, uh, about this year's festival float…"

"It's okay if you don't have time to help," she said quickly. He always built the basic structure for her floats, but he never liked participating in the events. He seemed to hold Sealena personally responsible for the disappearance of his wife and daughter, and anything to do with the Serpent Queen just stressed him out.

Which was why she hadn't shown him the picture of her dressed as Sealena, even though it was by far the sexiest she'd ever looked in her life.

"A float for the parade! That sounds fun," Sebastian started. "I've never built one before."

Oliver glared at the man before he cleared his throat. "No. I'm in. Like always," he told her.

She wasn't sure what had spurred the commitment that he usually tried to weasel out of, but she'd take it. She'd take any opportunity to spend time with him, and secretly, she hoped he'd eventually move forward from some of the things he was struggling to hang on to, like his pain and clinging to the past. Start to open up and enjoy life again, like he used to. "Great. Thank you."

"Yeah, I'm just a little worried about these dimensions

you texted me," he said, showing her his cell phone. "Did you really mean to go this big?"

She nodded. "I measured the street, taking into account the pedestrian viewing area—it will work," she said, answering the argument she knew he'd have.

"Means we can't use the float base from last year," he said, running a hand through his hair and staring at the dimensions.

"I thought maybe you could build a new one?" she asked hopefully. Now that he'd committed to helping, she was pushing her luck.

He sighed, but nodded. "No problem."

"I can help. I'm pretty handy with a hammer," Sebastian said.

"I got it," Oliver countered.

Sebastian raised his hands in peaceful retreat. "It's all yours."

"I should go," Oliver said again.

"Tell Tess I'm looking forward to seeing her later today."

"Will do." Oliver nodded and waved as he headed back down the street toward the diner. Carly watched after him, perplexed by the odd interaction. His attitude had been almost territorial; she wasn't sure why he seemed so put off by Sebastian. Maybe just that the two of them were so obviously different.

"So? What do you say? Think you could help me with a crash course in all things Sealena before the store opens?" Sebastian asked, stealing her attention. His charming smile and easygoing demeanor were back.

She checked her watch. They had forty minutes. They'd barely scratch the surface, but they had to get started if he was going to help make the season a successful one.

"Of course. Come on in." She moved back to let him

enter and sighed, knowing her special delivery bacon-and-egg breakfast sandwich had just become lunch, or quite possibly dinner.

BETWEEN TOUR GROUPS that afternoon, Oliver pulled his pickup truck in front of the local hardware and outdoor store. Every year, he helped Carly with her float base for the Sealena Festival parade. Except the first year after Alison and Catherine had disappeared. It had been too hard, too soon. That year, breathing had been difficult, getting out of bed had been nearly impossible, and moving through the motions of everyday life had felt almost futile. Only Tess and the support from Carly had pulled him through.

So as difficult as it was for him to get on board with anything to do with the sea serpent queen, he wouldn't let Carly down.

He climbed out of the truck into the bright, warm July sunshine and headed across the busy parking lot. Residents took advantage of the milder, more agreeable weather to perform home repairs and garden maintenance, and the store was always running out of supplies. Better to grab the stuff he needed now.

No matter what kind of design Carly was planning for that year, he'd need the basics. He'd get started on the new, larger platform that week between tour groups. It was almost a relief that he had to construct something new instead of just reconstructing the old one. He didn't have much else to occupy his thoughts and time, the lighthouse repairs and new paint having been done weeks before in preparation for the high tourist season. It would be good to stay busy that week.

Pushing through the front door, he entered the store and headed for the hardwood section. Taking his measuring tape from his pocket, he double-checked Carly's dimensions and shook his head. He hoped she knew what she was doing. He filled a trolley with supplies and, ten minutes later, headed to the counter.

The woman behind the register barely noticed him as he unloaded the supplies, deep in hushed conversation with another cashier. "Apparently, he's twenty-nine and has a marketing degree from Alaska Pacific," she was saying.

Marketing degree from a private university? They could only be gossiping about one man.

"All I know is that he's gorgeous," the other cashier said. "And if I wasn't happily married with my fourth child on the way..." She laughed, patting her pregnant stomach.

"He'll definitely be turning some heads," his cashier said, finally noticing him. "Oh, hey, Oliver," she added.

"Hey," he mumbled, but now *he* was distracted by thoughts of the newcomer. Had Carly thought the guy was attractive too? He'd noticed her cheeks flush when Sebastian had approached. She'd obviously met him before, but the man didn't seem to be her type. That slick, charming, polished salesy type. Not that Oliver could truly say he knew what Carly's type was. He couldn't remember the last time she'd dated someone. She'd been in a serious relationship years ago, but since that breakup, she hadn't mentioned anyone special in her life, hadn't introduced him to anyone. He hadn't really given Carly's dating life much thought before.

He suddenly was now and it caused an odd feeling to wrap around him.

He still didn't understand the green hair comment, but the way the guy had looked at her and the casual familiarity he'd addressed her with had rubbed Oliver the wrong way. As if they shared an inside joke or something. Was the new man in town attracted to her?

It didn't matter. Or at least, it shouldn't. He and Carly were best friends. They had a history… She had been his wife's best friend and part of their family. There were some lines you just didn't cross.

Not that there hadn't been times when he'd been tempted to.

Carly was beautiful and smart and caring, and she'd not only been a source of support and a shoulder to cry on, but she'd also stepped in to help him with Tess when he'd been so lost in his own grief that he'd struggled to raise his then seven-year-old. He didn't know what he would have done without Carly.

But a deep friendship was as far as the connection went. As far as it could ever go. He'd never risk losing her by doing something stupid like giving in to the urge to kiss her that came out of nowhere sometimes when he saw her laugh…or watched her with Tess…

"A hundred and fifty-three dollars," the cashier said, interrupting his thoughts.

Oliver handed over the cash, and gathering the supplies, he headed back to his truck.

An hour later, he unloaded the items in the large wood-working shed behind the lighthouse, refusing to read too much into his newfound motivation to get to work on the float base right away.

Before someone—Sebastian—could replace him.

The man was good with a hammer. Yeah right. Those manicured hands didn't look like he'd done a day's hard labor in his entire twenty-nine years.

Oliver got to work clearing a large enough space to build a bigger platform. It meant moving around a few other things he was working on. A birthday gift for Tess—a stand-up paddleboard he'd recently started—and the covered sailboat that had sat unfinished for three years.

Would he ever finish it? Every time he was in there, he asked himself the same question, and every time, he didn't know the answer. He had an existing contract that demanded that he did...if he ever wanted to get paid for it.

But the sailboat side business had been Alison's idea. Alison's dream. After they'd built her sailboat together, she'd had the idea of starting the family business. She came up with the most beautifully elegant yet practical and cost-effective boat designs and Oliver was the one wielding the hammer. They'd even recruited Catherine and Tess, and within three months, they'd built and sold their first sailboat to a cruising company in Anchorage. Then more orders had arrived. They'd fulfilled three and business was actually starting to look like a really lucrative side hustle, something they could build a new family legacy on—until Alison and Catherine went missing and the fabrication of the current project had been permanently on hold.

*Manslaughter due to poor construct...*

The hurtful accusations on social media years ago still rang in his mind whenever he saw the covered ship hull in the corner of his shed. The investigators in the missing persons case had actually contemplated the idea that Oliver had purposely sabotaged Alison's boat...

When they hadn't found it, those suspicions had faded away, but not from his own mind. Oliver knew he hadn't purposely been negligent in the sailboat's construction, but what if he had accidentally—an oversight? What if there had been a defect that had contributed to the disappearance that day? He knew in his gut that wasn't the case. But his lack of confidence combined with the ache he felt in his chest whenever he even tried to lift that sheet was reason enough to abandon the project. Tess was disappointed that they'd let their family's plans—Alison's plans—fade into the past, but Oliver just couldn't find the passion for it anymore.

Small woodworking projects were what he filled his time with now.

And this yearly float.

He sighed, grabbing his tool belt and getting to work. The physical labor in the thick humid heat of the shed actually made him feel better, or at least silenced his thoughts about the past, about Carly...about this new Sebastian guy.

But he'd just finished the platform when a knock sounded on the shed door and he could smell the expensive cologne wafting on the air, announcing the man's presence. Glancing up, he saw Sebastian, scanning the exterior of the shed. He ran a hand along the wooden door frame and Oliver had to resist an irrational urge to tell the guy not to touch anything.

Not *anything*.

"Hey," he said, setting his hammer down and wiping his dusty hands on the front of his jeans. "Can I help you with something?"

"Told you I'd stop by," Sebastian said, entering and still scanning. His suit looked a little too tight, stretched across his muscular upper body, and the pants were slim-fit and too short, in Oliver's opinion, exposing bare ankles above his leather shoes.

Maybe that was the style these days. He wouldn't know, not having worn a suit since...the funeral.

He hadn't expected the visit so soon, but may as well give the dude his abbreviated tour and send him on his way. "Let me show you around," he said, leading the way outside.

Sebastian followed close behind as they walked across

the overgrown grassy field toward the lighthouse. "Actually, could we start with the house?"

Oliver's gut twisted as he turned to face him. What the hell did the guy want to see the house for? "Most people prefer the lighthouse tower." His home was off-limits, and obviously, this newcomer hadn't been briefed.

Sebastian nodded. "I'd like to see that too, but if you'd indulge me, there is a reason for my interest."

His chest tightened. "Which is?"

"All in good time," the man said good-naturedly, tapping him on the chest.

Oliver's fist clenched at his side, but he nodded and forced himself to relax. Technically, the house was under the town's ownership as a historical property. His family had always lived there rent-free, but they'd never owned the building or the land it was sitting on.

The fragility of his situation had never hit him before that moment.

He changed direction and headed toward the living quarters attached to the lighthouse through a small garage. The four-thousand-square-foot interior was three stories high and its design was just as impressive as the octagon-shaped tower, with its rounded bay windows and upper loft. He opened the door and stood back to let Sebastian enter.

"This place is quite something. A lot better maintained than I was expecting," Sebastian said as he walked through the open-concept living area.

Oliver's shoulders tensed. He didn't like the way this newcomer to town was assessing something that had stood there for generations. That had been in his family for years. The man had an air of arrogance that didn't fit Port Serenity's profile. It was no surprise he'd been second choice. "My family has always kept her in good shape," he said.

"All new appliances?" he asked, glancing into the kitchen.

"A few years old," Oliver said tightly. In addition to his salary from the Coast Guard Aids to Navigation program, the town provided a budget for any upgrades the house or the tower required, but Oliver had purchased the higher-end appliances himself. He liked to cook and Tess liked to bake—the kitchen was the heart of the home.

Sebastian scanned up the stairs. "Six bedrooms, right?"

The guy had obviously done his research. "That's right."

"And it's just you and your daughter currently living here?"

Oliver's gut twisted again as he nodded. He didn't like that this man knew so much about the lighthouse. About him. It wasn't difficult to find articles online about the history of this place or about Oliver himself; it was one of the reasons it was hard to move on with his life. His past was forever a simple Google search away. There was no escaping or forgetting.

"How many bathrooms?"

"Three," Oliver said tightly. "Care to tell me what's happening right now?" It felt as though the house were being appraised by a real-estate agent for potential sale.

Sebastian nodded. "Of course. Truth is, one of the things I was successful in implementing in the last community where I worked was turning their lighthouse into a successful B and B."

"A B and B?" This was his home. Sure, he'd been wondering how much longer he might stay there…but he didn't like the idea of turning his home into a vacation rental. The lighthouse was a town landmark, not some tourist trap. This guy should know that the town would never go for that.

"The mayor thought it might be a great idea," Sebastian said confidently. He lowered his voice as he added,

"He also thought that maybe you'd appreciate the opportunity to move on."

Just how much did this guy know? Or *think* he knew? Unfortunately, probably a lot. His wife and daughter's disappearance had been a source of local mystery and intrigue for months. The press had been all over Alaska, interested in reporting the story, and there had been investigators as far as Anchorage who were looking into the case.

Looking into *him* and his potential involvement.

He'd had to deal with whispers and rumors circulating through the small town for months, the most harrowing of Oliver's life as he grieved the loss, bombarded with suspicion and questioning that had nearly broken him.

If it hadn't been for Carly, and her belief in him and his innocence, he may never have made it through.

"Just something to think about," Sebastian said in his silence, handing him a new business card. He checked his watch. "I'm meeting Carly for dinner, so the tour of the lighthouse will have to wait, but I'll be in touch."

He was meeting Carly for dinner? Why did that make Oliver even more uncomfortable than the business proposition the guy had just dropped on him?

He followed the man outside and watched as he headed toward his flashy rented convertible. He climbed in and waved as he drove away.

Oliver didn't wave back. He stared at the business card in his hand, unsettled emotions running through him.

Suddenly, he felt as though time was running out and decisions he'd thought he'd get a chance to make were suddenly no longer his.

# CHAPTER FOUR

SKYLAR HAD TOLD her that the Sirens Bay steak house, just outside of town, was posh and sophisticated, but Carly hadn't expected the level of elegance from the new restaurant along the coast. With its wooden A-frame exterior and ceiling-to-floor windows providing a fantastic view from any table in the place, it was definitely more upscale dining than anything they had in Port Serenity.

She glanced at the pale blue sundress and wedge heels she'd worn for her dinner with Sebastian and felt slightly uneasy. Was the outfit fancy enough?

She wasn't big on fashion and she was even less about expensive, lavish restaurants. A cheeseburger from the diner would have suited her just perfectly, but Sebastian had insisted that their first business dinner together be held somewhere nice.

And besides, he'd said, he could expense it.

Carly wasn't quite sure she was cool with taxpayer money paying for her meal, but she wanted to get off on the right foot with Sebastian. So far, he seemed genuine in wanting to help increase tourism and businesses within the community, but he was from a big city and wasn't really familiar with how things worked in the small Alaskan town. She wanted to make sure his goals aligned with those of the community. Having been on the tourism board for years,

Carly felt she was best suited to ensure a clear understanding with the newbie.

"After you," Sebastian said, holding open the restaurant door for her to enter.

He was definitely a gentleman. He'd brought her flowers and opened the car door, but Carly hoped it wasn't blurring the lines too much. She appreciated being treated appropriately, but she needed to make sure this business date was more business than date. After spending the morning with him in the store, learning about Sealena, she knew the two of them would never be more than just friends and colleagues. While he was handsome and charming, she just didn't feel the same butterflies or spark with him as she did with Oliver.

Though, she hadn't always felt those for Oliver either. When he and Alison were together, she'd always thought of him in a platonic way. Seeing him with Alison had somehow created a shield, preventing her heart from even considering the possibility. She wasn't sure when that shield had lifted or when things had changed. Gradually, over the years, as she'd become more involved in his life, gotten to know him on different levels and saw a rare vulnerable side that he showed few people, her feelings had shifted. She'd tried resisting them, but they only grew stronger all the time.

Unfortunately, there was nothing she could do to stop them and nothing she could do to act on them.

Inside the restaurant, Carly surveyed the diners at the other tables. Suits, elegant-looking dresses, heels, jewelry sparkling under the large chandeliers hanging from the ceiling. "I feel underdressed."

"You look beautiful," Sebastian complimented her.

Carly blushed, immediately regretting her insecurity.

She hadn't said it to get a compliment. She really wasn't helping her cause.

"You're not good at taking compliments, are you?" Sebastian said.

Carly shifted uncomfortably. She never had been. Growing up, she was the bookworm, nerdy one and Alison was the beautiful, popular one. The two of them had been the best of friends despite—or maybe because of—their differences, but Carly had always been aware of her shortcomings next to Alison.

It had taken a lot to overcome her insecurities… Maybe she never fully had. Maybe that was one of the reasons she couldn't open up fully to Oliver about how she felt. Fear of his rejection because of the circumstance was one thing. Fear of his rejection based on simply not feeling the same attraction to her was on a whole other level. He'd loved Alison. She was nothing like Alison. Therefore, how could he possibly love her in that way?

Instead of answering Sebastian's loaded question, she smiled at the hostess as she led the way to their reserved table in the corner. Discreet, cozy and slightly too intimate.

Sebastian either agreed or sensed her discomfort as he said, "I'm sorry—could we maybe move to a different table? Maybe near the window with better lighting?"

Carly sent him a grateful look as the hostess nodded and brought them to a different area of the restaurant.

"This okay?" he asked.

"Perfect. Thanks," she said, sitting when he pulled out her chair.

When he took his seat across from her, the hostess handed them both menus. "Your server will be right with you," she said and smiled before walking away.

Carly surveyed the food options. There were very few.

A single sheet listing only three appetizer selections, three main course selections and three desserts—that all sounded mouthwatering. No prices listed next to the choices meant this bill would give the tourism office accountant a minor heart attack.

"Should we start with wine?" Sebastian asked, reaching for the wine menu, which boasted many options. Again, no prices.

Carly supposed business meetings could include alcohol… but she saw her opportunity to put the focus back on the intention of the evening. "Actually, I'm good with sparkling water."

Sebastian smiled and nodded, looking slightly relieved. "Me too."

The waiter approached and they ordered their sparkling waters and salads to start. Then Sebastian launched immediately into talk of his plans for the town. "I may not be a resident with long-standing roots in the community, but I think that helps to bring a new perspective," he said.

Carly nodded slowly, but hesitantly. It could also bring an off-brand perspective, one that could take the town in a direction that could fail or, at the very least, destroy the reputation they'd built over the last three generations. Port Serenity thrived because everyone was usually on the same page. They worked together to achieve goals that were for the greater good of the community, even if that meant sometimes sacrificing individual needs or desires.

Would a city guy like Sebastian understand and, more importantly, appreciate that?

"I have been studying all the material you recommended," he continued enthusiastically, a welcome change.

Most of the tourism board members were older, had sat on the committee for decades, and, well, they were losing some of their excitement for the position. Sebastian's energy was slightly contagious and her eyes widened. "All of it?" He'd left the store with quite a lot of material that morning.

He laughed and nodded. "Benefits of being a speed reader, I guess."

She smiled sincerely, admittedly impressed by the effort. "Well? What did you think?"

"I think that Port Serenity has a very rich and layered history. And that the town has only scratched the surface of the things they could be exploring and offering to tourists."

Carly leaned forward, her curiosity piqued. This was exactly the kind of thinking that had been lacking on the recent committee. No one wanted to discuss new ideas. Sticking with the old tried, tested and true was safer, even if it was costing them in new generations of tourists. "Such as?"

"The maps of the town and the surrounding areas show a lot of fantastic wilderness that is currently difficult to navigate."

Her enthusiasm dampened slightly and her gut tightened. "Some of that is on purpose." They allowed tourists to come and appreciate their magnificent wildlife and everything the backwoods had to offer, but they also wanted to preserve nature as much as possible. As soon as the backwoods were more easily accessible and tourists were given access, the pollution went up and the unspoiled landscape needed to be altered and changed. Paths cleared and marked. Garbage and recycling bins added. Most likely a parking lot and pay booth, if the town wanted to capitalize financially on the developments.

Sebastian nodded, reaching into his pocket for something.

A map.

He had actually brought a map with him. Carly relaxed

a little. She had been stressing for nothing. This was obviously a business meeting for him too.

Moving aside the flowers and candles from the center of the table, he unfolded the map and stretched it out. He pointed to several areas along the mountains. "Most of this area is undeveloped and should absolutely remain that way. But what about here?" he said, pointing to the area that led to the falls.

The glacial waterfalls had once been a well-kept secret. In winter, spring and fall, only locals dared to go to them, as the hike in could be treacherous and the frigid water, while breathtakingly beautiful, was too cold to get in…but in summer, the attraction was becoming popular with the tourists. Word of mouth had spread about their beauty and the refreshing plunge from the rocks. Several blog posts from visitors had turned it into an off-the-beaten-path must-see in Port Serenity.

She nodded. "I could see these being a great attraction. People already know about them, so promoting them wouldn't be jeopardizing any sacred lands or places only locals know about."

Sebastian looked pleased that he'd gotten something right. "So, I'd have your support in suggesting the falls and this area from the coast all the way inland—" he gestured to the map "—to the committee for developing?"

Carly felt a sense of pride that he wanted her support, that she was involved and getting a bigger say in these things. She'd sat on the tourism board for years, but rarely did it feel that decisions were truly in her hands. They voted as a committee, but with the previous tourism manager, it had always felt so ceremonial, like the real decision had already been made between him and the mayor.

Maybe Sebastian was the right choice for the community.

"You have my support," she said as the waiter arrived and shot them an annoyed look.

"Sorry," she mumbled, helping Sebastian clear the map from the table. They put the flowers and candles back in the center as the waiter placed their waters and salads in front of them.

When he walked away, Sebastian raised his glass to Carly and she clinked hers against it. "To one proposal decided…and many more to come," he said.

Thank goodness they were on the same page. She sipped the bubbly water and relaxed, feeling the uneasiness settle. The town was in capable hands with Sebastian Grant at the helm.

BY NOW, HE suspected Carly and Sebastian would be enjoying dessert and planning world domination.

Oliver swung the hammer, driving the nail through the plank of wood.

Damn.

He pulled it out and reached for a new one. Despite all efforts to keep his thoughts and hands busy that evening, Oliver couldn't push the idea of Carly and Sebastian dining out together from his mind.

It was just because he didn't like or trust the man. That was all. He didn't think the man had Port Serenity's best intentions in mind and he knew Carly would see through the bullshit, but it still made him slightly uneasy. His best friend might be swayed by the man's charm—at least for a while—and he didn't like the idea that she might get hurt. Personally, or if the guy destroyed generations of progress the town had made.

Oliver finished hammering in the nails in the float base and stood back to examine it. At ten feet long and five feet wide, it would definitely check off Carly's requirements for bigger and better that year. It would also require a lot more work to fill the space. After the base was handed off, Carly usually recruited some friends, including Tess, to complete the design aspect, and that year, he suspected she'd need all the help she could get.

Maybe he'd even offer an extra set of hands.

He pulled out his phone and snapped a photo of it. Opening a text to her, he attached the photo and started to type... then deleted it.

He wouldn't interrupt her evening.

Even though he really, really wanted to.

Instead, he locked up the shed and headed into the house. His stomach growled. He hadn't eaten anything since breakfast.

Carly must not have eaten hers. Otherwise, she would have commented about the message he'd written on the back of the receipt for her.

Too busy educating Sebastian.

"Tess! Where you at?" Maybe they could head into town for dinner...go to the diner or The Noodle Hut on Main Street. Not that he was hoping to run into Carly and Sebastian at the more popular local restaurants. He just didn't feel like cooking that evening, that was all.

"In here!"

He followed the sound of her voice to the living room and found her tangled in Scotch tape and ribbon. "What are you doing?" A long run of Christmas-themed wrapping paper was rolled out on the floor and a large metal cage sat on it.

"Trying to wrap this for Darcy."

"You're giving her an empty cage?" He immediately scanned the room in case there was supposed to be something in the cage. He wasn't a fan of rodents. Tess had been asking for a guinea pig for years and his answer was always the same.

A big *hell no*.

He didn't deny her much, but the idea of having a furry little creature loose in his house gave him the heebie-jeebies.

"Relax, Dad," she said, sensing his anxiety. "Callan and Rachel are giving her two new rabbits for her birthday and they said I could give her the cage. We only had Christmas wrapping paper upstairs, but I think she'll think it's funny," Tess said, tearing off a long stretch of tape and trying to secure the paper in place.

"Let me help," he said, entering the room now that there was no sign of a critter present. He lifted the cage so she could cover it more easily with the paper.

"Thanks," she said, folding the ends and securing it. Then she took a long strand of red ribbon, wrapped it around the cage and tied a large bow.

"Perfect," he said, setting it down on the table. "When's the party?" He remembered Rachel giving her the invite the week before, but he'd been too preoccupied with the start of tourist season to pay much attention to the details.

Tess shot him an exasperated look. "I told you ten times already. It's tomorrow."

"What time?"

"Boat sails at noon," she said casually, avoiding his gaze.

"Boat?" His tone was anything but casual and he didn't even try to hide the worry in his tone.

"The party is on the family tour boat. You already said I can go," she said, preempting any argument from him.

"Yeah, I know..." He ran a hand through his hair. He actually couldn't remember agreeing to this. He suspected any conversation they'd had about it must have been while he was suitably distracted. But Darcy was her best friend, so there was no way he wouldn't let her go. Though he would have preferred the party be somewhere on land, it wasn't his call to make. "Of course you can go."

She looked relieved. "Speaking of birthdays, what were you working on in the shed?" she asked mischievously.

He suspected she suspected he was making her something for her birthday. No doubt she'd already peeked around the shed for evidence of it. His daughter was a little snoop. Every Christmas, she found all the presents hidden for her in the closet or the attic. She'd unwrap them all and rewrap them again before Christmas morning. She had no problem ruining the surprise and she could win an Oscar for her performance.

"I was actually working on the parade float base for Carly," he said.

His daughter's eyes lit up. "She showed me her design. It's going to be badass." Her hand covered her mouth as the word slipped out.

Oliver hid a grin as he shook his head. His youngest was a firecracker for sure and he loved her spirit. He just hoped he was up to the challenge of helping her channel the passion and determination into something productive and safe. "I'm sure it will indeed be badass." He hadn't seen the design yet, but Carly's store floats were always the best ones in the parade. She poured her heart into everything she did and it showed.

"Where is Carly, anyway? I tried texting her a few times about an idea I had for teaching Sealena School next week, but she hasn't responded," Tess said, gathering the discarded ends of wrapping paper and ribbon.

So, she was ignoring her phone. That didn't mean anything other than she was being polite. Still, he couldn't stop the image of her and Sebastian gazing longingly at one another over a shared milkshake with two straws from appearing in his mind. Apparently, his idea of modern dating looked like something out of an Archie comic.

He sighed. "Ah... I think she had a business dinner."

"With that Sebastian guy?" Tess asked, wrinkling her nose.

He immediately felt justified in his own dislike of the guy. Tess had an impeccably accurate sense about people. "Yeah. He's the new tourism manager and they are going to be working together."

"He wears pants that are too short and no socks with his dress shoes," Tess said.

Oliver hid a grin. "You met him?"

"He was leaving the store when I arrived for Sealena School today," Tess said.

"Other than his questionable fashion sense, what did you think?"

Tess thought for a moment. "Well, in fairness, he was carrying a lot of books about the community and Carly seemed different..."

His gut twisted. "Different? Different how?"

Tess shrugged. "Happier or something. I don't know."

Happier or something. Carly deserved to be happier or something, so why did that make Oliver definitely not happier...or something?

# CHAPTER FIVE

SHE WAS FORGETTING SOMETHING.

The next morning, as Carly hurried through the restocking and store opening procedures, the nagging feeling that she'd forgotten to do something important weighed on her.

All the new stock was brought out and displayed. She'd placed a new order for all of the items they were getting low on. She'd Windexed all the tourist fingerprints from all the glass display cases… She scanned the store. Then, spotting the bag from the diner with her breakfast in it from the day before, she sighed.

That must be it. She'd forgotten to eat her bacon-and-egg sandwich with double bacon. It probably wasn't the best idea to eat it now after it'd sat out all day. She picked it up and opened it. She took the sandwich out and sniffed. Then gagged.

*Nope. Can't eat that.*

She tossed it back into the bag and noticed writing on the back of the receipt. Taking it out, she read the note in Oliver's handwriting.

*Two mai tais on the beach sounds perfect right about now…*

Still dreaming of running away. She smiled and sighed simultaneously.

This, they could do. This game of make-believe. Dreaming of a vacation they'd never take and hiding behind texts and diner receipt messages to talk about the impossible possibility. In person, they never talked about things like this. They never flirted or joked or toyed with the idea of doing something crazy together—like running away to a secluded beach, abandoning their responsibilities, forgetting the past, enjoying the moment together.

Only from behind the security of messages did Oliver ever go along with her playful teasing that hid a secret lingering hope...

Pulling out her cell phone, she texted:

I may need more than one.

Knowing he'd understand.

That was the thing. They did understand one another. Without having to say it, he understood she'd be there for him in any capacity he needed and she knew without him saying it that he'd only ever need her friendship.

Some days, she wished for less understanding. With less understanding, there could be a harmless mistake, like an ill-timed, impulsive kiss or a touching of hands... But the way their relationship stood, there was no room to fantasize in real life. Only in messages.

Tucking the receipt into her pocket because she couldn't bring herself to throw it away, she tossed out the sandwich in the back room as the door to the store opened and Rachel entered. She was dressed in a blue-and-white-striped off-the-shoulder top and flowing white pants, with wedge heels and a blue-and-white hair bandanna completing her fashionable look.

"Someone's ready for the birthday party," Carly said, admiring her friend's style and courage. She looked like she belonged on a yacht, not a small tour boat, but she owned the look with confidence and pulled it off flawlessly.

"You're still coming, right?" Rachel asked, approaching the counter.

"Yep. Melissa will be here to take over at eleven thirty." It would be the first time in two years that Carly had left the store in the hands of someone else. But the young girl was doing great—she was a master at upselling—and she was responsible.

The store would be fine. Still, there was that nagging feeling that she hadn't prepped something properly. Had she checked the float? Made sure there was enough till tape to get Melissa through the day? Because sometimes that was a pain in the butt to change…

"I can't wait to see Darcy's face when she gets your gift," Rachel said excitedly.

Her stomach dropped. That was it. She'd forgotten to pick up the *Stranger Things* merchandise she'd ordered for Darcy from the pop-up store in Seattle. She'd had no idea what to get the little girl until Rachel had mentioned it, and Carly had begged her to let her get the coveted backpack and T-shirt featuring the cast.

She'd ordered it weeks ago and had recently received the shipping notification that it had arrived in town. She'd meant to go to the post office the day before. It was on the other side of town, almost an hour away with tourist traffic, in the same building as the mayor's office, but she'd been distracted with Sebastian.

Rachel looked slightly panicked as she studied her. "Did you forget?"

"No…of course not." She'd find a way to get it before the party. A quick glance at her watch revealed it would be an almost impossible feat.

If Rachel sensed she was lying or panicked, she didn't seem to notice. "Oh good, because she hasn't stopped asking if we could order the items in her online shopping cart and I'm running out of excuses for why not."

"Nothing to worry about," Carly reassured her.

"Okay, so the real reason I came in..." Rachel retrieved a book from her purse and clutched *Love at Sea* to her chest. It was less than two days old and looked like it had been through a war zone. Rachel was one of those readers who believed books were meant to be enjoyed; therefore, she dog-eared pages, wrote in the margins, highlighted text and broke the spine with disregard. Carly held her books in a more reverent way, but she let people enjoy their reading as they would. No judgment.

"I had two more last-minute RSVPs for book club Tuesday."

"So, that makes everyone in town?"

Rachel laughed. "I'm sorry—I can't stop talking about this book. Have you finished reading yet?"

"Not quite. I was out last night," she said. Should she tell Rachel about the business meeting/dinner date with Sebastian? Her friend would definitely read far too much into it and she was already encouraging Carly to date and put herself out there. Carly had never confided in anyone except her cousin Skylar about her feelings for Oliver, and while she and Rachel were close, she wasn't quite ready to share that with her yet. If ever. There didn't seem to be much point in talking about something that would never happen.

And without a concrete excuse to keep Sebastian in the friend zone, Rachel was sure to try to play matchmaker. Probably best to keep the info about dinner to herself for now...

Luckily, Rachel didn't seem even the slightest bit curious about Carly's previous evening's plans, as she was still only concerned about the book. "Carly, you're killing me. You own a bookstore!"

Carly laughed. "I'm busy selling the books, not reading them."

"I can't wait any longer. Ready or not, you're getting a spoiler. Listen to the opening scene from the third book," she said excitedly.

Carly sighed, knowing there was no deterring her friend.

Rachel flipped to the back of *Love at Sea*, where an excerpt from the upcoming third book, *A Lasting Passion*, was included as a teaser and read:

> *"The fisherman's home is exactly how I'd pictured it. A small, modest white bungalow near the water's edge, secluded, surrounded by trees with a slight yard. Veggies grow on a plot of soil and a tire swing hangs from a magnificent tree, swaying empty in the breeze as fall leaves decorate the ground below. Inside the shed, I can see several canoes and fishing gear hung on hooks. Outside, fish salt on the rack.*
>
> *The house holds an eerie loneliness, but I'm haunted by the sounds of spirits all around me. Laughter. Gentle, tiny voices.*
>
> *He used to have a family here.*
>
> *I remember when there used to be others on his fishing vessel...then it was just him.*
>
> *Time is different here on land. It ticks away one's life, replacing moments with memories, each one leading to the last. The fisherman's family have grown, moved away... They have their own families and so the cycle continues. His wife perished from too many days in this cold, isolated small town.*

*My bare feet move across the ground, the over-grown grass tickles my ankles, my toes seep into the cold, wet earth. A breeze blows across my flesh and my hair covers my face. So many new sensations at once. Overwhelming, yet exciting.*

*I approach the front door and slowly turn the knob. It's not locked, so I enter. He's not home. He's out on the water. I'm safe. I won't be discovered.*

*I breathe in the scent of the home—a faint musky smell of old, dated furniture and window drapings combined with the lingering smoky scent of a wood-stove recently snuffed out. As I move, the wood pan-els beneath my feet creak and moan as though tired from years of supporting the burden. I run my hand over the soft, worn fabric of an armchair that holds the fisherman's scent. I picture him seated there in the dim light of the fireplace, alone, and my chest aches.*

*There are photos on the wall in frames of mis-matched shapes and sizes. Black-and-white photos, then sepia, then color—generations of family. All smiling. All hiding all sorts of secrets that families cannot escape. I stare at the image of the fisher-man's wife with her pale skin and light blue eyes, her blond hair and thin, frail-looking frame. She's hauntingly beautiful with sorrow reflecting in her expression that not even the thin-lipped smile can fool. She had everything, yet she was sad here in the Alaskan wilderness with only the fisherman's love to try to save her.*

*Frailty can't survive here.*

*In the kitchen, bread sits on a cutting board on the counter along with a sharp-edged knife. Old cof-fee still sits in the pot and dishes are in the sink. The fisherman eats the same sandwich and drinks the same coffee every day. I open the lid and dip my finger into the dark liquid, grimacing at the strong, bitter taste on my tongue.*

*Maybe I'll like the sandwich.*

*I move down the hall toward his bedroom. The quilt on the bed looks homemade—and unrumpled—as though no one has slept there for a long time. The closet door is open and I see the clothes hanging inside—both his and hers. A vanity is still covered with bottles of colorful liquid and a silver hairbrush, the past perfectly preserved.*

*His life is lonely. I can feel it within the walls. I can hear it whispering in the items that hold a thin layer of dust. Abandoned and forgotten...like the fisherman's heart.*

*I shouldn't be here, but I've made the decision and now I have to see it through.*

*Hearing the front door open, my heart races and a flurry of odd sensations rush through me. Fear, anxiety, apprehension—I've never felt these things before. I'm not sure what to do with my pounding heart and trembling knees.*

*What will he do when he sees me? What will he say?*

*I step out of the bedroom as he appears in the hallway. His expression is empty for a long moment, then gradually becomes expectant, as though he's not surprised to see me standing in his home. He knew he'd see me there someday.*

*A real person. A real woman. Not a sea serpent. A thing of many legends. Not a mythical being he's only imagined.*

*I am standing there, in front of him, and I'm the one frozen in fear."*

Rachel looked up from the pages in absolute awe. "You know what this means, right?"

Carly hid a grin. "Sealena has no problem breaking and entering?"

Rachel released an exasperated sigh. "It means Sealena is on land in the third book! She's using her thirty-day pass to be with the fisherman!"

"Wow," Carly said, trying to sound suitably surprised and intrigued.

"I can't believe the third book is going to be the last. What am I going to do with myself once this series is over?" Rachel said dramatically.

Carly laughed. "I'm sure you'll survive."

Rachel shook her head. "I've actually signed the petition going around."

Carly's smile faded. "What petition?"

"For the author to write more books in the series."

More books? She frowned. "It's a trilogy. It was always meant to be a trilogy."

"Well, maybe Y.C. Salwert shouldn't have written such an engaging series," Rachel said. She glanced at her watch. "Oops. I gotta go. I've left Callan to do the decorating. I was supposed to be out grabbing the cake," she said with a laugh. "I'll see you at the party?"

"Yeah, I'll see you soon," Carly said distractedly as Rachel left the store.

More books. The fans wanted more books.

Right now, Carly had her own issues. She had to somehow get into town, pick up the gift from the post office, get it wrapped and get to the docks before the birthday party. The boat was leaving at noon and it was already after ten.

She bit her lip and tapped her fingers along the counter. Then, without further hesitation, she texted Sebastian:

Could I ask a huge favor?

The tourism office was in the same building as the post office. If he was there and could pick up the package for her, it would save her a lot of time and she might just make it. It wouldn't be wrapped in the Sealena-themed birthday wrapping she'd intended, but she'd bring along a bow to stick on the shipping box. It was what was inside that mattered to Darcy anyway, right?

Dots that he was replying appeared immediately, as though he'd been waiting for her to text, then:

Anything for my partner in crime.

The message was slightly flirty, which made her slightly uneasy to be reaching out so soon after their business dinner. She didn't want to give him the wrong impression, but she was desperate, and he was the only one who could get her out of this jam. Not an ideal situation to be indebted to a man she was determined to keep things professional with, but she had no other choice.

She couldn't show up at Darcy's birthday party without the gift, even if it was on its way. That would be lame. She didn't want to disappoint the child, especially after she'd begged Rachel to let her get the *Stranger Things* items in the first place.

After a quick call to the post office authorizing the

pickup, she texted Sebastian the details and a copy of the shipping delivery notification.

I'm on it. Meet you at the docks just before noon?

Damn, how could she ask him to go through all that trouble and then not invite him along? It wasn't another date or anything, just a friendly gesture of thanks. And it would be good for him to get to know Callan more, as he did own one of the tour boat businesses in town...

She was justifying, but she was stuck and it would be a dick move not to invite him after he helped her out. She knew Rachel would be thrilled and read it completely wrong, but Carly would deal with that. She sighed as she texted:

Thank you so much... And if you're free, you should tag along.

*Please don't be free.* She liked Sebastian a lot, but this was sure to give him the wrong impression.

Three dots, then his message appeared.

Was hoping you'd ask. :)

Oh no.

OLIVER LOWERED HIS sunglasses from his ball cap over his eyes as he climbed out of his truck parked near the dock just before noon. He opened the passenger-side door for Tess and helped her hop down as she struggled under the weight of the large gift she carried. Dressed in her swimsuit and flip-flops, her long hair poking out the back of a ball cap, she was practically vibrating with excitement.

"Sure you got that?" he asked, slinging her bag over his shoulder as he shut the truck door.

"Yep," she said, racing off ahead of him toward the pier, where a group of kids eagerly waited to greet her. She was a popular, well-liked kid and he was grateful for the friends she had. They were a good group, and while they'd never replace Catherine and the bond Tess had with her sister, her friends helped fill a void in a lot of ways.

Still didn't calm Oliver's unease about this birthday party on a boat.

The *Sea Secrets* fishing and tours boat bobbed along the edge of the pier, birthday balloons and decorations visible, and the sound of the Radio Disney version of hip-hop music came from within the cabin as they headed toward it.

He knew his fear was unjustified. Callan was a trained coast guard officer who had been on the elite drug operation squad. He'd navigated top cruising speeds, chasing after criminals on rough open waters for years, and he'd worked on the tour boat with his family since he was a child. He had a boating license before a driver's license and the man was skilled at any and all lifesaving techniques. They weren't going out too far from the marina, they all knew first aid, and Tess herself was a competent swimmer.

And yet nothing eased the worry gripping him as he forced a smile and greeted Callan, who was standing next to the boat. "Hey, man. You couldn't have asked for a better day for the party," he said politely, extending a fist bump. The skies were blue and the breeze was mild. The ocean was calm, rated a force one, with less than half-meter waves, according to the nautical forecast he'd checked a dozen times already that day. No predicted change for the next few hours.

Nothing to worry about.

Callan nodded. "We lucked out." He took Tess's bag from Oliver and slung it over his shoulder, where six other backpacks already hung. "Did she remember sunblock?"

"Should be in the bag. She already applied a layer at home." Being on a boat with its cool breeze could be deceiving when it came to the UV strength of the sun. Oliver always insisted on SPF 50 and a swim shirt—which she had already removed.

He frowned and shook his head. What could he expect when none of her friends were wearing one? He waved her toward him and she begrudgingly ran back. "Hug?"

"'Bye, Dad." Tess leaned against him for a quick side hug and then hurried on board to join her friends.

Oliver sighed as he waved. Guess it was better than nothing. Another year or two and he'd be lucky to get the half-hearted, half-a-second side hug.

Callan eyed him. "You're welcome to join us," he said.

"Oh no. I'm sure Tess would rather I didn't." He may not be the coolest dad on the planet, but he knew not to crash his daughter's fun.

"You sure?" Callan asked when he continued to peer on board.

"Yeah. Absolutely. Have a great day. Be careful." The tour boat was old but well maintained. The upgraded communication system was top-notch…

If only that was enough to slow his thundering heartbeat.

It was only a few hours. She would be fine. She'd be better than fine. She'd come home hyped up on sugar, with an amazing takeaway bag, and insist they immediately start planning her own party for later that summer.

"Oliver? You coming along?" Carly's voice on the dock behind him made him turn.

She was dressed in a two-piece swimsuit, visible beneath a tight white tank top and cutoff jean shorts. Flip-flops and a wide-brimmed hat completed her casual, summery look. One that shouldn't have his mouth going dry at the sight. It wasn't the clothes but the curvy body underneath that had his gaze drifting over her as though it had a mind of its own. Perfectly round, soft-looking breasts appeared above the tank top, and long, tanned legs extended below the shorts. Her toes were a pretty pink color and he couldn't remember if she'd ever painted her toes before. She must have, but he'd never noticed.

He was noticing now. Noticing so much…

She waved a hand in front of his face when he just stood there, taking her in. "Earth to Oliver," she said with a laugh.

He snapped out of the odd trance her pretty pink toes had put him in and cleared his throat. "Just dropping off Tess. You're going?" He should have suspected she would. She and Rachel were close and Carly adored Darcy. She often held sleepovers at her place with the two young girls. She was an honorary aunt of sorts and the kids loved spending time with her. She'd make a great mother if she ever wanted children of her own. Did she? Was she wanting to have a family? Husband too? How had he never wondered about that? They were best friends, but he was starting to see that the relationship had definitely been one-sided in his favor for a long time. He thought he knew her, but all of a sudden there seemed to be a lot he didn't know.

And wanted to know…

"Wouldn't miss a chance to eat birthday cake," she said with a smile.

"Who's manning the shop?"

"I've left Melissa in charge for today."

Her smile faded slightly and he could tell by her tone she wasn't completely confident in that decision.

"I mean, what's the worst she can do, right?"

Oliver nodded. "Right."

"No, I mean it. Tell me—what's the worst she could do?" Carly asked with a fake hint of desperation.

Oliver laughed and some of his tension eased. Carly had that effect on him. His best friend was like a miracle drug some days. One he was afraid to become too reliant on, lest he become addicted, because what if it suddenly wasn't available anymore? Realizing he wasn't in the know about her future goals had him suddenly sweating that he might not be a part of them. Sure, they were best friends now, but what if she met someone, fell in love, got married and had babies of her own... Where did that leave him?

He shook his head as the thoughts spiraled. *Man, pull it together!*

Unfortunately, on a more immediate level, thoughts of her interaction with Sebastian still plagued him. How had the date gone? Would there be another?

He wanted to ask, but how did he without sounding jealous? 'Cause he definitely wasn't jealous. He was just curious...

"Maybe I should call and check in before we set sail," Carly said, reaching for her phone in the back pocket of her jean shorts.

Oliver stopped her. "I'm sure the store will be..." His voice trailed as his gaze shifted past her and he saw Sebastian walking down the pier toward them. The man was dressed for a day out on the water, wearing khaki shorts, a white polo shirt and sandals. And the large birthday present he carried solidified Oliver's suspicions. He frowned.

What the hell was Sebastian doing going to the child's birthday party?

Carly caught his stare and looked slightly flushed as she waved at Sebastian.

Obviously, their date had gone well.

"He helped pick up the gift I'd ordered for Darcy from the post office this morning while I made sure Melissa was set up…and then I kinda felt obligated to invite him," Carly said quickly in a hushed whisper.

"That was nice of him," Oliver said, his back teeth clenching. Why hadn't Carly asked him to pick up the gift? He was the one she usually relied on for emergencies like that. If she'd chosen Sebastian to save the day, then she must have a connection with him already.

"He was at the mayor's office anyway…"

"No need to explain. I get it," he said as casually as possible.

"Are you annoyed I didn't ask you to drive an hour across town to pick up the gift?"

As a matter of fact, yes. "Why would I be annoyed by that?" he asked.

Carly released a slightly exasperated sigh. "I don't know, Oliver. You tell me."

"Nothing to tell. I'm not."

"Good."

"Perfect."

Callan, who'd been quietly observing the two of them, cleared his throat. "You know, Oliver, I'd actually really like it if you came along. I wanted to talk to you about…a few coast guardy things," he said.

Carly's eyes narrowed suspiciously, but Oliver sent the man a grateful look. "Sure, I can tag along." That way, he could make sure Tess was okay, that's all. His change of heart had nothing to do with Carly and Sebastian.

"Hi, everyone! Sorry I'm late," Sebastian said, joining them.

"You're just in time," Callan said politely, extending a hand.

The two men shook hands and Oliver gave an odd wave to the guy in greeting. Sebastian offered a curt head nod in return. Obviously neither of them was thrilled to see the other.

"Thanks for grabbing the gift," Carly said, smiling up at the other man.

Oliver tried to decipher the smile. Flirty or simply friendly? Grateful and polite? Or seductive and meaningful? Man, he couldn't read her when it came to this guy at all. It was frustrating as hell. And even more frustrating was the fact that it was frustrating.

"Not a problem," Sebastian said, sending Carly a definitively flirty look.

"You even wrapped it," she said, turning the box over in her hands to appreciate the *Stranger Things*–themed paper. "Where did you even get this?"

Sebastian looked sheepish. "I'd love to let you think I pulled off this impressive feat, but the box was already wrapped. I just took the shipping labels off and covered that spot with a bow I stole from a welcome gift box of chocolates the mayor's wife gave me."

Carly laughed. "Well, you totally could have let me believe you'd done this, so thank you for your honesty."

Oliver's head swiveled back and forth. What the hell was going on? He thought he might be physically ill watching the friendly banter happening in front of him. Carly couldn't seriously be into this guy, could she? Sure, he was good-looking and successful and had been there when she needed him... Wait—where was he going with that thought?

"Should we go?" Callan asked, hopping onto the deck of the boat.

"Good idea," Carly said, moving toward it. She balanced the gift on one arm as she judged the distance from the dock to the deck.

Oliver's hand shot out to help her on board the same moment Sebastian's did. Both men locked eyes in a silent battle of wills.

Who would Carly choose?

She laughed as she ignored both, and after handing Callan the gift, she propped her hands onto his shoulders and hopped into the boat herself.

"Nicely done," Callan said, a smirk on his face.

"Where's Rachel?" Carly asked, obviously having reached her fill of testosterone.

"In the cabin, putting out the food."

"I'll go see if she needs help," Carly said.

Oliver watched her disappear into the cabin and he heard the sound of her soft, vibrant laughter a moment later. A sound that warmed him with a new awareness. He loved that sound. There were days he actually lived for that sound. He used to be lighthearted and fun, but in recent years, that side of him had dulled and only Carly ever brought it out. He realized now it wasn't so much him wanting to make her laugh as needing to hear the laugh himself.

Damn.

"Well, it was great to see you again, Oliver," Sebastian said dismissively, climbing onto the boat deck.

"I'm actually coming along too," he said smugly, jumping expertly on board.

"Oh. Great," Sebastian replied, though it was obviously anything but.

The tension between them still lingered, amplified after their last conversation about Sebastian's intention to turn Oliver and Tess's home into a B and B. Had Sebastian mentioned their conversation to Carly? Had he told her about his plans? She would have said something, texted him... Surely, she didn't know. How would she feel about it when Sebastian did share his intentions with her?

Oliver didn't think for a second that his best friend would think it was a good idea.

"Hey, can one of you untie that rope?" Callan asked, pointing to the rope keeping the boat secured to the dock.

"Aye aye, Captain," Sebastian said in a pirate-sounding voice before leaning over to untie the boat while Oliver resisted every urge to push the man overboard.

If she was purposely *trying* to make Oliver jealous—and she absolutely was not—it was working.

Carly watched from inside the cabin as he and Sebastian chatted with Callan out on the deck as he drove the boat. She couldn't hear what they were saying with the loud kid-friendly music playing on board and the sounds of the girls' squeals of laughter as they tried to play water twister on the swaying back deck, but she could read Oliver's body language and he was more than a little annoyed that she'd invited Sebastian along for the party.

"So...you two?" Rachel asked, curiosity in her tone, catching Carly's stare.

"Me and Oliver?"

"You and Sebastian!"

"Oh. Um...nothing. Just working together on the town's

new marketing plan, that's all," she said, accepting a glass of wine from her friend.

"But you invited him to come to the party today." Rachel raised her eyebrow, daring Carly to bullshit her.

Carly sighed. "Full disclosure—he saved my ass. I'd forgotten to pick up the gift at the post office and he was there." Better to be honest than have Rachel think there was more to it than that.

"Handsome, smart, successful *and* dependable. You're not doing very well arguing your case for why you shouldn't date him," Rachel said, opening the fridge and retrieving the birthday cake—shaped like Sealena, of course—before starting to put candles on it.

Carly knew Rachel had a point. Sebastian would be a great catch for any woman in town, but she just didn't feel a spark with Sebastian. Not like the one she felt with just a simple look from Oliver.

Like now.

His gaze landed on her and lingered a beat before he gave an awkward little wave, as though embarrassed for having been caught looking at her.

If only he got it. He could look at her as much as he damn well wanted!

She sighed as he returned his attention to the conversation with the men, then helped Rachel with the candles on the cake.

"I'm just saying," Rachel continued. "Why not give Sebastian a chance? I mean, sure, you two are very different— some might say from different worlds, like Sealena and the fisherman, but…"

Oh, hell no. They weren't comparing her love life to the fantasy romance series. She held up a hand before Rachel could really make her case. "I'm in love with Oliver," she hissed. Admitting it was the only way to get Rachel off her back.

Her friend's eyes widened and her mouth gaped. The lighter lingered on the candle until Rachel flinched. "Ow! Hot!"

Carly took the lighter before her friend burned the boat down.

"Oliver?" Rachel echoed in a loud whisper.

Carly nodded as she finished lighting the candles on the cake.

"Since when?" Rachel asked, fully engaged.

Forever maybe? "I don't know… A few years, I guess?"

"A few years?" Her voice rose.

"Shhhh…"

"Does he know?"

Carly shook her head so violently, her braid nearly fell into one of the flames. This conversation was getting dangerous. "Let's talk about it later."

Rachel looked annoyed to have to put a pin in the juicy conversation, but she nodded. "These candles are burning fast," she said, picking up the cake.

"Poor kids. Hope they don't mind the taste of wax," Carly muttered as she followed Rachel out onto the deck.

No one—kids or adults—seemed to mind and the entire cake was devoured in no time. Hyped on the sugar rush, Darcy and Tess begged Callan to set up the banana boat to pull behind them.

Carly noticed Oliver stiffen slightly as the long, yellow inflatable was tossed out into the water and Callan secured it to the back of the tour boat. They were moored just outside the marina and the water was calm and still, the bright sun the biggest hazard to safety that day, but still, when the kids all prepared to jump in for the ride, Carly kicked off her sandals and peeled off her tank top and shorts.

Oliver wasn't dressed for the water—his tagging along had been such a last-second decision—and she knew he'd feel more at ease with Tess being out there if an adult was out there too. Callan had to drive the boat and Rachel wasn't a huge fan of the water.

Besides, it wasn't exactly a hardship for her to participate. She loved water activities and she hadn't been on a banana boat ride in forever.

As she folded her clothes on the boat bench seat, her cell phone chimed in her shorts pocket. Retrieving it, she read the message from Oliver.

New swimsuit?

He actually noticed? Oliver Klein, the man who hadn't noticed she'd grown her hair long again after a shampoo commercial had tempted her to cut it short two years ago, the man who hadn't noticed she'd recently lost fifteen pounds and now had biceps courtesy of her boxing trainer at the gym, and the man who had yet to notice the new car she'd bought six months ago despite it sitting parked in her driveway—*that* man noticed she was wearing a new swimsuit?

Smirking, she started to teasingly text back:

Test driving it before that trip to Bali...

Before she could hit Send, a new message from him appeared.

Sales tag is still hanging off the back.

Of course. She blushed, annoyed at her assumption and grateful she hadn't sent her own text. She deleted it and then quickly reached around and pulled the tag off the suit.

Her cell chimed again.

What now? Had she left the price sticker on the bottom of her flip-flops too?

That color makes your tan pop.

She swallowed hard as she stared at the message. Okay, that was definitely a better comment. Maybe he *was* eyeing her in the two-piece she'd bought on impulse the day before, when she hadn't known she'd have both Oliver and Sebastian on board the boat with her that day. But hell, maybe the daring, revealing bikini was worth it if it had finally caught Oliver's attention, finally made him notice her as a sexual being and not just his best friend, his daughter's role model, a woman he'd kept in the friend zone for years... Her heart raced. What did she do? How should she respond?

She read it again and sighed.

This one was not from Oliver. It was from Sebastian.

Of course.

Frustration on overload, Carly tucked the cell phone into the pocket of her jean shorts, and kicking off the flip-flops, she dived straight into the water with the kids.

The cold splash stopped her heart momentarily, until her limbs grew accustomed to the feel of the cool waves wrapping around her. She swam toward the banana boat and struggled to climb onto the wet, slippery rubber ride behind Tess.

"Yay! Carly's coming!" the little girl said, pumping her arms in the air before gripping the handles in front of her as the boat started to move and they gradually picked up speed, bumping and cruising along the surface of the water.

Carly's mother always said that children had more fun when adults participated in the activity, and no doubt her mom was right about that.

But right now, kids or no kids, Carly would be out there on the ride, hoping the thrill of excited adrenaline coursing through her, the salt spray in her face, the wind in her hair and the uncontrollable laughter escaping her as she held on for dear life to the yellow rubber handles could replace the feelings of conflict simmering in her heart and mind.

At least temporarily.

CARLY WAS WEARING the hell out of that swimsuit.

The light denim-blue color with the white trim made her skin look healthy and smooth.

His friend had always had a fantastic body, but rarely did she put it on display. Every time they went to the lake or the public pool with Tess, she usually wore a modest one-piece or a cover-up. She wasn't one to flaunt her beauty. He'd always marveled at her combination of soft curves and athletic frame, and he'd noticed her recent weight loss and muscle gain. And that day, he was getting the full, un-filtered view of her efforts at the gym.

And to say he wasn't attracted would be a lie. His body was certainly reacting. His sweaty palms mixed with the condensation on his beer bottle and his shorts felt uncom-fortably tight in the crotchal area.

While he was definitely enjoying this new, more confi-dent version of his friend, he couldn't help but wonder what was spurring it. Was all of this—the two-piece, the pedi-cured toes, the tight white tank top that had him drooling—for Sebastian?

Damn, it *was* jealousy he was feeling. Where had it come from all of a sudden? He didn't like it. In fact, it could take a hike anytime now.

He watched Carly laugh as she held on behind Tess on the yellow banana ride. Her braid had come loose and her long dark hair was flowing away from her face as the wind blew and the bright, carefree, happy smile radiating from her took his breath away. *She* was breathtaking.

How had he not noticed that before?

Tess looked so happy and—more importantly—safe, sitting there with Carly. His best friend had always been close to his girls, but in the last three years, Carly had truly stepped into the role of Tess's female role model, confidante and friend. He didn't know what they would have done without her.

*Would do* without her.

Which made the idea of leaving Port Serenity seem like an impossibility. Given no other choice, he may be able to leave the family legacy lighthouse and even the town and community that had always felt like home…but leaving Carly made his heart drop into his stomach.

He used to think it was just because they were best friends who relied on one another, but now he wondered if there might be more to it…

"She's something else, right?" Sebastian's voice next to him made his jaw flinch involuntarily.

He glanced at the man, holding a beer bottle of his own, his eyes locked on Carly out in the water. If the new two-piece was for Sebastian's benefit, it had certainly caught the other man's attention as well. Oliver didn't like the way the guy was eyeing Carly, but what could he do? They were friends with a complicated history, and up until that moment, he'd been ignoring any other potential connection they may share—or could share. He'd never voiced any feelings to Carly. Hell, he'd never really acknowledged them to himself.

"We're just really great friends," he said. If he was starting to develop more than friendly feelings for Carly, Sebastian wasn't going to be the first to know.

"Oh, I know. She told me all about it at dinner last night," he said, taking a swig of the beer.

She had? Carly had revealed something like that to this guy? What exactly had she said? And why did the idea that she had confided in Sebastian upset him? Worse, why did her acknowledging that they were just good friends—the same thing he always claimed—bother him so much?

"She has so many fantastic ideas for next year's tourism, and I think, up until now, she's been really underutilized by the board committee," Sebastian continued.

"Did you tell her about your intentions for the lighthouse?" he asked, unable to keep the edge out of his voice.

"Not yet. That's still…in the works. Keep that between us, okay, buddy?"

Oliver's hard stare drilled into the guy's profile, but he seemed completely unfazed as his gaze drifted back out toward the water—toward Carly.

"You know what? That looks too fun. Callan, stop for a sec. I'm going in," he called out, and Callan immediately slowed then stopped the boat. "Hold my beer?" Sebastian asked, handing it to Oliver without waiting for a response. It was either accept the bottle or let it crash to the deck. Sebastian quickly tore off his shirt and kicked off his loafers and dived into the water in the khaki shorts that were not meant for swimming.

Oliver clutched the bottle so tight he thought it might smash anyway.

"Whew!" Sebastian said as he resurfaced, wiping the water away from his face and slicking his dark hair back. "Alaska waters are no joke," he said before swimming off toward the banana ride.

Oliver's teeth clenched so hard it gave him an ache in his jaw. Seeing the guy climb onto the back of the banana behind Carly and wrap his arms around her waist made Oliver's stomach knot in a dozen different ways.

When Carly's gaze drifted toward the boat and landed on him, her expression held a hint of disappointment.

Damn, why hadn't he jumped in? He should be the one on the back of the banana with Carly and Tess, relaxing and enjoying the day instead of freaking out and worrying and keeping this guard up around his heart that wasn't serving him. If he wasn't careful, he was going to lose the only person besides his daughter who meant anything to him.

Meant everything to him.

That realization hit him hard and he swallowed the lump of unease in the back of his throat as the boat picked up speed again, this time with Rachel at the helm.

Callan appeared next to him as they watched the group being towed. "Hey, man, I think you need to decide if you're willing to always be the *hold my beer* guy," he said, tapping Oliver on the shoulder before waving to the group.

The words echoed in Oliver's mind as he continued to watch the fun he wasn't a part of. Was he willing to sit by and let someone else enjoy the happiness and love he potentially wanted for himself? He wasn't sure, but he knew his feelings for his best friend were definitely changing and developing into something a whole lot deeper, and he was running out of time to figure out what to do about it.

# CHAPTER SIX

THESE NUMBERS COULDN'T be right.

Standing behind the counter in the bookstore the next morning, her coffee cup between her hands, Carly recalculated the cash register receipts.

Nope, she hadn't added wrong. The day before had been the highest Saturday sales in months. Not surprising to see a rise in sales during tourist season, but these numbers were incredible.

Melissa really could hold down the fort. Which was good because Carly's life was about to get a little busier, and knowing she could trust the young girl was a big relief.

Not only had the store done record sales, but everything was restocked and clean. Melissa had even repositioned the sales merchandise to be front and center when visitors entered the store. Carly had always been hesitant about displaying sale items that way for fear they would cannibalize new product sales, but it had worked in reducing the extra old stock.

She counted the float for the day just as her phone chimed with a new text message. Picking it up, she expected to see her morning text from Oliver, but Sebastian had beat him to it. Carly's disappointment only reconfirmed her feelings for both men.

Thanks again for inviting me yesterday. I had a great time.

Carly put the phone down without answering. She'd struggled to have a fun time with the awkward tension between the two men and the conflict she was facing. On one hand, she had Sebastian, a man who was clearly attracted to her and would act on it if Carly opened that door, and on the other hand, she had Oliver, a man who sent her mixed signals and was afraid to open himself up to a new relationship. Unfortunately, she had to follow her heart, not theirs, and hers was always firmly with Oliver.

Her phone chimed again and this time it was him.

Was thinking we need to get started on the float this weekend. Hope you have a full crew.

Once again, not a declaration-of-love text, but he was right. They did need to get started on her design if she hoped to have the float ready for the parade in three weeks.

Assembling a team now.

She texted back, just as one said team member walked through the door.

"We need to get this author to agree to a signing," Rachel said, clutching her copy of *Love at Sea* as though she was afraid someone would steal it from her.

"God morning to you too," Carly said with a tight laugh. "Do you go anywhere without that book?" She was only half kidding. Her friend really was obsessed. It wasn't healthy.

"I've read it twice already. I can't believe I have to wait so long for the next one." She pulled out a stool at the counter and sat. "But maybe we wouldn't have to wait so long if we could convince the author to give us exclusive ARCs," she said, her eyes widening. "But to do that, we'd need to know who she is."

"I told you, she—or *he*—is a recluse. They refuse to do any appearances or interviews or appear at any signings or book club chats."

Rachel huffed, tossing her hair over her shoulder. "That's ridiculous. These are bestselling novels. The publisher should force her, him, whomever it is, to do promotion."

Carly shrugged. "I guess the publisher is happy that the books are selling so well and the mystery of the author's identity only adds to the hype."

Rachel eyed her from behind green-rimmed cat-eye glasses that Carly knew were nonprescription. She owned a similar pair. "Do *you* know who it is?"

"Nope," Carly said, reaching into the box behind the counter and stacking more copies near the register. By noon, they'd all be gone. It was still baffling to her how quickly they flew off the shelf.

"Oh, come on. You mean to tell me the publisher hasn't given you any clues?"

"None. The books arrive from the press just like all the others. I stock them. They sell."

Rachel's lips pursed. "And you're not at all curious about who it could be?"

"I respect the author's right to anonymity. I get it. I've seen the way authors can be tortured on social media. For as many fans as they have, there are just as many critics. And even the fans can get crazy. I saw one author having to defend her release schedule because four books a year wasn't fast enough for her avid fan base." Carly shook her head. As a lifetime reader, she'd never fully understood the world of publishing, but she sympathized with authors with impossible deadlines and reader expectations.

Y.C. Salwert was right to keep their identity a secret, for no other reason than to avoid being stalked by Rachel.

"It has to be someone local, though..."

Rachel was obviously not giving up. She tapped her long, manicured fingers against the counter, thinking. "Do you know anyone in town who writes other types of books or articles on the subject?"

"Besides you?" Carly asked with a raised eyebrow.

Rachel scoffed. "I wish I could write this well, and believe me, if I was Y.C. Salwert, I'd be screaming it from the top deck of my luxury yacht. Come on, think. Who could it be? You went to school here—was there anyone in your English class with exceptional writing talent?"

"Not that I can remember. Other than this Y.C. Salwert, the only other local star is Francine Cumins, who writes the children's books."

"Could be her, I guess." Rachel bit an acrylic thumbnail. "And it would make sense that she wouldn't want anyone knowing her identity. These romances aren't exactly PG... Maybe she's worried about her fan base..."

Carly snapped her fingers. "You know what? That makes sense. I think you cracked the mystery."

But Rachel still looked unsure. "Seems too easy though... and now that I think of it, Francine said in an interview once that she didn't write for adults because she has carpal tunnel and longer novels weren't possible for her."

"I wish I could help," Carly said. She checked her watch pointedly, but Rachel didn't take the hint.

"Well, what about the patrons?"

"What do you mean?"

"Well, I can't imagine that the author wouldn't come to the store to see the book on the shelf on release day. I mean, that's a dream come true, right?"

Rachel was on to something and Carly felt sweat pool a little on her lower back. "Assuming they live here in Port Serenity."

Rachel nodded emphatically. "They have to. This level of detail about the town and Sealena and the history is far too rich and accurate for someone who isn't a Port Serenity native, and the newer details in the second book, like the reconstructed statue, are things only residents would know."

Wow, Rachel missed nothing.

The chime above the front door sounded and Skylar entered.

Carly shot her cousin a grateful look, desperate to escape Rachel's questioning. Truth was, she did know who the author was, and it took everything she had to keep the secret. The author wasn't ready to come out to the world yet for good reason. But keeping the information from Rachel was getting tougher all the time.

"Hey, Skylar. Not working today?" she asked.

"Day off, just heading to the diner for breakfast with Isla, so thought I'd stop in to say hi."

Carly smiled. It wasn't so long ago that Skylar and her fiancé Dex's sister, Isla, didn't get along, but the Christmas before, the two had reconciled their differences when Isla had suffered a brain injury in an ice climbing incident. It had only taken a brief stint of amnesia for the two women to realize they were actually more alike than they'd ever realized. "Isla's home?" She was surprised. The young heir to the Wakefield legacy was rarely in one place for long, traveling the globe in search of adventure.

"Her and Aaron just got back from a backpacking trip in Australia. She's starting her social work program online this fall, so they plan to be in town for a while. Gotta say, I'm happy to have Aaron back for an extended time."

"No doubt." The elite rescue swimmer for the coast guard was an invaluable member of the team and he'd been taking longer vacations to travel with Isla these days, but Carly always felt better knowing he was on active duty, and as captain of the team, Skylar depended on him.

Skylar turned toward Rachel and nodded toward the book. "What are you clinging to like a life preserver?"

*"Love at Sea."* She turned the book toward Skylar. "Have you read it yet?"

Skylar wrinkled her nose. "No."

"Are you here to get a copy?"

Skylar scoffed as she shook her head. "You couldn't pay me enough to read that series."

Rachel gasped. "Are you serious?"

"Sealena's not my thing," Skylar said. "And romance novels aren't either."

Rachel refused to accept it. Climbing off the stool, she headed to the shelf containing the first Sealena book. "I don't want to give you spoilers, so this is the first book."

"There's more than one book?" Skylar asked.

"It's a trilogy." Rachel opened the book to the opening meet-cute scene. "Listen to this and tell me you're not intrigued…" She cleared her throat and read dramatically:

> *"The sea is angry tonight.*
> *Its soul howls as it casts looming, ominous waves crashing into one another. It's the pollution that has caused this peaceful, majestic being to cry out in protest. The mass dumping of garbage into the waters, killing its creatures, harming its very existence.*
> *Humans will never realize the impact they have on this world, and the ocean is the biggest part of it,*

*with its mysteries and secrets that are beyond human comprehension.*

*Four generations of my kind have protected these waters, both sides, but someday, we will be forced to make a choice.*

*The sea rages and I do what I can to protect the tiny ships at its mercy.*

*It's my calling. It's my legacy.*

*Yet I struggle with the morality more and more.*

*Why do these thoughtless humans deserve to be saved when they are destroying my home, the home of millions of sea creatures? My ancestors believed it was our duty, our obligation.*

*Legend has it that we haven't always been this way, but we were sentenced to this solitary life of savior as penance for deeds of long ago."*

Rachel paused for breath and flipped a few pages. "Let me get to the good part... Ah, here we go," she said as she started to read again.

*"The ten-foot fishing vessel looked no bigger than a toy as it was thrashed about on the surface. Its dark shadow above me rode out the storm, fighting against the current... It would eventually lose. The sea claimed many—and I could only save a few.*

*Swimming upward against the tumultuous current, I summon the strength of my ancestors—the fierce, strong Serpent Queens that came before, feeling their strength course through me, making me infinitely stronger. Generations of my kind are connected, each stronger than the last...*

*I see the boat as a wave cascades over it, swallowing it whole.*

*I dive below the surface and scan through the dark depths. In the distance, I can see its smashed and damaged hull—and the lone, lifeless body suspended in chaos.*

*With all my strength, I raise my arms outward and will everything I have for the waves and tide to stop roaring. I send out my peaceful message to the waters all around me, calming it, halting its rage. My arms shake and my body feels tired as the sea continues to fight back.*

*It's stronger than ever, and with the waning moon, I'm weaker.*

*But I keep pushing, gently coaxing, commanding my own will, silently reasoning with the ocean to subside...*

*Rest, my love. Rest.*

*A stillness envelops me as the waves die down and the howling wind becomes a mild, gentle breeze.*

*I swim fast toward the sinking figure—a man— and, reaching him, I bring him to the surface, where his broken ship bobs along the smooth surface. He's alive, so I leave him on the deck and, knowing this reprieve won't last, that the ocean's favoring is temporary, I guide the boat back toward the marina.*

*The Port Serenity lighthouse beacon shines in the distance, illuminating a path in the dark, cloudy night sky, cutting through with a ribbon of light, a symbol of hope.*

*I bring the vessel as close as I dare, then watch as it slowly drifts toward the shore.*

*As I turn away, I see the fisherman stand. His legs*

*slightly unsteady, his gaze bewildered as he searches out over the water.*

*I can hear his thoughts.*

*How?*

*I know I should go. Quickly. But I find myself unable to move. In a trancelike state, I'm drawn to this mere mortal...*

*My body aches and a deep longing clutches my chest. The water around me starts to churn as my emotions are spiraling beyond my control. What is this feeling? What is happening to me?*

*My gaze is locked on the fisherman—I'm unable to break away, and when he sees me, I'm trapped.*

*His expression is one of fear mixed with a relief of knowing.*

*I've seen it on the faces of the few who have spotted me.*

*But in his, there's also something else—an unusual acceptance, as though he'd always expected this moment, been waiting for it.*

*I try to break the spell but it only grows stronger, the heartbeats of my ancestors beating alongside mine, deep within my chest.*

*Overhead, the sky clears and the thin, waning moon shines brightly overhead, its power a force greater than all else.*

*I know what's happening now. I'd always known it would occur someday. But nothing could have prepared me for the curse of what cannot be."*

Rachel stopped reading and sighed. "Tell me that doesn't get you," she said to Skylar.

Carly glanced at her cousin. What would she think? Skylar had never been a Sealena fan, with her family's history of feuding with the Wakefields over Sealena's becoming the town's mascot, and she knew her sensible, no-nonsense cousin wasn't the romantic type.

Skylar shrugged. "The writing is great. Just not sure I'm buying the whole sea creature–human love story angle."

Rachel sighed. "It's a metaphor for forbidden love. You can't read it for what it is. You have to dig deeper into the hidden messages of passion and desire and how it transcends all forms."

Carly busied herself with stocking the shelf with more copies as her friend continued to explain to her cousin why she should give the novels a chance.

*Good luck, Rachel. This is one person you will not convert.*

"Okay, fine… I'll read it," Skylar said.

"What?" Carly's mouth gaped. "You will?"

Skylar sighed. "Why not?" She reached toward the shelf and grabbed the first book—and the second.

Carly could think of one reason why not. One very good reason.

ACCORDING TO EVERYTHING Oliver had read online the night before, Sebastian and the town were well within their rights to evict him from the lighthouse. Possession didn't really hold up in this case, when the land and the lighthouse belonged to the community as historical landmarks. Oliver had spent hours, up well past midnight, researching the legalities of what Sebastian was presenting, and unfortunately, with the automation of the lighthouse procedures and Oliver's position on the Coast Guard Aids to Navigation team being more of an honorary role, it didn't appear he had a great case to argue.

He sighed as he uncovered the float platform in the shed. The base was ready to go and Carly was on her way to go over her design idea. His palms sweated slightly and he felt an odd stirring in his chest at the thought of seeing her.

This was ridiculous. It was Carly. His best friend. There was nothing to be worried about.

The day before had been…weird. After much tossing and turning, replaying it all in his mind , he'd come to the conclusion that he was just freaking out a little about the possibility that things could change.

His attraction to Carly had always been there, but now it was being amplified by testosterone-fueled male competition. He saw Sebastian as a threat to his current status—his home and his friendship with Carly were compromised.

That was all.

So why did his heart race and his mouth go dry seeing her enter the shed moments later?

Dressed in a pale yellow sundress and ballet flats, her long dark hair in her usual braid hanging over one shoulder, she practically glowed like a ray of sunshine.

Glowed like a ray of sunshine? Jesus. What the hell was wrong with him?

"Hey, looks good," she said, nodding toward the float base.

She was avoiding eye contact. Did that mean she was annoyed about yesterday? Had the tension between him and Sebastian ruined her day?

He cleared his throat and tried to formulate an apology that didn't sound too lame. Nothing surfaced. "Did you bring your design?" he asked instead. He wasn't great with words. Especially ones from the heart—apologies, confessions of feelings… He was more an acts of service kind of guy. So, maybe he could show her he was sorry by being more involved with the float build that year.

"Yes, I did," she said, reaching into what looked like a new purse and retrieving the plans. She approached the float base and rolled them out.

Oliver approached and the scent of her familiar perfume filled his senses. He loved that sweet, mild scent that was uniquely hers. He'd never admit it, but he'd spent almost an hour one day at the perfume counter trying to identify the smell when he was going to buy it for her for her birthday, but nothing was quite right.

"What do you think?" she asked in his silence.

"Wow, this is quite the elaborate design," Oliver said, looking at the hand-drawn scale of the float Carly intended to build.

"I want to go big this year. We usually win the parade contest, but this year I want to really wow the crowd with the display, not just bring home the trophy. Tourism has taken a hit recently, and now that visitors are flocking back to town, I want to celebrate their return and show them their vacation to Port Serenity was worth the trip."

"Yeah, I can see that," Oliver said and paused. "Are you sure the store budget can accommodate the ambition, though?"

Carly refused to meet his gaze as she nodded. "It'll be fine."

"It's also going to require some extra hands," he said. "I'll help."

Carly looked slightly surprised by the offer but nodded. "Okay, well, other than you and Tess, I've recruited Rachel and Skylar and Dex. Callan has a full tour schedule, but he offered to help when he can." Carly paused and looked away. "And Sebastian's going to help."

Oliver's jaw clenched. "Wonderful," he said tightly.

Carly turned toward him. "Come on—give him a chance. He's new to town and could use some friends."

"I have enough friends," he grumbled. One, really. Her. And he wanted to maintain that status. He already felt Sebastian driving a wedge between them and he didn't like it.

Carly grinned and touched his hand where it rested against the float. "Where's that local hospitality spirit I know you're capable of?"

Oliver's gaze was transfixed on her hand on his and her words sounded far away. She quickly lifted it and laughed strangely. "I'm sure you two will figure it out," she said.

She turned and surveyed the work he'd already started with the flatbed they were using. Oliver had created the base with wood and chicken wire, and he'd just been waiting on her design to add fabric and lights. "Thank you again for getting started on this."

"No problem. Parade's three weeks away, and with your design idea, we'll be cutting it close."

"This really is huge," she said, eyeing the platform and biting her lower lip.

"Rethinking this now, aren't you?" he asked with a grin.

"No." She squared her shoulders. "We can totally get this built in time." Her cell chimed with a text and he watched as she reached for it and read. A smile crept across her face and his gut tightened. "I have to get going," she said, putting the phone away.

"Hot date?" he asked before he could stop himself.

Carly cocked her head to the side and folded her arms across her chest.

Uh-oh…he was in for an earful. Why had he said anything? It was her life; she could date whomever she wanted.

Unfortunately, the idea of her dating anyone other than him was making him slightly nauseous.

Carly's piercing gaze burned into his. "Is there something you want to say?"

He shook his head quickly. He'd already said too much. Or not enough. He couldn't decide. These feelings were new and confusing. "No. Just be careful with guys like that..." She'd only just met Sebastian and she didn't know the real guy. The one he presented himself to be around Carly wasn't the complete picture, and he didn't want her getting hurt.

"Guys like what? Smart, successful, interesting...complimentary?"

That last one hit its mark. "What's that supposed to mean? I compliment you."

"Really? When?"

Since when did she want him to? His heart raced, as he knew they were heading into slightly dangerous and very foreign territory. They'd never talked like this before. They'd never challenged one another with...expectations. Friends took each other at face value. They were direct and said what they meant. This gamesmanship that seemed to be happening was for relationships. Had she, too, sensed a shift? How long ago? Had he been blind to her feelings and intentions all this time or was this a new thing for her too?

She tapped her foot as she continued to wait.

Shit. She was really expecting an answer. "Um...the other day on the boat. I said I liked your swimsuit." Just the thought of the swimsuit now had his heart racing. He wouldn't admit to the thoughts he'd been having about it the night before, alone in bed.

She shook her head. "Nope. You asked me if it was new."

He sighed. "I thought the compliment was implied."

"You told me the tag was sticking out!" Well, one thing was new—this exasperation from her. He'd never seen her frustrated with him like this. Carly was always calm and even-tempered. This side was a little terrifying, but only because it was attractive as hell.

And Oliver was sweating bullets. What exactly was happening right now? The tension around them was nearly suffocating and the urge to word vomit exactly how he felt about the swimsuit was overwhelming. He swallowed hard. "Well, would I be a good…friend if I didn't tell you that your tag was sticking out?"

She huffed, but then reluctantly sighed in agreement. "Okay, fine. But it wasn't a compliment."

He swallowed again. Now or never. Say something!

"Well, um…it was a really great swimsuit."

She nodded, looking like it hadn't blown her mind, but she'd take it. "Thank you."

His shoulders relaxed. "So…we're okay?" He wasn't sure what else to say or how to broach the subject. He still hadn't fully wrapped his mind around his feelings and he wasn't sure it was the right time to try to bring up the new awkwardness that seemed to surround them.

What if it was just him feeling this?

"Of course we're okay," she said, but he sensed a slight disappointment in her tone. As though she'd been expecting more.

But what exactly?

"I really have to go," she said, turning to leave.

He shoved his hands into his jeans pockets and nodded. "Yeah, see ya later." Disappointed in himself for not having the balls to say what he was feeling, he could sense that the longer he didn't say it, the harder it would be.

She paused at the door and turned back. "For the record—not a hot date. Shopping with Skylar."

She certainly didn't owe him the explanation, but damn if it didn't make him feel a lot better.

NOW THAT OLIVER had taken care of the boring part of the float-building process, Carly couldn't wait to hit the local craft store to buy all the items she needed to accomplish her elaborate vision.

But as she drove across town, she couldn't shake the interaction they'd just had. The sizzling tension between them moments ago had never been there before and she wasn't quite sure how to process it. For years, her attraction to Oliver had simmered and she'd been forced to keep it hidden, keep her growing feelings to herself, but lately, she felt as though she might explode if she had to keep repressing it.

As though this thing with Sebastian had made her realize that she had been putting her future on hold, waiting for something she couldn't have. Or at least, she'd thought she couldn't have it.

Moments ago in the shed, she'd felt a shift.

For several days, things with Oliver had been strained, different, but she'd chalked it up to his dislike of Sebastian. She'd credited the new awkwardness to the fact that almost every time they'd been together lately, Sebastian was there too.

This time, they'd been alone and there had definitely been sexual tension between them when he'd voiced his concerns about her dating. This wasn't just about Sebastian...

But what exactly was it about? Was Oliver starting to develop feelings for her as well?

It was too much to hope for, but she couldn't deny there had been a moment in the shed when she thought...

The sound of a horn honking behind her snapped her out of her thoughts and she saw the streetlight had turned green.

She sighed, waved her apology to the car behind her and, moments later, pulled into the lot of the Crafts and More store.

She saw Skylar's car parked in the far end of the lot, so she pulled in next to it. She waved, but her cousin didn't see her, her nose stuck between the pages of *Forbidden Love*.

Wow, her cousin really was reading it.

Climbing out, she tapped on the window of Skylar's car, careful not to startle her, and her cousin held up a finger, indicating one more page. Carly watched her flip the page and waited as her cousin finished the current chapter she was on and reluctantly put the book down.

"Sorry, I was in the middle of the scene where Sealena has to save the family adrift on the life raft," Skylar said, climbing out of her car.

"You're enjoying it?" Carly asked.

Skylar shrugged. "Verdict is still out. I haven't made it to the good stuff yet, but let's just say, I wish I could bring it to work to read on my breaks."

Carly frowned as they headed toward the entrance. "Why can't you?" Skylar did have downtime during the day.

She laughed.

"Carly, my crew of eight men are just dying to find reasons to tease me. I'm not giving them ammunition."

"People shouldn't be shamed for what they like to read." She paused. "And for your enlightenment, six out of those eight crew members have already read *Forbidden Love*," she said, opening the door to the store.

"Shut. Up."

Carly shook her head amusedly. "You'll never get names

out of me, but just know even a certain retired captain purchased a copy."

Skylar's eyes bulged. "My dad has read this series?!"

Carly laughed. "Feel better now?"

"Honestly not sure how to feel about my dad reading sexy scenes," she said and shuddered.

"As if he's not having sex of his own..." Keith Beaumont had recently set sail for a three-month sailing trip with local meteorologist Monica Mallard, and Carly suspected there was more happening beneath the stars than just navigation.

"Please stop," Skylar said as they stepped inside the air-conditioned store. "So, do you have a list?"

Carly handed it to her and Skylar scanned it. "'Fringe and skirting, floral sheeting, three five-foot arches, festooning, paint...'" she read. "Maybe we should have borrowed Oliver's truck."

Carly's cheeks flushed at the mention of Oliver and she cleared her throat. "The arches come in pieces, so we should be able to fit everything into our two vehicles."

Skylar flipped to the other side of the page, where the list continued. "Maybe in two trips," she said. "This is a lot of stuff."

"I want the float to be the biggest in the parade."

"Pretty sure you'll accomplish that. Please tell me you've recruited more hands than just Dex and I?" Skylar said, looking slightly worried about her commitment to help.

"Don't worry. I've got a group of nine."

Skylar looked like she was mentally calculating who the nine could be. "Would a certain newcomer to town be among that group?" she asked casually, though the question was loaded with unconcealed curiosity.

Her cousin knew about her business dinner date with Sebastian earlier that week, and despite Carly's insistence that it was just business, Skylar was definitely intrigued about the new man, insisting he was totally into Carly.

She knew Skylar and Rachel were right about Sebastian's intentions and it did give her pause, but there was nothing she could do other than set clear boundaries and continue to express that she wasn't interested in a relationship with him. Once he settled into town and met other women, he'd be fine. He'd move on to one of the many turned heads.

"Sebastian is helping, yes, but like I told you, we're just friends and business associates. I want him to feel welcome in town and he's trying to learn more about the community, so participating in the float build is a great way to do that." She paused in the first aisle, next to the selection of paint. "I want as many different shades of blue as possible for the water. We need white for the waves and greens and golds for our Serpent Queen," she said, picking up paint cans and piling them into the cart.

Skylar eyed the swiftly growing pile. "Seriously want that much paint?"

Carly shrugged. "Whatever we don't use, I can donate to the community center. They are hosting a graffiti contest in September, repainting all the recycling bins throughout town, so it won't go to waste. Can you grab the gold? I can't reach," she said, standing on tiptoes and straining to reach the top shelf.

Skylar, with her taller, five-foot-seven stature, reached it with ease.

"The other shade too," Carly said and laughed at Skylar's look. "Yes, I know it's overkill, but I want an impressive float."

"And it has nothing to do with the new tourism manager? Wanting to impress him?" Skylar asked, obviously not willing to let the more compelling conversation about Sebastian drop.

Skylar knew about her love for Oliver but thought Carly was wasting her time and energy. Skylar liked Oliver, but she suspected he wasn't ready for a new relationship and she hated to see Carly pining for the man. And in the last two years, Skylar had been vocal about her opinion.

Unfortunately, there was nothing Carly could do about it. And this whole thing with Sebastian only solidified it. Sebastian was gorgeous, successful, funny, smart, interesting—a gentleman—and yet she felt nothing. Not one iota of a spark with him. She liked him. They'd be friends.

But no one other than Oliver had her heart.

Which made her cousin worry about her. A lot. Skylar would love to see Carly date someone else, find happiness and stop waiting around. Whether Sebastian was a perfect match or not, Skylar and Rachel were sure to push her in that direction.

"It's true that I want to make sure Sebastian sees what effort we put into tourism events." She'd say that much. It was important to show the community's drive and spirit and reinforce the things they were already doing right. "Oh, but I've paired him with you and Dex for the float team."

Skylar sighed. "Do I need to ask who you teamed *yourself* with?"

"Probably not," she said, pointing to the containers of gold-and-green glitter. "Grab those. Please," she added.

"Everything will be covered in glitter. Even us," Skylar said.

"Everyone could use a little sparkle in their life."

She and Skylar added the glitter to the already heaping cart. Then they headed to the fabric section, where Carly selected reams of green and gold material for parts of the Sealena figurine. She wanted movement on the float, not just a cardboard cutout. With several wind machines, she wanted to create the image of a real storm and show Sealena in all her fierce glory.

"What's left?" Skylar asked.

"Just the arches. I think we will need to get those from the warehouse," she said.

They headed toward the cashiers, and Carly put in her request for the arches as Skylar started to unload the cart. The young cashier smiled, seeing all the supplies. "Parade float?"

"Yep," Skylar said.

"Carly's are always the best."

"She does pour her heart into it," she heard Skylar say as she rejoined her.

"The warehouse guy is going to get them ready out back. We'll swing around to get them." She handed the cashier the ticket with the item code on it. "Three of these, please."

The cashier's eyes widened as she rang them in and saw the final bill. Over four thousand dollars. "Sure you need three?"

Her design required it and she was sparing no expense. She nodded, opening her purse.

"Carly—are you sure?" Skylar said, lowering her voice. "The store's budget is usually a quarter of that."

She waved a hand, taking out her wallet and retrieving her own personal credit card, not the store's business card. She ignored Skylar's raised eyebrow as she paid for the items. "Thank you," she said, tucking her wallet away.

Not before Skylar noticed it. "Oh my God—that's gorgeous!" She reached for the pale coral-colored wristlet and Carly sucked in a breath as her cousin saw the expensive logo clasp.

"I got it on sale," she said, feeling her cheeks flush. She wasn't one for extravagance or name brands. She still wore the jeans she'd had in high school—the side perk of never growing taller—but the wallet had been a splurge. Something she'd decided to treat herself to.

There had been a matching purse, but she didn't want to be too flashy. The wallet could be hidden in her oversized, three-year-old bag.

Skylar's face held a look of suspicion as she nodded and reached for the shopping bags. "Well, I'm happy to see you spending money on yourself as well as this float."

"I'll expense most of it," she said, struggling under the weight of the bags as they headed outside and across the parking lot to their vehicles. They put the bags in the back of Skylar's car and the two of them climbed into Carly's vehicle to go around back for the arches. Carly reached into her bag for her new sunglasses as the midday sun blared directly into her line of vision.

Skylar stared at her. "Okay, what's going on?"

Carly pretended not to understand as she put the vehicle in Drive and headed around the back of the store to the loading dock. "Nothing. Why?"

"The wallet, the Gucci sunglasses… Trust me, I'm here for it. But level with me—did you win the lottery?" She lowered her voice. "You can tell me and I swear I won't tell anyone—or hit you up for a loan," she said with a grin.

Carly sighed and shook her head. She knew her spending more on two items than she had on herself in two years must look odd to those who knew her well. "I just realized you're right when you tell me to reward myself, to treat myself to nice things sometimes."

Skylar didn't look convinced, but she sat back in the seat and let the subject drop as Carly stopped the car in front of the open warehouse door.

The arches were propped against the side of the building

and a young teen stood ready and waiting to load them onto the roof rack for her. He wasn't much bigger than Carly, but he had surprising strength as he lifted each one himself and placed them carefully onto the top of the car. He secured them with the rope and bungee cords that she provided.

A few minutes later, the arches were secured and Carly handed the young warehouse worker a tip for his help. He was working hard that summer and deserved the recognition. Too many young people didn't know the value of hard work these days.

The young man's face lit up as he tucked the money into the apron of his smock. "Thanks, lady! Have a good day!"

Carly smiled as she climbed back into her car.

Skylar shook her head. "I'm not going to pressure you for answers, but if one of our long-lost relatives died and left us an inheritance that you're not telling me about, I'm going to be pissed," her cousin said, teasing in her tone.

But there was also something else. A slight hurt that Carly was obviously keeping something to herself. They were so close and shared everything.

But for now, Carly just wasn't ready to share this particular secret yet.

"I promise you, if that was the case, you'd be the first to know."

# CHAPTER SEVEN

HE NEEDED TO chat with Tess.

Which would be easier if he knew what to say. He still had no idea what was happening with these new feelings for Carly appearing out of nowhere, but something in him had shifted. And before he could explore what that was, he needed to talk to Tess about their future. Did she envision it being just the two of them forever? Or was she open to him finding happiness again with someone? With Carly?

He shook his head. Where on earth had that sudden deep desire for his friend come from? Did she return the feelings? In the shed earlier that day, there had definitely been chemistry, a sexual tension that had never existed before—or maybe he just hadn't noticed? Or chose not to notice? He'd always admired and respected her. She was the only person in town he trusted—the only person in his life, really. He'd always loved being around her, but now that attraction seemed to be pulling him a different way. He still longed to be around her easygoing, caring, upbeat nature, but now there was also a desire to touch her, kiss her, see what those lips tasted like, feel the soft silkiness of her skin, breathe in the scent of her hair...

He felt his body stir and he cleared his throat as he headed down the hall toward Tess's room, where the sound of a new pop album floated out into the hallway.

As he neared the door, he heard her singing off-key and grinned.

Tess was so much like her mother. Alison loved to sing too. She couldn't carry a tune in a bucket, but she didn't care. She said a singing person was a happy person. Tess was the same. Spirited, full of life and uninhibited. In Tess, he would always have a piece of Alison.

His gut tightened. Would Tess ever be okay with someone else being in their lives? Taking over that role? No one could replace her mother, but maybe his daughter could learn to love and respect someone else. Someone she already did love and respect in a different way.

He tapped on the door and waited for her "come in" before entering.

"Hey, Dad," she said.

Inside, she was packing items into her backpack for the weeklong summer camp at the Marine Life Sanctuary starting the next day. She'd attended the camps at the conservatory every year since she was four years old. She loved learning about marine life and the environmental efforts that Dr. Ann Sweeny and her small team of researchers were implementing and studying here in Port Serenity. Every year, there was a new focus for the camp and the kids learned something different. Dr. Ann kept the learning fun with games and activities, but she also taught the kids some complex things. She took them out to the observation cabin across from the docks to study creatures in the wild, as well as teaching research methods in the lab.

Tess always enjoyed the camp, and each time it ended, she was more convinced than ever that a career in marine biology was the future she wanted. Oliver thought his daughter would be perfectly suited for the job, but knowing she would be choosing a life near the water and its unpredictability made him slightly uneasy. He'd never deter Tess from following her dreams, but he secretly hoped that as she got older, that dream might shift to something safer, something preferably on land. He watched her pack her hat and sun cream into the bag and felt the same pride he always felt seeing his daughter be responsible.

He did a few awkward-looking hip-hop dance moves to the upbeat music before saying, "Can I turn this down just a bit?"

Tess nodded, a slight frown appearing on her face. "Everything okay?"

"Yeah, we just need to talk for a sec," he said, suddenly second-guessing if they really did need to talk. Nothing was going on between him and Carly, except some supercharged sexual tension, and he still wasn't sure he was going to act on it in any way—or if she was even really up for it. Maybe they should figure it out before they talked to Tess.

Tess looked sheepish as she lowered the volume on her music. "I know what this is about, and before you get upset, I couldn't just leave it out in the cold."

Couldn't leave *what* out in the cold, exactly? He quickly scanned the room. "What are you talking about?"

Tess's expression changed to one of wide-eyed innocence. "Nothing. What are *you* talking about?"

Oliver sighed, his own topic on hold. "Tess, what kind of animal do you have hiding in here?" Could be a dozen animals hiding among this mess. Even ones she knew nothing about. Clothes littered the floor. Magazines, papers and books were strewn everywhere except where they belonged on her desk. Her bookshelf was in disarray and he didn't even dare look under the bed.

"I'm finding him a home, but I couldn't just leave him outside," she said, slowly opening her closet. Inside, a tiny, frail white-and-orange kitten lay curled up on a T-shirt, a bowl of milk beside him. In Oliver's favorite cereal bowl. Mystery solved as to where it had gone.

Oliver's heartstrings tugged involuntarily—the thing was adorable, but he had to stay strong. They weren't adopting a kitten. Even if it was the cutest little thing he'd ever seen.

Shit.

He moved closer and peered at the sleeping, purring animal. His fur looked matted and he was far too thin. "How long has he been in here?"

"Two days. I found him in your shed...when I was absolutely *not* snooping for my birthday gift."

Oliver rolled his eyes.

"But just off topic, my favorite color is teal green—in case you ever need that information."

He sucked in a breath. Wow, his planned conversation had taken two quick detours in record time. "Acknowledged. Now, you say you are trying to find him a home?"

"I told Darcy about him and said if anyone mentioned a missing kitten, to let me know right away."

Didn't sound like she was trying too hard. "Tess, you know we can't keep him."

"Why not?" she asked.

Unfortunately, he had no real answer. It wasn't like a dog that required daily walks and took up a lot of space, or a guinea pig that needed a cage and a place to set up. A kitten couldn't be that much work...

He shook his head. "Look, let's sleep on that, okay?" He really wanted to get to the point he'd come in to discuss.

She nodded, grinning as though she knew she'd just adopted a kitten. He was such a softy and the thing was too cute. He'd set some ground rules before officially agreeing, but they both knew they now had a pet.

Tess sat on the edge of the bed and swung her legs. "Okay, what did you want to talk about?"

Oliver thought hard for a moment. How did he bring this up? His gaze fell on the kitten and he nodded slowly, the unexpected animal giving him an unexpected lead-in. "I wanted to chat about our family dynamic."

"Okay…"

"Take the kitten, for example. Bringing him into our lives—*if* I decide we can keep him—will change things."

"Make things better," she said.

"Perhaps…but also complicate things. He'll need food and water and a litter box that will need cleaning. Essentially, he'll need his own space and toys."

"That stuff won't take up much room."

"Right… But he'll also need lots of love and attention."

"Not a problem," she said happily.

"But that could limit my ability to spend a hundred percent of my time with you," he said.

She laughed. "I can share your attention, Dad."

Could she? "I'm just saying, for the last few years, it's just been you and me. I'm happy with that… I'm just curious about how you feel?"

Tess's expression changed slightly and a look of perceptiveness crept across her features. "Well, I think adding to our family will be strange at first…but more people—or kittens—to love and care for is never a bad thing, right?"

Oliver nodded slowly, a small sense of relief washing over him. "Right."

"How do you feel about the idea of changing the family dynamic?" she asked.

Wow, he'd been wanting to feel her out, and here she was,

flipping the script on him. "I'm not entirely sure, but I just wanted to open the dialogue."

She smiled. "I'm glad you did."

"You are?"

"I think it's about time we consider…expanding," she said with a grin, hearing the kitten stir. She got up, picked him up and cuddled him into her chest.

"Okay then," he said. Was his little girl giving him permission to move on with his life, explore the possibility of a future with someone else, bring someone new into their lives?

Or was she just really trying to convince him to keep the kitten?

Either way, Oliver felt a little lighter as he turned the volume back up on her music and left her to get ready for camp.

CARLY YAWNED AS she turned off the store lights and climbed the back interior stairs to her apartment later that evening. That day's store traffic had been insane, with several tour buses arriving in town from other parts of Alaska. The one-day tours were always hectic as groups swarmed the shelves for Sealena souvenirs. Restocking had taken hours, but at the end of the day, she was happy to see the sales numbers. While, so far, she was on board with Sebastian's new tourism ideas, she had meant what she'd said to Skylar; she wanted to also show him that the town's current strategies worked well.

She opened her apartment door and entered, the scent of Crock-Pot lasagna making her stomach growl. Prepping the meal first thing in the morning and letting it cook all day while she worked was the only way to ensure she ate a balanced diet during the crazy tourist season.

It was a trick she'd learned from her mom years before and a habit she still kept.

Hanging her purse and keys on the hook near the door, she went into the kitchen and lifted the cover on the pot. Steam escaped, followed by the delicious aroma of meat and cheese and pasta sauce.

She grabbed a bowl from the cupboard and dished up her dinner, packing the rest away into storage containers. There was always so much left over. The downside to living alone. But she refused to eat single-serving microwavable food. She wasn't prepared to solidify her fate as a spinster just yet.

No cats. No frozen dinners.

As she sat down to eat, her cell phone chimed with a new email. Picking it up, she saw the message from Heartbeat Books with the subject line: The third installment of the Sealena series.

Her fork suspended in midair, Carly's heart raced as she opened the message from her editor.

Dear Carly,
I hope the flurry of activity in Port Serenity this month is providing ample inspiration for your WIP.

More like a plausible excuse for procrastination.

I'm writing to check in on your progress as our deadline for the third book is approaching fast. Sales and marketing have already launched their extensive promotional campaigns and early sales reports are promising, but we want to make sure we maintain momentum. Therefore, I'm writing to ask if you could submit the book chapters to me as you've written them.

The fork clattered to her plate. *What?*

Unprecedented, yes, I know, but we want to release excerpts to exclusive promoters leading up to release date. If you could just forward anything you've written so far beyond the sample excerpt we've included in *Love at Sea*, that would be a great start.

Thanks, Carly! Waiting with bated breath for the conclusion of Sealena's love story!

XX

Paige

Senior Acquisitions Editor—Heartland Publishing

Her editor wanted new chapters. The problem was, Carly didn't have new chapters.

This entire series had begun on a whim, as a simple fanfic short story she'd submitted to DigitalPress, an online reader app, the year before. She'd never expected the story would hit a million readers and gain the attention of Paige Heartland, the editor at the small Alaska-based publishing house—or that it would have resulted in a three-book, six-figure deal that had basically changed Carly's life overnight a year ago.

She hadn't thought she was capable of the three-thousand-word short story, let alone a series trilogy, but the first book had flown onto the pages. Evidently, forbidden love was not much of a foreign concept to her. The first book in the series was essentially a thinly veiled fictionalized account of her own love life—her hidden desires, her longing for a love that could never be.

The editor had loved it. Readers had loved it even more.

It had given her the confidence and inspiration to write the next book, *Love at Sea*. It continued the heartfelt struggles of love from afar. Sealena and her fisherman were navigating an impossible connection that neither of them truly understood or knew how to resolve.

Readers were hooked but, unfortunately, also growing impatient. They were calling for the love story to come full circle. After hundreds of pages of sensual experiences and interactions that were soul connections, readers were demanding the real thing. No more fantasies. No more lusting from afar.

Which meant she needed to make good on the mythical themes she'd introduced and give Sealena her thirty days on land "hall pass" of sorts that had been the dangling carrot in the first two books. It was time to take the Serpent Queen out of her element and explore the connection on land.

She'd introduced it in the excerpted chapter…but then she'd stalled.

Now that Sealena was on land—what next?

As she set her phone aside, it chimed again.

Another new message from Paige.

Oh, and I'll need those chapters you mentioned you'd written already by tomorrow, the one-line message read.

Those chapters were still rough. Ideas, really. It was going to be a long night.

Eating quickly, not really tasting the food, Carly cleared away her dishes and put the leftover food into her fridge. Then, grabbing her new laptop, she sat at her desk and flipped to the second chapter, where the blinking cursor sat waiting for inspiration.

How was she supposed to write this final story when she really had no idea what would happen between Sealena and her fisherman? Longing, unreciprocated feelings and dancing around a real connection were things she knew— *write what you know* had definitely been working for her—

but how did she write a story about the two lovers actually coming together in a meaningful, impactful way that would meet reader expectations when she herself hadn't experienced that pleasure?

*Fiction is not real. Come on, Carly. Stop trying to write a fictionalized diary entry and just tell a good story.*

Sighing, she started to type:

*The fisherman stares at me for a long time, as though he's not sure he can trust what he's seeing. Maybe I'm just a hallucination, a figment of the overactive minds of men who spend so many lonely days at sea. He recognizes me, but he's unsure.*

*I've always stayed just out of sight, out of conscious realization. He's never been certain he's seen me, yet now I'm standing here, fully exposed, fully vulnerable.*

*There's a disbelief, a slight madness in his eyes, and I hold my breath in these new, air-filled lungs as I wait for him to shoo me away like some wild animal...*

*Instead, he turns away and I watch as he moves toward the old wooden dresser in the corner of the bedroom, where he silently retrieves a plaid shirt and a pair of shorts. He hands them to me, and for the first time, I realize I'm naked.*

*Humans cover their beautiful bodies with these fabrics. Mostly for warmth and modesty, I've noted, but as I put it on, I feel confined, restricted. If I want to stay in this world, I need to blend in, become one of them, but already, I feel a tightness in my chest about what that means, about the restrictions I'm about to accept. I've always pitied the humans for their fragile sensibilities, their need for these fabrics for their comfort. They break so easily, their skin so weak that it can't bear the elements of nature without crumbling. I don't like that I'm now no stronger than that. That I, too, am vulnerable to the wind, the rain, the cold, the heat...*

*Feeling powerless is decidedly the worst feeling of all.*

*How do these humans survive it?*

*My hands shake as I struggle with the buttons on the shirt. Too small and cumbersome. I've held eight-ton ships out of the violent thrashing of waves, and these tiny, round plastic buttons are defeating me.*

*The fisherman approaches.*

*"May I?" he asks. It's the first time I've heard his voice this close, usually muted by distance and the echoing of the wind. It's low and quiet, but full of depth.*

*I nod and he reaches for them. I watch as he buttons the shirt. He's taller than I am in this form and his body is thick and wide and strong compared to my thin, womanly shape. I'd have no chance in protecting myself from him should he choose to hurt me... I shiver at the thought.*

*He smells like the sea and I instantly crave home, the deep hollowness in the pit of my stomach now that the choice has been made and I've sealed my fate. Terror and panic overwhelm me, emotions I've never battled before, and I forget to inhale.*

*But the fisherman's eyes meet mine and the kindness reflected in his carries not pity, but admiration. As though he somehow understands the sacrifice I've just made, as though he understands the turmoil whirling within my core. As though he knows what it feels like to be lost and afraid.*

*The longer our eyes hold, the more my heart rate relaxes, my body stops its quivering and the ache for home in my chest subsides. If I could stare into his eyes—the windows to his soul—forever, I might be okay.*

*But he looks away and takes a step backward. "Are you hungry?" he asks.*

*Am I? I don't know. I've never felt that sensation before. I touch my stomach and feel a slight rumble, but it isn't until the smell of a fish stew cooking on the stove hits my nose that I truly feel the hunger churning inside. Suddenly, I feel empty. As though I've never eaten before. I sit at the table across from him and accept the meal with gratitude, shoveling the food in so fast, I nearly choke.*

*He watches me while I eat and I can see the questions rolling over in his mind.*

*Am I really here? How is this possible? Has he truly lost his mind now?*

*I want to reassure him that I am real. In the best way I can be. But I haven't learned to speak in his language yet. At least, not in a way he'd understand. My voice would scare him...*

*After we eat, he clears away the dishes and leads the way into the bedroom. My heart races. He tears the sheets from the bed and replaces them with new ones.*

*I stand there, unsure what to do. Mating in my world is far different than the human world, so I stand there waiting. Held captive by my choices. I'm here and there's nowhere else I can go until my time runs out. I'm at the mercy of this fisherman's kindness or cruelty.*

*He turns to look at me, and in the dim light of the room, illuminated only by a lamp that strikes a remarkable resemblance to me—the me I truly am— his expression has changed once again. Now it's one of acceptance, belief...dare I hope, happiness that I'm here.*

*He walks toward me and reaches out a hand to touch my cheek.*

*As though he has to make sure.*

*His shoulders relax when his flesh touches mine, but my skin torches under the contact. Humans have no idea the power their touch can yield. Their contact can harm, it can heal...it can entice.*

*I feel a tingling throughout my core and tiny little lumps surface on the skin I can see. What is this? My legs tremble as though they may collapse and my mouth fills with saliva as the fisherman's hand traces the contours of my face. He caresses every inch of it. Then his hand softly strokes my hair.*

*I'm frozen—not in fear, but in this foreign feeling wrapping around me. This intense desire that simmers beneath the surface of this humanly frame. I never knew humans could feel so many things all at once, so deeply, so strong, yet so tender and all-encompassing.*

*His gaze seems lost as it sweeps over me. He doesn't speak, just continues to feel, reassure himself that I'm not a figment of madness and despair.*

*What is he thinking? What is he feeling?*

*This tension simmering between us has my body on alert, my skin tingles in anticipation, but my heart pounds with a dreaded uncertainty. Will he accept me? Will he want me? I've made the ultimate sacrifice to be here with him... Will he reject me? Will it all be for naught?*

*How do I know what feelings are real when I've never felt them before? How do I take the risk of opening my heart to this lonely stranger I've admired and longed for from afar?*

*Does he feel the same attraction and passion for me? Or will my heart be shattered once the waning moon returns?*

Carly sighed as she sat back from the computer.
*Same, girl. Same.*

# CHAPTER EIGHT

THE TINY YET-TO-BE-NAMED white-and-orange fluffball was curled up on a mat in the shed the next day as Oliver ran a hand over the smooth wood grain of the paddleboard he was building for Tess. He'd carved a Sealena figure into the wood grain and he'd planned on painting it various shades of sea green and ocean blue. Teal now as well.

He sighed and shook his head. Her birthday gift may no longer be a surprise, but at least he knew what color to paint it. Maybe once she received it, she'd give up the new kayak idea.

SUP was an activity she'd been wanting to try and he'd already enrolled her in a weeklong session a short drive away in Sirens Bay, the best surfing and water sports area in this part of Alaska. The surf there was perfect for beginners and the lessons were done as a group with a certified instructor in an alcove, close to the shore.

Over the years of trial and error, he'd learned this was the way to approach things with his younger daughter. Redirect. Never say no; that only made her more determined and persistent to get her way. Offering other options often worked.

He hoped it did this time.

He stared at the intricate design of the Serpent Queen in the wood and sighed. If only she were real... If only there really was someone or something in these waters protecting those at sea.

Not just a fanciful woven tail.

Like this new romance series creating such an uproar around town. Not just the women, but the men, too, were buying and reading this new series. The mystery surrounding its author held almost as much appeal as the books themselves.

Oliver shook his head. He didn't get it. Nor did he suspect he would.

His cell alarm chimed, indicating quarter to the hour, so he put his tools away and covered the paddleboard. Then he locked up the shed, climbed into his vehicle and headed down to the docks. He parked on the pier and headed toward the Marine Life Sanctuary building, where he could see the summer camp kids in their matching teal blue camper shirts with the Port Serenity Wildlife Conservatory logo on the back, reaching into the water with small beakers. Obviously, some kind of experiment.

He hung back a little, watching Tess reach in to fill her own beaker, and he grinned. She loved the water and all its mysteries and secrets.

The brilliant scientist, in her lab coat over cutoff jean shorts and matching camp T-shirt, waved at him now as she motioned for the kids to take the beakers back inside the lab.

He waved in return and leaned back against the front of the truck to wait. He was five minutes early. But Dr. Ann surprised him by walking toward him. "Hey, Oliver, can we chat for a minute?"

"Everything okay?" he asked. Tess had a history of being a bit of a know-it-all at camp. Dr. Ann wouldn't be the first to tell him that Tess needed to listen more and talk a little less when it was interrupting other children's learning. It was the only complaint her schoolteachers had about her.

"Great. Tess is so amazing to have in the camp."

"But…"

Dr. Ann laughed as she shook her head. "No buts."

Oliver raised an eyebrow.

"Okay, so she's a little chatty," she said. "But in my camp, I encourage that. If she wants to share her knowledge, she can share away. Besides, she's hardly ever wrong."

Oliver sighed. "Tell me about it." Disagreements with his daughter tended to go in her favor nine times out of ten. Tess rarely made bad choices, and even when she did things he didn't necessarily love or agree with, she always pleaded a great case. She came to every discussion prepared to negotiate and persuade by having done her research. Alison used to say that someday what they found most challenging about her would lead to Tess's greatest strengths. Parenting Tess had just been easier when it had been the two of them in it together.

"So, what's up?" he asked.

"I, uh, was just wondering if you and Tess might be interested in…tacos," she said.

Oliver frowned. "Tacos?" Like as a fun lunch at camp? Or parents' day food item?

"I've been told my tacos are the best in Port Serenity—I mean, by my brother's assessment, at least," she said with an awkward-sounding laugh. "Tomorrow is taco Tuesday, so I thought if the two of you aren't busy, you might like to join me?"

Oliver swallowed hard, trying to decipher the invite. Was she asking him on a date? Dinner at her place? She'd included Tess, which was both better and worse. He cleared his throat. "That's really nice of you, but Tess and I have plans tomorrow night," he said. At least, they did now. He'd come up with something so that it wouldn't be a white lie.

"What plans?" Tess asked, approaching, her open backpack slung over one shoulder, licking a Popsicle, her hat falling off her head.

"You know...that thing," he mumbled.

Tess shook her head. "There's no thing. I checked your calendar. We're free."

The downside of linking his daughter's cell phone to his to keep an eye on her meant she also had access to his information. He shifted from one foot to the other, unsure what to say. Tess looked eager to have tacos with her summer camp instructor...but why? "Right. Tomorrow is Tuesday!" he said, unconvincingly. "I was thinking about the thing we have on Thursday." Real smooth.

Tess grinned, her mouth and tongue a bright purple.

"Great. Well? What do you say?" Dr. Ann asked.

"Sure. Tacos sound great," he said.

"Perfect. My place at seven?"

He nodded as he took Tess's backpack from her and helped her climb into the passenger seat of the truck. "See you then."

"Bring your appetite," Dr. Ann called as she waved and headed back toward the building, where the rest of the children were gathering their things and several parents waited for pickup.

When he was settled into the driver's seat, he shot Tess a look. "Care to explain what that was about?"

She bit off a piece of the Popsicle and said over the mouthful of ice, "You...need to...get back in the saddle."

Oliver nearly drove off the shoulder of the road. "Excuse me?"

"Get your groove back, your love on..." Tess said.

Where the hell had this come from? He cleared his throat. "Um, excuse me, what?"

She glanced at him. "You know—our chat. Yesterday. About expanding our family, bringing more people and pets into our intimate circle."

Intimate circle. Oliver ran a hand over his stubbly chin and fought for the right words. He had broached the topic with Tess to gauge her thoughts on the idea of him potentially dating, of moving on, but he hadn't meant for her to suddenly start playing matchmaker. Maybe he should have been more direct, clearer in the discussion. Maybe he should have been more specific that he wasn't into dating just anyone...

First, maybe she should clarify her thought process with this whole taco night thing. "You think I should date Dr. Ann?"

"Why not? I think she's pretty and smart, and she thinks you're cute."

Huh? "She told you she thinks I'm cute?"

"She didn't need to say it, Dad. I noticed the way she looked at you at drop-off this morning. There was definitely chemistry."

He sighed. She'd noticed chemistry. He hadn't. He hadn't dated in so long, hadn't even entertained the idea of dating in so long, that he didn't pick up on those social clues anymore.

For months, Alison had been flirting with him in home economics and he'd never clued in that she wanted him to ask her out. She'd finally been the one to ask him out.

"So, these tacos are a date?" He didn't like the idea. And he certainly didn't like the idea of misleading either Tess or Dr. Ann into thinking he was interested in a relationship. At least, not with the local marine scientist.

"If you kiss her at the end, it is," Tess said after some contemplation.

Kiss her? He wasn't going to kiss Dr. Ann. He wasn't going to kiss anyone—except maybe Carly…eventually. Someday. If he ever got the courage to figure out how to tell her about these growing feelings and if he could stop his daughter from setting him up on any more dates.

"There will be no kissing," he said firmly.

"Right. That could be awkward for you and gross for me. Best if I'm not there. I'll make a playdate with Darcy so you can go alone," she said, licking the remains of the frozen treat from the stick.

"You will not. You got me into this. You're coming along. And next time, don't ambush me like that." They had a rule—discuss things in private first. Seems his daughter suspected he never would have agreed to this if Dr. Ann hadn't been standing there.

Tess sighed. "Dad, you can't be alone forever."

"I'm not alone. I have you," he said.

"Only for another six years and two months. Then I'm headed to Hawaii."

He smirked. "Hawaii, huh?"

She nodded confidently. "That's where Dr. Ann studied marine biology. She says once I'm sixteen, I can work as a volunteer at the conservatory, which looks great on a university application. She said she'll even write my letter of recommendation."

Oliver ruffled her hair and grinned to himself. His ten-year-old had her future all carefully figured out.

If only Oliver had his so perfectly planned.

FIVE A.M. WRITERS CLUB was a thing. And Carly was its latest member.

Sitting at her laptop before the sun had risen the next morning, a fresh, steaming cup of coffee at the ready, she rotated her shoulders and quickly reread the chapter from Sunday's writing session.

Not bad. Not perfect. But that was what revisions were for. Right now, she needed to get the words onto the page so that she had something to send to her editor.

Taking a deep breath and a big gulp of caffeine, she started to type:

*That night, I can't sleep. I lie awake, watching the rise and fall of the fisherman's chest, listening to his deep, peaceful breath as he rests.*

*I've loved him from afar for so long, having him so close feels surreal. This mythical being from another world. His pale skin, dark hair and eyes the color of the sea are etched in my mind from years of watching him sail above the surface.*

*Our time is borrowed.*

*My kind can't sustain life above the water for more than thirty days. Choosing to use this once-in-a-lifetime opportunity now, to spend it with him, is something I know I'll never regret. But the time is already passing far too quickly. Each day is closer to the end.*

*He won't remember me once these days together are over. Won't remember the way we'd longed for one another when being together hadn't been possible.*

*The day he discovered me still haunts my thoughts. He wasn't afraid, there wasn't a look of terror in his eyes, like there is with so many others who see me lurking beneath. He hadn't tried to follow me when I swam away...but he was there again the next day. The same cove where I rest. Few venture that far north.*

*My language and his are different, but we don't need words to communicate—the connection between us is so strong it surpasses all obstacles.*

*If I could stay, would I?*

*Would I choose love above my ultimate duty of protecting these shores along Port Serenity's coast? Would I leave my world behind to stay on this land, knowing someday I'd age, I'd die, I'd be long forgotten?*

*Would I do that for him?*

*All I can do is wait to see if he'll ask...*

Carly sighed as she closed the laptop and sipped her now lukewarm coffee, her interaction with Oliver the day before still playing on her mind. It had obviously manifested itself in this new scene and this new source of conflict for Sealena.

Before, it had felt like there was no chance for her and Oliver, but now she wasn't so sure. The day before there'd been...something. And that foolishly gave her new hope and new conflict.

Checking the clock on the wall, she composed an email to Paige:

Dear Paige,

Exciting news that the promotion team believes in this story enough to ramp up their campaign. Full disclosure: this book is taking a little longer than the others, but I'm attaching several new chapters for your review. Be kind. These are still in first draft.

Have a great day,

Carly xx

She attached the new chapters she'd written and hit Send on the email. Then, getting up, she headed into her bathroom to shower and get ready for work. By the time she'd dried her hair, her cell chimed with a new message from Paige:

Carly! These pages are wonderful! Can't wait to read more.
XX Paige

Carly sighed in relief. At least her current turmoil was resulting in great fiction.

Exhausted from lack of sleep, she set up for the day downstairs, and before she knew where the time went, the first few customers were lined up outside. Smiling, she opened the door and lost herself in a sea of tourists.

She didn't check the time again until she saw Sebastian enter just before noon. He was definitely committed to his promise of learning everything he could about Sealena. He hadn't missed Sealena School in two weeks.

That day, he seemed even more energetic as he approached the counter with a coffee for her from the diner. "Thank you," she said, gratefully taking a gulp. These 5:00 a.m. wake-ups were going to be tough. By now, she could really use a nap, not more caffeine.

"I have great news," Sebastian said, leaning his elbows on the counter.

"What's going on?" she asked.

"The parade is going to be televised," he said proudly.

Carly's eyes widened over the rim of the coffee cup. "Really? Wow. How?" The local TV station wasn't far-reaching enough to warrant the effort of televising the parade. Everyone in Port Serenity who wanted to see it would be there live anyway.

"I have a contact at News Live Anchorage. I reached out yesterday and pitched the idea and she loved it. The network is also looking to showcase more local stories to help bring more visitors to all parts of Alaska, so they are in." Sebastian's smile was wide as he delivered the news.

"That's great," she said, feeling the excitement for all of twenty seconds before the pressure set in. "Just means we are really going to have to pull out all the stops this year." Her float would be impressive, but they'd need to make sure the entire parade was spectacular.

"I've already drafted this email for parade participants, encouraging them to go bigger and better…offering incentives for their efforts," Sebastian said, opening his email on his phone and handing it to her.

Carly read quickly. Sponsored gift cards…free promo in the local marketing guide…

She nodded as she handed the phone back. "This is wonderful. It will definitely entice everyone to put their best work in."

He looked happy as he hit Send on the mass email and tucked his phone away. "I did good?"

"You did good," she said.

Now she needed to make sure her parade float was the most impressive display Alaska—and the world—had ever seen.

No pressure.

WITH TESS AT camp that week, the lighthouse tours fell on his shoulders, and by the third one that day, Oliver was struggling to muster the enthusiasm. Funny how the tour information seemed to get shorter with each one.

But if people wanted to know the history, they could read all the poster boards on the lighthouse walls and the artifact descriptions.

Outside, he lined the group up for the obligatory photo and barely waited until everyone was in place before flashing the pic. "Okay, thanks for coming! Photos will be mailed out in the next few weeks," he said.

As the crowd dispersed—some to hike the coastline trail around the lighthouse, others to sit in the picnic area along the shoreline—one woman lingered. With her cell phone, she snapped a dozen photos of the lighthouse and the surrounding plot of land. Then he noticed her talking into a recording app.

Her clothing didn't exactly scream tourist on vacation. There were no Sealena-themed T-shirt or knee socks on this woman. The polished dress capris and flowy white blouse with expensive-looking leather flats on her feet gave him a slight uneasiness as he approached. He'd seen enough tourists to know this woman wasn't one. She'd been quiet on the tour, taking everything in, but now she seemed full of questions as Oliver approached.

"Anything I can help you with?" he asked.

"All this land belongs to the lighthouse?" the woman asked, gesturing to the entire plot on which the lighthouse stood.

"The land belongs to the community as well as the lighthouse, yes," he said, feeling the hair on the back of his neck stand up. "Let me guess—real-estate developer?" He'd cut straight to the chase.

She extended a hand toward him. "Eliza Delton from Delton Vacation Properties. Nice to meet you," she said politely.

He'd like to say the same, but inside, he was raging. That

slimy Sebastian had sent a property developer out to take a look at the land before he'd even pitched the B and B idea to the tourism board? The man's arrogance had just crossed a line into cocky and Oliver's opinion of him took a further nosedive. "How can I help you?" he asked again because he wanted this woman gone before Tess got back from camp. He wasn't ready to tell his daughter about this just yet. And he certainly didn't want Tess finding out this way. He hoped a rumor wasn't already spreading through town.

"I just wanted to come out and see the land before my company put together its proposal for expansion," she said, pulling a notebook out of her oversized purse and sketching the lay of the land.

He could save her the trouble by offering a copy of the blueprints, but he wouldn't. "Expansion?"

"Some cabins. The main house will only accommodate eight to ten guests at most with some renovations, so we'd likely put another six or seven cabins along the back of the property," she said. "But I'm not really at liberty to say any more than that."

Things were being planned around him, as though he didn't matter. As though he would get no say in the decision.

She shut the sketchbook and took a final look around. "I think that's all I need for now. Thank you for your time," she said.

Oliver simply nodded as he watched her head toward a rental car parked in the gravel parking lot and drive away. Unsure how to feel, he needed to busy himself, otherwise he was going to head straight to the tourism office and demand that Sebastian give it to him straight. Was he losing his family home or not?

Inside, he headed into the laundry room, where a load

of wash had finished drying. Taking everything out of the dryer, he folded the items. Then, picking up the basket, he carried it into Tess's room. He had to shove the door open, as there was yet another pile of clothes and toys blocking his access.

He sighed as he entered and scanned. Unlike his older daughter, who had been meticulously organized and neat, Tess was a tornado of chaos, most of all in how she kept her room. But she claimed to know where everything was.

He set the laundry basket down on her bed and sat, his shoulders slumping as he tried to process all the conflicting emotions he was suddenly dealing with. His gaze landed on a picture of Tess, Catherine and Alison on her nightstand. He reached for it and stared at the photo he'd taken of the three of them at the local fairgrounds the spring before the disappearance. Cotton candy in hand, the three of them wore goofy smiles. Tess looked so little then... If only Alison could see how much she'd grown.

Would his wife be proud of how he was raising her? How would she feel about the prospect of him moving on, potentially away from the home they'd built? He wasn't sure that part was a choice he'd get to make.

He set the photo back down and, picking up the clothes, he approached the dresser. He rearranged the mess of clothes sticking out and tucked the clean stuff inside.

No wonder the drawers were overflowing; Tess had stashed dozens of books in there...

He lifted the stack of Nancy Drew books, planning to add them to her bookshelf, and frowned, seeing the Sealena-themed fantasy romance underneath. Obviously hidden. Where on earth had she gotten it? She'd never be brave enough to take it out of the library, and Carly would have told him if Tess had bought a copy from the store. He didn't think Carly would have loaned it to her without asking him first, or at least letting him know.

He flipped through the pages.

He'd heard a lot of people talking about the series around town and its mystery author, but he'd had no interest in checking them out. Romance wasn't his genre of choice. He looked at the animated, hand-drawn image on the cover— an image of Sealena in the water, staring off at a fisherman in his boat in the distance, with the title *Forbidden Love*. He turned it over and read the back cover copy:

*Sea serpent queen Sealena has one purpose in life— to protect the waters around Port Serenity, Alaska, and all those who dare to venture into the frigid North Pacific. Generations of her kind have been rumored to lurk beneath the ocean's surface and her solo existence is a lonely one. When she sees a local fisherman plagued by grief and sorrow, her world is turned upside down as a strange, yet undeniable force draws her to him. She can't seem to break the spell of attraction she feels for the human, but a love between them could never exist... Haunted by this forbidden love, Sealena is desperate to find a way to connect with her fisherman, risking everything she's always sworn to protect.*

Oliver frowned as he flipped through the pages. How sexy was this book?

He noticed a section of several dog-eared pages, and his heart raced. Tess had already learned about sex at school, they'd had several awkward chats...but was she getting a sexual education from these books? He held his breath as he started to read:

*Every night, the fisherman sits on the small front porch swing. He whittles away, carving small woodland creatures into blocks of wood. I love watching his skilled hands move as he carves away at the old pieces of trees to create these wonderful figurines. We sit there for hours in silence, enjoying being with one another, without him fully aware of my presence in the water just a few feet away. I don't want to scare him. I don't want to intrude.*

*But I can sense that he knows I'm there. I see him look out at the water sometimes and notice his small smile. I know he likes having me there and, each day, it feels as though our connection is growing stronger. I long for his touch, his kiss, his arms around me, but my fisherman maintains a distance and I can't find a way to connect our worlds.*

*In the mornings, he goes back out to sea to fish. But this morning, he's left a gift along the shores where I hide. I see the carved figurine of myself, only it's a different version of myself—one that fits into his world.*

*I pick it up and stare at it. Is this how the fisherman still sees me? Is this the only version of me he'll ever accept? Will I have to change who I am for him to accept this connection as real? How else could we possibly be together?*

Oliver sighed in relief as he closed the book. At least it wasn't a graphic sex scene that his daughter had flagged.

Unsure what to do, he slipped the book back under the Nancy Drew collection in the dresser drawer where she'd hidden it. Until he could figure out the best way to handle the situation, he'd leave his daughter to it.

NEWS ABOUT THE televised parade had definitely spurred excitement in town. Carly's cell phone hadn't stopped chiming with new messages all morning from people "replying all" to Sebastian's mass announcement the day before.

So far, it seemed that the town was embracing Sebastian and his ideas. His pitch to turn the glacier waterfalls into a tourist destination had been approved by the committee, thanks in part to her support, and plans were already moving forward to have the spot open in time for next year's tourism season.

As Carly hung a Last in Stock sign above a table of random items, the door opened and Skylar entered the store. "So, turns out Rachel was right—these books are seriously addictive," her cousin said, sounding almost annoyed at having been wrong. Or just not having read them sooner.

"Really?" That was a real compliment coming from the biggest Sealena critic in Port Serenity.

"Yes! The writing is so engaging I could keep flipping the pages for hours and not get bored. And the backstory the author has created for Sealena makes her so endearing and sympathetic. We've always known her as this creature lurking in the water, saving ships, but this new, deeper version of her is fascinating."

Carly grinned. "You know she's a myth, right?" She couldn't help but tease her cynical cousin, who had always had a tough time getting on board with the town's mythology.

Skylar swiped at her playfully. "When's the next one releasing?"

"October fourth," Carly said.

"And how do you know that?"

Oops. The book hadn't been announced yet. Carly thought quickly. "Oh, well, as a store owner, I'm given the release dates ahead of time...for promotion and stuff." Her cheeks were flushed and she could see that her cousin wasn't buying it. Skylar could always tell when she wasn't being completely truthful or was hiding something from her. They'd always been as close as sisters.

"Right...yeah. That makes sense." Skylar paused. "You know what I thought was uncanny as I was reading, though?"

"What's that?" Carly asked casually, avoiding her cousin's piercing stare as she readjusted several items on the table.

"The similarities between you and Sealena," Skylar said.

Now she was sweating. "What?" She scoffed. "That's silly." She headed back behind the counter and pretended to restock the till tape.

"Like the physical description of Sealena when she becomes human in the preview of book three—five-two, slim build, long dark hair and green eyes."

Shit. She hadn't realized she'd given the humanized version of Sealena her characteristics. Must have been subconscious. "That could be the description of practically half the women in town," Carly said, waving a hand.

"Okay, well, the whole plot of *Forbidden Love* sounds very familiar as well... Two souls connected but forced apart by circumstance?"

"Skylar, you don't read romance, but that is a very common trope," Carly said.

"A fisherman who is grieving the loss of his family? Closed off from the world? A wood-carver?" Skylar moved closer with each word. "The fisherman is Oliver!"

"Shhh," Carly said as a patron entered the store. "I don't know what you're talking about. Oliver doesn't fish," she said.

Skylar's eyes narrowed. "Okay, what about the turquoise

pendant Sealena wears around her neck?" Skylar's eyebrows rose as she eyed the one Carly was wearing.

"That's really coincidental," she said, her voice tight.

"Unless it's not… You're Y.C. Salwert, aren't you?"

Carly scoffed. And scoffed.

"OMG, you are!" Skylar's eyes widened with excitement as though she'd been bluffing, but now Carly had confirmed it.

Carly sighed and desperately pleaded with her cousin. "You have to keep this to yourself," she whispered.

"Why? This is incredible. I never knew you wanted to be an author," Skylar said, lowering her voice.

"I didn't. Not really. I kinda just fell into it," she said.

"You fell into a six-figure, multibook contract for a mega bestselling series?" Skylar asked incredulously.

"Sort of, yeah. It started as a fanfic out of frustration one night."

"Frustration about Oliver?"

Carly nodded. "Do you think everyone else in town can see the similarities between me and Sealena and Oliver and the fisherman?"

Skylar thought for a second. "It took me a bit to see it and I think I only did because we're so close, and, well, I started to suspect something was up with the recent spending. Putting the puzzle pieces together made me fairly confident in my accusation," she said with a laugh. "Hey, why are you so freaked out that I know? This is great! I'm proud of you."

"You are?"

"Yes, and so would the rest of Port Serenity be if they knew. Why the secret?"

"It all happened so fast and I had never expected the series to do so well. I guess a part of me wanted to keep the focus on the books. The mysterious author element seemed to help with sales, so the publisher was on board with keeping my identity a secret," she said.

"But don't you want people to know?"

Carly thought for a moment. She wasn't sure. As Skylar had pointed out, there were parts of herself—a lot of herself—within those pages, and announcing herself as the author might feel too personal. "I don't know… Maybe, but not yet," she said. Then she pointed a finger at her cousin. "And not a word to Rachel!"

Skylar nodded emphatically. "Oh yeah, no, that makes sense. She'd never be able to keep this to herself."

As Skylar placed an order for the third book in the series, Carly still felt on edge. Skylar now knew—how much longer before everyone else figured it out?

# CHAPTER NINE

Dr. Ann lived on the eastern coast of Port Serenity, directly across from the lighthouse on a small inlet that was easier to get to by boat than car. She claimed to love the solitude and being surrounded by nature. She had a simple motorboat that she used to get back and forth to work every day, but Oliver opted for the dirt side road path to the woman's house that evening for their taco Tuesday nondate.

In the passenger seat, Tess bounced as they traversed the bumpy, uneven terrain. "The boat would have been easier," she said.

"Off-roading's fun," he countered.

"Tell that to my bladder," she said, squeezing her knees together and doing a squirmy-looking dance.

Oliver laughed. "Hey, you were the one who wanted to do this, remember?" He wouldn't admit that the ride was doing a number on his bladder as well. Only his sweating over the fact that he was being ambushed into his first evening with a woman in years made him forget that he too had to pee.

Tess turned in the seat to scan him and frowned. "You didn't put gel in your hair like I told you to."

"I was out," he said. He hadn't put gel in his hair for three years. The old container sitting in the bathroom drawer was probably sticky goo by now.

His daughter leaned closer and sniffed him. "You didn't put on cologne either," she scolded.

He sighed. "Are you saying I stink?" He refused to act like he understood where this was coming from. She wanted him to look nice, smell nice, for Dr. Ann... Because she wanted this to be a date. Oliver was determined to keep it as platonic as possible.

"Dad! You need to put some effort in."

"Actually, I don't." He pulled the truck into the lot next to Dr. Ann's modest bungalow and cut the engine. "I know what you're trying to do, Tess, but it's not going to work."

She pouted, but then her little face lit up with a mischievous grin.

Damn, he'd just inadvertently issued a challenge to his ten-year-old.

"Come on. Let's go," he said. The faster they could eat, the faster he could make a polite excuse to call it a night.

It had been a day—with the property developer's untimely visit and finding the romance novel in Tess's room—and he wasn't exactly in the mood for this.

As he climbed out of the truck, he saw Tess lean around the seat to grab something from the back. When she emerged, her face was covered by the biggest bouquet of wildflowers he'd ever seen, fastened with her hair ribbon. "Where did they come from?"

"I picked them from the yard." She tried to force them into his hands but Oliver refused.

"You picked them. You can give them to her."

He was already regretting this evening. He pulled at the collar of the shirt Tess insisted he wear. He should have continued to ignore her suggestions and gone with his comfy cotton T-shirt. The dress shirt, the flowers—it was already too much.

How was he ever going to start dating again when right now just looking presentable and being polite for an evening with a woman was more than he was comfortable with?

Dr. Ann opened the door with a wide smile. She was wearing a T-shirt and casual-looking lounge pants and Oliver had never felt so relieved in his life. She hadn't dressed up for the occasion. He sniffed the air around her—no perfume and no extra makeup beyond what she'd been wearing when he'd picked Tess up from camp. All good signs. "Hi. Come on in."

"Hi, Dr. Ann," he said.

"Oh please—just Ann," she said.

Tess entered first, handing her the flowers. "These are from Dad," she said.

Ann took them and smiled, smelling them. She winked at him over the bouquet. "Thank you, Oliver. Very kind."

Now he felt bad that they weren't from him and she knew they weren't from him.

They were just flowers. People brought flowers to other people for lots of different reasons. Anniversaries, birthdays, Mother's Day…funerals.

His gut tightened as his real aversion to the flowers emerged.

Alison and Catherine's funeral had been full of flowers. So many flowers…

He hadn't been able to look at them the same way ever since. To him, they symbolized pain and grief.

He cleared his throat and forced away the thought. He was there; he needed to try to relax and enjoy the evening. Which was not a date in his mind and he hoped he could softly, gently explain that to Ann once Tess wasn't within earshot.

The food cooking in her kitchen did smell amazing and

his stomach growled as the scent of meat and cheese and peppers reached him.

Ann laughed, hearing his stomach. "That's a good sign, at least. Food's ready. I'll just pop these into a vase of water and we can eat," she said.

Surprisingly, dinner went better than he could have hoped. The food was delicious and it seemed they both kept the conversation and spotlight on Tess. They talked about camp and all the things she was learning. They talked about her upcoming birthday and the kind of party she wanted to have—a backyard inflatable bouncy castle, to Oliver's relief. They chatted about Ann and Tess's shared passion for the Discovery Channel and all things Shark Week, and Oliver was truly relaxed by the end of the meal. Ann had been friendly, but not flirty, and she too hadn't seemed to want to discuss anything too private or deep.

Sitting on the outdoor deck, furnished with a wicker table set and decorated with tiny lantern string lights to set a nice, cozy atmosphere, Oliver and Ann sipped on wine after dinner. Her home backed onto a small lake, which she'd turned into a private observation area to study more basic water species. It was quiet and peaceful as the sun set over the surrounding wilderness and Oliver could definitely understand the appeal of living there.

"Can I go feed the fish in your lake?" Tess asked.

Ann nodded. "Of course. The feed is in that bucket. Just be careful if the water's edge is muddy. I wouldn't want you to slip and dirty your dress."

Tess nodded. "I will." She grabbed the bucket and hurried off toward the water. Oliver watched as she tossed some food into the lake, but he saw her keeping one eye on them. Obviously, she was hoping if she left them alone, they might start to connect on a different level. His daughter was sneaky.

"She really loves marine life," Ann remarked with a chuckle. "She reminds me so much of myself at that age."

Oliver turned in his chair to look at her. "You always knew you wanted to be a marine biologist?" he asked. A safe enough topic.

"Since I was five years old and my parents took me to Hawaii on vacation. We went to the aquarium, and then diving, and I was hooked."

Oliver nodded, sipping the wine.

"I guess your future was predetermined as well?" Ann asked.

"In a way, yeah. I mean, I could have done something different. But this felt right at the time."

Ann studied him. "At the time?"

Oliver sighed. She'd caught that. How much did he want to reveal? Talking to Ann felt nice, comfortable, but he wasn't sure opening up about anything serious or personal was the right way to convey this wasn't a real date and wasn't leading anywhere beyond friendship. "I'm not sure it's the right fit anymore...but I don't know."

She nodded her understanding. "I'm glad you came over. You and Tess," she said. "It gets kinda lonely and quiet out here."

His chest tightened slightly. "Ann, I—"

"But I have to tell you, Oliver, I'm not interested in a relationship."

His mouth gaped. She wasn't? Well, why had she invited them to dinner? He was relieved, but he'd been planning to be the one to break that news. Now this felt slightly awkward.

"I'm sorry, but Tess kinda..."

"Guilted you into inviting us for dinner?" he asked in wry amusement. He should have known. "Let me guess. She told you I liked you and that I was lonely."

Ann laughed as she nodded. "Yep. I take it you got the same pitch?"

"I got that you thought I was cute. Tess caught a vibe."

Ann laughed and then covered her mouth with her hand. "I'm sorry. I didn't mean to laugh—you are definitely cute, but there was no vibe."

Oliver sagged against the cushions in relief. They'd been bamboozled by his daughter. Ann wasn't interested in a relationship with him either. For the first time that evening, he really settled in to enjoy himself. Pressure off, he even kicked off his sandals and crossed his ankles.

"Truth is, I'm seeing someone," Ann said, lowering her voice.

"Really? Who?" Port Serenity was a small enough town that if the doctor had been dating, there would be chatter. Everyone thought of her as a brilliant but slightly neurotic doctor. Most men in town were intimidated by her. Man, he hoped some dude wasn't going to show up and read the situation wrong.

"Another marine biologist, stationed in Hawaii," she said.

"A long-distance thing?"

"It's torture," Ann said, sounding distressed, "but it's always been that way, and with both of us on long-term contracts where we are researching, I don't see the gap closing anytime soon."

"You've never met face-to-face?"

"Nope." She sighed and Oliver heard the hint of longing. "Only Skype calls and texts."

"Why don't you take time off and go visit?" he asked. She must have vacation time she could take.

"Truthfully? Because I'm terrified." She laughed. "I'm afraid that once we meet, we'll realize what we have isn't so special. Silly, right?"

He shook his head. "No, I get fear." Fear of relationships was something he understood very well. He'd experienced it from every angle—disappointing someone, getting disappointed, hurting someone or getting hurt, dating...sex. He gulped, especially at the last one. He hadn't been with a woman sexually in three years. The only woman he'd ever been with was Alison. What if he'd completely forgotten how to do it or, worse, was shitty at it? "Do you think you ever will meet?" he asked, needing to keep the subject of her love life at the forefront. "Does he want to?"

"He does... Recently, he's been talking about it more and more, but I don't know. I like things as they are and I don't want to risk ruining it." She took a deep breath. "What about you?"

"What about me?" he asked, sipping more wine.

"Do you think you'll ever be ready for another relationship?" she asked, curling her leg under her on her chair.

"I have no idea," he said, an image of Carly popping into his mind.

"But you came here tonight," Ann said gently. "So, maybe part of you isn't completely opposed?"

"That was all Tess." He stared into the wine. "I know she'd like me to start dating, find someone in theory, but I'm not sure she'd really be ready for it, you know?"

Ann nodded gently. "Sounds like you may be deflecting a little."

"Or a lot," he agreed with a laugh. He ran a hand through his hair. "It's tough to move on, I guess."

"It's been three years. Alison would want you to be happy," she said.

He knew she was right. Alison would be damn well pissed off if she knew he was still alone after all this time. She'd want him to open himself up again. Find new love. But he just couldn't imagine a future—a life—with someone else.

Again, thoughts of Carly popped into his mind.

Except maybe her…but how did that happen when they'd been friends for so long? How did they make that transition? He had no idea.

Tess hurried up to them, a wide smile on her face. "You two seem very chatty," she said with a grin.

Oliver sighed and set the wineglass down. He stood, and wrapping his arm around Tess's shoulders, he smiled at Ann. "It's getting late. We should go, but thank you for dinner and the conversation."

"Anytime," Ann said as she stood. She hugged Tess and touched Oliver's shoulder.

As they walked back toward his truck, Tess glanced up at him. "No spark, huh?"

Oliver shook his head. "Sorry, kiddo. Unfortunately not."

There was only one woman he'd recently felt a spark with, and that fire might take a blowtorch to ignite.

OLIVER PACED THE sidewalk outside the Sealena Bookstore and Museum early the next morning. He checked the time on his watch and flinched as hot coffee spilled from the top of the cup he was bringing for Carly. Eight fifty-six… He peered inside, but couldn't see her.

Odd. She was usually in the store early, setting up for the day.

Had she had a late night? Out with Sebastian again?

An odd sensation flowed through him. When had Carly become interested in dating? He couldn't remember the last time she'd had a boyfriend or even a casual date. It was strange, actually, as she was a beautiful, smart, caring, interesting woman...

Oddly, he'd just assumed that they were both going to be single, best friends, relying on one another for the rest of their lives. But that was hardly reasonable. Of course, Carly might be interested in a relationship, marriage, kids.

Maybe she just hadn't found the right person.

Maybe with Sebastian appearing in town, she now had...

Tension crept across his shoulders as he once again peered inside. Where was she?

The interior light flicked on and he saw her opening the window blinds at the back of the store. He moved away from the window and attempted to casually appear as though he were just arriving.

He waved as she approached the front door, stifling a yawn.

Definitely a late night.

She unlocked the bolt and flipped the Closed sign to Open as she opened the door for him. "Hey, Oliver. Sorry to keep you waiting."

He shrugged. "I just got here."

She frowned. "You've been here fifteen minutes. I saw you from my bedroom window," she said with a look. "What's wrong?" she asked as he stepped inside.

"Nothing. What makes you think something's wrong?" Besides the fact that he was practically buzzing from too much caffeine and anxiety, which had been mounting over the last few days and was nearing a breaking point.

"The pacing. The tension in your shoulders. The crazy bedhead." She grinned, glancing up at his hair.

Oliver caught his reflection in the window and sighed. He did have bedhead and Carly knew him too well to fool her. He sighed, handing her the coffee cup. "It's Tess." He'd start there—it was easier than trying to decipher his own conflicting emotions right now, and he really did need his friend's advice regarding his daughter's new reading interests. Her stunt with Dr. Ann had him wondering if the book might be influencing her a little.

Carly's expression changed to one of worry. "Tess? She okay?"

He nodded quickly. Scanning the store, he reached for a Sealena book from the display. "It's this," he said with annoyance. "She's reading it."

He still didn't know how to handle finding the book under Tess's Nancy Drew mysteries in her dresser, dog-eared on rather...interesting pages. Should he ask her about it? Pretend he didn't see it? The adult content was relatively mild—from what he'd quickly scanned. But he wasn't sure these adult fairy tales were the right message for her at this age. She'd definitely been more interested in these things lately. Not boys. Just his love life. It was slightly unnerving.

But he also didn't want to censor what she read. He allowed her to make her own choices, guiding her toward what he felt was the right decision. It was the way he and Alison had agreed to raise the girls. It worked perfectly with Catherine—the more independence they gave her, the more mature and levelheaded she was. She'd self-policed her actions and Oliver always knew they could trust her to make safe, healthy decisions, whether they were around or not.

Tess was a little different. His firecracker daughter seemed to struggle sometimes with making the decision he'd like her to make. Her adventurous streak sometimes overpowered her safety guide. She was far from a troublemaker and Alison used to call her the free-spirited one. But with Alison around, Oliver hadn't worried. He knew Tess had an amazing role model in her mother and older sister to help guide her or help her get back on track if she did stumble or make a mistake.

He questioned if maybe a stricter, more rigid approach to raising her now, on his own, might be a better way…

Carly's cheeks flushed slightly, confirming his suspicions that there may be content within the pages that could be a little advanced for Tess's reading level.

"Where did she get it?" Carly asked, gulping the hot coffee, then wincing as the liquid must have burned the back of her throat.

"That's what I was hoping you could tell me."

She shook her head. "She didn't buy it from me. And I didn't loan her a copy, if that's what you think," she said slightly defensively.

"I didn't think so." He ran a hand over his face. "But you've read them, right?"

Carly nodded, the flush still in her cheeks. He wasn't quite sure why she'd be embarrassed about it. Carly read everything. It was part of her job. And there was no guilt to be had in reading romance. Hell, he'd read his own share of romantic suspense years ago when Alison liked to read them. She sometimes asked him to read passages to her at night.

"How sexy are they?" he asked, flipping through the pages again himself. That was really all he wanted to know. And not because he didn't want Tess reading about sex, but because he needed to be prepared for a conversation about…anything she might have read. How much ice cream would be needed for any conversation about the books?

Luckily, Carly shook her head. "These aren't too sexy.

There is…relations…but the author has kept them tender and heartwarming and mostly off the page," she said.

His shoulders sagged in relief. "So…no whips and chains?"

Carly laughed over another yawn. "You're safe."

Oliver put the book back and followed Carly to the counter. She set the coffee cup down and started to count the float in the cash register. "Tess is getting older. I guess it's natural that she's interested in reading more mature content. I assume she didn't tell you?"

He shook his head. "Found it in a drawer—while putting away clothes," he added quickly on Carly's look. "I wasn't snooping." Not that he was beyond snooping if he deemed it necessary. With Catherine, she was an open book. She told him everything. They could trust her to come to them. Tess was a little different. She was a little more secretive and selective about what she told him. She was definitely an "ask for forgiveness, not permission" type of kid.

"Well, I'm sure there's no harm done."

"Except that she has all of these romantic notions in her head…" he mumbled.

Carly frowned. "What do you mean? Is she starting to show interest in romance and boys?"

He laughed wryly. "No. Thank God. She's just interested in my love life all of a sudden."

Carly's hand tipped over her coffee, spilling it over the counter onto his lap. "Your love life?" she asked. "Shit. Sorry."

He jumped up quickly to save his pants as best he could as she grabbed some paper towel and started to dry up the mess. He took it from her and cleaned the side of the counter. "Not that there is one," he said. He sighed. "She set me up on a date last night," he said.

"With who?" Carly's tone echoed the sentiment he'd felt thinking of her out with Sebastian. Maybe they were still on the same page of growing old alone together. Or together together... He shook his head. He couldn't get sidetracked by those thoughts at the moment. One thing at a time.

"Dr. Ann," he said. "When I picked her up from camp on Monday, she ambushed me into saying yes to dinner."

"Dr. Ann ambushed you?"

"No. Tess."

Carly frowned. "So, she wants you to date?" she asked before sipping what was left in the coffee cup.

"If only. She wants me to fall in love."

This time, coffee sprayed from Carly's mouth, hitting Oliver in the cheek.

"OMG," she said, reaching forward to wipe the liquid from his face. He laughed, but when her fingers touched his skin, a warm tingling sensation had the grin dying on his lips.

She quickly pulled away, but not fast enough. There had definitely been a spark between them just now.

"Sorry... Here," she said, handing him a towel.

He dried his face and shook his head. "Anyway, it was just awkward and weird..."

"Good," Carly said, then blushed. "I mean, not good, but..." Her voice trailed off and she stared at the counter, avoiding his gaze. "You know what I mean."

He didn't, actually. "Speaking of dates...late night last night?"

Her head swung back up to look at him, curiosity on her face. "Are you implying something?"

*Yes.* He shook his head. "Just wondering how things are going with Stan."

She cocked her head to the side. "Sebastian?"

He waved a hand. "Same thing."

She sighed. "I wasn't out with Sebastian."

"Good," he said before he could stop himself.

Carly shot him a look. "Good?"

"You know what I mean," he said, throwing her words right back at her. If she couldn't quite verbalize why it was good that he hadn't been on a real date, he certainly couldn't. He'd been struggling to make sense of these new emotions brewing within him for days, and it wasn't as though he could talk to her about them.

Their gazes met and held for a long beat, before Oliver was acting solely on impulse. He couldn't talk about it, but his body was on a mission to show her. He reached across the counter and his hands gripped the sides of her face as he leaned toward her. "I want to kiss you," he said.

"You do?" she whispered, sounding just as confused by it as he was.

"I don't know why but suddenly it's all I want to do," he said, words coming a lot easier than he'd expected.

"So? Are you going to?" she asked.

"Do you want me to?" he asked.

"I've been waiting for you to for a few years now, so I'd say, sure, why not?" she said softly, moving closer to him. Her gaze flitted between his eyes and his lips. She licked hers and the sight nearly killed him.

When had his best friend started stirring these feelings of desire and yearning within him?

He leaned closer and his lips were just an inch from hers when her words registered. "Wait...a few years?"

She nodded and he saw her swallow hard. "I'm good at keeping secrets," she said, and her eyes pleaded with him to make all her waiting worthwhile.

It had been a long time since he'd kissed a woman, but

Oliver was determined to give it his best shot. His hands gripped her face as his mouth crushed hers. He pulled her in closer and savored the taste of her coffee-flavored lips, the soft fullness of them pressed against his. Instant desire ran through him along with a welcoming sense of relief, as though his body and his heart had been waiting for this moment, anticipating it. How long had he been subconsciously repressing this urge?

His hands slid to the back of her head, his fingers tangling in her soft, thick hair as he deepened the kiss, wanting more, needing more, completely surrendering to the moment. He wouldn't think, just feel. Be in the moment with her right now.

Carly's arms encircled his neck, drawing him as close as possible, and he wished the counter wasn't between them. He wanted to sink into this passionate embrace even more—wanted to press his entire body against hers and feel every inch of her against every inch of him. He wanted to wrap his arms around her and hold her tight.

Damn, it was only a kiss, and yet his entire body stirred with a new awakening. His chest was tight as he struggled for air, but he didn't care. He could stand there kissing her forever. This woman he'd always thought of as just a friend had him feeling things he hadn't in so long; it felt like he was being saved from drowning, as though she were breathing new life into him with this kiss.

She teased his bottom lip with her tongue, gliding it along seductively before slipping it between his lips, making the connection even more intimate, even more real. Damn, Carly—where had she learned to kiss like this? He'd never have expected the teasing torture she was putting him through. And this wasn't just a peck or a friendly kiss that they could forget about. This meant something.

For both of them.

Not breaking the contact with his mouth, Carly climbed onto the counter, and kneeling on it, she moved her body closer to him. He gripped her waist, steadying her so she wouldn't fall and bringing her body closer. Her breasts pressed against his chest and her hips rested against his as she tilted her head and deepened the kiss even more. Her hands fisted his hair, holding him in place as though fearful this might be their one and only kiss and she was desperate to make it last.

He held her tight and all other thoughts vanished except for how to please her, give her what she wanted, what she deserved, what she'd waited for—that part still blew his mind.

Reluctantly, he broke away a moment later and, out of breath, he rested his head against hers. "A few years, huh?"

"It was definitely worth the wait," she whispered against his lips, kissing him again softly.

Oliver's heart felt nothing but a deep sense of peace, the conflict he'd been fighting seeming to have melted away with her kiss, with her acceptance, with the knowledge that they were both feeling this strong connection that surpassed friendship but had a strong foundation in their platonic love for one another. But he needed to know for sure… "What's happening between us?" he asked.

"I'm not sure, but I know I want it to happen again," she said, staring into his eyes with an expression he'd never seen before. One that had his heart racing. "Over and over."

He nodded, happy they were on the same wavelength. "Over and over." He could definitely oblige that request.

IF SHE WAS still asleep, having slept through her alarm after an all-nighter writing session, Carly did not want to wake up. But the taste of Oliver's kiss still lingering on her lips told her the moment had happened; it had been real. Just seconds ago, she'd been kissing her best friend, the secret love of her life, and she'd let go of all inhibitions and uncertainty and just been in the moment.

One she'd waited forever for and one that hadn't disappointed.

Oliver was a fantastic kisser—gentle yet passionate. He'd delivered just the right amount of strength and dominance to be sexy, but just enough retreat to let her take control as well. It was as though they'd been kissing one another for a lifetime. It had felt right. And the best part was, he seemed ready to take this leap with her.

She'd felt things shifting between them lately and she knew Sebastian may have been the catalyst, opening Oliver's eyes to what he wanted, what he wasn't prepared to lose out of fear and uncertainty, but the kiss had taken things to a whole new level. It wasn't the kiss of a man afraid of losing his best friend; it was the kiss of a man prepared to fight for what he wanted.

He wouldn't have to fight too hard. Carly had long ago surrendered to her feelings for Oliver Klein.

He'd reluctantly left her for a tour group arriving at the lighthouse, but her phone chimed with a text as she counted and recounted (getting lost in distraction) the float in the cash register. She picked it up and smiled as she read:

No regrets?

None. You? she texted back.

Only that I had to leave.

Carly's heart filled with hope as she hugged the phone to her chest and a tiny squeal of excitement escaped her. This was what she'd been longing for and now the opportunity to take the relationship to another level was within her grasp.

She tucked the phone into the back pocket of her jeans as her gaze landed on the Sealena romance book display. Her smile faded slightly. Tess was reading her books. She wasn't sure how she felt about that. Not that she thought there was any content in there that the young girl shouldn't read, but what if Tess noticed the same similarities that Skylar had? Would the little girl connect the two?

And now that things were steaming up with Oliver, how long could Carly keep the truth from him about her being the author? That moment hadn't been the right time. She'd been caught up in the emotion of the kiss and what it meant for them, but if they were really going to do this—move forward with a deeper connection—she'd have to tell him. And Tess.

How would Tess feel about them together?

Oliver had said she'd set him up on a date and that she suddenly wanted him to fall in love, but would she be okay if that person was Carly? She and Tess loved one another, but would the little girl find the whole situation weird?

As much as Carly wanted to scream it from the rooftops, it might be better to keep the kiss with Oliver to herself for now.

Which might be hard to do since she couldn't erase the smile from her face.

Unfortunately, the inevitable business of the season got in the way of any more kisses and Carly had to satisfy her Oliver craving with text messages for the rest of the week.

Oliver on Thursday morning: Thinking of you. In fact, haven't thought of anything else.

Carly: Likewise. Mostly about kissing you again.

Oliver: Implied.

Carly: Confident now, huh?

Oliver: Just hopeful and desperate.

Carly: Maybe I'll make you chase me a bit.

Oliver: To the ends of the earth and back.

The sudden switch in their interaction had her on cloud nine. Every day for years she'd started her day with a text from Oliver, almost hoping that one day he'd say the things she longed to hear. And now they'd reached that place. Her cell phone had suddenly become the most precious thing on the planet.

Oliver on Friday morning: Dreamt of you last night.

Carly: That's intriguing. Elaborate please.

Oliver: We were sitting on the docks, holding hands and watching the sunset.

Carly: And...

Oliver: And I awoke thinking that we should do that someday...once these damn tourists leave.

Carly: Definitely...once the damn tourists leave.

Two days without seeing Oliver in the past would have

been a normal occurrence and she'd have been okay with it, but now two days felt like forever. She couldn't wait to see him, as though now he'd look different somehow. She knew the way they'd look at one another, the way they'd interact, would be different, and it filled her with so much excitement and anticipation. She no longer had to hide her feelings from him, and therefore, she couldn't wait to show him all the things she'd been keeping to herself, say all the things she couldn't before.

Now that there was a potential future with Oliver, she wanted that future to start right away.

# CHAPTER TEN

THE NEXT DAY was the first official float building meet-up. They wouldn't all be able to work together all the time, but by some miracle of timing, they'd all been available that day to begin the project together.

Dressed in her favorite pair of loose, comfy jean overalls and a bra top beneath, Carly stood on the float platform and addressed her crew, including Dex's therapy dog, Shayla, who would no doubt be an adorable distraction that day. "Thank you all for volunteering your time to help with this year's float. This is an ambitious build and I appreciate each and every one of those hands," she said, trying to keep her gaze off Oliver. It was nearly impossible and it drove her crazy that the first time the two of them were together was with so many people around.

Maybe they could sneak away...

Oliver was positioning fans in the corner of the room to circulate the air and help the paint dry faster. When his gaze met hers, he sent her a secret look and a wink that had her pulse racing. It was such a relief to know that in the last two days, his feelings hadn't changed, he hadn't let fear change his mind about them. Wearing a pair of work coveralls, his bare chest visible beneath, he looked incredibly sexy. He'd shaved that day and she was fairly certain he'd put gel in his hair—it was still messy the way she liked, but more of a deliberate, controlled mess.

What she wouldn't give to run her hands through it…

"Carly…you okay?" Tess asked when she'd obviously drifted off into fantasy territory of thoughts of Oliver. The little girl was in a full hazmat suit, ready to get to work.

"Yes, sorry," Carly said with an embarrassed smile. "You all have your teams and assigned tasks, so let's get started!" She climbed down as the teams gathered. Dex, Skylar and Sebastian were in charge of decorating the arches with sea florals and corals and sea creatures. Some were store-bought, others they were fabricating from colored cardboard. Callan, Rachel and Darcy were working on the ocean base and the layered waves they were constructing out of wood, painting them with the various shades of blue Carly had purchased. Rachel had a great eye for color and detail, so she knew the waves would turn out perfectly with the right amount of contrasting white. And she, Oliver and Tess were in charge of the key structure on the float—Sealena.

She planned for the sea creature to stand eight feet tall on top of the ocean waves at the base, meaning the overall height of the float would be over fifteen feet. She wanted to make sure people could see it from all angles and any viewing position along Main Street.

After turning on the music, she headed toward Callan, Rachel and Darcy. "You guys okay? Know how you're going to tackle this?" she asked.

Callan nodded. "Piece of cake. I'm no stranger to a skill saw and Darcy is going to draw the shape of the waves before I cut."

Carly high-fived the little girl. "Big ones. Menacing-looking ones."

Darcy nodded, accepting the responsibility. "I'm on it."

"How about you, Rach—all good?"

"I'm already mixing colors over here," Rachel said,

perched over the rainbow of paint colors. As usual, she'd brought flair to her float-building attire, wearing a cute painter's smock, her red hair tied in a bandanna.

Carly knew she could depend on the team. She gave them a thumbs-up sign as she made her way toward Dex, Skylar and Sebastian. Unfortunately, they were off to a slightly slower start. The three of them stood around the first arch, looking a little confused. Even the dog had a perplexed look as she pawed at a string of decorations. "What's happening?" Carly asked.

"Just a little unclear on the arch's purpose," Dex said, eyeing it.

Skylar nodded. "We know you want it decorated in sea elements, but we're not seeing your final vision."

Carly nodded, reaching into her pocket for the hand-drawn design. "The arch will serve as the basis for the sea floor beneath the waves…" She continued to explain her design idea, but she could feel Oliver's gaze on her, which was very distracting.

How on earth were they going to keep their budding relationship and attraction in check that day when Carly felt the sexual tension simmering between them nearly as suffocatingly hot as the humidity of the summer day?

When she approached her own team, Tess was nearly vibrating with excitement and it helped to ease some of the underlying chemistry between her and her other teammate. "I had an idea for Sealena's crown," the little girl said, unrolling her own design.

Carly smiled as she scanned it. "Perfect. Do you want to get started on that while…your dad and I start building the tail?"

Tess nodded, happy to have her design approved. "I'm on it. Can I work by Darcy?" she asked.

Meaning Carly and Oliver would be in that side of the shed alone…

"Yes!" they both said simultaneously.

Tess sent them an odd look, but then, grabbing her supplies, she hurried over to the other side of the shed where her friend worked. The two of them were instantly giggling and enjoying themselves.

"Did you have to look so freaking hot?" Oliver murmured, close to her as he positioned their tarps on the floor.

Carly swallowed hard as she sniffed the air. "You're wearing cologne," she said.

Oliver moved closer to her as she unrolled the gold-and-green fabric. "Why did you invite so many volunteers?"

Carly laughed. "We'd never get this done on our own. Now, focus," she said in the sternest voice she could muster given the fact that she too wished they were alone in the shed.

"Sure you wouldn't rather be on Sebastian's team?" Oliver asked with a mischievous grin as he knelt on the tarp and opened several paint cans.

"For the record, I was never on team Sebastian," she said, unable to keep the serious tone of desire from her voice. He was the one she wanted. The only one she'd ever wanted.

Oliver's eyes reflected the sentiment when they met hers. The long moment of simmering heat had sweat pooled on the base of her back, until she broke away. "Stop looking at me like that and get to work," she said.

With a televised parade happening in a matter of weeks, they needed to put their hormones on hold and get this float finished…but as soon as everyone had dispersed for the day and Tess had blessedly gone to Darcy's house for the afternoon, her hands and lips were immediately on Oliver.

As he closed the shed door, Carly's arms went around his neck and his arms went around her waist. His lips found hers and he kissed her hard and desperate. Like a man giving in to a craving. Frantic, passion-filled and hungry, he continued to possess her mouth until she was gasping for air. Pulling away slightly, she still pressed her body close as she asked, "Think anyone could tell?"

"Yeah," he said, his lips now against her neck, leaving a trail of kisses from her ear to her collarbone.

Her body tingled as goose bumps surfaced despite the hot, muggy air inside the shed. "Does that bother you?"

"Nope," Oliver said, his one-word answers signifying there were better things he'd like to do with his mouth than talk.

"What about Tess? Think she sensed anything?" She wanted to push all thoughts out of her mind and give in to the glorious sensations coursing through her at the feel of his lips against her flesh and the way he was gripping her waist, but she wanted to be sure he was sure. That he wasn't getting cold feet about them, wasn't worried about the others—especially his daughter—finding out. Because Carly wasn't sure they could keep this to themselves for much longer. The attraction between them that day had to be noticeable. She'd caught quite a few curious looks from Rachel and Skylar and several disappointed ones from Sebastian as they'd watched her and Oliver work together.

"Tess was the one encouraging me to open up," he said, sliding his hands lower to grip her ass. Her eyes widened in shock at the forwardness she'd never have expected from him, but certainly welcomed.

"So, I should stop overthinking right now?" she asked.

"Definitely stop overthinking," he said against her lips, before kissing her again. He lifted her off her feet, carried her across the shed to the float and set her down on the platform.

"Wet paint," she said too late.

Not that it mattered once Oliver's mouth crushed hers again. Carly wouldn't have cared if every inch of her was covered in the dark serpent-green-colored paint, and not just the ass of her jean overalls.

She moaned as her arms encircled his neck and she pulled him in closer to deepen the kiss. A kiss she'd thought about constantly over the last two days. Like the first one, the moment almost didn't feel real, yet she definitely wasn't imagining the taste of Oliver on her lips and the feel of his hands on her face. He smelled like cologne and sweat and his coveralls felt damp beneath her hands. She slid her hand in through the opening at his chest and explored the contours of his muscular, smooth chest. He was the kind of man who was naturally strong and sculpted without hitting the gym and Carly had always loved his build. He was definitely her type and she took the opportunity to touch his broad shoulders and wide chest, irritatingly restricted by the material.

His tongue separated her lips and dipped inside her mouth, exploring every inch and tangling with hers with a desperate hunger, as though he too had been deprived for far too long. He was such a great kisser, making her wish she'd been brave enough to make her move sooner, but he'd had to be ready.

He pushed himself between her knees and pulled her body toward his. She could feel the effect the kiss was having on him pressed against her leg. It may have taken him a while to get there, but he certainly seemed ready now.

But for what? Her heart raced. They'd shared their first kiss just days ago. Was this moving too fast, too soon? Or had the years of friendship been all the foreplay they both needed? They were both mature adults who knew what they wanted…

If he was ready to take things further, so was she.

He reached for the clasps on her overalls and unhooked them. The denim bib fell forward and the straps slid back off of her shoulders. Oliver pulled away to take in her body in the teal-green bra top that cupped her breasts nicely and exposed her thin stomach. He inhaled deeply. "Carly, this body isn't fair."

"Took you long enough to notice," she said teasingly, slowly unzipping his coveralls down to his stomach.

"I was a fool, clearly," he said, sliding his arms out of the fabric and lowering the coveralls down to his waist.

Carly eyed the muscular chest and six-pack abs, her pulse picking up speed at the sight. He was so incredibly hot. She'd always thought so and now she was getting to enjoy the view unfiltered. She no longer had to sneak peeks at him when he wasn't looking or try to conceal the attraction she had for his physique. She ran a hand along his chest, lower down over his stomach, and saw him swallow hard. "I love your body," she said. "So strong and sexy…"

Oliver slid a thumb under the strap of her bra top, sliding it slowly down over one shoulder. Then his finger traced the shape of her collarbone before he placed a kiss there. "You're so soft," he said, sliding the strap back up. He reached for the base of the bra top, and sliding his fingers below the fabric, he carefully lifted it over her head.

Her nipples instantly hardened at the exposure to the air and the intense desire running through her. Oliver took her in, a lust-filled expression on his handsome face. Carly reached for his hands and covered her breasts with them, desperate to feel his touch, to have his hands explore her body. Oliver massaged gently, then ran his thumbs over the hardened buds, increasing the pressure. She gripped his hips and a moan escaped her at the pleasure he was evoking. It had been so long since a man had touched her this way. Too freaking long, but she was glad to have waited for the man she really wanted. No one else could have made her feel this way. No one else's touch would have ever been enough.

Slowly, his fingers moved away and grazed against the sides of her body, tickling her as they went. Goose bumps covered her skin despite the heat and humidity in the shed as he lowered his head between her breasts and kissed every inch of each one. She was practically panting when his mouth wrapped around her nipple and sucked.

The things this man could do with his mouth.

She clutched his head, fingers gripping his hair, commanding him not to stop. It felt so incredible and she never wanted him to quit.

He broke contact with her breast and reached for the overalls around her waist. He tugged at the fabric and she propped herself up to allow him to remove them the rest of the way. Her heart thumped in her chest as their clothing became scarcer. Were they really going to do this? Go all the way?

She wanted to.

Oliver grinned seeing her Little Miss Sunshine days of the week underwear. "These were a joke gift last Christmas," he said, teasing her.

She shrugged. "Turns out, they are quite useful."

"Except today's Saturday, not Tuesday," he said, nodding to the little blue cartoon creature boasting Tuesday's ray of sunshine.

Carly laughed. "Are we really going to talk about my underwear?"

Oliver gripped her waist and pulled her toward him. "I could talk about your underwear all day long…but I'd rather see them on the floor."

She swallowed hard as she nodded her consent, not trusting herself to vocalize it. She once again lifted her body to allow him to remove the underwear and she noticed his hands shook slightly as he did.

Was he nervous? She was. It had been a long time for both of them…and they were friends crossing a line they'd never crossed before.

"Oliver?" she asked.

"Just don't want to push you for too much…too fast," he said, staring into her eyes.

"Believe me, this is so long overdue," she said, touching his face with her own trembling hand.

With more confidence, he finished removing her underwear, sliding the fabric slowly down over her legs and tossing them onto her overalls on the floor. Then he finished unzipping his coveralls and stepped out of them, revealing he was completely naked beneath.

Carly's eyes widened at the sight of his exposed cock, but then she shot him a teasing grin. "Maybe I should put underwear in your stocking this year?"

He shrugged. "It gets so damn hot in here." He pressed his naked, muscular body to hers as he kissed her again. "Especially today."

She kissed him back, slowly, their mouths lingering as though unsure how to proceed. They kissed and their hands roamed and explored for a long, torturous time.

Now what?

Oliver moved away and his eyes burned into hers, asking the question they both knew the answer to. They were about to cross a line they'd never considered before...but there was no sign of hesitation in his expression.

She hadn't been with a man since her last long-term relationship. And that relationship hadn't exactly been exciting and passion filled. The sex was...good, but it didn't fulfill all her fantasies. She'd accepted it for what it was, burying any deep desires for intense passion and the kind of sex she'd only read about in her romance novels.

Oliver climbed onto the platform and positioned himself between her legs. He took her hands and raised her arms above her head as he lowered his mouth to hers again. His kisses were driving her mad. Her legs trembled slightly as she clenched her vaginal muscles to try to calm the aching throbbing there.

Oliver kissed her cheeks, her forehead, her nose, before lowering his lips to her neck just below her ear. He kissed gently, softly, his breath and slight stubble tickling her in the best way. He continued his trail of kisses down her chest, along her collarbone, down the middle of her breasts. Carly writhed beneath him, arching her back, desperate to feel their bodies pressed together.

His free hand caressed the length of her body and he slid his fingers along her wet folds between her legs. His gaze met hers for a long beat before he lowered himself down her body. His head disappeared between her thighs and he kissed along her inner thigh from her knee all the way to her groin. Then he did the other side.

Carly's entire body felt like it was on fire with need. She craved more; she was desperate for release. So many years spent waiting and wanting...and now they were here, at this moment. She wanted it to last, but it also couldn't come fast enough.

When his mouth connected with her pussy, she couldn't

suppress the moan that escaped her. It felt so incredible to be pleasured this way…by a man she trusted so fully, so completely. She was so connected to Oliver in so many ways—emotionally, spiritually…and now physically. It made the sensations vibrating through her that much more impactful.

She was vulnerable but in the best way. Oliver already had complete control over her heart. She was willingly giving him control over her body in that moment.

His fingers plunged inside her as his tongue licked and flicked her clit. He clutched her upper thighs as he savored her with a desperation that she'd never had the courage to entertain.

"Oh my God, Oliver, that's so fucking incredible."

His head snapped up at the sound of her swearing and a grin appeared on his gorgeous face. "Did you just say the f-word?"

"You're driving me insane."

"Let's see how many other dirty words we can get to escape those sexy lips," he said, lowering his head back to her.

Her eyes closed and her back arched as he slid another finger inside her body and continued to pleasure her with his mouth. She was so close to the edge and her entire body was begging for release.

One he wasn't allowing her to have.

Slowly, he pulled away, leaving her close to the edge, the space between her thighs burning with intense desire. Oliver moved back to hover his body over hers and she searched his expression.

"You're not getting release that easy," he murmured against her lips. He pressed his thick cock against her and ran his thumb along her bottom lip, licking his own mouth. She swallowed hard. "Let me feel this mouth, Carly."

She could happily fulfill that fantasy.

She playfully bit his bottom lip and he allowed her to flip their bodies so that she was on top, but when she started moving down his body, he stopped her. "Give me your ass," he said, motioning for her to bring her ass back over his face.

She did as he instructed and the sixty-nine position had her even more exposed and vulnerable, but she'd never felt so sexy and confident in her life as she lowered her upper half downward, lifting her ass seductively into the air as she gripped Oliver's cock and swirled her tongue along the tip, which was dripping with precum. It tasted sweet and warm and she was instantly craving more.

She took him in her mouth and sucked, using her hand to stroke along with the motion of her mouth, moving up and down over the shaft.

Below her, Oliver gripped her ass cheeks as she rested her pussy on his face. He sucked and licked and teased with his fingers as they continued to pleasure one another. She could feel her orgasm build as she felt him getting closer. His cock strained and grew tight and his grip on her tightened, the pace of his own actions growing faster and more intense, the closer he got to his own orgasm.

"Carly, I'm coming," he said a second later.

She let herself go as she pushed him over the edge, feeling the rippling of her own release just as she tasted his cum on her tongue.

Oliver's body twitched under her and hers trembled over him. He reached for her waist and she sat up, turning her body to face him. Taking her hands, he pulled her toward him. She lay beside him on the platform and he held her close, kissing her forehead.

"I think we're going to need to repaint," she said.

"Worth it," he murmured.

Definitely worth it.

# CHAPTER ELEVEN

PUTTING HER CLOTHES back on moments later, Carly felt her cheeks still flushed as she mostly avoided Oliver's gaze, but sneaked several peeks in his direction.

She'd just been intimate with her best friend. The man she'd been in love with for so long. Really intimate. They'd gone from zero to a thousand in a matter of days. The last few weeks there had definitely been a new chemistry sizzling between them, something simmering just below the surface. A recently acknowledged attraction from him and the kiss in the bookstore had moved things forward, but now they'd taken a huge, giant leap, fueled only by hormones and passion and the sexual buildup of the last few weeks.

Her best friend had surpassed all expectations. His confidence and skill had surprised her. Not that she'd assumed Oliver was a bad lover, but he was usually so reserved and slightly grumpy; she hadn't expected the complete transformation to sexy love god… Oh, man, she had to stop writing her Sealena stories before she started saying that shit out loud.

He'd driven her wild with his kisses, his touch, the way he'd made her orgasm… She was hot again just thinking about it.

But had they gone too far, too fast? In her mind, the physical connection was long overdue, as they'd had years of friendship to talk and share personal things, connect on other levels, and the whole thing had felt natural, felt right... But that day, things had definitely escalated. What did it mean? Had it been too impulsive? Did Oliver regret it now that the heat of passion was over? Worse, was this now just a physical thing—a friends with benefits situation? While that would be better than just friends, Carly wanted more, and for her, this transition had signified a move in that direction, but maybe Oliver was seeing things differently.

She had no idea what to say or do, so she was leaving it in his court as she slowly got dressed, taking her time with the buttons on her overalls.

She heard the sound of Oliver's coveralls zipper, then the clearing of his throat... More throat clearing... *Oh my God, Oliver, say something!*

"So, um, that happened."

She lifted her head to look at him. His face was flushed as well and his lips looked slightly swollen from their kisses. His hair was messed up and he looked sexier than she'd ever seen him. Her love for him had only grown through their intimacy. There was definitely some truth in the claim that once women had sex, they felt things even stronger, deeper... But she couldn't tell him all that in response to what he'd just said, so she went with, "Yep."

He nodded slowly, putting his hands in his pockets. "How are you feeling about it?"

They were going to debrief after their wild, impulsive passionate sex? She'd rather less talking and more touching, kissing... This gap between them now felt cold and slightly terrifying. The act had been amazing for her, but what if it hadn't been as mind-blowing, earth-shattering for him?

"How should I be feeling about it?" she countered.

"Good, I hope," he said nervously. "I mean, I hope I didn't cross any lines or…"

She stopped his rambling by taking a step toward him and wrapping her arms around his neck. She needed to close the distance between them, reassure him and herself that the direction they were headed in was a good one— the one she wanted to go in. "I feel good."

He looked relieved. "You do? You sure?"

She nodded, then searched his expression. "And you?" That was the big question. She knew how she felt. How she'd always felt. This was up to Oliver. He was the one who'd never shown this kind of interest before, the one who may not be completely ready to go all in.

"I feel good too," he said gently, lowering his lips to hers.

Carly sank in relief into his arms as he continued to kiss her—with less intensity now, but a delicate passion that had her knees weakening and her heart soaring. She'd wanted this for so long and now it seemed as though they were both on the same page.

He pulled away slightly and stared into her eyes. "So… what now?" he asked.

"Well, I'd like to continue moving in this direction… see where it leads." For her, that had always been the hope, the only choice. She was in love with him, and while she wasn't going to reveal that just yet, she didn't want to take a step back, didn't want to retreat. Now that he'd shown his feelings, she was determined not to let him retreat either. Luckily, she sensed he didn't want to.

"I think that's a good idea," he said, holding her close.

"Okay. Well, that's the plan, then," she said.

"Simple. Easy. No pressure," Oliver said, kissing her softly between each word.

Simple. Easy. No pressure.

They could do that, right?

ENTERING THE HOUSE hours later, after repainting the finish they'd destroyed on the float base, Oliver still felt as though he were in a dreamlike state. Had that really happened?

He'd kissed Carly. Held Carly. Saw her naked. Been intimate with her.

Before that week, they'd shared hugs and a forehead kiss or two, then they'd ramped things up a bit with the kiss in the bookstore, but now they'd launched forward at warp speed. But he didn't regret it a single bit. It may have seemed quick, but in truth, they'd been dancing around this connection for years. He'd sensed she'd wanted more from him, but she'd never voiced it or acted on it and he'd taken that reprieve. Now he realized he no longer wanted her to hold back. He didn't want to hold back either. He wanted to go all in with her. Keep seeing one another and see where it led.

Simple. Easy. No pressure.

He hummed to himself as he entered the living room, where Tess sat on the floor with the yet-to-be-named kitten. The small puffball was a great addition to their family. It was sweet and no trouble at all. Tess was fully in love, and Oliver had to admit, it was nice to have company during the day when he worked in the shed between tour groups.

Tess had a handful of treats and had somehow taught the kitten to roll over. Oliver laughed, watching the display. Only his daughter could train a cat. "That's impressive."

"Pumpkin is very smart," she said.

"Pumpkin? Is that the name we're going with?"

"Unsure. Testing it out to see if it fits… Stay tuned," she said. She glanced up at him and sent him an odd look. "Why do you look like that?"

His heart thumped as he quickly glanced down. Had he forgotten to zip his coveralls fully? Were there traces of

Carly's makeup on his lips? He ran a hand through his disheveled hair. "Look like what?"

"Like you just got into the chocolate ice cream before dinner."

He hid a grin at the accurate assessment. He definitely felt as though he'd indulged. He shrugged. "Who knows? Maybe I did," he said with a wink.

Tess had encouraged him to get back in the love saddle and he knew she'd be happy that he and Carly had taken their relationship to another level—at least, he hoped she would be—but for now, he wanted to keep this feeling to himself. It had been far too long since he'd felt it.

He sat on the floor next to her and the kitten. The orange-and-white animal immediately approached him and rubbed her head along his leg.

"You were right. Expanding our family was a great idea," he said.

Tess grinned at him. "Told you. And who knows? Maybe we can expand to include Carly too?"

Oliver's mouth dropped and he stammered. "Carly? What…does she have to do… I mean, Carly?"

Tess laughed at his discomfort. "Dad, the vibe between you two today was obvious."

"Obvious, huh?" To everyone? Probably. They hadn't exactly been hiding their attraction as they worked together. They'd laughed and flirted and touched more than they usually did. They hadn't come out and said anything, but he'd caught the looks Callan and Dex had been sending their way and he also saw the disappointed expression on Sebastian's face.

"And also…you smell like her perfume," Tess said with a raised eyebrow.

Busted. He ruffled his daughter's hair and his shoulders

relaxed. "So…if there was something happening between Carly and me, you'd be okay with it?"

Tess nodded, scooping up the tiny kitten as it yawned and closed its little eyes. "I think I'd be okay with it. And I think Mom and Catherine would be too."

Hearing the validation from his daughter was the last hurdle Oliver's heart needed to take the plunge. Simple. Easy. No pressure. That might be a problem when he was suddenly all in for chaos. Passion. And commitment.

TESS HAD THINGS well under control at Sealena School the next day and Carly's pride watching the little girl was suddenly combined with something else. She loved Tess. She always had and being her main female role model all these years was an honor that Carly had cherished and taken seriously.

What happened to their dynamic now? If Carly and Oliver were going to be together, what would that mean for Tess? How would the little girl feel about a new woman in her dad's life? In hers? Would the transition be an easy one, as they already loved and respected one another, or would it take more time to integrate into a different role?

Whatever Tess needed, they'd do. Just like they'd agreed on slow and steady for their new connection, they'd take the same cautious, careful approach with Tess.

Carly watched as the ten-year-old expertly explained the mysterious artifacts they'd discovered in the waters surrounding Port Serenity that pointed to Sealena's possible existence while also having other plausible explanations. The goal of Sealena School wasn't to trick people into believing the Serpent Queen existed by showing items to fulfill the prophecy, but to educate and open minds to what could possibly be lurking below the surface of the ocean.

It was a fun, informative addition to the bookstore, and the kids who visited town loved it.

Sebastian looked a little less enthused as he sat among the children in attendance that day, but Carly suspected his mood had more to do with the float building the day before. He'd been polite and friendly when he'd entered the store, but he hadn't brought her usual coffee or lingered at the counter to flirt with her. He too must have sensed the connection developing between her and Oliver, and Carly was grateful that she didn't necessarily have to have that conversation…

He was such a great guy, but he wasn't the right one for her.

Feeling a hand on her hip, she turned and grinned as Oliver dragged her away from the room and toward the back of the store. Dressed in faded jeans and a light gray Henley, rolled at the sleeves, his hair messy just the way she loved it and five-o'clock stubble along his jawline, he was the best thing she'd seen all day. She'd always found him handsome, but since they'd started making out, her attraction had doubled. He looked happier now, and while the brooding look had definitely worked well for him, this new expression increased his hotness rating. Or maybe it was because she knew she was the reason for it.

"You're early," she whispered, not wanting to interrupt Tess's lesson.

"Wanted to sneak in a few kisses before I picked up Tess," he said, wrapping his arms around her waist.

Carly moved them between several shelves, out of view of a few customers browsing. She wrapped her arms around his neck and stood on tiptoes to kiss him. Soft, gently at first, then with more passion. He tasted like peppermint gum and his cologne wafting on the air between them awakened her senses. Before that week, he never wore cologne, and while she'd always loved his natural scent, the effort with the cologne meant something to her. He wasn't taking their relationship for granted; he was stepping things up a notch for her.

His hands slid up the length of her body to grip her rib cage, holding her tight against him as he deepened the kiss. She was out of breath and desperate for air, but she didn't dare stop kissing him. This was new and exciting and her whole world seemed to have been turned upside down in the best way that week.

She could stand there, lost in Oliver's embrace, all day.

"Hmm-hmm," a voice interrupted, and the two of them broke apart quickly.

Carly's cheeks flushed, noticing they had an audience of several browsers. Two older women, wearing matching Sealena T-shirts, looked at them with amused expressions as one pointed to the display of books they were blocking.

"Sorry. Excuse us," Carly said, hiding a grin as she ushered Oliver out of the row and toward the counter. "That was close. Luckily it wasn't Tess who caught us," she said, still a little worried about what the little girl would think when she found out. They couldn't keep this from her for long.

Oliver shook his head. "She already knows—or suspects, anyway," he said.

Carly's pulse raced. "Is she okay with it?"

He nodded. "Amazingly supportive."

Relief flowed through her. Having Tess's support meant everything. It was the next best thing to having Alison's. Deep down, Carly knew her friend would want Oliver to move on and be happy, find a forever with someone else, give Tess another chance at the family she deserved. But it still made her heart lighter to know that there was no resistance from the other person most affected by their union. "I'm so glad. Maybe we could all go out to dinner tonight?" Really have a discussion about what was going on, be up front with Tess...

"Actually, Tess is sleeping at the wildlife conservatory tonight—it's an end of summer camp thing that Dr. Ann has arranged, a sleeping under the stars kind of thing, for everyone who attended camp this summer. And I was wondering if I could take you on a date. A real one. A first one."

Carly smiled, her heart feeling so full, she thought it might explode. "I'd like that, but don't expect to get lucky on the first date," she teased.

Oliver kissed her again. "Let's pretend it's the second one, then."

AFTER DROPPING TESS off at the Marine Life Sanctuary that evening for the sleepover, Oliver drove across town toward Main Street, feeling more nervous than he'd felt in a long time.

Which was foolish.

He was going on a date with Carly. She was his best friend and someone he spent a lot of time with. They'd discussed practically everything two people could discuss and in recent days they'd grown intimate. So, being nervous about burgers and milkshakes at the diner seemed ridiculous, but his hands sweated against the wheel and his mouth was dry.

They were good at being friends. They were good at being intimate. But would they be good as a couple? What if they weren't as compatible as they thought? What if they had different ideas about the relationship and how things should go? What if when they found themselves under the pressure of a label, things felt strained?

His heart raced and he swallowed hard, but when he pulled up in front of her house and saw her standing on the sidewalk, dressed in a beautiful, pale yellow sundress and strappy heels, her dark hair piled high in a loose bun on her head, exposing her long, thin, sexy neck, all anxiety melted away. She was beautiful and breathtaking, but still Carly. The woman he'd always cherished and depended on. The woman he trusted like no one else. The one who made him laugh on his worst days and who was there for him through so much.

He had nothing to worry about with things changing between them, because at the core of their relationship, there was a strong foundation of trust, respect and love. It took most couples a long time to build that and they were starting off with it. They were lucky.

He was lucky.

Parking next to the curb, he climbed out of the truck and hurried to the passenger side to open the door for her. "You look beautiful," he said, almost wishing he'd worn something less casual, but he was a jeans and button-down type of guy and, hopefully, Carly loved him the way he was.

"Thank you," she said, kissing his cheek before climbing into the truck.

He got back behind the wheel and turned to face her. "I was going to suggest the diner, but you look too amazing."

She shook her head. "I'm craving a burger and a milkshake. I haven't eaten all day," she said, to his relief.

He wasn't a fancy restaurant kind of guy and he appreciated that Carly wasn't the type to insist on fine dining either. How many nights had they laughed for hours over burgers and milkshakes? Just because the relationship dynamic had changed didn't mean he had to.

Only made him appreciate and feel comfortable about the situation even more.

"Well, I guess we could walk, then," he said with a grin. The diner was less than a block away.

Carly laughed and reached for the door handle. But he stopped her, reaching for her hand. She turned back to him, her eyes sparkling.

"I know it's out of order, but could I steal a kiss first?"

She smiled and nodded as she leaned toward him. He reached for her face and brought his head closer to hers. She smelled so good, and with sweet honey-flavored lip gloss on her lips, she tasted even better. Her skin felt smooth and soft and he felt his body stir.

Better to end the kiss on a brief exchange, otherwise walking to the diner might be a little problematic.

He reluctantly pulled away and cleared his throat. "That's enough of that…for now," he said, readjusting himself in his pants.

Carly grinned as she climbed out of the truck. He met her on the sidewalk and she instantly reached for his hand. He folded his fingers with hers and waited to see if any feelings of hesitancy or insecurity appeared. This was the first time he was out in the community with anyone other than Alison. His first real date on display for everyone to see, question or judge.

He didn't care. He wanted to be with Carly and that was what mattered. Others would talk and have their opinions, but they would no matter what. He was used to the town's gossip, but at least this time, they'd be talking about his happiness.

They entered the diner a few moments later and he led

the way to their usual booth. The same fifties-style decor with its pink-and-green booths and old records on the wall, the same old classics playing over the speakers, the same smell of grease from the grill. He wasn't sure why he'd expected anything to be different. Nothing had changed except for the transformation within him, the new feelings bubbling to the surface that were a challenge to contain.

New, exciting feelings that had him more optimistic than he had been in a very long time.

Carly slid into the booth and, instead of sitting across from her, Oliver slid in next to her. She laughed and he shrugged. "The other side of the booth is too far away." He hoped his sudden obsession with her didn't scare her, but now that he'd opened himself up to this—to her—he wanted to enjoy every moment, he wanted to be next to her and show her that he was truly all in.

Show her and the rest of Port Serenity.

Curious eyes were definitely drifting their way as they picked up their menus. Behind hers, Carly muttered, "People are staring at us."

"They are staring at you because you look stunning," he said. It was a good thing that he had the diner menu memorized, because he didn't want to take his eyes off her. From a distance, the dress had been beautiful; up close, it was knocking him on his ass. Or rather, the way it hugged her body was—soft, satiny material that plunged low at the chest, revealing the swell of her gorgeous breasts, and then tapered in at the waist, before falling over her shapely hips and curves.

She swiped at him playfully and he caught her hand and brought it to his lips. He stared into her eyes as he kissed her palm softly.

Her mouth gaped and she swallowed hard, gently pulling her hand back. "That's enough of that…for now," she said.

He laughed, loving that he was having the same effect on her that she had on him. Knowing they were in sync with their feelings went a long way in reassuring him. This wasn't one-sided anymore. He hated that, for so long, it had been, that she'd been in this alone. He should have noticed, he should have been brave enough to let himself be aware of her feelings.

He couldn't change the past, but he could start now in giving her the life and love she deserved.

"Hey, you two!" Lindsey, their usual server, said as she approached, new electronic order pad in hand. She eyed them with open curiosity and Oliver decided to just put it out there.

"Yes, we are on a date," he said loudly, for the benefit of everyone in earshot.

Carly squeezed his hand, but looked happy at the announcement as she nodded.

The other patrons smiled and returned to their business as Lindsey said, "About damn time, I'd say."

"Me too," Carly mumbled teasingly, and he squeezed her hand.

"Well, wine is on the house—what else can I get you two?" she asked.

Oliver looked at Carly to go first, then seconded her order of a cheeseburger with a chocolate milkshake—they'd skip the wine for now.

Lindsey nodded, then frowned as she struggled with the electronic pad.

"What's wrong?" Oliver asked.

"This damn order system. I preferred my pad and paper."

"Why not just use that, then?" Oliver asked.

Lindsey sighed, rolling her eyes. "New tourism manager in town is recommending these to all businesses, and of course the Wakefields jumped on board."

Beside him, Carly frowned, seemingly unaware of this plan of Sebastian's.

There was more than one she was unaware of and Oliver shifted slightly in his seat. He should tell her about that. Soon.

Lindsey nodded. "Be careful. He'll be automating your inventory system soon enough," she said, typing in their order again. "Okay, think I got it." She crossed her fingers and walked away.

Oliver hated to bring up the other man on their date, but he had to ask, "So...the whole you and Sebastian thing...?"

Carly raised an eyebrow as she turned in the seat to face him. "I told you there was never a thing." Her voice softened as she leaned closer. "There's always just been you."

Oliver's heart skipped at the words and he wrapped his arm around her, settling back in the booth to enjoy his first date in forever, with the only woman he could see a new forever with.

THE DINNER DATE had been everything Carly had been hoping for. Laid-back, casual, fun, but with a new air of energy around them that had her feeling like they'd embarked on a whole new journey together. They'd chatted like they always did, talked about all the familiar things—the tourist season, Tess, the new kitten Oliver and Tess had adopted—but this time they did it while holding hands and sharing long, desire-filled looks.

By the time Oliver walked her back to her apartment, Carly felt like she was floating on air.

"Well, thank you for the best first date I've ever had,"

she said on the sidewalk in front of the steps leading up to her place.

"Likewise," he said. He was still holding her hand and he leaned in to kiss her cheek.

She gripped his face and pulled him toward her for a real kiss. They were standing on the sidewalk on Main Street with lots of locals and tourists around, but she didn't care who saw. His declaration in the diner told her he didn't care either.

They weren't hiding anything. From anyone. Not anymore.

He pulled back slowly and rested his head against hers. "I guess this is where I say good-night?"

Her heart raced. He was leaving this up to her. Did she say good-night or did she invite him inside with no illusions about what would happen? Tess was spending the night at camp, so he didn't need to go home... The idea of spending the entire night in Oliver's arms was too good to pass up. Who knew when they'd get this opportunity again?

"Or you could come up?" she said.

Oliver didn't hesitate. "That sounds like a better idea."

She nodded and, taking his hand, led the way up the stairs to her apartment, where she fumbled with the house keys. New nervousness mixed with a sense of apprehension as she unlocked the door and they entered.

She'd left the living-room lamp on and there was a warm glow inside. She closed and locked the door behind them, and when she turned to look at Oliver, his expression had her breath catching in her chest.

Within seconds, they were moving toward one another, hands and lips frantic as they removed items of clothing as they kissed. Her dress, his shirt, her shoes, his pants, all fell in a trail along the way to her bedroom.

Inside, Oliver backed her toward her bed and they toppled onto it, rolling as they struggled to remove underwear and her bra, all while keeping the connection with their mouths. He swore against her lips as the bra clasp stuck. Laughing, Carly broke free and undid it, tossing the bra onto the floor.

Completely naked, she moved back onto the bed and Oliver climbed on next to her. He reached for her, but his gaze fell on something on her bedstand and he paused.

"What's wrong?" she asked, following his gaze to the Sealena books on the tabletop.

He grinned. "Any dog-eared pages in there?" he teased.

She narrowed her eyes. "What if there are?"

He gripped her hips and pulled her beneath him, then forced himself between her thighs. "Just wondering what kind of expectations I have to live up to."

Oh, if only he knew the truth, that the books were based on him and her connection to him and the longing she'd always felt for him. The fantasies of the sea serpent queen were her fantasies for Oliver.

She reached up and touched his face, drawing him closer. "You have already lived up to all of my wildest fantasies. Now, stop talking," she said before crushing his mouth with her own.

Passion overtook, and within seconds, they were both panting and aching for one another. Oliver's hands massaged her breasts, caressed every inch of her skin, and Carly was desperate to have him closer—as close as possible.

"Oliver, I want you inside me," she said.

"You sure?"

They'd been intimate, but this would be taking things even further. Uniting their two bodies would be another level of emotional commitment. But Carly was more than ready for it. "I'm sure. I want you. I've never wanted anyone the way I want you. Make love to me, Oliver," she said.

He didn't need further encouragement. He climbed off the bed and retrieved a condom from his jeans pocket. Opening it, he slid it on over his long, thick shaft. From the bed, Carly's mouth watered as she watched. Her desire for him mounting, she clutched her legs together to keep the sensations at bay.

Oliver climbed back onto the bed and moved toward her, running his hands along her inner thighs as he gently spread her legs apart. Carly trembled with anticipation as he wedged himself between them and rested his lower half against her. Supporting his upper body with his arms, he stared down at her as he ground his cock against her body. His eyes closed and a moan escaped him. "This won't last long," he said apologetically.

"I'm halfway there already," she said, gripping his ass and pressing him against her opening. She could feel his hard, thick cock against her body and she craved the feeling of having him inside her, filling her completely. "Oliver, please…"

She didn't have to say anything more.

Oliver positioned himself at her opening and gently eased into her body. His head fell back at the sensations and Carly gripped his forearms as she wrapped her legs around him, giving him full access to go deeper.

He did and she moaned in pleasure as he filled the tight space. He moved in and out and she rocked her hips in a steady rhythm, keeping pace with him as his moves became faster, more urgent…

"Carly, oh, Carly," he said, and the sound of her name on his lips drove her wild. It was her making him feel this way. She was fulfilling her fantasies of being with him and it was beyond her wildest dreams.

He stared down at her and their gazes held as he continued to fuck her harder and harder until they were both moaning and giving in to the uncontrollable sensations enveloping them, making them one, uniting them...

He plunged deeper and then slowly pulled back out, repeating the motions until Carly's legs trembled around him and her toes curled, the first ripples of orgasm mounting. "Oliver, I'm coming," she said breathlessly.

He lowered his head to her neck and placed desperate kisses there as he picked up his pace once more, bringing them both over the edge. He bit down on the flesh at her collarbone as his cock throbbed within. Carly's own orgasm had her crying out in pleasure as the two held tight to one another.

As the feelings cascaded and slowly subsided, Oliver's body went limp and he rolled off her, pulling her against him. He kissed her mouth and then touched her cheek as he stared into her eyes. His expression was unreadable and slightly conflicted and Carly's heart raced.

"Everything okay?" she asked.

"It is now," Oliver said. "I'm just sorry it took me so long to get here. To this moment with you," he said.

"You're here now," Carly said as she snuggled closer, feeling happier than she'd ever allowed herself the hope to be.

## CHAPTER TWELVE

BEING WITH CARLY was unlike anything Oliver had ever experienced. They had a natural chemistry and the way their bodies moved in sync from years of knowing one another had made their lovemaking seem effortless. There was no awkwardness as they tried to figure one another out, no hesitancy, no struggle to get out of their heads and just be in their bodies.

Even lying next to her in her bed felt right.

Her back was turned to him and he admired the shape of her body in the early-morning light streaming in through the window. Unable to resist touching her, he trailed a hand along the curves of her side, the soft, warm skin making his own body instantly spring to life. The night before he couldn't get enough of her and it didn't seem as though their hours of passionate lovemaking had done anything to extinguish any of the desire and lust he had for her.

Damn, how had they been friends for so long without him realizing this burning need for her that was now consuming him so completely?

His fingers reached a delicate spot on her stomach and she wiggled in response to the tickle before slowly rolling toward him, her sleepy gaze so freaking irresistible when her eyes opened.

"Sorry, I couldn't help myself," he said, brushing her hair away from her face and peering down at her. If he thought she was beautiful at other times of the day, first thing in the morning, she was completely breathtaking. Messy hair, no makeup, sleepy expression and a look of peace had her radiating. He couldn't tear his eyes away. He wanted to commit this moment—this look—to memory.

"How long have you been awake?" she asked, moving closer and snuggling into his naked body. Neither of them had bothered to put on clothing the night before and the uninhibited way they could be around one another spoke volumes.

He pulled her in tight. "About an hour."

"You've just been lying there, staring at me?"

"Yep," he said with a laugh. "In the least creepy way, of course."

She covered a yawn with a hand. "Was I snoring?"

"Nope. But you do talk in your sleep," he said.

Her eyes widened slightly as though she feared giving away some deep, dark secret. As if Carly could ever have anything to hide or be ashamed of. She was the most honest, altruistic person he'd ever met. And she had the worst poker face in the world—she could never successfully hide things from him. "What did I say?" she asked carefully.

"Just that I'm the best lover you've ever had," he said teasingly. In truth, he hadn't been able to decipher her mumbling. Just random words strung together that obviously made sense in her consciousness, but he couldn't resist teasing her.

She swatted at him playfully. "Well, maybe that's the truth."

It warmed his heart to hear it. He'd hate to think that after years of her waiting for this connection that she might be disappointed in him. He wanted to please her in every way she'd ever fantasized.

And he wanted to continue that right now...

He bent to lower his mouth toward hers and she immediately turned her head to the side, gently shoving him away. "Wait—let me brush my teeth first."

He laughed, forcing her back down and tilting her face toward his. "Get over here, silly woman," he said, pressing his lips to hers. She tasted so good—even first thing in the morning.

She moaned as she deepened the kiss, wrapping her arms around his neck and bringing him even closer. Her tongue slipped between his lips and explored his mouth, tangling with his. He loved kissing her, the way it made him feel. The last week his entire world had shifted; he found renewed hope and passion in Carly's kiss.

He rolled on top of her and massaged her breasts with his hand as he continued to kiss her. She felt so good; her body was incredible. It took nothing for her to turn him on. Her hands massaged the muscles at his shoulders and down his back, coming to rest on his ass. She held him in place as she raised her hips toward him.

She broke away and stared up at him. "I want you again," she said, and he could feel the wetness between her thighs.

He groaned as he captured her bottom lip with his teeth. As much as he wanted her, he could feel his semi was about as good as it was going to get. His cock hadn't seen much action—any action—in years, and after several rounds the night before, it wasn't exactly cooperating.

"The will is there, believe me, but I think I need to recharge," he said with a hint of embarrassment.

Carly grinned. "I broke you already?" she teased, reaching down between their bodies to wrap her hand around his cock. She gently stroked his half-erect penis up and down, gently at first, then with more intensity.

The feel of her hand around him while she continued to kiss him senseless felt incredible, but it just wouldn't go.

Frustrated, he pulled away slowly. He may not be able to because of all the previous orgasms, but that didn't mean he couldn't pleasure her. "Do you have a vibrator?" he asked, desperate to see her come.

"I've been single, pining over you for the last three years—what do you think?" she said, slightly out of breath. "Top side drawer."

Oliver moved away to retrieve it and grinned when he found the bright pink, battery-operated dildo in the drawer. It was at least twice as big as he was, ribbed along the plastic shaft, with little rabbit ears at the base for additional clitoral stimulation. He held it up and shot her a look. "How is any guy supposed to compete with this?"

"Exactly why I stayed single and celibate—until it was worth it not to be," she said, grinning up at him.

"Well, I'm happy for the backup, but hoping I won't need this very much." Though if they kept having sex so often, the toy would become his new wingman, because bringing Carly to orgasm was the best feeling on earth.

He pushed her legs apart and settled between them. "Have a favorite setting?" he asked, turning it on. The thing was a little intimidating with its different speeds and vibration patterns.

"Surprise me," she said, giving him that seriously seductive look that he'd only recently been privy to. Damn, he hated that he hadn't had that look in his life until recently. But they couldn't go back in time. Change the past. They were together now. That was what mattered.

He adjusted the vibrator to a slow, steady pulse and pressed it against her mound. Instantly, her back arched and a moan escaped her. He moved it slowly along her folds, teasing the opening. He saw the wetness form and his mouth watered as he circled her opening deliberately slowly. He teased her clit with the vibrations and her moans grew more desperate and urgent.

There was no way he was letting her come that fast. Having this power over her was a high like no other. When they were having sex, they were on equal footing with the give-and-take of pleasure, but now she was at his full mercy and he wanted to give her the best orgasm of her life…eventually.

He moved the vibrator back to her opening, sliding it inside. Deeper and deeper as her legs widened and her folds welcomed it. She moved her hips up and down, grinding against it as the rabbit ears found her clit and pulsed. He saw her body clench around it and he was so desperately jealous of the machine.

He needed to get in there…

He slowly moved the vibrator in and out of her body and lowered his mouth to her.

Carly moaned when the heat of his breath touched her and she gripped his head, holding him there between her legs.

While the vibrator fucked her, Oliver sucked and licked her clit and along the wet folds. She tasted so sweet and delicious, he felt himself harden even more. He knew he'd never come again, but the turned-on way his body felt had him feeling incredible. Satisfying her, watching her get off, was the most intoxicating thing he'd ever experienced.

He adjusted the tempo on the vibrator and Carly's moans turned into more desperate pleading. She clutched the bed-sheets at her sides and arched her back. Her legs trembled on either side of him and he pressed a hand to her lower stomach, holding her down in place.

"Oliver, this is torture," she gasped as he slid the vibrator out, halting the orgasm that he knew was mounting.

"What do you want, Carly? Beg for it," he said, slowly gliding the vibrator over her lower stomach.

She twitched and placed a hand between her thighs, touching herself. "Please, Oliver. Make me come," she pleaded.

He held her hands together and placed them over her head on the pillow before easing the vibrator in and out of her body. "How bad do you want it, Carly?"

"Bad. Very bad... Please, Oliver. I'm aching..."

Having this control over her was something so beyond anything he'd ever felt before. The vibrator might be the one doing the work, but he was deciding when and how she came. Having her lying there, vulnerable, trusting him, being open to anything he wanted to do to her, was a power trip and it brought him even closer to her.

"Oliver, I need to feel the pressure inside me," she said.

Her mesmerizing dark eyes had him giving in, no longer able to tease her. He slid the vibrator back inside and turned the knob until the sensations were powerful and commanding. The rabbit ears pressed against her red, swollen clit, vibrating with force, and Carly cried out in release as her orgasm had her body trembling on the bed. She sucked in a deep breath as her back arched and her fingers tangled in the bedsheets.

Oliver leaned over her and kissed her hard as she rode out the rippling sensations. Finally, her body settled and relaxed and he slowly turned off the vibrator and eased it out of her body.

"That had to be the best sex of my life," she said.

"In that case, we'll have to keep this thing close," he said.

Carly grinned a satiated smile up at him. "Not feeling at all fazed by the machine's backup capabilities?"

"Not in the least," he said, kissing her lips. "I'm already envisioning a lot more fun we could have with it."

THE INSPIRATION WAS certainly flowing that morning. It was the first 5:00 a.m. writing session that she hadn't needed as much caffeine to get moving. After her night with Oliver, Carly was filled with new energy and motivation for Sealena's love story.

Sitting at her desk, her coffee going cold next to her, she furiously typed the next few chapters of her book, which detailed Sealena's days on land, the deepening connection between her and the fisherman, the way their lives intersected, and how they were learning to trust one another, how to love one another.

Carly's fingers could barely keep up with the thoughts flowing in her mind:

> They say nothing can last forever.
> But they haven't seen the way the fire burns deep between us when our bodies connect. Lovemaking in his world is different than in mine. It's tender, yet passionate. It's uncontrollable, yet measured. There's a rhythm that flows between our bodies, connecting our souls.
> In my world, I dominate everything I touch. With my fisherman, I surrender.
> I give up control, power, a need to overwhelm, and just release into the sensations flowing through me.
> He runs his fingers along my skin and goose bumps surface, a tingling that feels like the ocean waves caressing my skin. He kisses my lips and his mouth

*tastes salty like the water I command. He's the best of both worlds.*

*He lifts me into his arms and carries me into the bedroom. His motions are confident but careful, as though he might break me.*

*Break me—Sealena—goddess of the sea, protector of men, queen of the depths.*

*With him, I am fragile.*

*It's both terrifying and liberating. As though I can let go, relax, let someone else take care of me. It's foreign yet welcome. But how long could I surrender my power, before the deep, burning urge within me takes over, ruins everything?*

*It can't be suppressed...*

*My ancestors have tried.*

*I'm not the first to fall in love with a mortal. A mere human. Someone who shouldn't hold the mesmerizing power over me.*

*Generations of my kind have tried to bridge the gap between ocean and earth, connect our two worlds... and failed.*

*Despite the love my fisherman has for me now, it can't last. This spell he is under isn't real. It has a time limit. One that gets closer to expiring every day. I have to let him go after thirty days or he will be forever lost...as will I.*

*His madness has started to develop already. I see him gazing out to sea in a trance, weighing the life he has against the one he thinks could be.*

*There's no life underwater for him, yet my spell will make him believe he too has a choice. He doesn't. Our souls have intertwined as he is the balance to my watery being. In thousands of years, this happens once and only once. He is the chosen one.*

*And while his love for me is real—it will destroy him. Therefore, my love for him needs to set him free. It's the true test of my love.*

*Once it's over, it's over.*

*But for now, I give in to this powerful force between us and I allow the fisherman to touch me, kiss me, make love to me.*

*Hovering above me, he clutches my hands in his, raises them above my head on the soft pillow and enters my body. I feel his thickness fill me in a way I've never experienced. He moves with a tantalizing rhythm that steals my senses, a desperation within him so strong, it seems he's unable to control the passion brewing inside him.*

*He stares into my eyes and kisses my lips as his hips rock back and forth and his manhood demands to be satisfied. The lack of control, my full surrender to him, makes the feelings of pleasure spiraling inside me that much stronger.*

*He continues to make love to me until we are both spent and satiated and we fall into each other's arms, clinging to one another, clinging to this moment, terrified to see another day begin and end...*

*Nothing lasts forever—except me. I'll endure through this generation and next, watching his descendants be born, grow and wither, long after my fisherman is gone. Nothing lasts forever, but the memories...*

Carly sat back and sipped the cold coffee in her mug, rereading the last scene. Then she composed the email to her editor and attached the new chapters, feeling confident that Paige would love them.

Definitely some of her more powerful writing and she had this newfound passion and connection with Oliver to thank for it. He'd always been the inspiration for her books and he unknowingly continued to be…

She'd have to tell him soon. She couldn't keep a secret like this from him much longer.

She bit her lip. How would he react? Would he be upset that she'd written about him metaphorically in this way? Would he want to read the books? How would Tess feel? Had the little girl already made a connection? She wasn't sure how she felt about all of that. She'd written them never really giving it much thought—no one was supposed to know she was the author, least of all Oliver.

Her email chimed with a new message from Paige and she marveled at her editor's response times. The woman must work 24/7.

Opening the email, she read:

Just took a quick glimpse, but holy heat, Carly—your readers are going to love it!
XX Paige

Oliver may not be happy when he found out about her and the books, but at least her editor was happy and, for now, with her deadline looming, that was all Carly could concern herself with.

She'd find a way to break it to Oliver. Soon.

THAT WEEK, THE group worked tirelessly to finish the parade float. At least, most everyone did. Sebastian had shown his face just once that week and had only stayed a few minutes, having the excuse of a meeting with the mayor.

Carly wasn't upset. She understood. The man had really only volunteered to help with the design to get close to her; that had been obvious, and when it was clear that her heart belonged to Oliver, Sebastian had gracefully backed down—unfortunately, leaving them one key member short for completing the design tasks.

But like the amazing friends they were, everyone else had stepped up to the challenge, and by Saturday, the float was almost finished. The platform was covered with fabric and rows of blue lights, meant to give the impression of the glowing sea. The big cardboard waves had been positioned, looking even more menacing and real than she'd envisioned. Rachel's artistry had really brought them to life. And the sea arches were also in place, featuring the layers of the ocean that she'd wanted to portray—colorful sea creatures and coral and seaweed hanging from them really gave the impression they were suspended in the water. All the tiny sailboats they'd positioned along the base added a layer of perspective, and as Carly stood back to admire the hard work, tears of pride actually formed in her eyes.

Though, it was also hard to even look at it that day without thinking about what had happened on it the week before. Carly flushed as the memory of her and Oliver's naked bodies meeting and connecting on the seafoam paint flashed in her mind.

"You're thinking about it too, aren't you?" Oliver whispered in her ear as he walked past, his breath against her neck making her shiver. Despite their busy schedules, they'd found a way to see one another at least a few minutes every day, either in the morning before Carly opened the shop or later in the evening, once she closed. They'd also had time working together on the float, but with other people and Tess around, they hadn't had a chance to have sex again since the weekend before.

She leaned against Oliver and tilted her head up toward him for a kiss, which he happily obliged. "Think you're recharged yet?" she asked.

His grip on her waist tightened and he pulled her back toward him, where she could feel his semi through the front of the work coveralls. "What do you think?"

"I think Tess needs to have a sleepover at Darcy's soon. Very soon," she teased.

"I'll plant the seeds of that idea immediately," Oliver said with a laugh, releasing her to go rejoin Tess, who was finishing the Sealena crown.

It was the best part of the Serpent Queen. Tess had spent hours forming and painting the large, magnificent head-dress with its shiny sequins that took so much glitter paint, and its cutouts of various shapes that resembled sea life. It was going to give the silhouette of the serpent queen a beautiful profile from all angles.

The shed door opened, and to her surprise, Sebastian entered. He carried a bag of what smelled like sugar dough-nuts and balanced a tray of coffees in one hand. "Hey, thought you all could use a sugar and caffeine boost," he said.

Carly smiled gratefully as she approached and took the coffees from him. "Thank you. I'm sure no one will turn this down," she said, delivering the drinks to her exhausted paint-and-glitter-covered crew.

They all graciously accepted the snack and the break, except Oliver, who still wasn't exactly team Sebastian. Carly hoped she'd sufficiently put his mind at ease that there was nothing going on between her and the new tourism manager. Oliver should realize by now that she only had eyes for him.

But if he didn't want his coffee, she'd drink it.

"I also wanted to stop by and give an update about the televising of the parade," he said.

Carly frowned at the tone.

"Sorry to say that the network had a scheduling conflict— the reporter who was scheduled to come out and report live won't be able to after all," he said, sounding disappointed.

"Overpromised and underdelivered," Oliver muttered under his breath.

Carly shot him a look. She was disappointed too, but she knew some things just didn't work out. "It's okay," she said to Sebastian. Though she wondered if maybe he never had this nailed down the way he'd originally claimed or if he'd been talking big to impress her. Either way, it wasn't happening now and that was fine. Then her eyes widened. "Oh, but what about all the prizes and stuff offered to the parade participants?" The whole town had been putting in extra effort.

"Don't worry about that—we're still going to honor that commitment," he said, and she nodded in relief.

"Great. Well, we are just about finished, but we could use all the hands we can get to position Sealena onto the float." The eight-foot statue was huge and very heavy. They'd constructed it on the floor, but now they needed to secure her in place.

Sebastian smiled, rolling the sleeves of an expensive-looking dress shirt. "Put me to work," he said as they headed toward the float. "Oh, and if you're not busy one day this week, I was hoping we could get together to go over another proposal I hope to submit to the board."

Carly nodded. "Of course," she said, but there was something in his tone that made her feel slightly uneasy. And when she caught Oliver eyeing Sebastian with a hard look, her uneasiness grew.

Was it just the idea of her spending time, working with Sebastian that had Oliver still on edge—or was there more to it?

WITH THE SEALENA figure in place, standing fierce and proud, the focal point of the display, the extravagant float was done, and to her credit, Carly had really pulled off the impossible.

Not that it surprised him. Carly was amazing and she always put her heart and soul into everything she did. It was one of the things he'd always loved and respected about her. Oliver glanced at her now, wide smile on her tired face as she stood back to admire the group's work. She clapped her hands and shook her head as though she was amazed they'd actually pulled it off.

"It looks amazing. Thank you so much, everyone," she said, scanning the group, who all looked impressed by their handiwork.

Including Sebastian, who really couldn't take much credit, as he'd bailed on most of the work. Showing up on the last day with coffee and doughnuts with the disappointing news that the parade wouldn't be televised didn't exactly give him the hero status he'd clearly wanted. But if Carly was disappointed about the news, she didn't show it.

She had acted a little strange when Sebastian had asked for a meeting with her that week and Oliver hoped it hadn't had anything to do with him. He trusted her completely, and while he wasn't a fan of Sebastian, he knew he had nothing to worry about with the two of them working together.

What bothered Oliver was this new proposal the man had

mentioned. He hadn't heard any more about the B and B idea since the real-estate developer had visited the week before and he'd been foolishly hoping Sebastian had abandoned the idea completely, or had proposed it and been rejected...

Next to him, Tess tugged at his sleeve. "We should thank everyone for their help by hosting a cookout in the yard," she said.

Oliver nodded. "Sounds good to me." He'd already stocked the freezer with meats and hot dogs for the summer. During those warmer months with longer sunlight hours, he and Tess grilled every meal. "Everyone is welcome to stay for food and drinks," he told them all. He glanced at Sebastian and gave an odd little nod that meant, *yeah, even you.*

Carly beamed at him and he suddenly wished he could retract the offer and have Carly alone. All to himself.

"That sounds fun, but unfortunately, we can't stay," Skylar said on behalf of her and Dex. The coast guard captain had blue streaks of paint on her forehead as she removed the painting smock he'd loaned her and hung it on a hook on the shed wall. "We have a dinner with Dex's family tonight at the Sealena Hotel for his mother's birthday."

"Think we can show up like this?" Dex asked, teasingly. The man had more gold glitter on him than the float. He'd been in charge of holding the crown as they'd lifted the figure onto the float base.

Oliver laughed as Skylar shook her head. "Only if you want to lose your trust fund," she teased back.

"Well, we will get together for drinks some night soon. My treat as a thank-you," Carly told her cousin and her fiancé.

Skylar eyed her. "That's generous of you."

Carly looked away as she shrugged.

"Deal," Dex said, checking his watch. "Shit, we're going to need to shower together if we don't want to be late."

Skylar raised an eyebrow. "If we shower together, we will for sure be late."

Jealousy coursed through Oliver. He'd like to be taking a nice, long hot shower with Carly right about now. Lather up her entire body with soap and wash every drip of paint and glitter from every crevice…

When her gaze met his, he knew she was thinking the same thing.

He cleared his throat as he turned to Rachel, Callan and Sebastian. "What about you three?"

"We're in," Rachel said after a quick look at Callan, who nodded.

Sebastian checked his watch. "I can't stay…but thanks. I have a meeting."

Oliver couldn't say he was disappointed that the guy had other plans, but he suspected Sebastian was bailing because he wasn't thrilled about the connection between himself and Carly. They'd kept things PG around the others, but there had definitely been flirting and sexual tension and a few quick kisses. He'd seen Carly giggling with Rachel and Skylar at one point, so he assumed the ladies were in the loop when it came to all the juicy gossip.

Which was fine with him.

He had no hesitancy or reservations about the group knowing about the two of them. He was falling in love with his best friend and all he felt was happiness and renewed hope for his future.

His and Tess's.

"Okay, well, give me two minutes to shower and then I'll start the grill," he said as they all left the shed and the three leaving headed toward their vehicles.

"Should I get started on margaritas?" Carly asked him.

Oliver's heart soared even more. They were hosting their first impromptu get-together as a couple. Him at the grill, her at the margarita maker—perfect way to end a long, hot summer day.

Something he could definitely get used to.

CARLY SIPPED THE ICY, refreshing lime-flavored margarita as she stretched her legs out in front of her on the lawn chair next to Oliver's an hour later. The summer sun was setting and the smell of BBQ lingered in the air as they sat across from Rachel and Callan, enjoying the evening after a long day of hard work. An early-evening breeze blew her hair into her face and Carly tucked it behind her ear as she took another sip of her drink.

A few feet away, Tess and Darcy lounged on large bean-bag lawn chairs, munching on popcorn as they watched the latest kids' movie being projected onto the shed wall with an old projector Oliver had rigged for Movies Beneath the Stars. It was a wonderful setup and the girls loved it. The sound of their laughter filled her heart. She couldn't remember the last time she'd felt so complete. So happy. So at peace.

She'd been there with them a million times, but this time felt different. As though she were a part of it in a different way. Making and serving the drinks while Oliver made the food had felt like a whole new level of intimacy. Almost more powerful than the sex. They were operating as a couple, hosting their friends. Their connection and relationship on full display. She was no longer just a guest in Oliver's home.

Oliver reached for her hand between their chairs and a tingle raced up her arm at the touch. She squeezed his hand tight and he winked at her. She loved that they weren't trying to hide what was going on between them. They were both entitled to their happiness and it didn't matter what anyone else thought.

Rachel grinned at her over the rim of her margarita glass and she grinned back. She'd filled Rachel and Skylar in on the details of the budding relationship earlier that day...or at least, some of the details. The more intimate ones she'd kept to herself, much to Rachel's chagrin.

And her friend took Oliver's lightened, margarita-influenced move to take another run at her interview request. "So, Oliver..." she started. "Now that the float is done, I was wondering if maybe you might have time for that interview?"

Carly held her breath, but she didn't feel Oliver tense beside her the way she'd have expected. She knew Rachel had been hounding him for an insider story about the history of the lighthouse and his family since she'd moved to town and Oliver kept resisting. He was a private person and the invasion of his privacy by the local papers and law enforcement years ago had left their mark. He was now weary of these kinds of interviews—rightly so.

But Carly also couldn't fault her friend for trying. She was hoping to grow her blog about the town and it was great exposure for the community.

"She's relentless," Callan said to Oliver, with an affectionate gaze toward Rachel.

"Part of the job," she said with a no-offense-taken shrug.

Oliver sighed. "I'm not sure, Rachel."

She leaned on her elbows, her red hair falling over her shoulders. "Look, this place is so full of mystery and charm. I just think it would be such a fantastic story. And...there is this rumor circulating that the town might be considering converting this place..." She lowered her voice so the girls wouldn't hear.

Oliver nodded with a quick glance in Tess's direction. Obviously, he hadn't mentioned anything about it to Tess yet. Carly too had heard the rumor circulating around town that week, that there had been a property developer looking at the land around the lighthouse, but she hadn't heard anything directly, and she knew not to believe every whisper around town, so she hadn't brought it up to Oliver.

Was that what Sebastian wanted to talk to her about? This new proposal of his? She remembered Oliver's look when Sebastian had requested the meeting with her. Maybe there was more to the rumor than she knew.

"Reminding the community of the lighthouse's history and its origins and significance might help your case," Rachel continued, pleading *her* case.

Carly's stomach twisted unexpectedly at her friend's angle. Maybe an article like that could help if Oliver wanted to keep the lighthouse the way it was. But she couldn't help but be unsure of what was best for the community, despite her growing relationship with Oliver.

While this place was important to Oliver and Tess and his family, it was also important to the town as a community historical site, one that could be further utilized to draw tourists and provide more accommodations within the town. When she'd heard the rumor, her reaction had been torn.

The idea of him revisiting the past and recounting the old stories hadn't bothered her before, but now the idea made her uneasy for a lot of reasons. They'd just started to explore their new connection and were working toward a future together. Was it a good idea for Oliver to rehash the past? What kind of effect would that have on him? On them?

But Oliver had been resistant to Rachel's interview requests so far, so the likelihood that he'd agree now was slim. Either way, it was his decision and she'd support whatever he decided.

Rachel continued to stare at him expectantly and Callan just shrugged to say, *up to you, man*.

Oliver shifted in the seat next to her and took another swig of his margarita before answering, "You know what? Sure. Can't hurt, right?" he said, surprising her.

He glanced at her and squeezed her hand again.

"Right," she said, offering the best version of a supportive, encouraging smile she could with her own conflict about the subject simmering below the surface.

## *CHAPTER THIRTEEN*

THE NEXT DAY, Carly drove to the mayor's office for a meeting with Sebastian. He hadn't suggested a restaurant this time, so that made her feel infinitely better. This was all business, and as she entered his office just before noon, he was definitely in business mode. He'd redecorated the space with more modern furniture, and paintings of the town's landscape were new additions to the walls. He'd added a bookshelf that boasted a lot of marketing and business books and he seemed to really have settled in.

Dressed in a suit and tie, he looked more professional than she'd ever seen him and he definitely had a different air around him as he greeted her. "Hey, Carly, come on in. Thanks for meeting with me."

So formal. A little too formal given their previous interactions, but she sensed he needed to make the very clear distinction now that they were colleagues only. That was fine with her.

"No problem at all. I'm excited to see this new proposal," she said, but her chest was tight. If it was what she thought it was, she had no idea how she was going to feel about it.

"Have a seat," he said, gesturing to the one across from him. As she did, her heart raced. She could see the designs on his desk for the new lighthouse tourism site that she'd heard rumored throughout town.

So that really was the man's plan.

She sat and folded her legs at the ankles as she prepared to keep an open mind. And five minutes into the meeting, she found herself in the toughest position she'd ever faced.

In those five minutes, he'd already presented a strong case for the development and he'd only scratched the surface. Truth was, it was hard not to get excited about the idea. Not only had he successfully implemented the same structure in another city, but his plans for the Port Serenity lighthouse were actually really well-thought-out and carefully constructed for the betterment of the town, not just some quick marketing ploy from a city guy who didn't care about the community.

He may have arrived in town with a slight ego and edge, but in recent weeks, he'd really proved why the mayor had hired him. He'd put in real effort getting to know the town's history and the people. He'd learned about the Wakefields and Beaumonts and their generation-long feud, he'd studied the mythology of Sealena, and he'd even taken some boating lessons, planning to take up the hobby.

The proposal in front of her from Delton Vacation Properties was surprising and unfortunately causing her major turmoil. She wasn't sure how to deal with her conflicted state, so she pushed it off for now.

"Why don't you walk me through it?" she asked. He'd explained why he thought it was the right strategy for the community and how it had worked elsewhere, but before she could fully jump on board, she needed all the details.

Though she suspected the more she heard, the more convinced she'd be.

Sebastian nodded. "Right. So, the land the lighthouse currently stands on is sixteen acres. Only ten of it is currently being used. The idea is to turn the main house into a B and B, but then build smaller individual lodgings on the extra land. The vacation rental could then easily accommodate another thirty people at once."

"Easily making up for the capacity that was lost with the Bayview Inn closing last year," she said, biting her lip. That unexpected closure had really left them vulnerable to guests staying outside Port Serenity and therefore not fully benefiting from the vacation spend.

He nodded eagerly. "And the best part is that these modular builds are built off-site and delivered complete. So, on-the-ground construction would be a week or two at most. No long disruptions or drawn-out completion dates."

"This company—Delton Vacation Properties—how long does it take them to build one of these?" She pointed to the cabin on the proposal.

"Three weeks."

Carly's eyes widened as she peered at the beautiful spec designs. Each of the cabins was two-bedroom, one bath, with a tiny kitchen and living space, but featured a hot tub on the large wraparound deck. The top was flat and therefore had extra seating space, elevated to give a fantastic view of the coast and the town. She could envision watching a beautiful sunset from up there. The interior design could be dark or light wood with white accents and appliances that gave it a sleek, cozy yet modern look and feel. The supplies used throughout were high quality and would age well. The samples were decorated with local handmade quilts and artwork, utilizing the skills and displaying the talents of the locals.

Sebastian had really pulled out all the stops in getting these designs just right to gain community approval. Carly was struggling to find any fault with them. "That's definitely a benefit," she said. She already knew these cabins would book immediately, as soon as the marketing went out.

But this was Oliver's home. Tess's home.

The knot in her stomach tightened as her excitement rose.

Doing this was good for tourism, but they would be essentially kicking the family out of their home. Unfortunately, the Kleins had always lived with that possibility. That uncertainty. But there had been a level of mutual respect and trust that something like this wouldn't be sprung on them.

"Have you talked to Oliver about this yet?" He hadn't mentioned anything to her, but it would definitely explain some of his hostility toward Sebastian. Maybe that hadn't only been about Sebastian's interest in her.

"He's been made aware of my intentions, yes," Sebastian said simply. No indication of how Oliver felt about it. Though that should be up to her as his—girlfriend? Lover?—to decipher. Though, having her on the opposing side made everything that much trickier. She hoped he wouldn't see her involvement in this as a betrayal.

They'd need to discuss it. Soon.

Her gut clenched but she forced a deep, pragmatic breath. This was out of her control. Her job right now was to remove emotion and attachment and objectively offer her input and thoughts on the proposal as a member of the tourism board.

She cleared her throat. "What about the lighthouse itself?"

"It would still be functional and operated by the coast guard. It would be open for tours. Private access would be offered to guests staying on-site," Sebastian said confidently.

"An exclusive perk," she said, nodding. It was a great idea. Kind of like how theme parks offered early access to guests staying in their featured hotels. It was a huge draw for people.

"And…beyond vacation stays, in addition to the B and B capabilities, the lighthouse grand room is the perfect size to host events. Guests could book weddings, parties, anniversaries…"

"And locals could as well in the off-season," she said, loving the idea.

The lighthouse had always held such a romantic charm and she could envision that great room transformed into the most elegant of events with a spectacular view. Christmas parties for companies and all the town's corporate events… A community summer BBQ… So many ideas came to mind and her heart raced. The town held most things at the local community hall, but this would be so much nicer. The revenue they could make from these lighthouse grand room event bookings alone would justify the expansion costs within a year.

Guilt fought with her enthusiasm.

All this meant the man she was in love with having to give up his home, his family's heritage… But it was for the good of the community and Oliver hadn't been truly happy in the lighthouse for years. He'd recently voiced the idea that maybe it was time to move on, and he had his woodworking, which could turn into a lucrative business. That sailboat contract could ensure he wouldn't have to worry about financials—if he ever finished the boat and delivered it.

She was justifying…

Sebastian studied her, his dark eyes holding a rare look of empathy. He obviously sensed the object of her hesitancy. "You're worried about the impact this has on the Kleins."

She nodded. How could she not? Even before they'd taken their relationship to a new level, Carly had loved and respected Oliver and she adored Tess with all her being. This idea affected them in a huge way, and therefore, it also impacted her.

"Look, while they don't officially have any legal claims to the land, I'm putting forth a proposed payout that will cover the costs of their relocation and setup costs in a new home," Sebastian said reasonably. He'd obviously covered all angles, including the town's empathetic nature. Carly wouldn't be the only one with mixed emotions about this and Sebastian was definitely hoping to offset any resistance from the community by offering something to the Kleins in return. "And Oliver is more than welcome to continue running the tour groups. He knows the history better than anyone."

He wouldn't. Carly suspected if this plan went through, Oliver would rather make a clean break from the lighthouse. Maybe this would be best—having the decision taken from him. Then he wouldn't have to feel guilty and Tess would have a better understanding…

Oliver could focus on the woodworking business he loved and he'd never have to face another tourist season he hated.

She was really reaching, but she was desperate to feel better about this idea.

"So? What do you think? Do I have your support?" Sebastian asked directly.

Carly sighed as she hesitated. Did he have the support of Carly, the woman in love with Oliver? No. But Carly, Sealena Bookstore owner and tourism board member? Yes. "Is it okay if I talk to Oliver about this first?"

Sebastian shook his head. "We'd prefer to keep this under wraps for now. He's been made aware of changes happening."

She swallowed hard and nodded. "I think it looks wonderful. I think it's a well-thought-out proposal. And I think it could be a great boost for tourism." There was really nothing she could argue.

"Is that a yes?" Sebastian coaxed, his charming grin back on his face.

"It's a yes," she said, knowing it was the right decision.

So why had her heart just fallen into the pit of her stomach?

IF HE WANTED to move forward with a relationship—a life—with Carly, Oliver needed to make peace with the past. Telling his story and moving on was one way he could do that. He'd resisted Rachel's interview requests for long enough, and that day, he was determined to go through with it. It would mean opening himself up to the feelings he'd struggled to contain, but he needed to do that in order to fully be emotionally available for Carly.

Sitting in his kitchen two days later, with family photo albums next to him, he watched Rachel set up her recording app on her phone. She smiled encouragingly at him. "Ready?"

Not entirely, but maybe the time had come to open up and reconnect with the community. It had been three long years, locking himself and his emotions away, and maybe it was time, maybe it was okay to start living again. If he proved he had nothing to hide and that he was willing to discuss everything that had happened years before—without any resentment or hurt—it would lighten the load he'd been carrying.

He nodded, wrapping his hands around his coffee mug. "Let's do it."

"Okay…just a sec." Rachel hit Record on the app, announced the date and the interview and glanced at her notes.

"Let's start with your great-grandfather. Tell me about him. How did he end up here in Port Serenity? How did he become the lighthouse keeper?"

Easing in. Starting with safe facts and history.

Oliver cleared his throat. "Great-Grandpa Henry Klein was a lobster fisherman for most of his life. He suffered an injury with a fish hook and lost an eye," he said, retelling the details he'd heard through family stories. "He was off the coast of Port Serenity at the time and was taken to the local hospital, where he met my great-grandma Bertha, a nurse. The two fell in love and they settled here in Port Serenity." He opened the photo album and pointed to a photo of his grandparents—his grandpa wearing the eye patch he'd been known for around town.

Rachel looked at it and nodded. "If it's okay, I'll take some of these with me to scan in for the article?"

"Sure," he said.

"Let's continue."

"Well, the lighthouse keeper at the time was really old and he passed away shortly after my great-grandparents were married, and the position became available. My great-grandfather essentially volunteered to fill in until the community could find a replacement and, well, they never did, so he just kept doing it. He moved his family into the house a few months later."

"Interesting. So, you could say he was kinda grandfathered into the position."

Oliver nodded. "He had to learn everything on his own, without a predecessor to teach him the ropes, but he caught on quickly and found his own way of doing things. My great-grandfather had been a smart man, far beyond his years in terms of technology, and he'd designed some lighthouse features that made the process smoother. Unfortunately, he hadn't learned to read and write, so my great-grandmother kept the daily logs back then."

"Wow, so it was a family effort from the start?"

He nodded. "She only had the one son, which was odd back then, but the three of them lived here and ran things together."

"And then your grandfather William Klein took over once Henry died?"

"About five years before. Great-Grandpa showed him the ropes and it became his one true love."

Rachel looked surprised. "Not your grandmother Rose?"

Oliver shook his head. "That relationship was a little less romantic. My grandfather hadn't wanted to get married or have children. He was a quiet, mysterious sort with an obsession with the sea. But he also liked to drink at the local pub and, well, he and Rose hooked up."

Rachel laughed. "I'll try to find a nicer way to put it in the article."

"Yeah, well, my father was the result of that hookup, and when Rose told William he was the father, they got married. But there was never much love between them. Rose lived here and they raised my dad together until he was sixteen. Then Rose left. I've never met her. I believe she lives in a home in Anchorage." He'd never had the desire to reach out. His father hadn't spoken much about his mom. Neither of his grandparents had seemed very loving or hands-on with Oliver's dad. He was more of a burden, by the way his father told it.

"And your grandfather died of pneumonia at an early age, with only one heir, your father, right?" Rachel asked, consulting her own records.

"That we know of," Oliver joked. "As I said, he liked the local pub… But yes, he died at forty-two, when my dad was twenty-two. Dad took over from him. My parents met at church."

"Your family was religious?"

Oliver shook his head. "My mother was. My dad saw her go into Sunday service when he was running errands in town and decided to stop in. He sat next to her and said he fell in love with her angelic voice. She dragged him to church every Sunday after that and he said he only went to hear her sing."

"That's a nice meet-cute," Rachel said. "So, they had you and you were their only child?"

"Yes. My parents had wanted lots of children, but my mother had complications during childbirth. We almost lost her, so they decided to stop trying for more."

"You grew up in the house and the lighthouse has always been your home?"

Oliver's chest tightened. "Yes. I think it was always assumed I'd eventually take over." Growing up, he'd never really contemplated his future. He knew that the lighthouse would fall on his shoulders someday and he never really felt one way or another about it. It was just predetermined fate and he'd never questioned it or allowed himself to want more.

"Did you have a passion for the family business or was it more of an expectation? Out of obligation?" Rachel asked the question as though reading his mind.

"A bit of both. By the time I took over, the coast guard was officially in charge of things and I just became a member of the Coast Guard Aids to Navigation. I maintain the systems here, but they are all so advanced and automated now that there's not as much work as there used to be."

"Can you briefly detail that work for my readers? I'm sure

they'd love a glimpse into the operations side of things," she said. "This job is such a mysterious one for many people."

Oliver wasn't so sure the day-to-day was all that interesting, but he briefly explained things in terms most laymen could understand for the article. He explained how the lights no longer needed to be tended to on a daily basis, just quarterly or semiannually, but they still needed to be checked by a professional to ensure they could be depended on when needed. He outlined how technicians inspected the main and secondary optics, verifying the beacon's characteristics and checking the associated electronic support equipment as well as testing the sound signal's component and its Mariner Radio Activated Sound Signal system, needed in thick fog or bad weather conditions.

When he noticed her eyes start to glaze over, he laughed and stopped. "Not so exciting, huh?"

Rachel laughed. "I may edit some of that," she said. She pointed to the document on the table that held a timeline of events and notable changes in the lighthouse operation from 1916, when the first flashing acetylene lights were used to automatically replace burned-out electric lamps, to 1921, when the first radio fog transmissions started, to the late 1930s, when remote control operations were introduced.

"If it's okay, I'll add this timeline to the article as a side note as well, for those history buffs who want all the details," she said.

He nodded.

"For this article, I really want to focus more on the human element—you," she said.

Obviously, she'd picked up on his slight discomfort that they were approaching the more intimate details of his life and was stalling by detailing the technical.

"Do you enjoy this work?" she asked.

Did he? He'd never really thought about it. "I love—" loved "—that this career gives me the flexibility to be with family and a sense of pride and purpose to be protecting the community." Though, for a while now, he had been thinking of giving it all up, walking away from that sense of duty...

"But that community hasn't always been a source of support for you, has it?" she asked gently.

Oliver hesitated, unsure how to comment. It hadn't, but then, that was a long time ago and he wasn't sure how he could explain without dredging up old hard feelings. He didn't want anyone reading the article to think he was still bitter or angry.

Rachel cleared her throat. She hit Pause on the recording device. "Are you sure you're okay talking about the accident? We really don't have to."

Unfortunately, he felt as though he did. No story about the lighthouse—its history, its secrets, its past and potential future—could be told without unfolding the past. His family's story and life were entwined with the old buildings. They were woven together like a delicate tapestry and he'd agreed to give Rachel the story. "I'm good."

She nodded and hit Record.

"This lighthouse has seen some tragedy. Three years ago, your wife and daughter disappeared at sea," she said gently.

"We'd just finished building Alison's new sailboat. As a family, we'd decided to start constructing boats as a side business and Alison's was the first. It was a twenty-foot beauty with double mast sails and an engine for backup. All the safety equipment was top-notch..."

Why hadn't they used it? Why hadn't they radioed

for help if they'd been in trouble? It was one of the main thoughts that still plagued him.

He cleared his throat and continued. "Alison and Catherine had decided to take the sailboat out for the day for its first test run. The weather was perfect. The ocean was like a sheet of clear, pristine glass—smooth and peaceful, force level zero...maybe one. There was just the right amount of breeze and they were both qualified sailors and competent swimmers."

Oliver took a deep breath and continued.

"They packed a lunch and water and necessary supplies and planned to return by dark. I had a copy of their charted route for the day. They were prepared and had taken all safety measures."

Rachel nodded and voiced the part he couldn't. "But they didn't come home."

He shook his head. "By nightfall, I knew something was wrong. They never stayed out longer than they planned and Alison didn't love being on the water at night. She had a deep respect for the ocean and its mysteries and fully embraced the mythology and beliefs adopted by the town."

"Sealena?"

"Among other things. She always said she felt relief knowing there were unknowns lurking in the water around Port Serenity, but she never wanted to encounter one." He chuckled sadly. His wife had been such a beautiful dichotomy of strength and softness. She was fearless but held to strong beliefs that humbled her.

"So, what did you do?"

"Alerted the authorities right away and they didn't hesitate to send out the coast guard boat in search of the sailboat. But they found nothing that night and called the search off when the weather took a turn for the worse. They searched for days, but there was no trace of them anywhere."

"As if they'd simply vanished," Rachel said, almost in a whisper.

Oliver nodded. "The following months were hell. Tess and I were grieving but trying to remain hopeful, the worst possible combination, as the body doesn't know how to react, how to feel. Caught in this limbo of not being able to move through the stages of grief and come to a level of acceptance, when there was no closure. There was always the optimistic what-ifs that prevented us from moving on."

It had been torture to be in that state, knowing in his gut they weren't coming back but clinging to any hope that they might. And when he wanted to finally let go, Tess would pull him back with her desire to have her mother and sister return.

"And the investigation couldn't have helped," she said with a slight anger toward authorities that made him feel better.

"No. Once authorities couldn't locate the boat or the… bodies—" he stumbled over the word, his gut twisting "—I became a suspect. They questioned me and everyone who knew me. They searched the grounds all around the light-house." That had been one of the hardest days of his life— watching the search crew look for clues and answers in the wrong place, knowing they were wasting their time. He shook his head. "It's hard to grasp that a community that I once was a solid part of could ever think I would do something so terrible…" It still made his gut tighten to think about those days. Still made his heart hurt. Time had passed, people had put suspicions to rest, but without the closure of knowing, he had never fully felt like everyone believed he was innocent.

"What did they think happened?" she asked, leaning closer.

"I'm not sure. They wanted to charge me with maybe tampering with the boat in some way, but without the boat, there was no strong evidence to support that claim." It had, however, left him with the guilt and nagging thought that maybe he had done something wrong in the boat's construction, but he knew he hadn't.

"I can't imagine how tough that was." She reached across the table and touched his hand gently, taking a breath as though she too needed a quick pause. Then she said, "So how did you move on?"

"Life doesn't give you a choice. Tess and I finally had to get up in the morning and continue living. We hold Alison and Catherine in our hearts, but we've learned to accept that they are no longer part of our everyday. It was hard at first and it continues to be hard, but less and less all the time. Time heals even if you don't want it to." It was a new sense of guilt that had wrapped around him in recent years—the fact that he was less sad, less angry, that thoughts of them were less over the years. That he was moving on was a betrayal, but he knew in his heart it wasn't.

Rachel stopped the recording and sighed. "Thank you, Oliver. That was beautiful."

"It felt good to talk about it, so thank you." It had been tough, but he did feel a little lighter, sharing his side for the first time. Talking about his family's past, the history of the lighthouse and what it meant had also reminded him how important this place and its heritage was to him.

He walked Rachel to the door just as a vehicle pulled up in front. He waved, seeing Callan behind the wheel. The man climbed out and walked toward them as Rachel snapped her fingers and turned to him. "The photos. Can I borrow the photo albums to scan some of the images?"

He hesitated. "Um...okay. Just be careful with them." He went inside and brought them out for her.

"I'll guard them with my life," she said, noticing the image on the cover of one of the albums. "Is this your family crest?" she asked.

He nodded. "Yeah. We even have a set of family wedding rings with the crest on it. They were passed down through family generations." He hadn't worn his in years, even before the disappearance. It was unsafe to wear when he was working in the shed with tools all the time. Alison used to tease him about not wearing it, said the single ladies in town would get the wrong idea, but she'd understood.

Callan leaned over the album and peered at the image. He frowned, leaning closer to inspect it. "So, the crest and the rings are unique?"

"One of a kind... Well, there used to be a second one," he said. Alison had never taken hers off once it was passed on to her by his mother. She loved the sentiment, and Oliver had continued to offer to buy her a real ring with a diamond, something pretty and uniquely hers, but she insisted she loved the family heirloom.

"I know. I saw it," Callan said.

It wasn't the other man's words that caused the chill to dance down Oliver's spine, but the tone. One that said Callan had suddenly made headway on the unsolved disappearance that he'd just been about to lay to rest.

THE TEXT FROM Rachel had Carly reaching for the stool behind her before her knees could threaten to give way.

Callan might have found a lead into the disappearance of Alison and Catherine.

Her mouth was dry and her hand shook so violently that she nearly dropped her cell phone. He'd recognized the family crest, which had been the design for the wedding rings. Her heart pounded in her chest. The interview had opened up more than just old feelings...

She might actually find out what had happened to her best friend after all this time. Oliver and Tess might finally know.

Tears burned the backs of her eyes and the door opening a second later and the sight of Oliver had her stomach lurching. His expression was one of conflicted uncertainty, but also held traces of hope.

He headed toward her and Carly met him around the other side of the counter. He opened his arms and she stepped into them. As she rested her head against his chest, neither of them spoke. They just stood there in silence, holding one another, both lost in their own conflicted thoughts.

# CHAPTER FOURTEEN

How on earth was she supposed to write now?

For the last two days, Carly's emotions had been spiraling and her thoughts had been on nothing but what Callan had possibly uncovered about Alison and Catherine's disappearance. The cold case was now open again after all this time. She'd learned from Rachel that Callan had gone straight to the coast guard with the image of the ring he'd recognized and was working with several active members to try to locate the files from the year the two had gone missing, when he was an active member of the elite drug trafficking team. He'd refused to give any details to Oliver about where he'd seen the ring in case his memory was wrong, and he'd cautioned Oliver not to get Tess's hopes up, to keep the information to himself for now. Carly knew she wasn't the only one preoccupied with thoughts of the past.

It was as if she'd been transported straight back to that fateful day three years ago when the news had hit.

She and Oliver had barely said a word in the bookstore the day before, but there was definitely a new tension and anticipation that had made things a little strained between them. They were both so invested in this. They'd both lost people who were important to them. This new development was impacting them the most. They'd just started exploring the connection between them, but now Carly wasn't quite sure what was happening...

And her creativity and motivation were definitely suffering.

But the email from her editor asking for more chapters meant she needed to push through…and maybe, if she could channel what she was feeling onto the page, it might help her process everything. Writing had always been therapeutic for her.

Opening the manuscript to where she'd left off during her previous writing session—the night after the BBQ, when her world had seemed to be on the biggest high—she noticed she'd stopped on the climactic scene at the end of act two. The dark moment was next and, ironically, she was probably in the best state of mind to write it that day.

Taking a deep breath, she started to type:

*The storm had come out of nowhere.*

*That day had been mild and calm when the fisherman had left my side in the early morning to head out onto the water. But now, hours later, he hadn't yet returned, and dark clouds had settled above. In the distance, I hear the rumble of thunder and can see flashes of lightning, illuminating a sky as dark as midnight.*

*From the house I can see the large waves crashing against the shore. I shiver in the damp, cold interior as I stare out the window, my heart pounding and fear closing in around me with each passing second that I don't see him or the boat.*

*I can't stay inside. I'm going insane with worry as the ticking grandfather clock pounds in my head. I have to at least go to the shoreline and see if I can see him…wait for him.*

*Putting on warm clothing and boots, I head out*

*and down the trail toward the ocean's edge. Rain
starts to fall, big droplets covering my body, and the
ground beneath my feet is muddy and slippery as I
hurry, a sense of dread propelling me forward.*

*He will be okay. Maybe he's found an inlet to dock
and wait out the storm. I have to believe that everything will be okay. The power of our love connects
me to him in ways I've never imagined possible and
I need to stay positive and hopeful that he will navigate this storm and come back to me.*

*But as I reach the water and peer out at the dark,
angry sea, I catch sight of the boat in the beam of the
lighthouse beacon. About three miles from shore, the
small fishing vessel with my love on board is being
tossed about on the violent waves.*

*I freeze as fear overwhelms me. My feet sink into
the rocks beneath me and my voice is stolen on the
wind as I cry out to him. I watch as the boat bobs
up and down, crashing over each wave, fighting
against the tide, trying to make it to shore, but getting dragged farther out to sea on the current.*

*I wave my arms, but he can't see me and the ac-
tions are futile. I can't help him from here.*

*I remove my heavy, thick clothing and tremble as
the cold wind and rain bite into my skin. I tear off
the boots and, taking a deep breath of courage, I run
into the water and dive, the cold piercing me as I re-
surface, with only one thought echoing in my mind:*

*I have to save him.*

Carly sat back from the laptop and new tears burned in
her eyes as she stared at the cliff-hanger where she'd left
her characters to simmer. So much uncertainty hung in the

balance of how she would finish that scene. So much emotion whirling within Sealena as she took that plunge, not sure of the outcome.

Could this vulnerable version of Sealena save the fisherman? Would her love be enough? Could she have the happily-ever-after she deserved? If she did save him, how did they move forward with Sealena's own time ticking away…?

Authors often spoke of writing themselves into a corner and Carly certainly had with this book in the series. Impossible love. How did she make this work? How had she ever intended to make this work?

Her own conflicted heart pounded hard in the depths of her chest. Things had once again shifted between her and Oliver, with this new uncertainty creating unspoken drama between them. The issue of the lighthouse seemed small in comparison to this new development in the disappearance of Alison and Catherine. All discussions about anything else had been put on hold. They'd once again been tossed into the deep end of tumultuous waves that toyed with their emotions.

Carly wanted Callan to find answers, to give them all the clarity they'd been searching for—longing for—but then, what did that mean for her and Oliver? For all of them?

Would they be able to move forward with more confidence once the mystery of that day was solved or would the reopening of past wounds force Oliver to close himself off again?

And was she strong enough to continue fighting for a man haunted by his past?

TIME HAD HELPED to erase the memory of what it had felt like as they'd waited on news about Alison and Catherine. He vaguely remembered the quiet stillness as he and Tess had sat together, simultaneously hopeful and hopeless, as the search and investigation had played on. But now, these last three days, all of those emotions had come rushing back.

But this time it was almost worse because he couldn't tell Tess and he was trying to act as normal as possible around his daughter, while keeping this new knowledge to himself. He understood Callan's warning, but it was tough not to share this new hope with his daughter. Only the uncertainty and not wanting to disappoint her again with whatever the outcome was kept him silent.

And this time, there was Carly too.

She'd lost her best friend and the disappearance had been almost as difficult on her as it had been on him and Tess. She'd suffered as well, so he knew she was also holding her breath that Callan would solve this mystery for them. But there had also been conflict and questions in her eyes when he'd gone to see her three days ago. Questions he hadn't known the answers to.

Until things were settled, he had no idea what to do or what to say...

Things were back in limbo between them and he hated that he couldn't find the right words to reassure her of... anything.

He spent more time puttering around the shed those last few days, keeping his hands, if not his thoughts, preoccupied, avoiding the tourist groups and, most of all, Tess. If she sensed anything was up, she didn't mention it, and she was busy litter training Caramel (the kitten's latest name they were testing out), so at least he didn't have to feel too guilty for pulling away from her slightly in his sense of turmoil.

A knock sounded on the door to the shed just as Oliver finished spraying the last coat of teal-green paint on the stand-up paddleboard. If nothing else, he'd finished Tess's birthday gift in record time. He lifted the face shield of his mask as he turned toward the open door.

Callan entered and walked toward him. "Hey, man… it's looking good," he said casually, but Oliver could tell he was stalling. There was an air of heaviness about him, his usual confident ease burdened with bad news.

A tragedy made it impossible not to have a sense about these things. Oliver could sniff impending dread or doom a mile away. He removed the visor and set the spray can down with a shaky hand as he prepared for whatever news Callan was there to deliver. "What did you find out?" There was no way he could entertain small talk when, for the last three days, he'd been desperate for an update.

Callan ran a hand through his dark hair and stared at the shed floor. "There's no easy way to say this, man…"

Oliver's gut tightened. For years, he'd longed for any closure he could get, but he now realized, even without hearing it, that he still wasn't completely ready to know for sure that his wife and older daughter weren't coming home. He swallowed hard as bile rose in the back of his throat and he reached behind him to find stability in the work counter. "Just tell me, please."

Callan took a step toward him and said, "I went through the files of the illegal smuggling operations we busted that year, sorted through the room where contraband is stored…and found this." He extended his hand and Oliver saw the matching wedding band with the familiar family crest. Alison's ring. Oliver stared at his wife's wedding band, the one that matched the one he'd recently started wearing on a chain around his neck, and emotions threatened to strangle him. With a shaky hand, he took it from Callan and nodded, unable to vocalize a response as he clutched the ring in a tight fist.

"I convinced the department that it should be returned to you."

He appreciated that. This ring had been in his family for generations. He'd always thought one day Catherine or Tess might wear it... It had been on Alison's hand the day she disappeared and it was the only thing he had left of her.

He expected to feel closer to her, just holding the ring, but the cold truth was that the metal was just that—a reminder of what he'd lost that provided none of the comfort he sought. He didn't need to ask if they were still alive. He knew Callan had brought him all that was left. They were really gone.

"Do you want to know what happened?" Callan asked gently after a long silence.

Did he? Knowing that his wife and daughter hadn't survived that boating trip, that they were no longer out there somewhere, was hard enough to wrap his mind around, even though in his heart he'd known the truth all these years. Would knowing the details make things easier or worse? Would it be the closure he sought or just more pain?

He sighed and cleared his throat. After all this time, he needed to know. "Tell me," he said.

Callan pulled out a couple of wooden chairs and Oliver fell into one. He rested his face between his hands, elbows resting on his knees, as the effort to sit straight was almost too much. His knees bounced uncontrollably as he waited for Callan to speak.

"According to the records, the LA-based division of the coast guard found your wife's sailboat off the coast of California on July 6 at 4:30 p.m. Unfortunately, it wasn't yet registered, so they couldn't trace it back here."

Two days after they'd gone missing. California? How had they gotten so far? Why had they gone that far?

Callan continued. "Alison and Catherine weren't on board. The boat had been taken over here in the North Pacific by a smuggling crew when their own boat had caught the suspicion of the local coast guard vessel in the area. My crew." He paused. "Unfortunately, my records show there hadn't been sufficient evidence to apprehend the suspects at that time. Our orders were to observe and wait," he said, sounding disappointed. As though he knew that he may have been able to stop it if only the local crew had acted or investigated further.

Oliver's chest ached as he listened.

"When the suspects knew their boat was marked, they moved all the contraband on board Alison's sailboat and continued their mission south, where they were eventually stopped by authorities."

"Were Alison and Catherine still on board?" Oliver dared to ask, though his voice sounded thick and hoarse.

Callan shook his head with a deep sigh. "According to the men arrested, they hadn't intended to hurt them. They planned to release them once they hit shore, but Alison and Catherine decided to take their chances by jumping overboard."

So, they weren't injured or killed by the smugglers— maybe they were still out there somewhere. They were both strong swimmers... But if they'd survived, they'd have found their way back home by now. They'd have contacted him the moment they were safe. His heart was in his throat as he said, "They didn't make it." It wasn't a question, but he needed his friend to say it, to confirm the worst.

Callan shook his head again, a look of torment on his face as he delivered the worst of the news. "Afraid not. Their bodies were discovered in San Diego on July 8. A fisherman made the discovery, but without identification, they were listed as Jane Does." His buddy paused, then said, "I was able to confirm DNA matches with the California coroner's office this morning."

Coroner's office... DNA matches...to his deceased wife and daughter.

Who so bravely fought for their lives instead of remaining hostage to a smuggling operation. He swallowed hard, several times, but was unable to swallow the bile rising in the back of his throat. His mouth filled with saliva and nausea overwhelmed him. He'd barely made it to the trash can before he vomited.

Callan was next to him, offering support as Oliver's knees gave way and he sank to the cold, dirty shed floor. The room spun around him as wave after wave of nausea overwhelmed him, the sick feeling penetrating through his core. It was as though the disappearance had just happened yesterday, the pain and regret burning through him as though the wound were still fresh. He'd wanted to know what had happened that day. He'd tortured himself with what-ifs, and a lingering, lasting hope that had paralyzed him for so long. Prevented him from moving on with his life. But this permanency held its own level of torture. There were no more what-ifs, just the truth about what happened to his family that day.

Now that he knew it, did it really set him free?

IF HEARING THE news had been difficult, telling Tess had been the hardest thing Oliver had ever had to do in his life. As a parent, delivering this kind of devastating news had to be the most challenging in the world. And having to do it a second time was the ultimate in unfairness.

After Callan left him with a sincere apology and offer to support Oliver and Tess in any way he could, Oliver had spent a long time alone in the shed before heading into the house to have the difficult talk. He couldn't not tell her. She deserved the truth, the closure, as much as he did.

So, with as much strength as he could muster, he'd delivered a shortened, less devastating version of the events, simply explaining that her mother's boat had been pirated and her mother and sister had escaped but unfortunately hadn't made it to safety.

And now he sat on the floor outside her bedroom, listening to the sound of her crying, as she'd insisted on being alone with the kitten to process the new information. Feeling helpless, wanting to respect her need for space as she came to terms with the news, but wanting to be nearby if and when she did need him, Oliver rested his head against the wall, battling his own turmoil.

Emotions overwhelmed him—sadness, anger, torment and despair—and he tried to steady his uneven breath and control the spiraling thoughts and emotions. He didn't—couldn't—fault the coast guard and he didn't want to harden his heart with anger and blame. He needed to accept the unfortunate incident for what it had been. His wife and daughter had been in the wrong place at the wrong time.

He needed to be strong for Tess. Years before, he'd been a mess, and he'd always regretted not being there completely for her as she processed things. This time, *her* feelings, *her* healing, were the thing that he'd prioritize. Whatever she needed. Therefore, he needed to deal with his own as quickly as possible and then be the source of support she needed.

Whenever she came out of the room…

He heard the front door open and, a moment later, Carly appeared in the hallway. Her own devastated expression told him she knew. He was grateful that Callan or Rachel had delivered the news, because he wasn't sure he was physically strong enough to have explained things to her as well.

She walked toward him slowly, and placing her back against the wall, she slid the length of it and sat next to him. He reached for her hand and held it tight as they sat there in silence, once more grieving, processing and drawing whatever strength and comfort they could from one another, despite the conflict brewing in their own hearts.

# CHAPTER FIFTEEN

"I CAN'T BELIEVE Callan was able to figure this out," Skylar said the next day. Standing behind the counter of the bookstore, she poured two cups of coffee, carried one toward Carly and placed it on the counter in front of her. "I mean, when he came into the station the other day, asking to review the old records, I thought never in a million years would he find what he was looking for. There were dozens of smuggling operations that year. It was like looking for a needle in a haystack." Skylar paused and sipped her coffee. "But he was persistent. I don't think he left the office for two days, sorting through files and going over the photos of contraband and items held in the storage facility."

Skylar was clearly impressed by the former coast guard officer's diligence at finding answers and Carly was grateful too, but unfortunately, knowledge and closure didn't make things any better. It didn't bring Alison and Catherine back.

She sipped the hot liquid but it just tasted bitter on her tongue that day. She'd already let two cups go cold, her stomach unable to cope with food or caffeine. She was already unable to sleep, and her heart was so messed up, she feared adding caffeine would just fuel an anxiety attack. "It's just so hard to process, you know?" she said.

Skylar touched her hand. "At least now there's closure. No more wondering what happened," she said softly.

Carly nodded because it was impossible to explain how that closure really didn't make her feel much better. At least she knew Alison and Catherine were at rest.

"Where does this leave you and Oliver?" Skylar asked carefully.

A question she'd felt selfish asking herself, so she'd pushed the thought to the back of her mind. Things had already been somewhat complicated with the idea that the tourism board might vote to turn their home into a B and B—with everything going on, that conversation was yet to happen.

Now it felt as though any progress they'd made moving toward one another had been lost. Their connection had been put on ice, and once again, they were at this standstill of emotions that Carly had no idea how to break past. She knew Oliver and Tess were once again having to deal with the worst and she wanted to be there for them, in whatever form that took.

But sitting there with Oliver outside Tess's bedroom the day before, the silence speaking volumes, it had been obvious that Oliver's heart was once again locked away. She sighed as she shrugged. "I guess we are back in limbo."

Skylar frowned and shook her head. "Look, I don't mean to sound insensitive to their situation. Lord knows that family has been through so much pain and uncertainty—but so have you. And you've been Oliver's rock through it all. More than that, you've loved him and Tess unconditionally, not expecting anything back."

"Yes, but it's just so complicated…"

"It's also very simple. You love him. He loves you. You're both hurting and you both have healing to do. But that's something you can do together. Oliver pushing you away again in self-preservation is understandable…but unfair to you." Skylar's tone was gentle, but her words were full of truth.

Carly nodded slowly. She appreciated her cousin's support, but she had no idea how to put her needs and what she wanted ahead of what Oliver and Tess needed. For so long, she'd always thought of herself and her needs last. It was hard to start putting what she wanted ahead of everything else now.

Skylar reached out and touched her hand. "Look, when Dex pushed me away because of his illness, I didn't understand. I was angry. I thought he was rejecting me. He didn't realize that he could depend on me and that, together, we could have gotten through anything. Just like Oliver doesn't realize that what he and Tess need most right now is you and the hope of another chance at a future—together as a family."

Skylar may be right, but how did she find the strength to continue putting herself out there for a man who continued to protect his own heart?

SEBASTIAN GRANT HAD the worst timing.

Oliver didn't expect the newcomer to know what was going on with his personal situation, but he couldn't help but feel disrespected when the man arrived early the next morning with the proposal to turn him and his daughter out.

As he stared at the thick, typed proposal from the town's tourism board, heat coursed through him. He knew this was Sebastian's plan, but seeing it in action was tough. Especially given the other things that had happened that week.

"I wanted to give you time to review this before it goes out to the rest of the committee for their votes," he said, as though he were doing Oliver a favor.

Oliver had no interest in reviewing the plans for his

home. In light of recent events, he had no intention of letting the lighthouse be taken from him and Tess. His daughter had been through enough that summer. Losing the home she loved would be too much. If and when Oliver decided to move on, give up the family legacy, it would be on his terms. When he was ready. When Tess was ready. He wasn't going to let Sebastian bully him into accepting some deal he wasn't comfortable with. He took a step toward Sebastian and shoved the proposal back toward him. The other man looked startled as he said, "You can keep this."

Sebastian shook his head as he let the proposal drop to his side. "You can refuse to review all of this but it doesn't change things, Oliver. The town is looking for changes and this one makes sense. We both know the lighthouse operations no longer need you here and you really should think about what's best for the community."

Oliver folded his arms across his chest and glared at the man. "You've been here all of a month and you think you know what's best for this town?" The man's arrogance knew no bounds. He may be an educated charmer who thought he could trick other people into believing his intentions were genuine, but Oliver wasn't fooled. Sebastian didn't care about Port Serenity. He cared about his own career. Once he implemented the strategies he wanted here and padded his own résumé with his achievements, he'd move on. Oliver was sure of it.

"As we both know, this idea needs community support," Sebastian said with a shrug. "It's far from a done deal. Of course. But I feel confident that the residents here will see the value of what I'm proposing." He flipped open the proposal and started to outline the details. "Cabins along the property will result in a much better use of the space for visitors and I think the rental for events will appeal to locals. Everyone wins," he said.

Everyone except Oliver and Tess.

"And of course, you'd be compensated as well…"

He thought he could buy him? His anger simmered and he started to close the door. "Good luck with the proposal, Sebastian. As you said, you'll need community support and, well, you'll never get mine."

"Has Carly spoken to you?" the other man asked, and Oliver's stomach knotted.

"Carly supports this?" he asked, hating that this information was coming from Sebastian and not Carly. But in fairness, they hadn't spoken much over the past few days, and when they had, their thoughts had been on the disappearance. They had so much to discuss, so much to clarify, so much to figure out—and it seemed like this was another one of those things.

Sebastian nodded, extending the proposal toward him again. "Just take a look at it, Oliver. That's all I'm asking."

Reluctantly, Oliver accepted the proposal and shut the door. He sighed, his own feelings on the subject more confused than ever. Carly already supported this idea? And she hadn't said anything to him?

He sighed as he headed into the kitchen and tossed the proposal onto the table. He poured a cup of coffee and then sat down to read.

If he was going to have any shot at fighting this idea, he'd need to first be familiar with it.

CARLY'S FORCED SMILE was starting to fade with each customer; she was emotionally exhausted from the last few days. Between the store, the tension between her and Oliver and the impending book deadline, she was ready to collapse.

"Hey, why don't you take the afternoon off?" Melissa said, coming up next to her behind the counter as she handed a bag to the last customer. "I can handle things," she said.

Carly glanced at the clock and hesitated. This time of day got busy, but she really could use a few hours to herself. She wasn't exactly the best face of tourism in the store right now anyway.

"Okay...thank you." The young woman had really been a godsend that season and Carly wasn't sure what she'd do without her in the fall. She'd gotten used to having help around the store and Melissa seemed to really enjoy the position as well. "I'll just be upstairs, if you need me."

Moments later, she entered her apartment and couldn't decide what she craved most—a long hot bath or a nap. She yawned as she made her way into her bedroom, but before she could decide on either, a knock sounded on her door.

Making her way toward it, she was surprised to see Oliver standing on the other side. Surprised, but also relieved. They hadn't spoken or seen one another in days. He was dealing with so much and she sensed he and Tess needed some time and space. She was trying to be okay with that, but with every passing day away from him, with things left uncertain, things left undiscussed, the harder it was.

"Hey, you," she said, standing back to let him enter.

He looked as tired and emotionally spent as she was. And there was something else about his mood, but she couldn't quite decipher what it was. "Hi," he said awkwardly, avoiding her gaze.

Her heart pounded in her chest. "Everything okay?"

He stared at the floor. Then when his gaze met hers, she

knew nothing was okay. "You agree with Sebastian's plans for the lighthouse?" he asked, solemnly.

Shit. She'd been wanting to talk to him about this but the time hadn't been right. Now it seemed the opportunity to bring it up on her terms, when it was most convenient, had been stolen from her. *Damn, Sebastian.* She hadn't expected the man to submit his proposal so quickly.

But then, there really wasn't any reason to wait.

She swallowed hard and nodded slowly. "I don't not agree with them," she said gently. Her own personal feelings aside, the plans were the best thing for the town. Even if that wasn't what Oliver wanted to hear. "Have you looked at it?" she asked. Maybe he was reacting before reviewing. Without knowing all the details.

He nodded. "Cover to cover," he said, his voice hard.

"Well, can't you see the merits in the idea?"

"All I see is some city slicker trying to steal my home out from under me for profit."

Carly sighed and fought to control her patience. Oliver's prejudice about Sebastian was clouding his judgment. Carly didn't think for a second that he'd be this stubbornly opposed if it were anyone else proposing the idea. "You were thinking that maybe it might be time to move on as well," she reminded him. "You know that the lighthouse keeper position is more of an honorary job. It was just a matter of time—"

"But the decision should be mine," he said. "Or at least, I should have a say in it." He ran a hand through his disheveled hair in frustration.

"You do."

"Right. Along with the rest of the community and the tourism board."

She took a step toward him and reached out to touch

his arm, but he moved back slightly. His actions shocked her…and hurt her. Was he really this upset with her about something she was only partially in control of as well? Anyone in town could pitch these ideas to the mayor's office for consideration at any time. The fact that no one had challenged Oliver's position at the lighthouse up until now was almost a miracle. And the lighthouse wasn't bringing in the revenue it could for the town.

It had taken a newcomer like Sebastian to present the idea, but that didn't mean it wasn't the right one. Still, she could understand Oliver's resistance and inability to consider the idea.

What she couldn't understand, however, was his attitude toward her right now. "Oliver, I'm only one voice…"

"An opposing one," he said coldly. "And what hurts the most is that you didn't even tell me."

Her mouth gaped. "When was I supposed to bring this up? There have been more important things going on." She hadn't even found the courage or the right time to talk to him about them yet. Their relationship had been at a standstill these last few days and she was desperate to figure that out, discuss where they were now… This lighthouse issue had been put on the bottom of her priority list, especially since it wasn't something she could even control.

"You should have mentioned something. Given me a heads-up that Sebastian was going to drop this bomb," he said, folding his arms across his body.

Was he seriously acting as though she and Sebastian were conspiring against him? After so many years of friendship and, more recently, their growing connection, he should know better than to think she'd be on anyone's side but his.

"Um, why didn't *you* say anything to me?" she countered. "Sebastian said he mentioned this idea to you weeks ago." Oliver couldn't claim to have just heard about this. She knew he'd been approached. He'd kept this from her as well. At least she had good reason for not bringing it up. It would have been insensitive in light of recent events. But he'd had plenty of time to talk to her about how he was feeling about this.

Though, would anything really change her perspective?

Maybe this was one thing she and Oliver would never agree on, maybe even the one thing that could drive them apart? She refused to believe that. This was a disagreement. They'd figure it out.

"I didn't say anything because he told me I wasn't at liberty to," Oliver said.

Carly scoffed. "I'm your best friend. You could have told me. We could have discussed the option and—"

"And you'd convince me it was the right thing? Pressure me into it?" he asked.

Her nostrils flared and her eyes narrowed. "Pressured you into it?" Was the man serious right now? "When have I ever pressured you into anything?" For years, she'd kept her feelings for Oliver to herself, suffering and pining in silence because she hadn't wanted to lose their friendship or make him feel like he had to commit to her in a more serious way. She'd never asked for anything from their friendship. His words right now were unfair and they hurt.

"That's not what I meant. I just mean you think this is the right thing to do and you would have tried to convince me."

She sighed. "Maybe. Yeah," she said honestly. "I just think your judgment is being clouded and you're trying to hold on to the past. Not allowing yourself to move on and do what's best for you. Again," she said.

Oliver was quiet as he stared at the floor, contemplating her words. He sighed and she watched his shoulders rise and fall. When he looked up at her again, his expression was full of anguish. "I think maybe we are on different sides of this…and I'm not sure there's a way to meet in the middle."

What exactly was he saying? "Oliver…" She took a step toward him, but he held back. Her chest tightened and a lump rose in the back of her throat. "Let's take a minute and talk about this." Talk about everything. Clear the air and find a way to work through all of this together.

"I'm not sure I want to say anything more right now," he said.

"Okay, well, why don't we have something to eat? Just sit and take a breather?" she asked. They needed to cool off and just take a moment to think and prioritize.

But Oliver shook his head. "I can't." He took a deep breath. "In fact, I'm not sure I can do this, Carly."

Her eyes widened. "Do what?" Was he talking about them?

"You and me. I think maybe I rushed into things and…" He sighed. "Damn, I don't know."

He didn't know? Didn't know about her…about them. Was he truly ending this? Pushing her away again? Closing himself off after they'd opened up to one another?

He looked conflicted and torn as he stared at her.

Her heart was breaking in ways she'd never thought it could break as she stood there, not knowing what to say to change his mind or convince him that they could work this out together. She'd never known how to fight for Oliver Klein, and that day, she was too exhausted to.

So, when he headed toward the door to leave, she didn't try to stop him.

# *CHAPTER SIXTEEN*

THE NAP HAD won out once Oliver had left her apartment, but she hadn't exactly slept much. Lying on her bed, heartbroken, confused and distraught, Carly had tossed and turned, trying to rest, trying to quiet the conflict coursing through her. The last few days had been an emotional roller coaster and, as much as she wanted to close her eyes and shut the world out for a few hours, sleep and comfort had eluded her.

Arguing with Oliver was something she'd never done before. As best friends, they'd always gotten along and agreed about most things—or rather, she'd just been agreeable and gone along with whatever he wanted. She hadn't forced things between them or demanded anything from him out of love and respect, but she was also realizing it had been out of a sense of fear and not wanting to upset the status quo. She hadn't wanted to disrupt the peace between them or have any tension or conflict. That was why their relationship had remained stagnant all these years.

Well, she couldn't do that anymore. She'd voiced her feelings and gone after what she wanted with him. Things had progressed for the better, but she couldn't just be a puppet and agree with him on everything just to keep that peaceful, loving relationship.

Her mother had once said that couples who cared about one another fought. And Carly hadn't realized how much her mother was right until now. In her previous relationships, she'd never fought—she hadn't cared enough. But with Oliver, she needed to have a voice and be heard.

And if they were going to be together, he needed to hear her.

Unfortunately, he didn't seem to want to even listen.

Rolling over on her bed, Carly could see the sky darkening outside as night fell. She'd been lying there for hours, thinking about him, replaying their conversation in her mind, trying to decide if maybe he was right...but she just couldn't bring herself to agree with his stance on the subject or the way he'd used this hiccup to once again drive a wedge between them.

Oliver Klein may never be ready for a new relationship, a new love and future with her, and Carly needed to learn to accept that.

Sometimes, happily-ever-after just didn't work out...

Climbing out of bed, she made her way to the kitchen. Flicking on the table lamp, she sat at her laptop. These raging emotions might as well make themselves useful for something.

She opened her manuscript and picked up where she'd left off, with Sealena having dived into the unknown in an effort to save her fisherman:

> In the water, the waves crash against my body and I'm tossed around like a tiny, helpless ship as I try to swim in the direction of the fishing boat. I can see it in the distance but it feels impossibly far away.
>
> I used to be able to swim fast and strong against the currents, defying the angry sea, but in this human form, my limbs ache and freeze and tire.
>
> I've never felt the ocean's power like this. Fighting back. There was never any battle for me before. The

*waves and tide did as I commanded. Now I'm powerless against its demanding current. It's as though the ocean is taking its long-awaited revenge on me and my kind.*

*Punishing me for interfering in its will for so many years.*

*A large wave envelops me and my body crashes against a large, jagged rock. I feel my earthly skin tear. Blood seeps out of the wound at my side and turns the water around me a deep crimson. It aches and stings as the salt water covers the wound. I force a deep breath, forgetting I can't breathe under the water. Water fills my lungs and I struggle to propel myself higher, lifting my head above the tumultuous waves for a gasp.*

*I dive back under, annoyed at these useless human legs that won't work together to propel me through the water strong enough, fast enough... These small, weak arms tire quickly and the air in my lungs runs out too fast.*

*At the surface, I scan the dark depths and it's nearly impossible to see. There's no light illuminating the dark the way it did before. The lighthouse beacon seems to be lost in the thick fog overhead and the stormy weather.*

*These human eyes are burning from the salt and my nose stings, but I refuse to give up. I can't. I keep scanning the surface for any sign of the boat and I see the fisherman fall overboard as a wave capsizes the vessel.*

*My heart races and blood thunders in my veins. Renewed determination and a fighting spirit propel me to continue. I dive below the surface and kick my* legs as fast as I can. I move my arms through the water and I continue to search...

Long moments later, I spot my fisherman floating, his limp body suspended in the water, dipping farther and farther into its unknown depths. I swim faster, harder, against the unforgiving current toward him.

I need to reach him. I can't give up.

My strength lies within and I need to channel that courage and resilience to rescue the man I love. I need to believe in my own power and not give up.

I reach him and, wrapping my arms around him, I summon any remaining strength I have to swim back toward the shore. The waves continue to push and pull and I can't be sure of the direction I'm traveling in, but I keep moving.

What feels like a long time later, I drag his body onto the rocky coast, out of breath and exhausted.

I collapse next to him and struggle to take deep breaths in and out, shivering in the cold wind. I turn toward him and check to see if his eyes have opened. They haven't.

He's not breathing.

I lean over him and breathe into his lungs. I press against his chest. I repeat the motions over and over.

Come on! Wake up! I can't lose you!

I can't lose him.

Not this way. It was supposed to be a different ending for us—equally painful and heartbreaking, but at least he would live...

It can't end this way.

I fight and fight to save him until there's no strength left in my arms, no breath left in my lungs. I collapse

*against his limp body, lying on the cold seashore, and*
*weep tears that seem endless.*

*I couldn't save him. My fisherman is gone and*
*it's my fault.*

Carly's cheeks felt damp and she wiped the tears away
as she attached the chapter to an email for her editor.

Yep, some happily-ever-afters just weren't meant to be.

AN ODD-SOUNDING ringing woke her from a troubled sleep
the next morning. Peeling her eyes open, Carly sat up and
scanned the room. What was that noise?

It wasn't a ringtone or her alarm clock.

The noise continued and she pushed back the bedsheets
and tossed her legs over the side. She moved through her
apartment, the noise growing louder as she made her way
to the kitchen. Seeing her laptop open on the table, she saw
the Skype call trying to connect.

She moved closer and saw the image of her editor on
the screen.

Her pulse raced as she glanced down at her tank top and
shorts. A quick glance toward the window reflected back
that her hair was a mess and she knew she must have rac-
coon eyes from not having washed off her makeup before
falling back into bed the day before.

Maybe she could ignore it, send Paige an email to set
up a call later that day.

The noise stopped as the unanswered call quit ringing and
she sighed in relief before it immediately started again. This
time a little message bubble appeared on the side. URGENT!
her editor had typed.

Damn. She couldn't ignore it. She ran a quick hand through
her messy hair and wiped under her eyes. She'd just submit-

ted the most recent chapter hours before, with the dark moment and the completion of the book—the completion of the series—and she was nervous about the editor's comments. Paige usually sent notes by email, so an unexpected Skype call had Carly on edge.

She pulled out a chair and perched on it as she hit Connect on the call, plastering on the best fake smile she could muster. "Paige! Hi!"

"You pulled a Nicholas Sparks on me," Paige said as her face—her disapproving face—appeared on the screen. Her editor looked polished and professional, but if she was surprised to see an author disheveled and a hot mess, she didn't show it.

"A what?" she asked with a frown, still not quite awake. It had been a very late night and a very troubled sleep once she finally did pass out, well after 3:00 a.m.

"You killed the fisherman," Paige said, shaking her head in disbelief, her pretty blond bob swishing around her chin.

Carly's heart raced as she nodded and prepared to defend the decision. "It just seemed like the most realistic ending..." The entire series was about forbidden love, a union that could never be. Sure, it was sad and slightly depressing, but what had readers expected? The two of them were from different worlds and simply couldn't make it work, despite their love for one another.

Paige sent her a look that suggested she was crazy. "Realistic? Carly, you're writing fantasy romance—suspension of disbelief is assumed and an HEA is required."

If only it were that way in real life. "Yes, but it's the end of the trilogy and each book has ended on a cliff-hanger. No real HEA." Where else could the love story go? Sealena was on borrowed time, and if she had to return to the ocean and give up her fisherman eventually anyway, what was the harm in killing him off?

"About that—we'll come back to this awful ending in a sec—the publisher wants more books," Paige said with a slight hesitation. Obviously not so excited about that offer now that Carly hadn't quite delivered the promised story in the third installment.

Her heart raced. "What?" Had this petition circulating around town reached the publisher? Were they really giving in to what the readers wanted?

"I spoke to the higher-ups and they want to go to contract for three more."

She blinked. Three more? Carly hadn't thought more than one installment was possible. Then, when she'd turned it into a trilogy, she'd had to dig deep and plot out two more books...

"Readers want more," Paige said, flipping through a stack of papers on her desk. "Early preorder sales indicate that this third book is in high demand. It will be the biggest seller yet—or at least, it was supposed to be," she said, sending Carly a look.

Carly bit her lip.

"So, rewrite that ending, bring her fisherman lover back to life, and I look forward to a more uplifting ending," Paige said in an upbeat tone that left no room for argument. Carly knew she was bound to the terms of her contract and she did want to give readers the satisfying ending they wanted and deserved. Her loyal fans would be devastated by the current ending, and now, with the potential for more books in the series, she had to rethink things.

"Of course. I'll send a new ending over to you soon," she said with another forced smile. "And thank you for the opportunity for more books, Paige," she said.

"I know you won't let me—or your readers—down," Paige said. "Talk soon."

Carly sighed as she disconnected the Skype call and slumped back in the chair.

A more uplifting ending. Could she possibly put her own heartache aside to give the serpent queen an impossible happily-ever-after?

# CHAPTER SEVENTEEN

OLIVER'S SHOULDERS SAGGED, once again feeling the weight of the world on them as he climbed out of his vehicle and headed toward Callan's house early that morning. The day before, Tess had asked to spend the night at Darcy's and Oliver had been relieved to see that she was feeling better and wanting to see her friend. After his run-in with Sebastian, he'd appreciated the time alone to review the proposal without Tess there. He still wasn't sure how he was going to tell his daughter about all of this, but he needed to that day, before she heard there was a possibility that they were losing their home from someone else.

And Carly supported it—that was the part that hurt the most, the part Oliver couldn't quite wrap his head around.

She hadn't even spoken to him about it before cosigning Sebastian's proposal.

He'd gone to see her about it, hoping there had been a misunderstanding, but she'd actually argued that this might be a good thing. It had cut him deep and he'd reacted by shutting down again, shutting her out.

Maybe things had moved too quickly between them. He'd opened up and gotten hurt, and now he wasn't sure how they moved on from here.

The problem was, he didn't want to go back to being friends. The two of them together had felt right. They'd been friends forever and had shared a grief and sadness like no other, and he knew her feelings had only grown after that. Carly had developed a love for him in recent years as their friendship had changed and evolved. Just like his own feelings had over recent weeks.

This was the first time the two of them had really disagreed on anything and it was a big thing. How were they supposed to reconcile their differences on this? And how could they have a future together if they couldn't see eye to eye on something so important?

Knocking on the front door, Oliver scanned the yard. A tire swing hung from the tall maple tree, and the large trampoline, occupying most of the space, was one of Tess's favorite activities when she visited her friend. The two of them would bounce on it for hours, talking and giggling, then collapse on it when they'd exhausted themselves.

Maybe he should buy her one for her birthday.

But where would they put it if they ended up moving?

The door opened, and Callan, dressed in SpongeBob SquarePants pajama pants, coffee cup in hand, looked surprised to see him. "Hey, Oliver, what's up?"

Oliver's gut twisted instinctively before he said, "Here to pick up Tess."

Callan's frown had his knees all but buckling. "She's not here, man. Was she supposed to be?"

Yes. Yes, she was.

The ground seemed to shift under Oliver's feet and his mouth was dry, despite the instant sweat that pooled all over his body. Tess wasn't there. She'd said she was sleeping over at Darcy's… She'd lied? He thought back to the conversation the day before. She'd come out of her room, just as Sebastian had left, and had asked if she could go. He'd been slightly distracted, but he was sure she'd said Darcy was coming to pick her up with Callan.

He'd been sitting at the kitchen table and he'd hidden the proposal when she'd come in to give him a kiss goodbye… He'd been happy to get some alone time to sort through everything that was going on, but he'd hugged her tight and she'd left.

If she wasn't here, where was she? Where had she been for the last twenty-four hours?

"Easy, man. You look about to faint. Did Tess say she was hanging out with Darcy this morning?" Callan asked, laying a hand on Oliver's shoulder.

Oliver shook his head as he ran a hand through his hair. "Said she was sleeping over last night."

Now Callan's face was full of worry. "No, she didn't."

"Is Darcy here? Has she heard from Tess at all?" The two kids were best friends. If anyone knew where Tess was, it would be Darcy.

"She and Rachel are out shopping—let me text them. Come on in," Callan said, moving back to let Oliver enter.

Even the blast of air-conditioning did nothing to ease the heat coursing through him as he paced the hall while Callan texted. "Just take a breath and think. Maybe she said she was staying at another friend's house and you mixed it up?"

Oliver shook his head. It was definitely Darcy. It was the only place she did sleepovers. She didn't feel comfortable staying over at other children's houses. "It was definitely here," he said, pulling out his phone to text her.

Where are you?

Then:

I'm not mad, you're not in trouble, just please tell me where you are.

She'd never pulled something like this before; it was so unlike her. His heart raced. "Maybe the kids had planned a sleepover and didn't tell you and Rachel?"

Damn, he'd been…preoccupied and hadn't followed up with his little girl to make sure she'd arrived. She'd texted a quick good-night around 8:00 p.m., so he'd assumed everything was okay.

He never should have assumed. He should have been on it like usual. He should have confirmed with Callan and Rachel…

He'd been distracted. And now Tess could be anywhere.

But Callan shook his head. "I really don't think so. Darcy and Rachel had planned the shopping trip for a week, so I don't think Darcy would have made plans with Tess…" Callan's phone chimed, while Oliver's remained eerily quiet.

Unfortunately, the other man didn't have good news. "Sorry. She said she hasn't heard from her," he said while texting back. "I'll ask her to text Tess now and see if she answers."

Oliver's palms sweated as he dialed all the other local parents on his contact list, just in case.

Each parent had the same response. No Tess.

Damn, he never thought he'd be in this position, be that parent who didn't know where their kid was. His heart pounded in his chest and it was impossible to stop the shaking of his hands.

"Give me two minutes to get dressed and we will head out to look for her," Callan said.

Oliver nodded, not trusting his voice to speak over the large lump forming in the back of his throat.

*Tess, where are you?*

He paced the hallway as he waited. Then, reaching for his phone, he texted the only other person who might know.

Have you seen Tess?

Carly's reply was instant:

No, is she okay?

Not sure.

He quickly explained the situation to Carly and she said she'd join in the search right away. He wanted to text something else...but he didn't know what to say, and right now, his sole focus was on finding Tess.

Thank you.

Of course...and we will find her.

Five minutes later, he and Callan jumped into his truck and started the search along the side streets near Callan's home. They drove slowly, scanning the space between the houses, looking for any sign of her, but they found nothing.

Several neighbors were out walking and gardening and they asked if anyone had seen her, but no one had.

Oliver's chest tightened more and more the longer they searched and his phone remained silent. No texts or calls from her—what if she was hurt? What if she was in trouble?

Port Serenity was a safe place. Residents looked out for one another and the crime rate was low. But during tourist season, with an influx of strangers coming through town...

They headed down to Main Street next, and parking the truck, Oliver took one side of the street and Callan took the other as they went into every store and business, inquiring if anyone had seen Tess. Concerned faces and expressions of sympathy were all they received. No one had seen her in days and there was no sign of her on Main Street.

His worry hit its peak when they'd reached the city limits sign and there was still no hint of his daughter anywhere.

Gone without a trace. As though she'd vanished.

An overwhelming sense of déjà vu struck him and he bent at the knees, unable to breathe.

This couldn't be happening. Not again. She had to be okay. He couldn't lose her too.

The street around him spun and he felt Callan's hand on his back. The man's voice seemed far away as he was telling him to breathe, take deep breaths… Then he was guiding him back to the truck.

Oliver sat in the passenger seat and his vision wasn't focused on anything in particular as his gaze drifted out the window while Callan drove.

"I'm going to take you back to your place… Maybe she came home," he said.

His place. A place that may not be his much longer. Right now, that hardly seemed to matter. Without Tess, nothing else would matter. The lighthouse was just a building…

His daughter and the people he loved made it a home.

Callan pulled the truck in front of the house and, seeing a large group gathered there, Oliver felt his gut twist.

A tour group. The first one of the day. Eight expectant faces turned to look at him with various degrees of annoyance to be kept waiting.

"I can't…" he started.

Callan put the truck in Park. "I got this," he said, jumping out and approaching the group. "Tours are canceled for today…" He heard Callan tell the group, instructing them to leave and reschedule the experience.

No one seemed pleased, but no one argued with the six-foot-three, muscular former coast guard officer as they dispersed.

Oliver climbed out of the truck but a quick search of the house revealed Tess wasn't inside. He searched her room and discovered that Ginger (the latest name they were trying out on the kitten) wasn't there either. The pet usually slept at the foot of Tess's bed every night, but he hadn't noticed the animal hadn't been there the night before, as he'd had no reason to go into the room.

Most nights, he went in to check on Tess and give her a kiss...

The lump in his throat grew larger and he swallowed back the emotions clouding his judgment. He couldn't break down or think the worst. He had to stay positive. Keep searching with a clear head.

He scanned Tess's room. Where else could she have gone?

Callan entered the house and called out to him.

"Find her?" he asked, hurrying out to the front room.

"No, but I found this in the shed," he said, handing Oliver a note.

With a shaky hand, he took it and read the letter in Tess's handwriting:

*Gone to live on Fishermen's Peak with Ginger. Love you. P.S. Thanks for the paddleboard—I love it.*

Oliver blinked, then reread the note. She was going to live on the island? His daughter had run away from home? What...why? He frowned as he looked up at Callan. "Was the paddleboard gone?"

Callan nodded. "At least we know where she was headed," he said.

Grateful for a starting point at least, his fears of abduction mostly erased, now Oliver had to worry about whether his daughter had safely made it to the island several miles off the coast.

And why she'd decided to run away.

AN HOUR LATER, the coast guard rescue vessel, with Skylar at the helm, was leaving the dock, and Carly hurried down the pier toward a devastated-looking Oliver.

The sight of him made her chest ache. All morning, she'd been worried sick about Tess to the point where she'd closed the store to look for her. Getting Oliver's text about the little girl's whereabouts had been both a welcome relief and another source of worry. The night before, the weather hadn't been great. Had Tess made it to the island on the paddleboard before nightfall? Before the weather had gotten bad? Where was she now and why wasn't she answering her text messages and calls?

And why on earth had she run away?

She slowed her pace as she reached Oliver and he turned to face her. His worried expression had seemed to age him; the tired look on his expression and the sag in his shoulders had her heart breaking for him. She wanted to reach out and hug him, but she hung back, unsure, their argument and the way they'd left things lingering in the tension surrounding them.

They needed to put everything else aside right now as they waited to find Tess, to bring her back home safely... but there was so much uncertainty and pain around them.

"Don't worry. Skylar and the crew will find her," she said reassuringly.

But the moment was too familiar—those reassuring words were *far* too familiar. Once again, the two of them were standing helpless on the docks, while the coast guard looked for his family. Her family.

"Thank you for being here," Oliver said, his voice sounding hoarse as he stared into her eyes.

"Where else would I be?" she asked.

Despite everything, she loved him. She loved Tess. There was nowhere else in the world she would rather be right now than by Oliver's side. He should know that she always had, *would* always have his back. Be there for him no matter what.

But she hadn't exactly supported him in regard to the lighthouse...

Her stomach knotted at the realization of the source of Oliver's anger toward her. He thought she was turning her back on him in that situation. She wasn't. She just hadn't been able to tell him quite everything yet...

There was so much to say, so much to tell him and discuss, but now wasn't the right time.

They stood there in silence, watching the coast guard boat move farther away, heading to Fishermen's Peak. Lost in their own thoughts, their own emotions, they waited together.

The search for Tess lasted barely two hours, but they were the longest two hours of Carly's life. A small crowd of parents and a few local store owners who'd heard about Tess's escapade had gathered. All-too-familiar memories were haunting her thoughts.

Years before, standing there, waiting... It had been torture.

That day, old feelings had resurfaced and the pain of the tragedy had come sweeping back from where it had reluctantly been repressed.

When the news from Skylar came in that they'd found

her, she'd touched Oliver's arm gently, supportively, but his body language told her he needed space in that moment, so she'd kept her distance, allowing him to deal with the incredible sense of relief on his own.

She'd longed to hold him, to offer comfort and receive some in response, but she suspected his mind and heart were as conflicted as hers.

What mattered now was that Tess had been found. Safe. A little cold and wet, but okay.

Her paddleboard had been on the shore of Fishermen's Peak and her cell phone battery was dead. She'd done all the right things by staying put, instead of trying to head back out on the rough water. She'd stayed close to the shore and had lit a small fire.

They continued to watch the coast guard vessel approach, and when it docked at the marina, Oliver raced toward it. Tess was on deck and she burst into tears immediately upon seeing her dad. She climbed off the boat, wrapped in a thermal blanket and holding the kitten, and Oliver opened his arms to her. She ran into them and Carly's chest tightened at the sight of the two people she loved most in the world. She wanted to join in the embrace, wanted to hold them tight and never let go.

But her feet remained frozen on the spot as her conflicted heart told her the gesture may not be appreciated.

She was just grateful the little girl was safe.

There would be time to talk and try to figure out where they all went from here, but for now Tess was home, where she belonged, and that was all that mattered. She'd give father and daughter the time and space to talk and solve this issue before they discussed anything else. She just hoped that Oliver would give her a chance to explain everything, to clarify so much…

When Oliver glanced her way and their gazes met, there was a look of hope reflected in his eyes that made her heart feel a little less heavy as she waved, then turned and headed back toward Main Street.

A HOT SHOWER and fresh clothes later, Tess sat at the table, devouring a sandwich and a glass of milk, which she was sharing with the kitten, and Oliver struggled with the patience to wait until she'd finished her lunch to get to the bottom of what had happened.

Finally, she wiped her mouth and reached for a chocolate chip cookie.

Oliver moved the bag of cookies out of reach. "Start talking."

"You said you weren't mad," she reminded him, having seen his text messages now that her cell phone was recharged.

He took a deep breath. He wasn't mad. He was relieved and grateful…but he needed to understand why Tess had lied and why she'd thought her actions were okay. He sat across from her and handed her a cookie. "I'm not mad," he said calmly, shoving a cookie into his own mouth. He chewed quickly and swallowed hard. "Why did you go out alone without telling me? Why did you lie about staying at Darcy's?"

Tess stared at the cookie in her hand.

Something was definitely bothering her. Something serious had made her act this way.

Oliver's stomach tightened. Was it the new relationship with Carly? Tess had said she was happy about it, but maybe it was too much too soon. Knowing they were dating was one thing, but seeing him kiss another woman, hold another woman's hand, was quite another, despite how much

Tess adored Carly. That had to be it; there had been nothing else that could have triggered this in recent weeks. He cleared his throat when her silence was prolonged. "Tess, are you sure you're okay with me dating Carly?" Not that he even knew where they stood anymore after their argument. That day, standing together on the docks, waiting—it had brought back a lot of old memories, and having her support once again had meant a lot. He realized he'd been focused on all the wrong things, but was it too late? And if his daughter was struggling with the relationship, that would also need to be considered as they all moved forward.

But Tess's head shot up and she nodded quickly. "Yes, of course. I love Carly and I'm happy that you're happier now," she said, her voice soft.

"But maybe it's too soon?" Was he looking for his daughter to confirm it to help solidify his own conflicting thoughts? A week before, he'd been all in. He'd been 100 percent certain that Carly was what he wanted for his future. For their future.

But then, standing on the docks, every ounce of hurt and pain and sadness that he'd moved past as best he could had come spiraling back. The haunting memories, then memories of the love he'd lost, the family he'd lost… It made his heart ache. As though the wound had reopened. The seal had been ripped off and now he was left even more vulnerable and conflicted.

But Tess shook her head. "It's not too soon. It's been a long time and Mom and Catherine would want us to be happy, to start a new life. I know they'd be happy to know it was with Carly."

Okay, so this wasn't about him and Carly. That should make him feel better, but it didn't. Both because now the whole Carly thing was on him—his decision alone—and also because something else was upsetting Tess. Enough to have her lying to him and sneaking off dangerously.

He took a deep breath. "Okay, well, if that's not it, what is it? Something going on with your friends?"

He'd been hoping to have a few more years before teenage hormones and issues with peers started to play a major role in his daughter's moods and actions.

Again, she shook her head no.

Oliver repressed a deep sigh. "Tess, sweetheart, you're going to have to work with me here. What's going on?"

She looked up at him and the tears brimming her eyes made his chest tighten even more. His little girl never cried. Hadn't in so long. She was so tough and brave. Seeing her upset twice that day, to the point of tears, had his mind reeling even more.

If anyone had done anything to hurt his little girl...

"I heard you talking to Sebastian," she said, the words sounding strained over a sob. "About us having to move, about turning the lighthouse into a B and B, and I was upset. I decided to move out to the island so I wouldn't have to leave Port Serenity."

His stomach dropped. He should have suspected she'd have eavesdropped on that conversation. He stood and moved to sit on a closer chair. He turned hers to face him and sighed.

Tears ran down her cheeks and he struggled with the right words. He wasn't entirely sure what was going to happen with the lighthouse, with their home. He wasn't sure if the decision was even up to him. The community could vote for the B and B idea and they'd be forced to move. He wasn't even sure if he was still completely opposed to the idea himself. In recent months, he had been considering whether it was time to move on, let go... Being with Carly had also played a factor in that. If they did move forward together in a relationship, what would that look like? What would that entail? There was no rush to move in together or anything, but eventually, that was where things would be headed. At least, that was what he would want.

The apartment above the bookstore and museum wouldn't be big enough for the three of them, and he wasn't sure living in the lighthouse with her, starting over, rebuilding a new life, new future, was the right move. There were already far too many family memories in this home. Reminders of Catherine and Alison everywhere, and while he knew Carly would never voice it, it would have to be difficult for her to simply move into the life he and Tess had created, one that still held all traces of the past. Of Oliver's first love.

But it wouldn't be fair to Tess to remove those memories. This was her home…

He had no idea what the right thing to do was. Which was something else giving him pause and making him wonder if he was truly as ready as he thought he was.

"Is it true?" Tess asked in his prolonged silence. The apprehension on her young face broke him. She'd already been through so much more than any child should have to deal with. He hated that this was hurting her.

"I'm not sure. Sebastian does want to present that option to the town at the next community meeting. He thinks it will help tourism and, apparently, he had success with converting another lighthouse in California…"

"But the town won't want that. He'd know that if he actually belonged here. He'd know what this town was like," Tess argued. She wiped her tears with the back of her T-shirt and sniffed, her sadness quickly turning to annoyance and a fit of spitefulness emerging.

Definitely better than tears, but unfortunately, there was nothing he could say to make her feel better.

"You're right and you're totally justified in feeling that way. I'm just not sure what the community might decide. It is a possibility."

Tess eyed him. "Do you want to move? Would you be okay with this plan?"

He sighed. He wouldn't lie to her. "I'm not sure. For a while, I thought no way, but that was more pride and just not wanting to admit that Sebastian might be right, or that the idea would help us move on."

Tess's shoulders sagged. "I hadn't really thought about it like that."

He pulled her in for a hug and kissed the top of her hair, which still smelled like the salty sea after Tess probably neglected to shampoo it in the shower in her rush to eat. "Look, nothing is decided yet and I'm sure we will get a say in it as well. For now, we just need to be open-minded and think about all the pros and cons." He paused. "Either way, no matter what, we will be together. This place is just four walls and a roof. Home is us together."

She hugged him tight and he could still sense she wasn't happy about the possibility, but his brave, smart little girl was being open to it. "You, me and Carly," she said, and Oliver's heart once again skipped a beat.

## CHAPTER EIGHTEEN

SHE WAS TAKING a huge risk, but Carly had no idea how else to come up with an ending for the third book that readers would be happy with—and could lead to another three books. She'd spent hours the day before, after Tess was home safe, trying to rewrite that dark moment scene and a new alternate ending that Paige would be happier with, but she was coming up blank.

It was a challenge to think of happily-ever-after endings when her own relationship status was up in the air at the moment.

Therefore, she'd turn to the fans of the series for inspiration.

She positioned the chairs in the book club room in a circle and checked the online sign-up. The last-minute book club discussion she'd posted already had a full attendance, and based on the names on the list, she knew many hardcore Sealena fans would be arriving any minute.

If anyone could help her figure this out, they could.

She went into the front room and brewed two carafes of coffee and opened the boxes of sugary, delicious pastries she'd picked up from the bakery down the street. She scanned the selection, and reaching for a chocolate-dipped doughnut, she took a big bite, hoping the sugar high would help her get through that evening's event and the all-nighter writing session she was in for.

A few moments later, the door opened and Rachel entered. She wasn't surprised to see her friend was the first one there, her Sealena shirt tucked into a stylish short leather skirt and her long red hair tied in a braid over one shoulder. She was clutching her copies of the books as she approached, a suspicious look on her face. "A last-minute Sealena book club?"

Carly shrugged casually, chewing slowly. "Thought it might be fun, as the publisher has started releasing sample chapters of the third book, that's all." Two of the chapters she'd already submitted were live on the publisher's website with the preorder links, and so far, the comments from readers were encouraging.

"Okay…so it has nothing to do with the fact that you're stuck on an ending?"

Carly nearly choked on her doughnut. Her eyes widened as she struggled to swallow the dough.

"I knew it!" Rachel said, pointing a finger at her. "I've been trying to bait you into telling me for months!" She swiped at her. "I thought we were friends," she said.

"We are. Sorry, I was going to tell you…eventually," she said sheepishly.

"Does anyone else know?" Rachel asked, completely enthralled.

"Just Skylar," she said.

"Skylar? Are you shitting me? She didn't even want to read the books," Rachel said, looking hurt. "Why did you tell her?"

"I didn't. She guessed." First Skylar. Now Rachel had figured it out on her own. Was the writing that transparent? Had anyone else in town figured it out yet? It amazed her that no one had realized that Salwert was an anagram of Walters. She'd been stuck on a pen name and thought it would be fun...

Rachel reached for an éclair and took a big bite. "So, am I right? Are you stuck on the ending?"

Carly hesitated. Could she admit that to her friend and avid reader of the series? She sighed. "Yes. I've written myself into a corner here and have no way out. I submitted one possible ending..." She avoided Rachel's gaze as she continued. "But apparently, the fisherman can't die."

Rachel shook her head. "Absolutely not."

"I'm hoping the readers can offer some insight," she said, biting her lip. Because if they couldn't, she was hooped.

Luckily, all Carly needed to do was pose the question to the group moments later:

"We know the third book will deal with the relationship on land as Sealena's time is running out...but what do you think happens to ensure they can be together?"

And theories flew out at record speed.

"The fisherman is magical too..."

"Sealena finds a loophole in her thirty-day stay..."

"The waning moon holds a special magic that allows her to transform again..."

All fascinating ideas, and as Carly listened, she made notes, hoping one of them would strike the right chord.

Then, finally, one did.

"What if the fisherman and Sealena had a baby together?"

Carly's mouth dropped as she turned to see who'd voiced the perfect thought and saw Skylar standing in the doorway. All eyes turned to stare at her, still in her coast guard uniform, having come to the book club straight from work.

She waited... What would the room think?

Eyes lit up and excited discussion resumed around her,

everyone talking at once, all seemingly on board with that idea. Her heart raced as thoughts spiraled through her... She could make that work—somehow—and that would open the door for the further three books in the series.

Feeling more inspired than she had in days, Carly stood quickly. "Um, keep chatting among yourselves, keep enjoying the treats. I just have to run out for a moment..."

Rachel winked at her, obviously thrilled to be part of the inner circle of knowledge, but no one else seemed to be paying any attention to her as she moved past the chairs and headed out of the room. She smiled at Skylar and squeezed her arm. "Thank you," she whispered as she hurried upstairs to her waiting laptop.

The words flowing to her mind, she started to type, ready to give Sealena and the fisherman the love story of a lifetime:

*This is impossible, yet I can feel new life growing inside of me.*

She didn't pause for a break until the final chapters were done. Then, sitting back, she smiled, a sense of satisfaction and pride overwhelming her as she composed the email to Paige and hit Send.

Sealena had gotten her happily-ever-after. Now Carly just needed to find a way to get hers.

Too bad there wasn't a support group she could call on for that.

THREE DAYS LATER, Carly entered the tourism office on her way to the post office counter to mail the signed contract for the next three books in the Sealena series. The offer had arrived the day before, immediately after Paige had read the new ending and loved it. And Carly had immediately signed the new agreement without hesitation.

After finishing the book, ideas for the future of Sealena and her new family had popped into her mind and she was excited to get started on the next installment. What had once felt like a side hustle, a hobby, now felt like her true calling.

She was an author.

One with a very sizable advance coming her way that she knew exactly what to do with.

"Hey. In here," Sebastian said, poking his head out into the hall and gesturing for her to enter the office.

They hadn't spoken since he'd approached Oliver with the proposal, but there was really nothing she could say or do, and in the end, she still agreed it was best for the community.

As she entered, the office receptionist, Maya, exited, a flushed look on her face, and Carly caught Sebastian's gaze lingering on the other woman. Obviously, he'd moved on already.

He approached and hugged her quickly. "Heard about Tess. So relieved she's okay."

She nodded. "It was scary for a few hours there, but yeah, she's good." The little girl had been texting her over the last few days, wondering when they'd all get together again, and it had been difficult to respond, not knowing the answer herself.

But she told Tess she'd see her at the parade that weekend.

Which led her to her question for Sebastian. "Could you possibly drive the parade float?" Oliver had helped build it every year, but he always refused to drive it. Most years, he skipped the parade entirely. Carly suspected Tess would be attending with Callan and Rachel again that year.

It was disappointing, but she couldn't force things...

Sebastian looked surprised, but graciously didn't ask any questions. He simply nodded. "You got it."

"Thank you. I appreciate it." Carly sent a grateful look and waved as she left the office and continued on to the post office.

HE NEEDED TO make things right.

Over the last few weeks, his emotions had been a whirlwind, but the one constant was how he felt about Carly. Even when he was conflicted, wondering if it was too soon or whether he was truly ready to move forward with her in a new capacity, there had always been that love. Deep, burning, passionate and real.

Pushing her away had been a natural, automatic defense mechanism out of hurt and disappointment, but he knew it hadn't been the right thing to do. Carly had always been a rock for him, a shoulder to cry on, someone to make him laugh and the only person in the world he trusted, but it had been unfair of him to expect her to always agree or go along with what he wanted. That wasn't a relationship, and if he wanted to be with her—which he so desperately did—then he needed to learn to compromise, to open his mind and heart to the new proposal, and figure out how they moved forward *together*-together. As a team.

He hadn't heard from her in days. She was giving him and Tess space, but he sensed it was more than that. She was pulling away. He deserved it. He'd been so hot and cold, so selfish and careless with her emotions, with her heart. She'd never been anything but a support system for him and Tess and he'd taken advantage of that. Then he'd opened up to her, starting to give her hope of a future together, then shut back down again.

He needed to fix things and fast.

Unfortunately, he couldn't just go and apologize to her. Carly deserved more than that. Saying sorry wasn't enough after all the years she'd patiently waited for him to realize what she had to offer—that they were perfect together. He needed to do something, show her how he felt. Demonstrate the depth of his feelings.

And he may have figured out the perfect way.

Heading into the shed, he retrieved the extra buckets of paint left over from the float. The main portion was dry and covered and waiting for the event the next day, but there was something he wanted to add.

Opening the lids on the darkest blue and several lighter shades, along with the white, he stirred the colors and poured them into separate paint trays. Dipping the roller into the darkest one, he took a deep breath before rolling it along the frame of his favorite, reliable pickup truck. He just hoped he could pull this off without making a mess of things.

And he meant more than just the truck's paint job.

The next day, he paced the kitchen, a nervous wreck as he waited. The sound of a vehicle pulling into the lot had his heart pounding in his chest and his palms sweating.

"Is that Carly?" Tess's eyes lit up from where she sat eating breakfast. She'd barely slept the night before; she was so excited about the parade that day. It was a highlight of the summer for her, and this year, it held more stakes for Oliver as well.

"I think so," he said, taking her empty cereal bowl from Ginger (the name they'd decided to keep), who was lapping up the remaining milk, and placing it in the dishwasher. He needed a moment. He needed to try to figure out the emotions raging within him before he could say anything.

He knew what he wanted to say. He wanted to tell her he

was sorry and that he loved her and that the last few days had really had him spiraling with indecision, but things were clearer now—or at least getting there. He wanted to continue what they had started, building a life together, a love together...

The closure had been tough to receive, but now as the shock of the news faded, he realized it was what he'd needed to fully move on.

He wiped his palms against his jeans as he headed outside to the shed. He had the flatbed already hooked up to the truck for her and the parade float was ready to go.

He paused, hearing voices in the shed. Tess's. Carly's. And...Sebastian's?

What the hell was the other man doing there?

Sweat pooled on Oliver's back as he entered the shed.

"Hey," Carly said awkwardly, sending him a quick glance before continuing to inspect the float.

"Hey," he said, shoving his hands into his pockets. She looked so pretty in a blue flowing skirt and white tank top, her long dark hair curled and hanging loose around her shoulders. He had to resist the urge to touch her, reach out to hold her, kiss her, confess his undying love.

None of that would happen now with Sebastian there.

All he could do was stand there and hope they got another chance to talk soon.

Carly's eyes widened when she noticed the truck. "Oh my God. You painted your truck?" She trailed a hand over the finished design.

"Like it?" he asked, nervously. The dark blue paint with the waves and bubbles had taken him hours, but he'd wanted to surprise her.

"Like it?" she asked. "It's so beautiful!" She continued to stare at it. "I can't believe you did this."

He shrugged, shoving his hands into his pockets, despite the happiness he felt at her approval. "We really only use this truck for the parade anyway," he said and immediately regretted downplaying the act when her face fell slightly.

What he'd meant to say—what he'd wanted to say—was that he'd done this for her because she deserved the most fantastic float ever. That he'd done it to apologize for his mood and actions the last few days, and mostly, he'd done it because he loved her and he wanted to make her happy. But the words refused to surface.

Sebastian appeared next to her and checked his watch. "We should get going," he said, climbing into the truck.

Oliver's jaw tightened as he saw the man getting comfortable in the driver's seat.

"You're not driving it this year?" he asked Carly, nodding to Sebastian.

"Um…no. The extra size and weight makes me a little nervous, so I thought I'd ride back here during the parade and make sure Sealena doesn't fall into the crowd," she said with an awkward laugh, surely meant to ease the tension.

"I could have driven it for you," he said.

Carly's expression was full of frustration as she turned toward him. "The parade has never been your thing. You've refused to attend for years."

He swallowed hard. He deserved that. He deserved her tone and her cold shoulder. He deserved that she'd asked someone else to drive the float that day. He knew none of it was meant to hurt him—she'd just had enough of his bullshit.

Truthfully, he'd had enough of his own bullshit.

Unfortunately, now wasn't the right time to try to tell her or demonstrate that.

"You're right. Sorry about that. Tess and I will be there today."

Tess swung around to face him and her look of surprise matched Carly's. "You're going?"

He nodded. He needed to start letting go and embracing the community—whatever that meant for his future involvement in it. He forced a smile. "I heard they're giving out Sealena-themed foam fingers this year," he said.

Garnering him another look from the ladies.

Sebastian honked the truck horn, breaking the moment. "Ready to go?" he asked through the open window.

Carly nodded. "Yeah, we probably should. Parade lineup starts in an hour on Main Street." She hesitated as she walked around to the passenger side of the truck. "But I'll see...both of you there."

Oliver nodded as Sebastian pulled the truck and flatbed out of the shed and slowly headed down the street. Carly waved through the window, the look of confusion on her pretty face only making Oliver more determined to make things right.

WHAT THE HELL was happening?

If anyone had told her that Oliver—her best friend and love of her life Oliver, frustratingly infuriating Oliver—was going to attend the annual parade that year, Carly would never have believed it.

Yet he was going. And he was joking about Sealena-themed foam fingers?

She shook her head in bewilderment, staring out the window as they drove away from the lighthouse.

She'd been more than a little relieved to see him and Tess seeming much better that day than they had a few days ago. They were obviously coming to terms with the cold case being solved and so was she. In their own way, they'd all been forced to move on three years ago, learn to accept not having Alison and Catherine in their lives. So, while the revelation of what happened that day had been sad and disappointing, they'd all gone through the stages of grief once before, and now this round was passing more quickly. Knowing didn't change anything; Alison and Catherine had been gone a long time and they'd all known they weren't coming back.

"You okay?" Sebastian asked.

Carly nodded. "Yeah, fine. Thanks again for driving today." Dex was working the bar at the Serpent Queen Pub for the huge after-parade crowd expected to pour in. And Rachel and Skylar had adamantly refused to try driving the large float. But she wouldn't hurt Sebastian's feelings by admitting he was her fourth choice. She was just happy that Oliver didn't let the grudge between him and Sebastian cause any issue that day.

"No problem," he said, lowering the sun visor as the early-morning sun nearly blinded them. A picture fell onto his lap.

Ah, the photo… Oliver had always kept a family photo under the visor in a clear plastic case. It had been there for as long as she could remember. It was one of the things she found so endearing about him.

But her heart raced as Sebastian picked it up and quickly glanced at it. "Nice pic of the three of you," he said.

Carly frowned, reaching for it. It was the family photo, but added in the plastic film next to it was one of her, Oliver and Tess that they'd snapped with the old-fashioned tour camera the night of the BBQ.

She swallowed hard, staring at their three smiling, goofy-looking expressions. The smallest thing holding so much significance.

"Okay, I'm not going to say that I like the guy, or that I

think you've made the right choice, but I will say that you deserve to be happy. And if that's with Oliver, then you need to fight for that."

Carly glanced at Sebastian. "It's complicated."

"And I know I didn't help things with the B and B proposal and I am sorry about that."

Carly turned in her seat toward him and took a deep breath. Now was her chance to make a proposal of her own and she wouldn't overthink it or get cold feet. This was the right thing, what she wanted, and Sebastian was right—if she wanted a life with Oliver and Tess, she had to fight for it.

She cleared her throat. "About the B and B…"

"Yeah?" he asked, curiosity in his voice.

"I have a proposal of my own."

MAIN STREET WAS full of residents and tourists already by the time Oliver and Tess made it. The streets were barricaded and local police were rerouting vehicles toward side streets to bypass the floats lined up and ready to go. All of the local shops had closed for the day's event and would reopen once the crowd had dispersed. The mood and energy all around them was electric as everyone anticipated the best parade Port Serenity had ever held.

"Dad! I told you we should have left earlier. We're never going to get a good spot up front," Tess chided as they hurried through the busy crowds, standing three deep on the sidewalks on both sides of the street.

"Don't worry. I'll put you on my shoulders," he said, holding tight to her hand as they wove in and out of the crowd.

Reports hadn't been lying when they said Port Serenity's tourism was up to 90 percent of what it used to be that year.

He also knew that with the closing of one of the local B and Bs, the town was struggling to accommodate booking requests. Some tourists were staying a short drive away in Sirens Bay, which wasn't ideal.

Sirens Bay had a new mayor and a wealthy businessman had moved to the community the year before to open a high-end steak house. He claimed not to have any political aspirations or plans to build anything else in the small community, but the fear was that the town would soon try to compete with Port Serenity for the tourists. Sending them there due to lack of accommodations wasn't in the town's best interest.

It didn't bode well for Oliver's case about not turning his home into a vacation rental. But the last few days, he was changing his way of thinking. Maybe the new restructuring plans were in the town's best interest, and as he'd told Tess, home was where they were together.

Letting go of the lighthouse would be tough, but not impossible, and in time, he knew he'd learn to be okay with it.

Seeing an opening in the crowd as a group of teens decided they were too cool to watch the parade after all, Oliver quickly hurried into the opening. "See? Best viewing place available."

Tess sent him a look. "We got lucky."

The sound of the local high school marching band approaching in the distance had everyone around them turning in the direction of the oncoming parade. With Tess in front of him for her safety, Oliver peered down the street as the group approached.

The song was the "Ode to Sealena," which had been written by a local artist ten years before, and he couldn't deny the sound of it did give him a sense of pride. He may have had his issues with the mythical sea serpent queen, but there was just something about feeling like a part of something, and the town's folklore gave the community that. It bonded them and connected them all. Standing there now, hearing the music and seeing all the excited faces, Oliver knew he was truly part of something special.

Next was the high school's cheerleading squad, dressed in their green-and-gold uniform. *SS* on the front for *Serpent Squad*—the local sports teams were all called the Serpents. Tess's eyes lit up, seeing them as they stopped to perform a daring athletic stunt to a round of applause from the crowd. As the cheerleader flew through the air, even Oliver's heart was in his throat, until she was safely on the ground.

"I can't wait to be on the Serpent Squad," Tess said excitedly.

Oliver could.

The next to pass were the mayor and his wife in a convertible, waving to the crowd, and several of the local business owners tossing candies to the kids from their cars. Three large balloons passed overhead, held by dozens of volunteers. And then the promised Sealena-themed foam fingers were distributed by a large supply van, volunteers racing them out to the crowd.

He and Tess put theirs on and high-fived one another. She giggled and held his hand, squeezing it tight, obviously happy he was there. He couldn't deny that he was having a good time. It made him feel bad that he'd missed out for so many years, but he couldn't change any of that. He was there now and he was determined not to miss out on any other aspects of life.

Then, in the distance, the actual floats appeared.

The first one was from the local fish market. Their design featured various types of fish and Oliver laughed as the owner, dressed as a codfish, was chased around the flatbed by his cleaver-wielding wife, who was dressed as a cook. The older man struggled with the limited mobility of the costume and it was a close call several times.

The next one was from the conservation wildlife center and their display featured a lab setup with large fish tanks and specimens being cared for and researched. Along the side were sea life and environmental facts. Dr. Ann, dressed in her lab coat, waved to them from the platform and they waved back. Then Ann nodded toward a man he didn't recognize, also on the float. Her face lit up and Oliver clued in—the mysterious long-distance boyfriend. The man must have shown up for Ann. Oliver winked at her, happy for her.

But it only made him long for his own happiness with Carly.

He knew painting the truck and attending the parade were a start, a step in the right direction of showing her that he was ready to go all in, but they still had some things to figure out.

Following the conservatory float was the coast guard vehicle, the crew dressed in their uniforms and rescue gear, waving to the crowd. There was more than one swooning woman around him as they passed. There was a reason the yearly coast guard calendar featuring the brave and attractive crew was the biggest charity fundraiser in town.

Even Tess looked slightly gaga over the handsome men in uniform as they waved and handed out brochures about water safety to the children.

Oliver leaned over her shoulder and pointed to one of the safety rules. "Don't go out into the water unsupervised. Huh. That sounds like an important one," he said pointedly.

Tess rolled her eyes. "I get it. I won't do it again."

He ruffled her hair and laughed. He knew she wouldn't.

She was a great kid and he was going to have his hands full in raising her, but he was up to the challenge.

A few smaller floats passed and then he could see Carly's float turn the corner onto Main Street.

"There it is! She's coming!" Tess said excitedly next to him.

The crowd moved closer to the edge of the sidewalk as the large float neared. It was even more impressive, seeing it now. Carly's vision had certainly come to life in the biggest, most impressive float the parade had ever had. Sealena stood proud and fierce holding the small sailboats among the large waves that Rachel had painted to look amazingly real. The rotating device was working perfectly to create the storm raging around her on the arches, the sea creatures battling the tumultuous environment.

"It looks so good!" Tess said, clapping her hands along with everyone else as it passed in front of them. "I helped build that one," she told the family of tourists standing next to them.

The woman offered Oliver a warm smile, and once again, a sense of pride overwhelmed him. Despite what happened with the lighthouse, with their home, he needed to make sure they could stay in Port Serenity. Tess deserved that. And he wanted to stay. This was where they belonged.

His gaze fell on Carly at the back of the float. She didn't see them at first as she waved and smiled at the crowd. But then she spotted them and her face lit up. She blew a kiss at Tess, and when her gaze locked with Oliver's, his heart pounded loud, confirming all the feelings he had for his best friend.

Now he just needed to figure out a way to prove to Carly that he was all in—and hope that she was too.

## CHAPTER NINETEEN

CARLY HAD NEVER been so nervous in her entire life.

The next day, she arrived early at the community center where that month's town hall meeting was scheduled to start in half an hour. The parade the day before had gone amazingly well. Her store's float had been a crowd-pleaser and had won best float again that year. But she'd been so impressed by the efforts of the other stores as well. They'd all put so much time and thought into their designs, and the shops along Main Street had boasted record sales numbers as the parade crowds spent their afternoon shopping and eating at the local establishments.

The town had felt alive and vibrating the day before and Carly's pride in the community had only soared to new heights.

She'd barely slept the night before, lying awake thinking about what she was about to do, wondering if it was truly the right decision and if she was ready to take this leap of faith. She'd weighed all the pros and cons in her mind and went over all the details.

But she knew she was ready to commit to the community she loved in a bigger way.

Seeing Oliver and Tess standing in the crowd at the parade had only solidified her feelings. She was in love with Oliver and she wanted to be there full-time as a mom to Tess. They were already her family, the two people on earth she cared about most of all. Her feelings had only grown stronger over the last month, especially when they'd been tested.

She and Oliver might not agree on everything, but she knew his actions—painting the truck and being there for the parade—had been his way of apologizing and trying to make amends. They'd both hurt one another with their actions and lack of communication, but that ended that day.

Carly was ready to open up and reveal all the things she'd been hiding. She was ready to be brave and go with her heart. For the first time in her life, she was chasing a dream that meant more to her than any other.

She paced the hallway of the center as some volunteers positioned the chairs on the stage and along the floor for the attendees. These meetings were always full, standing room only, as everyone liked to be involved in major town decisions. Everyone liked to have their voices heard.

So, she suspected that day's agenda, which had circulated already, would bring in a full house.

Oliver and Tess would definitely be there, as the major topic of discussion directly impacted them, and Carly was nervous, but also excited to see them and see their reaction when the plans were presented.

She opened the top button of her blouse and fanned herself with her prepared statement. It was hot in there, and the closer it came to start time, the more sweat gathered on her lower back.

"Hey, you ready for this?" Sebastian's voice said behind her. He offered an encouraging smile as he approached and Carly was grateful for his support and friendship. He'd helped make this decision easier for her the day before with his advice and guidance. He really was a great addition to the town's tourism team and she hoped he decided to stay.

She liked him and she knew they'd be great friends and work well together to benefit the community.

Maybe one day, he and Oliver could even find common ground.

She nodded. "Definitely ready," she said, confidently. She was.

In twenty minutes, her life was about to change, and in Carly's opinion, it was long overdue.

OLIVER WIPED HIS palms against the legs of his dress pants as he sat in the front row next to Tess. The meeting was scheduled to start in five minutes and the community hall was standing room only as the entire community seemed to have come out for the big decision.

The mayor stood in the front at the podium, his wife seated on the stage behind him, looking polished and professional as she waved and smiled politely to members of the community.

As part of the tourism board, Carly and Sebastian sat up there too.

Seeing her made his heart pound. They hadn't spoken since before the parade the day before. Surprisingly, she hadn't attended the Sealena parade after-party at the pub. He'd been hoping to talk to her there, but Rachel had said she had something important she had to take care of.

Seeing her now, looking beautiful in a white blouse and tan pencil skirt, ballet flats on her feet and her hair in a high ponytail, revealing her gorgeous, vibrant complexion, his heart swelled. He missed her so much. He knew she had to do what was right for the community, despite her feelings for him. Despite her own personal feelings about the lighthouse and their home…

Tess clutched his hand in hers as the meeting started.

Hers was just as sweaty, and he whispered, "Whatever happens, we'll be okay."

She nodded, but he saw the conflict written on her face.

He wasn't sure how he felt or what he wanted the outcome to be. He'd gone back and forth in his mind for days. One minute he thought it was the right thing. And the next, he wasn't sure. One minute he was okay with the idea of moving on, letting go of the home he'd grown up in, raised a family in, had in his family for generations. And giving up his post, his responsibility to the community. But the next minute, he thought just the idea would break him.

Ultimately, it was out of his hands.

The mayor started the meeting, addressing the crowd, but Oliver was barely listening as he waited for him to get to the important part. His gaze was locked on Carly, but she was avoiding his, which told him everything…and made him really nervous that maybe he'd already lost more than just his home.

"In regards to proposal number three forty-two regarding the lighthouse reconstruction, the committee's decision was split," the mayor said finally, his gaze landing on Oliver and Tess before continuing, "but after tallying the votes from the public, it was a definite confirmation that the B and B is what would be best for the community moving forward. I'll hand it over to Sebastian for the rest of the details."

Oliver swallowed hard. There it was. He glanced at Tess and saw her struggle to control her own emotions, and that made his chest tighten even more. No matter what, he needed to be strong for Tess and build the best new future he could.

Onstage, the mayor took a seat next to his wife as Sebastian took to the podium to address the crowd. The rumble died down as they all stopped to listen to the details of the proposal.

"Thank you all for coming out today and for the overwhelming support of the proposal," he said confidently. "I'm so happy that you agree that it's the right move forward for the community and I promise you it will directly benefit everyone in this room, with increased tourism and a new event center."

He continued outlining the proposed expansion and all the things Oliver had already read about. He looked at Carly, who looked slightly nervous as she shifted in her seat. He frowned. What was up with her? She was definitely acting odd and she'd yet to look at him. Was she just nervous that she'd disappointed him? Was she afraid he was upset?

He wasn't. He understood. He respected her for making this decision that he knew couldn't have been an easy one. He wished they'd talked about it and that he could have been more open-minded before...

Sebastian paused for a breath, then smiled as he continued, "And I have another announcement that I think a lot of you will be thrilled to hear." He paused again for effect and the entire room was quiet. A pin drop could be heard as everyone waited for this surprise news.

Oliver's heart thundered in his chest, and next to him, Tess looked as though she were holding her breath.

"Author Y.C. Salwert has bought the proposed resort development plans," Sebastian said.

A gasp and muffled voices ran through the room. Oliver frowned, the name not ringing any bells immediately. Then he got it—the author of the fantasy romance Sealena series. That person had bought the land and the new development from the city.

He glanced around as the crowd continued their excited chatter and he noticed Rachel and Skylar share a smile across from him. Onstage, he saw Carly stand slowly and nervously release a deep breath.

"Which is actually me," she said at the podium. Her gaze met Oliver's and he had no idea what was happening. What was she saying? She was buying the lighthouse B and B? She was Y.C. Salwert? A bestselling romance author?

What? How? She'd never told him.

Next to him, Tess squealed in delight. Jumping up from her seat, she raced toward Carly on the stage and wrapped her arms around her waist. "I knew it all along!"

Carly laughed. "You weren't supposed to be reading those just yet," she chastised.

Oliver's heart swelled with pride and wonder at the woman he was definitely in love with.

All around him, people stood and cheered, her fan base excited for the revelation. Carly graciously accepted the applause and, taking Tess with her, she moved back in her seat, pulling the little girl onto her lap as the meeting resumed.

Their gazes met and held, and all he could do was send all the love he had in his heart in her direction and hope that she could feel it. Feel its depth and intensity from across the room.

She'd bought the B and B. He still couldn't quite wrap his mind around it. She'd obviously done it because she'd known the impact losing it would have on him and Tess, but what else did it mean?

The crowd barely listened to the rest of the meeting agenda; everyone was whispering excitedly about the new development, but mostly about the shocking revelation that

Carly was this mysterious author they'd all been obsessing about.

Oliver couldn't believe it either.

Once the meeting was adjourned, the crowds dispersed slowly, some lingering by the refreshment tables, some chatting in little groups around the community center, but all of them pretending not to be watching as Carly left the stage, Tess's hand in hers, and approached Oliver. His heart swelled and he resisted the urge to reach out to take her other hand.

Just barely.

"So, you own the lighthouse now," he said. Overwhelmed with so many emotions, he didn't quite know where to start.

"Well, the town still owns the lighthouse, but I'm personally funding the B and B and cabins that are being constructed. I couldn't let it go to anyone else," she said softly. "It's too important."

Their gazes met and held for a long beat, and Tess removed her hand from Carly's. "I'll let you two talk," she said, rushing off toward Darcy.

Oliver watched her, then turned back to Carly. "But is that what you want? To run an inn? What about the bookstore?"

"I'll still work there part-time, but I'm handing the management role to Melissa. Turns out she wants to take a break from university for a few semesters. And, well, I need more time to write anyway," she said almost sheepishly.

He shook his head, still in disbelief over that revelation. "I can't believe you never told me."

She shrugged. "It was easier when no one knew."

"Everyone knows now," he said with a grin, nodding toward the big group of women waiting outside the community hall door. "I think you have fans waiting."

Carly looked adorably mortified at the thought. "Think I could slip out the back?"

"Can't hide from them forever," he said.

She nodded and looked uncertain as she shifted from one foot to the other.

He couldn't stand it any longer. He didn't care who was there, who was watching; he needed to tell her how he felt. He cleared his throat and took a step toward her. "Carly, I was an idiot."

She shook her head, but he silenced her. "I was. For a long time. I was closed off and afraid of opening myself up again to love, to a new future, to you." He paused for a breath. "But I love you. I love you with every part of my soul and I can't imagine a life without you in it."

Her eyes welled with tears as she smiled at him. She took a step toward him and he pulled her into his arms. He kissed her forehead. "I'm sorry about everything," he whispered.

She looked up at him with only love and affection in her gaze as she said, "I love you too and there's nothing to apologize for. Life—and love—is messy and complicated."

"Can we navigate it together?" he asked, pulling her closer and lowering his mouth toward hers.

"I'd like that. Does that mean you'll continue doing my lighthouse tours?" she asked teasingly, standing on tiptoes to close the gap between their lips.

"Can I still live there with you?" he asked, his heart feeling like it might explode from happiness.

"I was hoping you would," she said. "I love you, Oliver."

He could hear her say those words every day for the rest of his life. "I love you, Carly, or Y.C. Salwert, or whomever you are," he said with a teasing grin.

"Just Carly. From now on, I'm not pretending to be anyone but me," she said, kissing him.

That sounded perfect to him because his best friend and the love of his life was perfect exactly the way she was. He held her tight and returned her kiss, feeling as though the new chapter in their love story had just begun.

# EPILOGUE

Dear readers,

When I started writing this trilogy featuring the tragic, heartwarming, tender love story of Port Serenity's fearless Serpent Queen, I never thought it would touch so many of you the way it has. I never thought it would touch me the way it has.

Sealena is me. Sealena is all of us. This story is mine. This story is all of ours.

Love is the greatest treasure of all. It is also the hardest joy to capture. It can be elusive. It can be cruel. It can break a heart over and over. But it can also uplift and heal and inspire, and in the end, it really can conquer all.

I've written this trilogy in the shadows, out of respect for a creature so powerful and majestic that I didn't feel worthy of telling this love story.

It turns out I didn't feel worthy of a lot of things when I started writing these books, but through them, I've discovered my voice, and within it, its power.

I am fearless. I am strong. I am worthy of love.
So are you.

Dear readers, I've heard your pleas for more Sealena stories and I'm happy to say that I will continue to write them. After all, her story is just beginning…

But I'll write them as who I truly am—Carly Walters—a woman no longer afraid to chase the dreams she wants and deserves. A woman no longer feeling inadequate or undeserving of love. Like Sealena, I can decide my own fate.

Thank you for believing in me and these stories that are so close to my heart.

XO
Carly

* * * * *

# ACKNOWLEDGMENTS

Writing this Wild Coast series has been such an educational experience as I've learned so much about the coast guard and its commitment to keeping our oceans safe. Thank you to my uncle, Coast Guard Captain Brian Legge, for all the research help! All mistakes are my own.

Thank you to my editor, Dana Grimaldi, for all the amazing feedback and notes that make every book stronger, and my agent, Jill Marsal, for always championing my work. As always, I'm incredibly grateful to the Harlequin art team for the beautiful covers for this series!

Thank you to my family for continuing to support this author journey and helping to balance my stressful deadlines with fun and adventure. And a big thank-you to my readers whose messages and reviews mean so much.

XO
*Jen*

# Love in the Alaskan Wilds

# CHAPTER ONE

HE HAD THE script memorized, but keeping the same level of enthusiasm with each new tour group he took up into the air was requiring energy Dwayne Madden simply did not have. He stifled a yawn as he took the same flight path for the third time that day.

How had he done these aerial-view-of-Alaska tours multiple times every day when he still worked for his family's business? Two weeks of it and he was starting to wish he'd taken his forced leave of absence from the coast guard somewhere south.

But it was July and his family appreciated his help during this busy season, so he infused enthusiasm into his tone as he said, "In the distance to your right, you will see the Chugach Mountain Range—the northernmost of the ranges that make up the Pacific Coast Ranges."

He navigated the helicopter over the valley, offering his three passengers—a family from Seattle—a breathtaking view of the Alaskan wilds and the small coastal town of Port Serenity. Dwayne felt a tug of pride seeing their reactions. Faces full of awe and wonder as they pointed and marveled over the scenery below.

There was no place on earth as beautiful as his hometown. Nestled between tall, rugged mountain ranges and featuring some of the world's most magnificent trails and rivers, with natural hot spring waterfalls, Port Serenity was a favorite tourist destination for many and a great place to grow up.

While he was getting tired of these daily sightseeing tours, he'd never get tired of the view.

He flew south and mentioned several other points of interest along the valley, but as they drew closer to the coastline, his chest tightened.

If only they could skip this part of the tour.

He missed his job with the Port Serenity Coast Guard. Missed his crewmates and friends. Missed the challenges and rush of adrenaline he felt on rescue missions. Missed helping people in need. He'd been avoiding the coastline while on the ground as much as possible.

Unfortunately, it was the part of the tour that guests enjoyed the most, so taking a detour wasn't an option.

He flew toward the rocky beach, the waves crashing onto the shore and the whitecaps visible from a distance putting him on full alert as he scanned by instinct. The weather was beautiful—sunny and warm without a cloud in the sky—but the wind had picked up and ocean waves were reportedly reaching thirteen feet high… He hoped locals and visitors opted for nonwater activities.

But it wasn't his concern. Nor would it be for another six days.

He straightened his headset as he continued the speech. "To the left on the hillside is the famous Port Serenity lighthouse. It is one of the oldest lighthouses in America, standing there for over a hundred years. While the coast guard has official control over it now, the fourth-generation lightkeeper still lives there." Oliver Klein and his daughter, Tess, lived in the magnificent structure with its tall light tower, the rotating beacon still a source of hope and guidance to all at sea. Unfortunately, the family had suffered a tragedy several years before when Oliver's wife, Alison, and his older daughter had gone missing after a day out on their boat, and Dwayne had heard recent rumors that Oliver might be planning to move on...away from Port Serenity and the memories that haunted him.

"Along the coastline to the left, we can see the Port Serenity Marine Life Sanctuary, a research facility that ensures safe and ethical practices in researching marine creatures in their natural habitat." It was one of his own favorite places to visit in town. There was always something interesting going on inside the lab—new species discoveries and weekly conservation presentations. "Be sure to check it out before you leave town," he told the family.

"Is that the coast guard station?" the father asked, pointing to the small, nondescript building. Along the pier, rescue vessels were docked, and he could see several crew on the deck of *Starlight*. Most likely a training procedure.

The helicopter pad came into view and Dwayne's stomach twisted at the sight of "his" MH-65 propellers rotating in preparation for takeoff. He'd left the post in the very capable hands of his crewmate Officer Dorsey, but it still made him uneasy to think that he wasn't the one the team could rely on in an emergency.

"Yes, that's it," he said, forcing the longing and regret from his tone as he delivered the spiel about the Port Serenity Coast Guard division and its long history of having a Beaumont as the commanding officer. The third-generation Beaumont in that role—Skylar—had been the one to suspend him from duty...twice in a year since she'd taken the helm.

"Do you think we could see Sealena from here?" the kid asked, perched on the edge of the seat, her nose glued to the window as she peered down at the ocean.

Sealena the Serpent Queen was rumored to protect the

oceans along the Alaska coast. The town had adopted the mythical creature as their own generations ago and now Port Serenity was famous for its "sightings." Visitors flocked to town during the warmer, milder months to visit the Sealena museum and bookstore, enjoy boat tours, watch the Sealena festival parade—which was scheduled for later that day— and enjoy a night at the themed hotel. Embracing the myth had brought the sleepy fishing village to life decades ago and ensured its prosperity for future generations.

Dwayne glanced back at the kid and winked. "You never know. Keep your eyes peeled."

While *he'd* never caught a glimpse of the half woman, half serpent creature, he had experienced the mystery and the unknown of these oceans, hills, mountains and valleys. Enough to know that there were some things that couldn't be explained.

ANNA ARMOS HAD arrived in Port Serenity with a map and a mission. One that didn't include this traffic jam. She leaned around the back seat of her Uber and peered through the windshield. "What's going on?" It was a small coastal town, and while it was tourist season, she hadn't expected the crowds lining both sides of the street.

"The Sealena parade," the driver said, stopping behind a long line of cars.

Handmade floats on flatbed trucks that were blasting local music were visible from the side road. A large Sealena-themed float went by—the papier-mâché Serpent Queen posed in a fierce stance, protecting sailboats in a storm, and Anna sighed.

Mythical sea creatures.

Sure, people might call the treasures her family searched for just as fictitious, but at least there were credible, reliable accounts of the lost gold and riches... Sea monsters were just ridiculous.

She checked her watch, then consulted Google Maps on her cell phone. It was a sixteen-minute walk from her location to Madden Heli-tours. Waiting to get through this traffic would definitely take longer. "Thanks. I'll walk from here."

Climbing out of the vehicle, she tossed her bag over her shoulder and headed along Main Street through the thick crowd. Port Serenity was a favorite Alaskan tourist destination in the summer months, and she would have avoided it this time of year if her mission didn't require warmer weather and better backwoods conditions. There was a small window of opportunity to find what she was looking for...

Admittedly, the town *was* quite beautiful.

She noted the breathtaking scenery of the mountains surrounding the town and the beautiful old buildings and structures as she walked quickly, dodging people on the sidewalk. Heat pooled on her lower back beneath her shirt as the bright midday sun beat down, and she was grateful for the cool breeze drifting in off the ocean. Her thick cargo pants weren't the best choice for the temperature, but they were practical for her purpose, with pockets for her bear spray, utility knife, map, sunscreen and emergency hydration pack. Who knew what kind of terrain or wildlife she might encounter on this trip?

She entered Madden Heli-tours a few moments later, and the blast of air-conditioning was a welcome respite. The office was small but held an air of professionalism that boasted pride in ownership. Comfortable leather furniture was arranged in the tour meeting area and a large flat-screen played videos and testimonials from happy guests.

She knew the business was family owned and operated. It was part of the reason she'd selected this particular company, hoping corporate policy was more a guideline rather than a rule.

Anna tied her long dark hair into a high ponytail, off her neck, as she waited behind a group of elderly people at the counter. A friendly woman behind the desk explained the tour packages to them and Anna took the time to scan their brochures. Sightseeing, heli-skiing in winter... Her gaze landed on the Treasure Lure tour. She picked up the brochure as the group at the counter moved aside to contemplate their adventure options.

"Can I help you?" the woman asked with a warm smile. She had to be in her late fifties, and she obviously took care of herself quite well. Her beautiful long hair was streaked with gray, but healthy and shiny looking. Her skin was flawless and her clothing was casual but expensive.

"Yes. Hi," she said, stepping up to the counter. "I called last week about a private helicopter tour. Anna Armos."

The woman nodded. "Welcome!"

"Thank you. I was held up by the parade. I hope that's not a problem." She'd been scheduled to arrive an hour ago and had anticipated heading out thirty minutes ago. She'd packed a few things for an overnight trip if necessary, but she didn't plan on being in town long.

"We did have to give your reserved time slot to another group, I'm afraid." The woman scanned the online booking system. "And we are fully booked this time of year... but let me see what I can do." She typed a few keys and lifted her glasses hanging around her neck to peer at the screen. She frowned and pursed her lips as she scanned the schedules and bookings.

Anna held her breath as she waited.

"I have one available time slot later today with tour operator Mike…"

"Um, actually, I was hoping to fly with Dwayne," Anna said quickly.

The woman looked surprised that she knew a member of their staff. "Oh…okay. Well, he's not on regular shifts…"

"Please. I heard he's the best," she said. She'd done her research and the only person who could help with her mission was him.

The woman beamed. "He's my son," she said, pride in her voice. Then she lowered it slightly. "He is the best, but I may be biased."

Anna laughed. "Well, if he's available, I can wait…" She didn't love the idea of prolonging her stay, but if it meant securing the coast guard rescue pilot as her guide, it would be worth it.

The woman scanned the system again and nodded. "I can get you out tomorrow morning with Dwayne around 9:00 a.m.?"

"Perfect!" Anna smiled, relief flowing through her. A 9:00 a.m. flight would have her back home again before all hell could break loose.

# CHAPTER TWO

A 9:00 A.M. FLIGHT? Had his mother forgotten that he wasn't exactly a morning person?

With his third coffee of the day in hand, Dwayne lifted his sunglasses up over his hat as he entered Madden Heli-tours the next morning.

He knew from his mother's text that it was a treasure-hunting tour—his least favorite. The economy of his small hometown was based on the Serpent Queen myth, and almost everyone in town made their living from tourism. His family was no exception.

But the Port Serenity that was available to tourists was just the tip of the iceberg. The town's secrets were protected by locals, and the treasure-hunting tour just felt…intrusive. As though outsiders had any right to lay claim to fortunes hidden on Alaskan soil.

Over the years, he'd seen many try…and fail.

And this…Anna Armos, his schedule report listed… was no different than all the others to flock to Port Serenity in the last eighty years since the Winters Lot treasure was reportedly lost in the wilds.

Except that she was late twenties and stunning, instead of late sixties and delusional.

Dwayne froze when he saw his tour guest enjoying a latte, sitting in the tour meeting area. Wearing hiking boots and khaki cargo pants, an army-green tank top hugging her curves, the woman had to be the sexiest real-life version of Lara Croft he'd ever seen. She'd certainly dressed the part of a tomb raider.

This morning's flight was actually starting to look up. He could definitely spend two hours in the air with this woman. Although, if she really did believe there was treasure in the Alaskan backwoods, she might not be the most sensible woman in the world.

"You must be Anna," he said, striding toward her, hand outstretched, his most charming smile on display. "I'm Dwayne. Heard you requested me."

She eyed him quickly, assessing him with dark, piercing emerald eyes as she stood, then nodded. If she was charmed, she hid it well. "Shall we go?"

Not wasting any time. He cleared his throat. "Of course. Whenever you're ready."

"I've been ready since nine...the time we were scheduled to leave."

Okay, so a little prickly. He checked his watch. It was quarter past.

Behind the counter, his mom hid an impressed grin as she pretended not to watch the interaction. No doubt she was enjoying another woman holding him accountable for his tardiness.

"My apologies for keeping you waiting," he said to Anna, opening the door and gesturing for her to exit first. His gaze slid lower as he watched her walk in front of him.

Prickly, but a fantastic ass.

She turned unexpectedly, her long dark ponytail nearly whipping him in the face, and caught his stare. She folded her arms across her chest and raised an eyebrow. "Do you check out all your tour guests like that?"

"Only the attractive ones," he said. He was busted anyway. Might as well admit it.

He caught the faintest hint of a smile playing at the corner of her mouth, but she was all business again. "I'm kind of in a hurry."

"I can tell. But treasure hunting takes time, so just relax and enjoy the ride," he said as they reached the chopper on the helipad. He opened the door and offered a hand to help her climb inside. She ignored it and hopped up without any effort, immediately reaching for her headset.

Impressive. Obviously, not her first time flying in a chopper.

Moments later, he was seated next to her and ready for liftoff. He communicated with the tower and prepared for flight. He gripped the cyclic in one hand, the collective in the other, and his feet operated the foot pedals that controlled the tail rotor. He opened the throttle completely to increase the speed of the rotor and pulled up slowly on the collective. Depressing the left foot pedal to counteract the torque produced by the main rotor, he continued pulling up slowly on the collective while depressing the left foot pedal until the aircraft slowly left the ground.

He glanced toward Anna and noticed her white-knuckled grip on the door. "You okay?" he asked through his headset.

"Just not a fan of heights," she said, her cool, polished exterior slipping slightly.

"Yet you booked a helicopter tour?" He couldn't suppress the chuckle that escaped him.

She shot him an annoyed look. "Facing a fear, I guess."

There was definitely more to it than that.

"So…what draws you to the Winters Lot fortune?" It was a considerably small treasure in comparison to most lost riches. Rumor had it that Winter Sullivan had been smuggling contraband into various Alaskan ports for his friend Earl Wakefield, collecting large amounts of gold in exchange for alcohol and cigarettes. However, on their last mission before Sergeant Beaumont busted the operation, Winter had caught wind of the trouble brewing onshore and had veered off course with his ship, docking on the side of what was now called Winters Mountain, just off the coast of Port Serenity. He'd taken all the money he could carry and hiked into abandoned caves nearby, where he'd hid the fortune. Over the years the amount of gold buried had escalated as the tall tale was passed down through generations and to the tourists who came in search of it. Eyes lit up at the prospect of discovering the secret caves from the air, catching a glimpse of the fortune, as the path was unhikable now due to erosion and climate change.

Anna shrugged next to him, peering out the window. "Just thought it would be interesting..."

His gaze slid over her. The hiking boots were worn at the toes and the edges of the pockets on her cargo pants were frayed, meaning she wore both items often. This wasn't just to look the part for that day's adventure. She wasn't snapping selfies for an Instagram profile...nor was she relaxing and taking in the sights.

Her gaze was surveying the ground below with the intensity of someone searching for something...

Did she really think she was going to find a lost treasure on this two-hour aerial journey when no other tour group ever had?

"Where are you going?" she asked as he headed south at the ridge, over the mountains.

"Along the treasure route," he said, nodding to the map on the brochure in her hands that his mother must have given her at the office. It detailed the route that Winter supposedly took from the coast inland to the caves.

Anna's eyes narrowed and all nervousness seemed to evaporate as she turned in the seat next to him. "We both know this is not the *actual* route."

Dwayne shrugged as though he had no idea what she was talking about, but the hair on the back of his neck stood up. "Sure it is. He docked the ship on the east side of the coast, in an alcove where the ship wouldn't be discovered, and then hiked all the way into the caves, through the Golden River Valley."

"Only he didn't. He couldn't have. Back then, those trails through Golden River Valley weren't crossable because of a large lake. The lake has since dried up and hiking trails cut through there, but in the late eighteen hundreds that wouldn't have been possible."

Dwayne sighed, pretending to look annoyed at her believing in all of this anyway, but his pulse was secretly racing. "Look, this is a fun tour. Most guests don't question the story and they just sit back and enjoy the ride."

"I'm not most guests."

Man, she was stubborn, and those emerald eyes were even more mesmerizing when she was fired up. He cleared his throat and looked away before they had a hypnotizing effect on him. "Well, I'm sorry, but this is the story…and the route that has been passed along for generations. I don't know any other…"

He stopped when she retrieved a different map from her bag and handed it to him. It was old, the edges torn, brittle looking. The paper was yellowed, and the ink was faded with age. Hundreds of different fold marks indicated it had been bent and crumpled many times, but he could clearly see the Alaskan landscape they were currently flying over.

"Lucky for you, I have the correct one," Anna said, her determination both a major turn-on and a huge inconvenience.

DWAYNE MADDEN HAD the worst poker face. He should never try his luck at the local casino, or he could kiss his inheritance goodbye. His too-handsome-for-his-own-good face was flushed and his sudden eye avoidance told her everything Anna had already suspected. He knew the route he took tourists on was bogus.

Well, he wasn't fooling her.

He glanced at her map and then back at his flight path... still headed in the wrong, opposite direction. "Where did you get that?" he asked casually.

"Passed down from family," she said simply. If he didn't know who she was or anything about her family's reputation for being the most successful treasure hunters in the country, that was on him. She wasn't about to fill him in. Men got a little...weird when they heard what she did for a living. Apparently, chasing something most people thought was a fantasy was too much for the guys she'd met to get on board with. Which was why she was still single at twenty-nine.

"Well, it's a nice antique drawing of old Alaska," Dwayne said. "But I can't take that path."

"Why not?" She refused to be deterred.

He sighed. "It crosses military airspace, for one, it's two hours off course, and there's nowhere to put the helicopter down for miles all around those caves. An aerial view of where they are supposed to be is all this tour provides."

She cocked her head to the side. "So, you admit that you're in the business of duping people?"

His jaw clenched. Ah, just as she suspected. He wasn't a

fan of the town's way of misrepresenting certain things to turn a profit. She liked him, despite her better judgment. In her line of work, people were best kept at a distance. Colleagues, collaborators…never friends. Only family was allowed to get close. And even then, that could be problematic.

"We give people an exciting, entertaining helicopter ride over some of the most breathtaking scenery on earth," Dwayne said. "That's all that we promise. If they happen to spot gold or a sea serpent swimming in the water, then that's a bonus."

He was stalling…and getting farther away from where she needed to be. "Look, I hired you for a private helicopter tour and I insist we go this route."

He scoffed. "Okay, princess."

Her mouth gaped. Okay, so maybe that had sounded a little rich-girlish, as though she were used to getting her way. Nothing was further from the truth. As a female in this male-dominated industry—a young, wealthy female—she met with a lot of pushback. From older, more experienced hunters to the hired help she employed on her expeditions, she struggled consistently to be taken seriously. Sure, she was chasing pots of gold at the ends of rainbows, but sometimes that pot was really there.

And in this case, she desperately needed it to be.

But playing the money or power card on Dwayne wouldn't work. She'd try a different tactic. "I asked for you specifically because I know you're not one to care about breaking the rules."

He shot her a questioning look, his gorgeous blue eyes transfixed on her, and she continued. "Two suspensions in the last year for breaking protocol on rescue missions suggests you like doing things your way."

His head swung toward her again and the helicopter jerked slightly to one side. "How do you know that?"

She shrugged casually, feeling the power dynamic shift. "I'm a princess, remember. Money buys knowledge." Her voice softened. "Look, I need your help because I know you can get me where I need to be."

"You hired the wrong guy."

"Dwayne, please… This is important to me," she said, daring to reach across and touch his arm. She wasn't ready to tell him just how important…

His gaze shot to the physical connection between them and she watched him struggle with the decision—obviously common sense in battle with an intrigued urge to do as she requested.

"Come on. Don't tell me you're not curious. All this time taking tourists along the wrong path… Don't you want to know if the story is true?" She had an insatiable thirst for discovery, searching and seeking answers. She thrived on deciphering clues and solving mysteries. Having grown up in a family of treasure hunters and surrounded by those always up for the challenge, she knew how to spot that spark of intrigue in someone…and she saw it in Dwayne.

He sighed his resolve, but the excitement in his eyes, the color of the ocean below them, was undeniable. "If we get a fine for being in an unauthorized area, you're paying it," he said, pointing a finger at her.

"Consider it done," she said with a wide smile. Money was never an obstacle for her. Money was never the ultimate treasure either…

"And you need to tell me how your family got that map."

Damn. That part would be tougher.

# CHAPTER THREE

ANNA ARMOS WAS LOOKING for something, but it wasn't Winters Lot.

Dwayne's gut was rarely wrong when it came to reading people, and Anna had personal stakes in whatever she was really searching for.

That map she held could have only come from one place—Winter Sullivan himself. Which meant Anna Armos had ties to Port Serenity and its past, making her even more intriguing than when she'd simply been a disillusioned but beautiful wealthy tourist.

She shook her head next to him. "Like I said, just something my family had. I come from generations of treasure hunters," she said simply, as though it were a normal, everyday career choice. "I think my grandfather found it in a museum or something…"

"Okay," Dwayne said, pulling on the cyclic and turning the chopper in the other direction. If she wasn't going to tell him the truth…

Anna's eyes widened. "What are you doing?"

"I agreed on two conditions," he said.

"Grr." She caught him barely containing a grin at her annoyance. "Fine! I'll tell you—just turn back," she said. "Please."

He did. "Start talking."

She took a deep breath, as though this story wasn't something she told many people. "Winter Sullivan was my great-great-grandfather. When he was found in the Alaskan backwoods—the authorities had discovered the ship after days of searching—he was sentenced to life in jail for smuggling and assisting the Wakefields in their questionable transporting of goods."

Dwayne nodded. That part he knew. Earl Wakefield was sentenced as well, by his best friend Castor Beaumont, and it had started the decades-old feud between the Beaumont and Wakefield families.

"In jail he drew the map of where he'd hidden the gold and contraband," Anna continued.

"Right. That's the map on our brochure."

Anna shook her head. "There were two. One he released to authorities looking to retrieve the goods and one—the real one—he kept for himself. When he died, the map was discovered among his items and my family started searching for it."

"With no luck?"

She shook her head.

"So, that's why this is so important to you? You want to reclaim your great-great-grandfather's assets. Your family obviously believes it's rightly yours." The fortune had been acquired by questionable means, but Winter had served his time for the crime, and after all these years, the Armos family could potentially lay claim to it.

If it existed.

She nodded. "Exactly."

Dwayne studied her, not entirely convinced it was the full story, but it was enough to get him to redirect the chopper. For now, anyway…

Two hours later, they were circling the location where the caves were supposed to be, according to her map. Anna peered out the window, scanning the tall, jagged mountains and lush green valley below.

This couldn't be it.

She consulted the map. "Where's the river that used to run through here?" she asked, pointing to the spot on the map. Maybe they still were too far north... The coordinates might be off.

"The landscape here has changed, just like it has everywhere," Dwayne said, rotating the chopper and getting closer to the mountaintops for a better view.

Anna bit her lower lip as she tried to locate other points of reference between real Alaska and the drawing.

"Remember, your great-great-grandfather was also drawing this map from memory without the same aerial view," Dwayne said as static sounded over the radio and then his mother's voice came over his headset.

"Tower to aircraft A-Star, what the hell are you doing?"

Anna's eyes widened and she grinned seeing Dwayne's face flush. "Just a slight detour...at the request of the client," he said, tightly, sounding like a twelve-year-old busted for breaking curfew.

"You are in a no-fly zone and need to evacuate immediately. Understood?" His mother's voice was calm and professional, but Anna suspected it was for her sake. If she wasn't in the chopper, his mother would be delivering an earful.

"Yes, ma'am," Dwayne said. He shot her a look. "You got me in trouble with my mom."

She laughed and it nearly caught in her chest. When was the last time she'd laughed out loud? Lately, she was so preoccupied with family drama and needing to find this site that there hadn't been much time to laugh. "Sorry?"

"No, you're not," Dwayne said with a wink in her direction that had her heart racing.

Her pilot was seriously sexy, and now that she was taking the time to notice, he was definitely her type. Strong, muscular, daring and confident. And he was going along on this search without too much protest.

"Well, you heard her. We can't stay in the air. I'm going to need to set down and we'll have to hike the rest of the way in."

At least he wasn't suggesting that they'd run their course and needed to head back. She nodded as he navigated the helicopter back toward the valley, out of the no-fly zone, and masterfully set the helicopter down in the open space, which she suspected they also weren't allowed to be in. He turned off the chopper and they grabbed their gear for a hike up the mountainside.

Moments later, they were on foot, their backpacks carrying only the necessary supplies, making for the steep incline toward the location of the caves as indicated on her map. Her calves burned and the heat of the midday sun beating down through the trees had her sweating, but the excitement of being this close to the treasure gave her hope and energy. Next to her, Dwayne seemed to be taking the trail with ease. He was in great shape—obviously a necessity for his career in the coast guard. She knew the training required to fulfill the position he held, which only increased her attraction to him. The man saved lives for a living—who wouldn't be attracted to that? Was he single? Damn, maybe she should have paid for that knowledge too.

She sent a look his way and dared to ask. "So…these suspensions—what happened?"

He shrugged. "Made a few bad judgment calls, that's all."

He was owning up to it, but she had a hard time believing that he'd made a call so bad it would warrant a suspension. From the information she'd gathered, no one had died or been injured in recent rescues. "Like what?"

He shot her a look. "Thought you knew all about me?"

"Not everything… And besides, I'd like to hear your version of events."

He seemed a little surprised that she cared to hear his side of things, and it struck her that maybe no one else had asked, which bonded them in an unexpected twist to this journey.

MAN, SHE WAS PERSISTENT. Oddly enough, her curiosity seemed genuine and made Dwayne want to talk to her about it. "Well, in one rescue, I didn't refuel before take-off. The people had been in the ocean for long enough and I knew time was of the essence. Unfortunately, it resulted in my coworker being stranded in the tides longer than necessary when we ran out of fuel." Protocol. It had come down to not following the rules.

"Was he hurt?" Anna asked, sounding slightly out of breath as they continued their trek up the side of the mountain.

"Aaron?" He scoffed. "Nah. Dude's a beast. An elite rescue swimmer—one of the best." He used to be slightly jealous of his buddy. The big hero on the team who received all the praise and credit. It hadn't helped when Aaron had swooped in on Dwayne's ex the Christmas before, but now he realized his friend deserved all the credit he received… and happiness with the love of his life, a woman who hadn't been the right fit for Dwayne.

Unfortunately, Dwayne still hadn't found the right fit. And having grown up in the small town, where everyone knew everyone, he'd dated half the available women his age already and knew to avoid the others.

His family name and money made dating tricky. It was tough to figure out if a woman was interested in him or his bank account. In fact, one of the appealing things about Isla Wakefield had been that her trust fund was bigger than his and her status in the community had rivaled his own.

"Was anyone else hurt?" Anna asked.

"No," he said, her question bringing him back to the present.

"Would they have been if they'd been in the water longer?"

He knew where this was heading. He'd tried to justify his actions in his own mind exactly the same way. "That's not the point. I didn't follow protocol."

"You went with your gut and it worked out. That's a good thing. Not something to be punished." She stopped for a breath, putting her hands on her hips.

He stopped next to her. "But what if someday my gut instincts are wrong?" He shook his head. He'd come to terms with the fact that Skylar and the crew were right. He needed to do things by the book or rescues could go sideways someday. He couldn't continue to take risks with other people's lives and safety on the line.

Which made it hard for him to decide whether he could continue working with the coast guard. It wasn't that he didn't want to follow the rules. It was just in the heat of the moment, he couldn't trust that he wouldn't go with his gut.

This day was the perfect example. He knew he shouldn't have allowed Anna to talk him into flying into a military no-fly zone. He knew he wasn't supposed to set the chopper down in the valley. But something about her insistence made him think that taking these small, harmless detours from the right thing to do *was* somehow the right thing to do.

His mother was not going to agree.

"Well, for what it's worth, if I was in danger, I'd want someone who knew when and how to break protocol to have my back," she said, blowing a strand of hair away from her flushed cheeks.

Damn, she was hot, and the fact that she was on his side had an overwhelming effect on him. Right or wrong, having a true ride or die was something he was lacking. Their eyes met and held, and instinctively they moved toward one another. Dwayne reached for her face and after only the slightest of hesitation lowered his mouth to hers.

Anna wrapped her arms around his neck and deepened the kiss, pressing her body closer to him on the uneven terrain beneath their boots. Dwayne's hands moved to her waist, drawing her even closer as his mouth explored hers. She tasted like peppermint and smelled like honey, and her muscular but curvy body felt incredible. She was exactly his type physically and his body was reacting to the kiss like he was fifteen years old. When her tongue teased his bottom lip, his heart raced. This impulsive, bold woman was a match made in heaven.

Adventurous, daring… Someone—the only one—who understood his actions. Didn't make them right, but it gave him a sense that maybe they weren't completely wrong either. At least, not to her. This odd sensation of not being alone…of having someone like-minded who could appreciate that sometimes reality required a different judgment call than the one the textbooks taught.

She tangled her fingers in his hair and continued to kiss him as though he had the air she desperately needed. Their connection and chemistry in that moment was undeniable and the instant spark between them caught him completely off guard in the best way.

A moment later, he reluctantly pulled away, breaking contact with her lips. Her eyes opened and she smiled. "That was a really great kiss," she said.

"Had you expected anything else?" he said, feeling a tug in his chest that was even more unexpected than their impulsive make-out session.

"So far you have delivered on all levels, Officer Madden," she said with a grin, slowly moving away from him. Her hips swayed distractingly as she continued ahead of him on the trail and Dwayne knew he'd just met a woman he'd not soon forget.

## CHAPTER FOUR

SHE'D PLAYED IT COOL, but that kiss had rocked her to her core. Heat coursed through her that had nothing to do with the blazing sun overhead or the exertion of climbing this never-ending mountain. Obviously, she was attracted to Dwayne. The man was gorgeous and smart and skilled. He was interesting and perceptive and offered her a challenge she usually didn't get.

But there had been something else in that kiss. Something truly unexpected. A spark that had ignited passion and desire, but also a connection that seemed to run deeper. As though their souls had connected as well as their lips. It was odd and unexplainable and definitely unexpected, but also undeniable.

She glanced his way now and saw him smiling, and her heart pounded in her chest. She'd traveled the entire world looking for valuable hidden treasures, but the one time she wasn't searching for the big score, she found something—someone—that she already knew was priceless. A man who had understood her need to go on this adventure without her having to fully reveal just how important the journey was.

As they finally reached a clearing, she caught sight of something several feet away and her heart raced for an entirely different reason. She hurried toward it, ignoring

Dwayne's calls behind her, no longer feeling the ache in her legs from the hike.

This was it. She'd found it. She couldn't believe it was actually here.

SLIGHTLY OUT OF BREATH, Dwayne stopped in front of a single-engine two-seater plane. Or at least what was left of it, partially hidden by the overgrowth, parts of it scattered across the clearing. "What's this?"

Seemingly transfixed, Anna ignored him as she started sorting through the wreckage.

"Hey, be careful," Dwayne said, moving closer. Years of decay and rust made the thing a major hazard. Not to mention, there was probably a dead body... At what stage of decomposition, he didn't know.

"Don't worry—the pilot ejected before the crash," Anna said, stepping carefully over the left wing to stand in the middle of the debris.

He frowned. "How do you...?" He paused, seeing the Armos family name and crest on the side of the small plane. "It belongs to your family?"

She nodded, lifting heavy pieces of the front of the plane. "Can you help me?" she asked, struggling under the weight.

He moved closer and took the heavy metal from her. She sent him a grateful look as she carefully climbed inside the cockpit. She moved slowly, scanning the small interior. She picked up an old bag and searched through. "Come on, old man... I know you took it with you," she muttered to herself.

What was she looking for? Obviously, it wasn't Winters Lot.

She lifted several seat cushions and peered inside. She rummaged through the entire vessel as if in a trance, as though she'd almost forgotten Dwayne was even there.

"Where is it?" she asked frustratedly to no one. At least, no one who could answer. Frantically, she re-searched the front area of the plane, tossing items onto the ground at his feet. He narrowly escaped a rusted old metal thermos.

"Okay, hey, enough. Time out," he said, carefully climbing into the wreckage with her and placing his hands on her shoulders. He looked squarely into her eyes. "Want to tell me what's going on?"

Anna sighed, a look of disappointment crossing her pretty features. "This was my grandfather's plane. He went in search of Winters Lot twenty years ago after my father died. They'd planned the excursion together, but then my dad got sick before he could go."

Dwayne nodded slowly. "Sorry to hear that."

"I was just a little girl, but the death hit me hard. My dad and I weren't exactly close—he was so obsessed with treasure hunting that he wasn't home much and he always said treasure hunting wasn't for little girls." She looked like the words still ate at her, and Dwayne suspected part of her commitment to her chosen lifestyle was an attempt to prove her father wrong.

"I'm sure he'd feel differently if he were here now," he said gently.

"I'll never know." She took a deep breath and continued. "Gramps decided to go anyway. Alone. No one could talk him out of it." She paused. "The plane wasn't in the best of shape. He ran into trouble, but wouldn't give up and land somewhere safely."

"He must have been a brave man," he said. Not unlike his granddaughter.

"He was a determined fool," she said, but the words were softened by her laugh. "He was my favorite person in the entire world. We did everything together. Which is why I know he took it with him." Her eyes resumed scanning the aircraft.

"Took what?"

"An heirloom compass. It was in our family for generations—the one thing of any value that Winter had to pass along. Grandpa and my dad always took it on their expeditions. A sort of good-luck charm. He'd almost forgotten it that time. I found it in the den on my dad's desk and ran out to the plane to give it to him."

"So, that's what you're hoping to find?"

She nodded.

"Was it valuable?"

"Not by any real standards. But it was old and rare and special." She sighed, hands on her hips, giving up the search. "And unfortunately, it has broken my family apart. My mother and her sister both believe that the other took it when they divided Grandpa's estate. No one believes me when I say Gramps had it with him."

"That's why this was so important to you."

She nodded. "I want my family to reconcile. If I can bring it home, the sisters can stop this petty fighting before our upcoming family reunion."

Dwayne nodded, feeling a warmth in his chest by her admission. She wasn't looking for some elusive treasure. She was doing this for her family. He understood, as family was important to him as well.

Which just made Anna Armos even more perfect.

"Well, let's keep looking." Dwayne joined in the search, moving pieces of the broken plane to search the ground below.

Unfortunately, an hour later, every inch of the wreckage was explored and there was still no sign of the compass.

He thought hard, then said, "You said your grandfather ejected before the crash…"

Anna nodded, running her forearm across her sweaty forehead. "He had a parachute and he jumped. Rescue crews found him and got him back to a hospital in Anchorage safely, but he'd suffered a brain injury—a slow bleed that made him confused. He was incoherent and not making any sense when he talked about the expedition. He said he'd made it to the caves and that he'd moved the treasure…" She shook her head. "Then he died in his sleep a week later. He didn't have the compass with him when they found him, so I thought it had to still be with the plane."

Dwayne thought about it. "If he ejected between here and the coast, the compass may be along the valley…"

"It could be, but… It's miles long and it was a long time ago. It would probably be covered by now or someone else may have found it…"

She sounded discouraged and he hated to see her lose hope. "We have the crash site and you know where he supposedly ejected. Let's look and see if we can narrow down his landing site."

Sitting in the grass, the two of them hovered over the map of the area, trying to figure out the best place to start their search.

"You think he actually made it to the caves?" Anna asked.

He shrugged. "If the plane crashed here and he ejected somewhere here…" He pointed to the area on her map. "Then he could have made it. In fact, he was fairly close…"

Her eyes widened. "I'm sure he would have tried," she said excitedly.

"So? Should we try?"

The expression on her face was all the answer he needed as they headed out on foot to make the treacherous descent down the other side of the mountain toward the caves.

And a long three hours later, they made it. Tired, sweaty and dehydrated…but they were finally there.

"These are incredible," Anna said in awe, scanning the interior of the large dark cave.

"I can't believe places like this exist and almost no one ever gets to experience them…" Dwayne said, taking in the breathtaking sight. He'd lived in Alaska his entire life and explored the backwoods, but he had never been to these caves. The dangerous terrain leading into them and their distance from civilization made him suspect very few ever had.

Anna looked around, disappointment on her pretty face. "Unfortunately, no treasure."

"No." He wasn't entirely surprised, but he realized a part of him had been hoping that the old stories were true…at least for Anna's sake.

He saw something glimmer behind a large pile of stones gathered near the back of the cave, and his heart raced. Moving toward it, he picked up the shiny object and dangled the old, tarnished chain. "But there is this," he said with a smile, feeling as though all their efforts had been worth it, even without the promised fortune.

Anna turned, and even from that distance, he could see tears glistening in her eyes when she saw the compass. "It was here," she said, her voice barely more than a whisper. She walked toward him and he met her halfway, giving her the cherished family heirloom.

"The mystery of Winters Lot lives on," she said, softly taking it and lovingly running a finger over the gold-embossed *W.S.* "Thank you, Dwayne."

"For what?"

"Everything," she said, looking up at him with appreciation and affection in those beautiful eyes. "But most of all, for following your gut."

# CHAPTER FIVE

OH, HE WAS in for an earful…

As they climbed out of the helicopter at the Madden Heli-tours landing pad much later that evening, Dwayne's mother was pacing inside the office. Even from that distance, he could see her face was flushed and her mouth moving as she practiced the lecture she was about to dish out.

It was the same since he was a kid. He always heard the lecture twice—once when he waited it out in his bedroom, thinking about what he'd done while she rehearsed downstairs, and then when she formally gave the speech hours later.

He turned to Anna as they crossed the parking lot. "You know what? You better not go in. I'll face the music alone."

"You sure? I mean, she looks really pissed," she said, nodding toward the office.

Dwayne swallowed hard and resisted the urge to bring Anna along for reinforcement. His mother would go easy on him in front of a paying client… "I'm sure," he said.

"Okay… Well, um…thank you. Again. And sorry for getting you in trouble," she said with the most adorable grin that said she'd get him in trouble every day of the week.

Damn, she was the most appealing woman he'd met in a very long time. Her daredevil, risk-taking, adventure-loving and the-hell-with-rules nature spoke to him. Standing there now with her hair a mess, dirt streaked across her forehead, but the happiest expression at having found what she'd been searching for, she was the most beautiful sight he'd ever seen.

"That's okay. I'm happy you found the compass," he said.

She looked as though there was something more she wanted to say…and he waited, holding his breath. Would she want to see him again? She was headed home… They'd only just met…

She cleared her throat and nodded. "Right. So, thanks again."

Dwayne watched as she headed toward the taxi station on the side of the road. Maybe he could ask her to dinner while she was still in town? Maybe she'd consider staying a few more days…

If the kiss earlier that day had been even half as powerful for her as it was for him…

"Dwayne! In here!" His mother's voice drifted across the tarmac. She was ready for him.

He sighed as he reluctantly turned away from Anna and headed inside. "Mom…"

"Hush," she said. "I don't want to hear any excuses. You're grounded."

"But it's the busy season…" Dwayne knew her decision was final, but he also knew she'd be punishing herself and the business if she stuck to her guns on this. They had multiple tours booked every day and she'd been planning on having him there for another five days.

"Believe me, I know. This isn't coming from me. It's coming from higher up. You were in a no-fly zone. It's out of my hands."

Dwayne sighed as he accepted his fate.

The coast guard had suspended him. His own family

had been forced to make the same call. Maybe he really shouldn't be flying helicopters for a living.

Unfortunately, he wasn't quite sure who he was if he wasn't a pilot.

ANNA HAD NO idea where the sweet little woman behind the counter had disappeared to, but inside Madden Heli-tours, Dwayne's mother looked commanding and not to be messed with. Those were the best kind of mothers—soft but tough when they needed to be… Anna knew from experience.

Still, this was her fault. She couldn't just let Dwayne take the heat for this.

She bit her lip as she stared at the taxi waiting for her. Could she really just leave? After the kiss they'd shared, she knew there was a connection between them, and while he hadn't asked her to stay or to see her again, she knew he'd wanted to.

She'd wanted to as well.

After telling the taxi to wait another moment, she headed back toward the office but slowed her pace as Dwayne exited again. His face held a look of surprise when he saw her. "You're still here," he said, and she clung to the hope she heard in his tone as she went out on a limb.

"I'd like to offer you a job," she said. She'd like more than that, but keeping things professional seemed like the least terrifying proposal.

His eyes widened. "Doing what?"

"Flying a helicopter for our family." They owned one and usually hired a different pilot for each mission, but having one permanently on payroll made sense. Or at least, she'd reason that it did…

"For treasure-hunting expeditions?" he asked, sounding

slightly amused by the idea, and her stomach clenched, as her own confidence waned.

"You're suspended from both jobs… Got anything better to do?"

"Not really…" he said slowly. "But I'm not sure your line of work is really for me."

Of course, it wasn't. She laughed a strangled-sounding laugh. "Never mind. It was an impulsive thought, that's all."

"No… I mean, where are you off to next?" he asked, but she wasn't at all convinced that he was actually contemplating the idea. He was just being polite and not wanting her to feel embarrassed.

"Isn't it obvious? I'm going in search of where Gramps could have moved Winters Lot."

He frowned. "You think he moved it?"

She laughed. "Well, it wasn't in the caves, was it?" He'd seen the empty caves for himself.

"No, but maybe it never was."

Her smile faded as her chest tightened. "You're saying Grandpa lied?"

"I'm saying that he'd suffered a brain injury," he said gently. "You said yourself he wasn't making much sense."

"That was before I saw the caves, found the compass and knew he was telling the truth about having been there." If that part was true, then the rest could be too. She had to have faith and at least try. Dwayne's skepticism was disheartening. She was used to disbelief by now…but she had been hoping he was different. That after that day, he'd have a different opinion. Or at least be open.

Instead, he said, "Right…but, Anna, he was injured…"

"Dwayne, this compass was a sign. He left it there on purpose, knowing I'd go searching for it…" Normally, she'd have walked away from him the moment he'd started questioning her or making her feel ridiculous, but a part of her was still clinging to that connection she'd felt in their kiss—that moment where she'd felt she'd found someone special, someone different.

He ran a hand over his face. "I'm not sure I can believe in hidden treasures and all that."

Her spine stiffened and self-preservation took over. She'd been wrong about him. She hadn't found the one person who might come on this life journey with her. "But you can buy into serpent sea creatures?"

"I don't exactly believe in the Sealena myth either," he said, as though that made things better.

All it did was make her feel bad for him. What kind of boring life would it be if there were no adventures? No taking leaps of faith on the unknown and impossible?

She nodded slowly. "Then what do you believe in, Dwayne?" she asked, not waiting for an answer as she turned and headed back to her waiting taxi.

# CHAPTER SIX

A WEEK LATER, Dwayne expected to feel relief as he entered the coast guard station for his first shift back. No more tour groups. No more forced time on the ground. And no more hours of free time staring at his cell phone, hoping to hear from Anna. She'd gotten what she'd come for and now she was moving on.

He needed to as well…except the job offer she'd casually thrown out—which he knew she was serious about—played on his mind. So did the fantastic kiss…and her question about what he believed in.

He'd had nothing but time the last five days to sit and contemplate it all. He wasn't any closer to answers, but he knew there was definitely something missing in his life, something lacking…something for a brief moment, he'd felt like he'd found.

"Hey, man, good to have you back," Aaron said as he entered the station locker room.

"Thanks," Dwayne said, pushing all other thoughts aside as he opened his locker and reached for his gear.

"You good?" his friend asked, studying him with a look of concern.

"Yeah…great. Training exercise today?" Once he was back in the air and back to being busy, he'd shake off the nagging regret he was feeling over the Anna situation. He'd only known her a day. These intense feelings couldn't possibly be real. He just needed to fill his time and thoughts with something else.

"Chopper leaves in ten," Aaron said with a grin.

"Not without me," Dwayne responded with his usual banter as he shut the locker.

Twenty minutes later, they flew over the coast toward the south mountain ranges and Dwayne's chest tightened as he saw the area where he'd explored with Anna. Of course, fate would be messing with him like this. Just when he'd started to push her out of his mind, the reminder was there.

He couldn't believe they'd actually found her grandfather's crash site...or the caves or the compass. What were the odds? Especially after all this time...

He knew he'd hurt her with his disbelief of the legend about Winters Lot, but it was a lot to ask—to believe in the old stories. Or that her grandfather had actually found it and moved it.

If there really were hidden treasures around the world, wouldn't more of them be found? He'd read about a few discoveries over the years—old sunken ships and gold panning successes...but an actual treasure?

He shook his head. It was a little much to wrap his mind around and Anna deserved someone who was all in—who believed as strongly and passionately as she did.

Focusing on the training mission, he pushed all other thoughts aside as he operated the helicopter through the narrow openings between the mountains. Since Isla Wakefield's emergency the Christmas before, falling into a glacier cave, the team was really focused on training for the tougher rescues they might encounter. His team needed his focus and concentration right now.

But an hour later, training exercise over, he turned the chopper around to head back and something in the scenery below caught his attention. A river running north of the caves where the compass had been hidden. That hadn't been on Anna's map. Must be a glacial river formed due to climate change. Before there would have been just a sunken valley...

One that would have been accessible from the caves and not too far of a distance...

He shook his head. This was ridiculous. He couldn't actually be entertaining this...

Yet the image of Anna's determined expression had him indeed entertaining it.

So much so that in the locker room half an hour later, he reached for a draft pad and pen and sketched the area as best he could from memory, adding in the coordinates and location.

"Whatcha got there?" Aaron asked, coming up behind him.

Dwayne tucked it away. "Nothing..." He might be willing to suspend disbelief and follow through on a hunch, but expecting Aaron to would be asking way too much. "Hey, do you think Isla would mind if I go through some of the old Wakefield photo albums and scrapbooks?" Isla's family had kept amazing records of the town generations ago. News clippings, photographs, documents from the town's claiming of the Sealena myth... Stories about the smuggling and the search for Winter Sullivan.

Aaron nodded. "I'm sure she'd be happy to help you find whatever you're looking for."

Dwayne smiled. "Thanks, man."

What he was looking for was the key to the secret of Winters Lot.

BRINGING HOME THE compass had worked to reunite the family. Anna's mother and aunt were so surprised and remorseful that they'd never believed her all these years, and they were happily making up for lost time on a girls' weekend in the Bahamas. They'd invited Anna to come along, but her thoughts were preoccupied with the treasure.

And, more annoyingly, Dwayne.

It wasn't new for her to meet that kind of skepticism and disbelief. She was more than used to it by now, but she'd foolishly thought for a second that Dwayne was different.

But he'd turned out to hold the same narrow-minded opinions as every other guy she'd ever met. Growing up, she'd always seen treasure hunting as exciting, exotic… She'd never looked at the career from the viewpoint of others until she'd gotten older and her story was often met with snickers or whispers behind her back. She'd never let their taunting hurt her. Anna knew who she was.

She squared her shoulders.

She'd never allowed anyone's opinions about her and her career bother her before and she wouldn't start now.

If only there hadn't been that connection…

"Miss Anna, there's someone here to see you." Pedro, the family's gardener, popped his head in through the open office window.

"Oh, thanks. I didn't hear the door." Occupational hazard of being engrossed in her maps and old documents. Her grandfather's journals from the weeks between his injury and his death were hard to decipher. In one story, he talked about finding the treasure in the caves and the next he was rambling on about some cutaway ledges in the side of a valley. Which valley, she had no idea. She hadn't seen one from the air…

Reluctantly leaving all the documents on the desk, she stood and headed toward the front door, just as it opened. Her mouth gaped, seeing Dwayne enter her family home behind Pedro. The older man shot her a wink as he left them alone.

"Dwayne? What are you doing here?" She hadn't heard from him since she'd left Port Serenity. Not that she'd expected to. They'd had one day together. One kiss. One shared experience that had changed the course of her life...

"I was thinking about what your grandfather said...about moving the treasure."

She sighed, hands on her hips. "And it wouldn't be physically possible in his injured state. Yes, you've expressed your opinions." He wouldn't be the first man to feel a need to explain. Some people just couldn't let it go.

But Dwayne shook his head. "Actually, I'd like to take back my earlier assessment."

Her eyes widened, but she folded her arms across her chest as he continued. He might have a different opinion, but she wouldn't get her hopes up quite yet.

"He could have moved the treasure...if he hadn't had to go far."

Okay, he'd succeeded. She was definitely intrigued. "What do you mean? When we flew over the area, there was nowhere he could have hidden so much loot."

Dwayne's smile was wide as he took a step toward her. "Except in the river."

"There's no river on the map."

"But there is one now...and my research into the geographical records shows it would have been there twenty years ago. The start of one, anyway. A river that would have been crossable and that would have held ledges..."

Her eyes widened. "And Gramps knew the river levels would only rise over time..."

"Making the treasure that much more hidden."

Her heart raced as she nodded, excitement flowing

through her at the lead and its source... Then her eyes narrowed. "I thought you didn't believe in all of this?"

Dwayne took a step toward her and reached for her hands. She reluctantly unfolded her arms and allowed him to hold them. "I was wrong. I never should have shot down the idea, and the more I thought about it, the more plausible it seemed."

Anna swallowed hard as he stepped even closer, his gaze gentle and full of remorse.

"And thinking about you...and that kiss, made me even more desperate to figure out where the treasure could be, so that I could add value to the search."

Her heart pounded in her chest and she swallowed hard. "You want to help?"

"I put in a leave of absence with the coast guard. Do you still need a helicopter pilot?"

She hesitated. He'd actually taken a leave of absence? Sure, he was here now, but was he really into this or was he just trying to get close to her? "I don't know, Dwayne..."

"Oh, I also wanted to give you this," he said, reaching into his pocket and handing her a photocopy of a tattered old black-and-white photo. Her eyes widened seeing the man in the photo holding up the family heirloom compass.

"Is this...?"

"Winter Sullivan," Dwayne said with a wide grin.

Choked up, she stared at the photo of her ancestor for a long moment, needing a second to regain her cool. Finally, she glanced up. "You think you've redeemed yourself, don't you?"

"Little bit," he said with the sexy grin of his that had plagued her memory all week.

"You're right," she said, stepping toward him and wrapping her arms around his neck. "But don't think you'll get to keep some of the treasure when we find it," she murmured against his lips.

"Don't want any. I already have what I was looking for," he said softly before kissing her.

Anna's heart warmed at the words. She knew that, together, they'd definitely find the treasure, but even better—this was the start of a lifetime of adventures.

\* \* \* \* \*

# Get 4 FREE REWARDS!

**We'll send you 2 FREE Books plus 2 FREE Mystery Gifts.**

**FREE**
Value Over
**$20**

Both the **Romance** and **Suspense** collections feature compelling novels written by
many of today's bestselling authors.

---

YES! Please send me 2 FREE novels from the Essential Romance or Essential Suspense
Collection and my 2 FREE gifts (gifts are worth about $10 retail). After receiving them, if I
don't wish to receive any more books, I can return the shipping statement marked "cancel."
If I don't cancel, I will receive 4 brand-new novels every month and be billed just $7.49 each
in the U.S. or $7.74 each in Canada. That's a savings of at least 17% off the cover price. It's
quite a bargain! Shipping and handling is just 50¢ per book in the U.S. and $1.25 per book
in Canada.* I understand that accepting the 2 free books and gifts places me under no
obligation to buy anything. I can always return a shipment and cancel at any time by calling
the number below. The free books and gifts are mine to keep no matter what I decide.

Choose one: ☐ **Essential Romance**       ☐ **Essential Suspense**
(194/394 MDN GRHV)              (191/391 MDN GRHV)

Name (please print)

Address                                                                                Apt. #

City                                State/Province                          Zip/Postal Code

Email: Please check this box ☐ if you would like to receive newsletters and promotional emails from Harlequin Enterprises ULC and its affiliates. You can
unsubscribe anytime.

Mail to the **Harlequin Reader Service:**
**IN U.S.A.:** P.O. Box 1341, Buffalo, NY 14240-8531
**IN CANADA:** P.O. Box 603, Fort Erie, Ontario L2A 5X3

Want to try 2 free books from another series? Call 1-800-873-8635 or visit www.ReaderService.com.

---

STRSMAX22R3